Highland Moon

"All of you is very . . . very . . . nice," she said.

He chuckled and nuzzled her throat. "And what do ye like best about me?"

"I like your thighs—I mean your eyes." She giggled. "You have eyes like a fallen angel." His hand dropped to the bodice of her gown. She could feel the heat of his palm through the layers of clothing. And suddenly it was hard to breathe.

He's beautiful, she thought, *the most beautiful man I've ever known.* A lock of his hair fell forward, and she caught it between her teeth and tugged gently.

"Dinna begin what ye canna finish," he said.

"Don't go," she begged. "I want you here with me . . . I want you . . ."

A hunger deep within her cried to be filled. *Just once,* she thought, *I want to know what it's like to be loved by a man like this.*

Highland Moon

JUDITH E. FRENCH

AVON BOOKS  NEW YORK

HIGHLAND MOON is an original publication of Avon Books. This work has never before appeared in book form. This work is a novel. Any similarity to actual persons or events is purely coincidental.

AVON BOOKS
A division of
The Hearst Corporation
1350 Avenue of the Americas
New York, New York 10019

First Avon Books Printing: July 1991

AVON TRADEMARK REG. U.S. PAT. OFF. AND IN OTHER COUNTRIES, MARCA REGISTRADA, HECHO EN U.S.A.

Printed in the U.S.A.

RA 10 9 8 7 6 5 4 3 2 1

For Colleen, with all my love

Prologue

London, England
February 2, 1723

Torrents of rain poured from the gray skies and soaked Ross Campbell's feathered bonnet and his *breacan-feile*, the full belted plaid that swathed his tall, broad-shouldered frame from his chin to the tops of his high fringed Shawnee moccasins. The icy wind raised gooseflesh on his sinewy, scarred arms and drove needles of freezing rain down the back of his neck. He swore a foul Gaelic oath and reined his mount closer to an overhanging building, hoping to shield the stallion from the force of the storm.

The big horse flattened his ears against his head and turned into the wind. Snorting, he bared his teeth and raised one iron-clad hoof to paw impatiently at the slippery, mud-covered cobblestones. Muscles rippled beneath the stallion's sleek black hide as he arched his powerful neck and shook his sweeping mane and tail.

Ross swore again in English and peered into the deluge. The figure of a man appeared through the mist at the entrance to an alley. Ross transferred his reins to his left hand and smoothly drew his broadsword with his right.

"Colonial?" The man's voice was thin and so

1

heavily accented with London street cant, Ross could hardly understand him.

"Aye." The stallion wheeled to face the man on foot, gave a fierce squeal, and reared on his hind legs. Ross threw his weight forward and tightened his knees around the animal's sides. The horse's front hooves struck the stones, and he danced sideways, fighting the bit.

The Londoner darted forward and held out a scrap of paper. Ross clenched the stallion's reins in his teeth and grabbed the missive. Without another word, the messenger turned and ran.

Sheathing his sword, Ross again took the reins in his right hand. He spoke soothingly to the agitated horse as he unfolded the damp paper and tried to make out the scrawled words. *Noon. Saint* was clear enough. The ink had smeared on the third word. Ross struggled with the unfamiliar handwriting. *M-a-r.* Was the next letter a *y* or a *g*? The next few letters were nothing more than a blot, but . . . "Saint Mary . . . Saint Mary-le-Wood." Ross grinned wolfishly. "Saint Mary-le-Wood." He leaned forward in the saddle and clicked to his horse. He had the hour and the church. Now, all he needed was the lady.

Chapter 1

As long as the moon shall rise,
As long as the rivers shall flow,
As long as the sun shall shine,
As long as the grass shall grow.
                    Native American promise

The Church of Mary-le-Wood
London, England
February 2, 1723

Anne Fielding Scarbrough, the Marchioness of Scarbrough, stood wet and utterly miserable before the church altar. Her gold and silver chine silk gown was water soaked and splashed with mud; her eyes were red and swollen from weeping, and her right cheekbone bore a purplish-green bruise that paint and powder could not hide.

Her stepfather, Lord Langstone, stood unsmiling on her left, gripping her arm as though he thought she would pick up her skirts and fly over top the assembled guests to freedom. Her mother, Barbara, sat in the first row, splendid in her cherry-colored Watteau gown and red jeweled high-heeled slippers. Barbara's blond hair was curled and twisted into a fashion statement, her hands heavy with rings. Not a drop of water

marred her coiffure or her satin gown. Trust
Mother to look her best, Anne thought, but then
she's not been locked in a tower for five months
or dragged through the rainy streets to her wedding in an open carriage.

Anne unconsciously fingered her antique gold
necklace as she stared at the shriveled clergyman
in his musty crow-black robes. His wrinkled face
showed no trace of Christian charity. His bleary,
colorless eyes were filmed with cataracts, his thin
lips drawn down at the corners of his mouth. Did
he know she was being forced into this marriage?
Would he care if he did?

To her right stood her betrothed, Baron Murrane. Stubbornly, Anne would not look at him.
She could smell the damp wool of his cloak; she
could feel his small blue eyes boring into her, but
she'd not give him the satisfaction of meeting his
cold gaze. Colonel Fitzhugh Murrane . . . the
butcher of Sheriffmuir. He was twice her age and
as heartless as a Tyburn hangman. She'd had her
choice of suitors. Dozens of men, young and old,
rich and poor, had courted her since Lord Scarbrough had passed on, leaving her a rich widow.
Any of them would have suited her better than
Fitzhugh Murrane.

Anne's chest felt tight, and her head was
pounding. She swallowed the lump in her throat
and blinked back tears. She would not shame herself by losing control in front of all these people,
and if she started to cry, she knew she wouldn't
be able to stop. She glanced down at her hands.
The nails she'd always been so vain about were
bitten to the quick. She tucked them out of sight
under her lace-covered prayer book.

Murrane's heavy hand closed about her shoulder and pushed her roughly to her knees. Bewildered, Anne looked up at the minister. He

scowled at her and continued his droning litany. His words seemed nothing more than a jumble of meaningless chant.

Anne fixed her gaze on the floor and tried to keep her teeth from chattering. She was cold . . . so cold. She didn't want to be here. She didn't want this crude soldier for a husband . . . but no one seemed to care. What was it Barbara had said? *You're making much of nothing. Marry the man Langstone's chosen for you. Murrane may be only a baron, but he's strong enough to protect you and your fortune. Give him use of your body, and when he walks out the door, take a lover. It's what I always did.*

Anne was vaguely aware that her stepfather had released her arm and moved away. His footsteps on the stone tiles echoed in her ears. Murrane coughed and cleared his throat. Behind her, she heard the rustle of petticoats and the shuffling of shoes. It's happening, she thought. I'm taking marriage vows for the second time, and I've never known a man's love. Never known passion except in a dusty book of poetry. Sensible, meek, shy Anne. Better I had been a feather-heeled jade like my mother. At least I would have known the joys of bedding a man of my own choosing. The fingers of her left hand tightened around her amulet. If only it were magic, she wished. If only—

"Anne!" Murrane leaned close, and she caught a whiff of smoked mackerel on his breath. "Answer!"

She blinked. What?

"Do you, Anne, take this man to be your lawful husband?" the cleric repeated.

She pursed her lips.

Murrane's hand dropped to her elbow, and his gloved fingers dug into her flesh until she winced with pain. "Answer," he growled.

She drew in a ragged breath. Tears blurred her vision. "What?" she murmured dumbly.

Murrane swore softly.

"Ah-hemm." The minister sniffed in disgust. "Do you, Anne—" he repeated.

"She does, she does," the bridegroom flared.

The cleric ignored him. "Do you, Anne, take this man to—"

The roar of a flintlock rocked the church. Women screamed. Murrane let go of Anne's arm and whirled about, scrambling to his feet. Anne turned to see a howling wild man on a giant black horse charging down the center aisle directly at her. The rider's long black hair fanned out around him from under a feathered Scots bonnet, and his black eyes flamed like the coal pits of hell.

Murrane reached for his sword, swearing a foul soldier's oath when his hand came up empty. He darted off to the left out of Anne's line of vision. The minister heaved his Bible toward the terrible apparition, tried to run, and tripped on his own robes. He toppled backward and lay thrashing about on the floor with his feet tangled in Anne's gown.

Anne froze, facing certain death under the flying hooves of the madman's horse without uttering a sound. She stared helplessly as the marauder gave another spine-chilling whoop and threw something into the far front corner of the church. The object exploded in midair with a cloud of smoke and fire. The wedding guests panicked and began to scramble for the doors.

Anne didn't move. She watched as horse and rider thundered down on her. Her heart was pounding erratically, her knees were locked, and her muscles felt as though they were made of whey. She willed her lips to offer a dying prayer, but her tongue seemed glued to the top of her mouth.

For an instant it seemed to Anne that everything was happening in slow motion. She could taste the fear in her mouth . . . She could smell the acrid scent of black powder . . . She could hear the shrieks of the frightened cleric . . . She was acutely aware of the cold, hard stones beneath her knees. And most of all, she was conscious of the colors around her: the ebony hide and the startling white of the horse's eyes and bared teeth; the intense blue and green of the horseman's plaid; the flurry of scarlet, azure, and gold finery of the fleeing crowd.

In the last seconds before the black horse reached her, Anne found the strength to stand. I'll not meet my end on my knees, she thought, raising her chin in a hopeless show of defiance.

A heartbeat before she would have been crushed under the animal's hooves, the rider yanked back on the reins and the stallion reared, pawing the air above her head. The madman's heathen black eyes stared into hers. "Be you Anne?" he demanded in a deep steely voice.

"Yes," she squeaked.

"Then it's ye I seek." He wheeled the big horse and leaned from the saddle to snatch her up in his arm.

"No!" she cried. Realization struck home as he dragged her up in front of him. Belly down across the horse's withers, her skirts and hoops askew, she kicked and screamed and lashed out with balled fists.

Laughing, her abductor pinned her in place with one hand while he drew his sword with the other. The blade flashed over her head, and her ears rang as sword struck sword. She caught a

glimpse of Murrane's angry face before the mad
Scot threw another bomb. Anne clenched her eyes
shut and buried her face in the horse's hide.

"Hii-yii-yii-yiee!" the horseman screamed.

Anne felt the stallion's muscles tense and then
explode beneath her. She gasped as the wind was
knocked out of her by the force of the plunging
animal. Iron-shod hooves thundered across the
stone floor and down the aisle out of the church.
Someone shouted, and Anne felt the horse rise
into the air. She opened her eyes to see the top
of a man's head as they flew over him. The stallion landed running. Rain and wind tore at her
hair and exposed skin as they galloped wildly
down the street with a yelling mob in hot pursuit.

"Let me go!" she cried in desperation. Her captor's only reply was another burst of savage
laughter.

Men and women scattered before them. Anne
lifted her head to see a wagon full of hay blocking
the intersection. She gave a frightened squeal and
covered her face with her hands. When she
looked again, the wagon was gone, but she wasn't
certain if they'd gone around it, over it, or under
it.

"Hold tight, hinney," her kidnapper ordered.
His voice held a strange accent, one she couldn't
place.

"Please," she moaned. "I'm not—"

"Not now, woman!" She heard the grate of
steel as he drew his sword and hacked his way
past two city watchmen wielding oak staffs. The
horse gave a quick burst of speed, then stopped
so suddenly her stomach lurched.

Anne knew she was going to be sick. She
gagged and choked, but nothing came up. She
felt as though she were being jolted in two.

The Scot backed the big horse into a deserted coal yard and shoved the gate shut. In a flash, he was out of the saddle and lifting her down. She dropped to her knees in the mud and was sick again. This time she choked up a mouthful of bitter liquid.

"Hist now, hinney," he said gently. " 'Tis sorry I be for your discomfort, but there was no time to make things easier for you."

She wiped her face with the back of her hand, and it came away streaked with paint and powder. Her hair had come loose from its pins and hung around her face like a dockside trollop's. Slow, hot anger pushed back her awful fear, and she turned her head and glared at him through the pouring rain. "If it's ransom you want, I can pay it," she spat, "but if you mean to kill me, have the decency to do it now before I drown!"

His deep laugh was a rumble above the rain. "Nay, lady. Ye need have no fear of me. I'll not harm a hair on your head." He grinned. "And I want no ransom, although I admit my fortune could use it. My name is Ross Campbell. I've come from your sweetheart, and I'm sworn to deliver ye to him safe and sound."

She staggered to her feet. "What?"

"Your betrothed. He hired me to rescue you."

"You tried to cut my betrothed's head off with your sword in the church," she accused.

"Not him," Ross said. "Your true sweetheart, Bruce Sutherland."

Anne tried not to dissolve into hysteria. "There's been some . . . some mistake," she said between chattering teeth. "I don't have . . . have . . . a sweetheart, and if I did, it wouldn't be Bruce . . . Bruce Sutherland. I've never met the man."

"Ye know each other well enough, I vow. There's nay need to be coy with me. Bruce told me all." Ross untied a second plaid from a waterproof bag behind his saddle. "Wrap this around ye." He draped it over her shoulders. "We must make a run for the city gate. Ye'll need to get rid of those hoops an' such."

"Get rid of . . . of my . . ." Anne clutched at the thick wool and backed away. Mud oozed over the tops of her jeweled slippers, but she was so cold and wet it didn't matter. She was at the mercy of a madman. "Please," she reasoned. "I can pay you. I'm rich. If you'll just take me to my house—"

"Don't make a fuss, hinney, and cover your head, do. Your hair's all elf-locks. Fair to say, ye look like a drowned partridge. I've no wish to deliver ye to your love frozen solid."

"I told you, I don't know any Bruce Sutherland. You've made a mistake." Her words were carefully enunciated, as though she were speaking to a slow child. "I can pay whatever you ask, but I can't go with you."

He grinned. "Ye mean I've taken the wrong bride."

She nodded. "It appears so."

"Ah, I see the right of it now. There was another Anne at the church. I overlooked her and picked you."

"Yes, that . . . that must be what happened."

He pulled off his Scots bonnet and wrung the water out of it. "Do ye know many colonials, m'lady?"

Her eyes widened in bewilderment. "No," she admitted. "I . . . I know none at all."

"Good. I was afraid you'd met a flock of clodskulled Yankees and had a bad impression of

Americans." He shook out his bonnet and put the soggy hat with its dripping wet feathers back over his drenched mane of night-black hair. He set one moccasined foot on a bag of coal, folded his arms over his massive chest, and stared at her with the arrogance of a landless German prince. "I'm half Scot, half Delaware Indian, and half wolverine," he proclaimed. "I can outride, outshoot, and outdance any mother's son on this little island. I've got the fastest horse and the most gall you've ever laid those bonny gray eyes on. Women have called me rogue, but they've never called me stupid."

Anne blinked. She felt light-headed, as though she was going to faint.

"What I'm trying to tell ye, hinney, is that my daddy never raised no fools. Ye make a poor liar. You're Bruce Sutherland's Anne, right enough. You've doubtless taken a long look at that rich bastard back at the church and changed your mind about who ye want to wed. But that's not my affair. Ye can take that up with Bruce when I deliver ye to him." He glanced up at the downpour and grimaced. "The weather's against us, mistress. We'd best ride and take our chances with the storm."

"God's wounds!" she cried. "Are you so thick you cannot realize what you've done? I don't know who you're looking for, but I'm Lady Scarbrough. I'm a marchioness. You're in very big trouble, Master Ross, very big trouble indeed."

He grinned again, and Anne's breath caught in her throat. There was something very dangerous about that smile.

"Will they hang me, do ye think?"

"After they draw and quarter you!"

He scratched his head. "It sounds painful.

Mayhap we'd best be certain they don't catch us."
He took a step toward her.

"No! Stay away from me!" She whirled to run,
but the sucking mud pulled at her feet. She
slipped and fell facedown. A heartbeat later, he
had her. Anne opened her mouth and began to
scream. He clamped a broad hand over her mouth
and gathered her up in his arms.

"Hist that screeching now," he warned. "Ye
sound like an Iroquois squaw."

She caught the skin on his palm between her
teeth and bit down as hard as she could. He didn't
flinch.

Anne felt his face pressed against her cheek.
She couldn't see him because somehow, in the
struggle, the plaid was over her head.

"Hold your tongue, lass," he warned. He
didn't raise his voice, but his tone demanded caution on her part. "Mind your manners, or I'll have
to bind and gag ye, I swear I will."

Anne stopped fighting and let go of his hand.

"That's better. Now listen well, for I doubt I'll
soon have time to repeat myself. I've no designs
on your purse or your body. 'Tis fair-shaped
enough, what I can see of it, but I'm not a man
to reave from a friend's stable. You're as safe with
me as if I was your blood brother. I'm taking ye
to Bruce in Scotland."

Anne's heart sank. There was no reasoning
with him. No matter what he said, she knew that
he was carrying her off to her death. She made
no further protest when he lifted her petticoats
and took hold of her hoopskirts. There was a loud
tearing sound. He spun her as easily as though
they were partners in a country dance, then he
lifted her out of the hooped frame.

"A bride's finery is no good for riding, that's
certain," he said. "I'll take a little of this off for

good measure." He pulled a dirk from his waist and cut ten inches off the hem of her gown.

"You'll have to kill me first," she stammered. Fear thickened her tongue and made the rain and cold fade away. "Murder me and be done with it, for mercy's sake."

"For the love of God, woman! Have ye heard nothing I've said? Bruce Sutherland sang your praises right manfully over his jack of whiskey, but he never said ye were a lackwit. You're going to make me do this the hard way, aren't ye?" He jerked a leather thong from the top of his moccasin. Before she knew what was happening, he'd seized her wrists and bound them together in front of her.

"No," she groaned.

"Astride is easier on the gut than belly-down, hinney," he said. He lifted her up and set her on the horse in front of his saddle, then mounted behind her.

Anne gasped as one muscular bare calf touched hers. He tucked the thick folds of the woolen plaid over and around her, covering her from head to toe.

"Give me your word you'll not betray me, and I won't gag you," he rumbled into her ear. An iron arm encircled her waist and held her tight against him.

"Don't cover my mouth," she pleaded.

"An *aye* will suffice."

The stallion arched his neck, and his great legs moved under them. Anne heard the squeak of the coal yard gate and the sharp cadence of the horse's hooves against the cobblestones.

She stiffened her body, straining to stay as far away from Ross Campbell as possible. He chuckled softly and began to whistle and then to sing the words from an old ballad.

". . . Gae saddle to me the black, black steed,
Gae saddle and make him ready,
Before I either eat or sleep
I'll go seek my fair lady—
And we were fifteen well-made men,
Although we were nay bonny;
And we are all put down for one,
The Earl of Cassilis' lady."

Chapter 2

It was still raining. Anne pushed aside a fold of the woolen plaid that covered her head and saw three bound prisoners in an open wagon being drawn by a single water-soaked ox along the narrow, shop-lined street. An armed guard walked beside the great-horned red and white beast; four more guards walked behind the wagon. None of them looked particularly enthused or competent. Even the prisoners seemed more downhearted by the weather than whatever fate was in store for them.

One of the prisoners wore a battered sign around his neck that read *Highwayman.* He was a thickset balding man with no chin and a prominent nose. Anne thought he looked more like a tailor down on his luck than a *gentleman outer.*

"Don't even think of appealing to that lot to save you," Ross Campbell cautioned. "I could take those five with my eyes shut and a grizzly bear at my back."

Anne didn't mistake her captor's softly slurred threat for idle boasting. The slack-bellied guards looked more accustomed to lifting mugs of ale than the weapons on their belts. In contrast, this savage Scot seemed as deadly as a tightly wound crossbow. She could feel his rock-hard thews, could sense his readiness to spring into action. It would be useless for her to cry for help from these poor guards. Ross Campbell would scatter them like barnyard poults before a hunting hawk.

They'd been wandering around the city for hours, getting wetter and wetter. The heavy woolen plaid that had seemed so warm when she'd first wrapped it around her was now as wet and cold as her feet. Anne was beginning to wonder if her captor was stupid as well as crazy. If he had a plan for escaping London, he hadn't given any inkling of it yet.

"Where the hell are we, hinney?" he rumbled in her ear.

She jumped. Had he read her mind?

"Do ye know this part of the city?"

"I'm your prisoner," she reminded him timidly. "How should I know where you're going?"

"These streets are worse than rabbit warrens. I've never seen so many people all in one place."

She took courage from his weakness. "You've never been to London before?" she ventured, deciding he must be a bumpkin if he thought London was crowded today. The streets were nearly empty due to the heavy rainfall; even the beggars and footpads had been driven to find shelter.

"Nay, and I'll not come again if I ever find my way out of this foul-smelling—"

"You needn't worry about going anywhere again," she retorted. "I told you. You'll be drawn and quartered. What's left of you will feed the fish under London Bridge. This isn't the heathen Highlands of Scotland. We take a dim view of kidnappers here." She paused for a breath. Both of his hard bare legs were wedged against hers. She'd given up trying to avoid touching him—it was the only spot on her that was warm. "I know where we are," she continued. "This is Cheapside. If we go that—"

"—way," he finished. "I'll end up in the king's privy, or mayhap, Newgate Prison. Wasn't that what ye had in mind, mistress?"

"You're the one who asked me where we were," she reminded him. "You're the one who's lost. You haven't a chance of getting me out of the city. Release me, and you might escape with your neck."

"Hist, woman, ye have the tongue of a jay. A man cannot ask ye a simple question without loosing a flood of abuse."

Anne was shocked into silence. No one had ever accused her of being a scold. "Sweet Anne," they had called her, and "gentle Anne." If she was behaving abominably, it was this savage who had caused it.

Ross reined the stallion close to an overhanging house and called out to a man carrying a live sheep over his shoulders. "Can ye tell me the way to London Bridge?" he asked.

Anne tensed. "Please," she began throatily. "I—" She broke off abruptly as the Scot's hand around her waist moved higher under the plaid, and she felt the cold, hard blade of a knife beneath her chin. "Ohhh," she gasped.

"My wife is near her time," Ross continued smoothly. "Her sister lives just beyond the bridge. I'd have her there and abed before she slips the babe."

The farmer motioned with his head. "That way. Left when ya come t' Cannon, then right on Fish Hill. Ya cain't miss the bridge."

"Thanks to ye, good sir," Ross replied, urging the black horse into a trot. "Never fear, sweeting," he murmured to Anne. "I'll have ye safe in no time."

She ground her teeth in frustration. No matter how much she'd wished to avoid wedding Murrane, she hadn't wanted to be carried off to be raped and murdered by some Highland brigand.

A voice from her childhood echoed in her mind. *Out of the pot and into the fire*, her old Welsh nurse, Janet, had always warned. Anne shivered. She'd done that, right enough. If Ross Campbell wasn't spawned in hellfire, he gave a good imitation.

Why hadn't she agreed to marry Murrane months ago when her father—her stepfather, Langstone, she corrected—first informed her of the match? If she had, she'd have been far from here, safe in Murrane's stone-walled keep in Northumberland.

Without warning, she sneezed and then sneezed again. Her nose began to run, and she lifted her bound hands helplessly. "I need a handkerchief," she pleaded. "My nose is . . . My nose—" She sneezed again and burst into tears.

"For the love of God, woman." Ross caught a corner of her plaid and wiped her nose roughly with it.

"Oh," she moaned in total mortification.

"Hist your wailing. Have ye never been wet before?" The stallion snorted and shied away from the bloated body of a dead dog lying in the street. Ross patted the horse's neck and guided him wide around the carcass with soothing commands. The black laid back his ears and pranced stiff-legged on the slippery cobblestones.

Anne whimpered, clutching frantically at the horse's mane. When the skittish mount had leaped sideways without warning, she'd lost her balance and slid forward on the withers.

"Can ye not ride, woman?" He pulled her upright with an impatient jerk of his wrist.

"I ride well enough," she protested, "sidesaddle. I've never ridden astride. This devil-beast isn't even broken."

Ross chuckled. "He suits me well enough. My daddy always said a docile woman or a docile mount aren't worth feeding."

Anne squeezed her eyes shut. Another personal need was making urgent demands on her body. "I should have turned Catholic and taken the veil, like Janet wanted me to," she whispered under her breath. At least nuns were free to use to use a garderobe when they had to!

"What are ye whining about now?" he demanded.

"I—" A musket fired behind them. Above Anne's head, a wooden sign splintered, showering horse and riders with bits of wood.

"Halt!" a watchman yelled.

Ross let out a wild scream, drew his sword, and brought it down heavily across the stallion's flank. The horse lunged forward and galloped down the street. Two more shots rang out. The horse slowed his momentum and reared, snorting, into the air.

Anne kept her eyes shut. Her fingers were wound so tightly in the animal's mane that she couldn't have let go if she had wanted to. Ross leaned forward over her, crushing her with his body. She heard the terrifying sound of his sword swish through the air. There was a sickening thud and a man's groan. Then the horse was running again.

She opened her eyes to see four soldiers with pikes and muskets blocking the street in front of them. Ross never hesitated. The black horse galloped straight at them, then the Scot squeezed his knees into the animal's sides and pulled back on the reins. The soldiers scrambled aside as the horse jumped. A cry of pain told Anne that one man hadn't gotten out of the way of those terrible hooves soon enough.

Ross turned the horse south onto Fish Hill Street. London Bridge was only a short dash away. Another group of horsemen galloped toward them from Tower Street.

"Hang on," Ross shouted in her ear. He let go of her and pulled a tinderbox and a round leather ball from his saddlebag. Taking the stallion's reins between his teeth again, he struck a spark and lit the fuse on the ball.

Anne screamed as a pie seller loomed up before them. The black horse dodged left around the terrified merchant, leaped over a pig, and plunged through the center of a herd of sheep. Anne lost her seat and slipped forward over the horse's neck. She knew she couldn't hold on any longer. Her head hung only inches from the milling herd of frightened sheep—the stench of manure and wet wool filled her nostrils. One black-faced ram, climbing on the back of another in an effort to escape, banged into her chin with his muddy nose. "Help me!" she cried.

Pain shot through her as Ross seized her by the hair and dragged her back up on the stallion's withers. "I said hang on," he admonished.

It was a race for the bridge. The soldiers behind them kept up a steady fire of gunshots as they pounded down Fish Hill. Ross's horse jumped the last three ewes and a spotted sheepdog, narrowly avoiding a collision with a coach and four. Pedestrians scrambled for safety. A mule rammed into a gray mare pulling a farm cart, and the cart overturned, spilling cabbages and driver into the muddy street. The farmwoman came to rest in a puddle of water. She shook her fist and cursed as the stallion galloped by.

Anne got a strong whiff of something burning and realized that what the Scot had lit was another bomb. He'd lit the fuse, but he'd not thrown the explosive device. If he didn't throw it soon, they'd both be blown to bits.

The big horse stretched out and covered the ground in great, powerful bounds. The traffic had thinned; the cobblestone street was clear of wheeled vehicles. Ahead of them, through the pouring rain, Anne could see the buildings at the entrance to the bridge. It was fast growing dark, and her sense of distance seemed distorted in the misty twilight. She blinked away the water that streamed down her face and into her eyes.

Something was wrong.

"Look out!" she cried. To her horror, she realized that the bridge had been blocked with overturned wagons. Armed men crouched behind the wagons. In front, wearing the green and black livery of her betrothed, Baron Murrane, were two burly retainers with crossbows and square-tipped arrows. And in the shadows, behind the ale cart, Anne was certain she recognized Murrane himself. He raised a French musket and took aim.

"Stop!" she shouted. "Don't shoot!"

Fire and white smoke belched from the muzzle of his gun. Ross's stallion screamed and reared sideways as a bloody furrow plowed across his rump. The Scot yanked the animal's head to the right and dug in his heels. The black lunged forward toward the barrier. A crossbowman raised his weapon, and Anne shut her eyes as Murrane's men howled with the scent of victory.

Anne steeled herself for the flesh-shredding blow. The metal bolt shot from a crossbow carried enough force to pierce armor, and at this range it was impossible for the bowman to miss. Instead, she felt the stallion wheel hard to the right.

Anne opened her eyes as Ross Campbell gave another spine-chilling whoop and lobbed the bomb at the bowmen. The horse plunged through the alley between two houses. The pathway was so narrow that a jutting board grazed Anne's right knee. She heard another gunshot behind them and the clamor of angry male voices. The Scot laughed and rose in his stirrups. Anne's heart missed a beat as the big horse gathered his legs under him and leaped into empty space.

The last thing she remembered was plummeting headlong toward the black, turbulent waters of the Thames.

"She's so beautiful . . ."

So beautiful . . . so beautiful . . .

"How could she ever produce a child so ugly, when she's so beautiful?"

"Well, she's Barbara's right enough. Who can say about Langstone?"

"If she were mine, I'd drown her, or at least have the decency to put her out to nurse. I wouldn't keep her around where I had to look at her every day."

Eight-year-old Anne cringed at the brittle laughter and crouched lower behind the boxwood hedge. She didn't need to see the faces of her mother's friends to know who they were; she knew them by their voices.

"And that mouse-colored hair," Lady Mary whispered loudly. "Barbara's is spun gold, but Anne's is impossible. It was bad enough before she took the fever and it all fell out. Now she reminds me of a hedgehog."

"Truth to tell, Barbara's may have been gold at one time, but I've heard from a very reliable source that the color comes from a shop on Puddling Lane. Barbara's not as young as . . ."

Anne bit her lower lip to keep from crying. Tears spilled down her thin cheeks as she ran an ink-smeared hand through her shorn locks. Forgetting her slippers and her precious book of poetry, she stumbled up and ran toward the orchard. Her stockinged feet flew over the soft spring grass until she was far away from the

house. She flung herself facedown on the thick moss
and wept great anguished sobs.

It was true what they had said. She was ugly! Ugly
and slow-witted! As skinny as a rail. She never knew
what to say or do in company. No matter how hard
she tried, she couldn't please her mother . . . couldn't
make her father proud . . .

"Ugly. Ugly little Anne." Their taunts rang in her
ears. ". . . drown her if she was mine."

Drown her . . . drown her . . . drown her . . .

Anne choked up a mouthful of water and gasped
for breath. She tried to lift her head, but something heavy was pressing her down. She spit up
another great mouthful, and the world began to
spin. She was falling . . . falling. Down, down
into cold darkness.

The earth was moving under her. Not like before . . . not spinning. This time it was rocking
. . . swaying. She could hear the soothing rumble
of . . . rumble of wheels against a dirt road.

Anne opened her eyes and looked into the
seamed face of an old woman. Golden hoop earrings and thinning snow-white hair peeked from
under a flowered silk scarf. The woman's eyes
were black and bright as wrinkled currants, and
she smelled of cloves. "I . . . I . . ." Anne began.

"Shhh," the woman ordered. She laid a leath-
ery hand over Anne's eyes. "Shhh."

Anne sighed and closed her eyes. It was too
much trouble to argue. It was easier to lie still, to
let the sway of the bed rock her back to sleep. To
let the darkness pull her down again. She was
warm . . . warm . . .

The old woman was humming a strange tune.
From far off, Anne thought she heard the plain-

tive notes of a violin. The ghost music soothed her, and she surrendered to fitful sleep.

The orangery. She was in her father's orangery. A caged nightingale poured out a flood of sweet, clear notes. The air was filled with the scent of orange blossoms, and the colors of the trees, the rug, her azure morning gown were so vivid they hurt her eyes. Her mother walked toward her through the open garden door. The nightingale ceased singing, and Anne was overcome by sadness.

"An unwilling bride . . ."

Unwilling . . . unwilling . . . unwilling . . .

"But he's old, Mother," Anne protested. "Why must I marry now? I'm only fifteen."

"Lord Scarbrough is as wealthy as Croesus, and he's a marquis. You're a lucky girl to get him."

"But I don't want a husband. I'm content with my books and my flowers."

Barbara's tone grew curt. "You'll hold your tongue and take the man your father's chosen for you, you ungrateful chit. You've a decent dowry, but it's not as though Scarbrough's getting any beauty—"

"I know I'm plain, Mother, but—"

"Barbara! I've told you, I wish to be called Barbara, not Mother." Her blue eyes had become as hard as twin sapphires. "Plain as dirt and timid as a scullery maid. You must take after some of your father's people, Anne; you certainly don't take after me. The only thing I can boast of is that you're biddable."

"I don't mean to cause you trouble, but—"

"No buts, Anne. You'll take Lord Scarbrough and thank God for the opportunity. An old man is easy to please, especially if you've nothing about you to cause him jealousy. He'll die soon enough and leave you a wealthy widow. You'll be able to . . ."

Take the man your father's chosen for you . . . Plain

*as dirt . . . Don't take after me . . . Biddable Anne
. . . Anne . . .*

"Anne. Anne, open your eyes, hinney."

A face loomed above hers. Not the old woman's but a man's. Anne sucked in a sharp breath.
It was that devil of a Scotsman—the barbarian
who'd kidnapped her from her own wedding.
"You," she murmured. Her throat felt raw and
scratchy, and she ached all over. She stared past
the outlaw to the curved red roof above. "Where
. . . where are we?"

He sighed a sigh of relief and grinned. "With
friends, sweeting."

Anne swallowed and moved her hands restlessly over the covers. She was lying in a bed, but
the bed—the house—was moving. Confused, she
closed her eyes again and tried to remember.
"The Thames," she whispered. "We fell into the
Thames."

"Fell, hell!" he exclaimed. "We jumped. I
couldn't see any other way to get shut of that
popinjay you were about to marry. A lot he
thinks of you if he was willing to set his dogs on
us. A crossbow isn't particular. He could have
killed you as easily as me. The bastards shot my
horse."

"Is he—"

"It was only a flesh wound, no thanks to your
bridegroom." He squeezed her hand. "You gave
me a fright, hinney. You must have swallowed
half the river."

Anne touched the wall beside her built-in bed.
The narrow wooden boards were carved and
painted in bright red and blue and yellow flowers. The room was tiny, lit by a hanging brass
lantern and packed full of barrels and baskets.
Kettles and pots and a polished violin and bow

hung suspended from hooks in the curved ceiling. With every breath Anne took, she drew in the heady odor of drying herbs. "What place is this?" she asked weakly.

"Not to worry, lass," Ross replied. "You'll come to no harm here."

The room jolted to one side, righted itself, and bounced on. Anne heard the distinct squeak of a wheel. She remembered the soothing sound of wheels from her dream . . . or was it a dream? "We're in some kind of a wagon, aren't we?"

"Aye," he admitted. "Some kind o' wagon." He placed his scarred, callused palm across her forehead. "Ye were feverish before, talking out of your head, but you're cool enough now."

Anne moistened her lips. "I . . . I want to know where we are."

"A half day's journey from London on the Colchester Highway, if ye insist."

"But what is this? What kind of a . . ." She trailed off, intimidated by his insolent grin.

Ross leaned back on his heels, crossed his arms over his broad chest and began to sing:

> "By and by the lord came home,
> Inquiring for his fair lady,
> One did cry, another replied,
> She's gone wi' the gypsy laddies."

Chapter 3

J ust before dusk, the gypsies turned their wagons off the Colchester Highway onto a rutted dirt track that led into the woods. They followed that road for nearly two miles until it ended at a ruined manor house, one of many destroyed nearly a century ago in the battle between Royalists and Roundheads. Nothing remained of the great house but blackened walls. The men guided their horses past the tumbled-down chapel and around the ancient overgrown cemetery to a massive, timber-framed wheat barn.

The barn's roof had sagged and fire had claimed one wall, but the rest of the structure was sound. The gypsies halted their wagons in a semicircle around the open end of the barn and began to unhitch their animals. Immediately, dark-eyed children scattered to gather wood for fires, and the women began to unpack their cooking utensils. One man carried a monkey from his caravan and chained it to a wagon wheel.

Ross untied his black stallion from the back of one of the bright-painted *vardos* and led him to a stream for water. The tall Scot brought the horse back to the wagons after he'd drunk his fill and tied him securely to a tree away from the other horses. ''You're a sight, certain,'' Ross murmured to the animal. To disguise the big horse,

27

the gypsies had smeared whitewash on his head and chest to turn his shiny, black hair to gray. One ear had been covered with a dirty bandage, and his magnificent tail had been wrapped with cloth and tied with red yarn. Ross had exchanged his saddle for a worn packsaddle. He'd hidden his good leather saddle in one of the caravans and loaded the stallion with a huge bundle of baskets.

Ross grinned and patted the stallion's neck. "Your own mother wouldn't know you, Tusca." A boy brought a leather nose bag full of grain, and Ross tied it over the animal's head so the black could eat. "Much obliged," he said. "He earned his oats yesterday, and I've a feeling he'll do so again." With a final pat of the horse's rump, Ross joined two men on the far side of the fire.

"Well, Johnny Faa. Do I look Rom?" Ross spread his arms and laughed. When he'd joined the gypsies in London, after he and pretty Anne had nearly drowned in the Thames, they'd disguised him as well as Tusca. His black Indian hair and bronzed complexion made it easy for him to blend in with these fey wanderers, but his feet hurt in English shoes, and he longed to trade this womanish red scarf around his head for his own Scots bonnet. He'd come close to losing his bonnet in the river—one of his eagle feathers had washed away—but luckily he'd thought to tuck it into his vest when they'd made the jump into the water.

The men laughed and said something in their own tongue. The leader of the band, Johnny Faa, was middle-aged and wiry. The second, slightly younger, was his brother Tom, as round as an ale barrel and as sturdy.

"We knew ye must have *tacho rat*—the true blood—when we saw ye come up swimming." They laughed again. Tom had waded into the

Thames to catch Tusca's bridle and lead him from the water.

Ross exhaled sharply as he remembered the fierce current of the river. It had been close. Without luck, and the stallion's strength, the black water would have had him and the woman. As it was, the lass had nearly drowned. The force of the river had carried them far enough from the bridge so that their pursuers hadn't seen them climb up the bank.

Johnny Faa grinned, exposing white, even, foxlike teeth. Anne's pearl earrings dangled from Johnny Faa's ears, the price for the gypsies' aid and protection. Well worth it, Ross thought, whatever the cost of those huge pearls.

"Sara says your woman has recovered," Tom said, choosing his English words carefully.

"Aye, she's well enough. We'll take leave of ye come morning." Ross watched Johnny Faa's eyes for any hint of trickery, but he saw none. Either they had accepted his story—that he had carried off Anne from her wealthy family to be his bride—or it made no difference to them.

"Our fate takes us another way." Johnny Faa leaned back against a tree and idly ground one foot into the fallen leaves. "I could send one of my boys with ye, to set ye on the right course to Edinburgh."

Ross nodded. "True enough, but could ye give me a map, it would do as well. You've put your own people in enough danger for me already."

Tom pursed his lips and his eyes narrowed. "Most *gorgios* don't give a tinker's damn for Rom. You're different."

Ross winked. "It's my Lenni-Lenape blood."

"A map, then," Johnny Faa mused. "I have one, a good one, but . . ." He sighed. "Maps come dear, my colonial friend. I'm a poor man with many mouths to feed."

"I lost my pistol in the river, and I won't part with my sword, my horse, or my woman. Other than that . . ." Ross shrugged. "Name it."

"His lady has many rings," Tom reminded his brother.

"And a gold necklace," Ross said. "I'd—"

Johnny Faa thew up his hand with index and middle finger extended in the ancient sign to ward off evil. "No!" he cried. "Not the necklace. 'Tis . . . 'tis . . ." He shook his head. "Nay, friend, your lady has luck of her own. I'll not touch that necklace—nor should you. It's old, very old, and powerful. 'Twas that amulet that brought ye both from the Thames when ye should have drowned."

Ross hid his skepticism behind expressionless features. These damned gypsies were as superstitious as Shawnee, and he'd no wish to insult them. "A ring then," he said seriously. "Your choice. For a good map."

Johnny Faa grinned. "Two rings—the square emerald and the small ruby on her left hand."

"One," Ross replied. "The ruby."

"Both." The gypsy leader pulled a French flintlock pistol from the bag at his waist. "Take this as my gift to you, no charge. A man needs a good pistol."

Ross tucked the pistol into his waistband. "Done." He shook hands with the gypsy. "You're shrewd, but you're fair, Johnny Faa. You'd do well in the Colonies."

It was the gypsy's turn to shrug. "Who knows? Times are always hard for the Rom. It could be that our paths will cross again."

"If we don't set the snares, the pot will be empty tomorrow," Tom put in.

Johnny Faa looked up at the taller Scot. "Have you ever set rabbit snares, my friend?"

"Aye," Ross admitted. "A few."

Minutes later, the Scot was crouched beside an animal trail, carefully knotting a rawhide cord. The task was one he'd learned as a child from his mother, so simple it left his mind free to wander while his fingers kept busy.

Bruce Sutherland would be fit to be tied when he found out Ross had traded off part of the bride's dowry. Tough. Nothing had gone as Ross had planned since he'd landed on this godforsaken island. Sutherland would just have to bear part of the cost. A man had to have a map in unfamiliar country, and a good pistol was worth its weight in gold.

Daddy had no idea what was what when he'd sent his only son off to collect a title and a fortune in his native Scotland. Angus Campbell had inherited both, so the letter from that Edinburgh solicitor had stated. And Angus, being still laid up from that tussle with a black bear sow, had figured that sending his boy in his place was the right thing to do.

"No sense lettin' grass grow under their feet," old Angus had insisted. "We need the money too bad."

Ross agreed. His daddy had staked a claim on the Mesawmi River forty years ago when the woods were really wild. He'd fought off wolves and Iroquois, and finally married the daughter of a Delaware chief to get that land. He'd built a trading post and cleared virgin timber for pasture and a few crops, and he'd buried four children in the rich earth. And after all that, he wasn't, by God, about to hand over his land to any English lord who'd never set foot in America.

It had been Ross's idea to mosey into Williamsburg to try and get legal title to the land around Campbell's Trading Post. The officials there had said the land in question was part of Maryland territory and sent him north to Annapolis. There, on the Chesapeake, Ross had found out that what Angus thought belonged to him was part of some Englishman's grant from King Charles. And after Daddy had got done pitching a fit, they'd started trying to figure out a way to raise enough gold to buy their own land.

The inheritance seemed an answer to their prayers until he'd actually gotten to Scotland. Instead of a grand welcome, he'd been met by the sheriff and nearly tossed into debtors' prison. Somehow his daddy's cousin, Robert Bruce Campbell, had managed to spend money he hadn't had in the years before he died. The title "earl" was as empty as Robert Bruce's castle strongbox. Ross had escaped the sheriff by a whisker and a lucky left punch.

Ross rose from his crouch and stretched. The rabbit trail looked well-traveled. He'd be surprised if he didn't catch one by morning. Whistling, Ross started back toward the gypsy encampment. A hot meal and a good night's sleep would be just what he needed. He was certain Sutherland's Anne would squawk like a chicken when she found out he'd promised more of her jewels to Johnny Faa. He'd wait until they were ready to ride out before he told her. No sense courtin' trouble, Daddy always said. And women were all trouble—red or white. Not that he didn't favor the ladies. He did, but he'd learned young enough that a woman could complicate a situation as easily as a snapping turtle in a birchbark canoe.

* * *

Anne glared at the old gypsy woman and pushed past her to the door of the wagon. "I'm not his sweetheart," she declared indignantly. "I never laid eyes on him before he kidnapped me at the altar!" She threw open the door and jumped down from the back of the caravan to the ground. Gypsies of all ages turned to stare at her in the firelight. The man playing the violin let his bow fall, and the dancers stopped in mid-step to gawk.

Anne hid her fear behind a growing fury. She spied out the best-dressed man in the motley crew and marched toward him with head high and back ramrod straight. "I demand to be returned to London," she proclaimed. "I am the Marchioness of Scarbrough, and I will be treated with the dignity I deserve."

Behind her, a child twittered. Anne's cheeks grew hot as female giggles were replaced with deep guffaws. "I am," she insisted. "I am Lady Scarbrough."

"And I," rasped a deep male voice with a familiar Scots burr, "am the Prince of Wales."

Anne whirled around to see Ross Campbell strutting toward her. He was decked out in gypsy costume like some drunken mummer, with a red scarf knotted around his head and golden hoop earrings in his ears. "You!" she spat.

"Annie, love."

Before she knew what was happening, he'd seized her and kissed her hard upon the mouth. "Ohh!" Her outcry was muffled by his lips. She was too stunned to move. Her breath caught in her throat as unfamiliar tingling sensations traveled from her lips to the tips of her toes. A wave of heat enveloped her, and she swayed and nearly fell when he let go of her shoulders.

He stared into her eyes. "Are ye all right, hinney?"

Anne ducked her head in shame; they were all laughing at her. Worst of all, he was laughing. Not out loud—he was laughing with his eyes. They gleamed in the dancing firelight like black onyx gemstones. "How dare you?" She wanted to shout it, but it came out a squeak. Her mouth still tingled from his kiss. Her heart was pounding so hard she was afraid it would burst through her breast. Swallowing, she tried to wipe away the feel of him with the back of her hand. "I am . . . I am . . ." she whispered hoarsely. "I am Lady—"

"The lady of my heart," he supplied loudly. The faintest odor, the trace of a taste on her lips, made her realize he'd been drinking. With a lopsided grin, Ross caught her hand. "Come, come, hinney, dance with me." He nodded to the musician, who began to play again.

"No." She shook her head. She couldn't dance. She wouldn't. Had they all gone mad to think the Marchioness of Scarbrough would dance their heathen dances? Bad enough the old woman had taken her bridal gown and given her these horrible, gaudy gypsy clothes. Bad enough she would not allow her to leave the wagon without a scarf over her head. Now they expected her to perform publicly for them like some common actress before this wildman ravished her body in full view of them all.

Ross leaned close. "Don't be afraid," he murmured. "I'll protect ye."

Her mouth dropped open in astonishment. He would protect her? This Scots marauder whose touch still burned the flesh on her shoulders, whose devil eyes branded her with each careless glance? Who in God's name would protect her from him? "No," she repeated dumbly. "I can't."

"Suit yourself then." He led her aside and deposited her on a blanket on the ground between two women. "Sit here and don't cause trouble," he ordered. With a wink, he returned to the circle of firelight and began to clap to the beat.

A young man in a blue dotted headscarf joined Ross. He began to dance, and Ross followed. The Scot tossed off his shoes and danced barefooted, quickly catching on to the twirling, stamping pattern of the gypsy music. A woman kept time with a tambourine as others in the group clapped and called out encouragement to the dancers. More men and children joined the dancing. The music grew faster and faster until Anne could feel herself drawn into the wild, pulsing rhythm.

On and on they danced. The children fell giggling to the ground, and one by one the men threw up their hands in surrender until only Ross Campbell and the leader Johnny Faa were left. Anne knew the gypsy's name because the women were shouting it as they clapped. "Johnny Faa! Johnny Faa!"

The musician's bow flew over the strings until the violin seemed to take on a life of its own. The high piercing notes of the instrument echoed from the shadowy corners of the barn and brought tears to Anne's eyes. Emotion rose in her chest, making breathing difficult. She couldn't take her eyes off the Scot as he leaped higher and higher, swirling, his hands moving in sweeping gestures, his eyes telling a story without words.

Suddenly the musician gave a final flourish and the women cried out. Both dancers sank onto the hard-packed floor of the barn, clothes soaked with sweat, gasping for air. Cheering, the other men ran toward them and offered each man a drink from a goatskin bag. Ross turned toward Anne and fixed her with a long stare, then he raised the goatskin in salute before he drank.

She blushed and turned away, unable to rid herself of the throbbing in her veins, unable to wipe away the memory of that brief kiss. She stumbled to her feet and walked away into the darkness beyond the wagons. She had to put distance between her and her kidnapper, had to clear her head enough to think of a way to escape.

Away from the fires, Anne felt the bite of the night air. The thin cotton blouse gave little protection against the wind, and the bright yellow woolen shawl was old and tattered. She shivered but she kept moving, afraid of the unknown but even more frightened of the man behind her. She could still taste his kiss, still feel his possessive touch. And God! Oh, God, deep down inside, some part of her had liked it!

What was wrong with her? Why had her body betrayed her? She was no green girl but a woman grown—a widow. She'd been kissed before.

Anne moistened her top lip with the tip of her tongue. The trembling in her limbs would not stop. Her stomach still felt as though she had swallowed a butterfly. Was this what her old nurse had referred to as the "thunderbolt"? Was she, Anne, more like her mother when it came to men than she'd ever wanted to admit?

Barbara had fallen easily into the arms of any handsome man who took her fancy. Her conquests were legendary. Barbara enjoyed the physical pleasure a virile man could give her—she'd never hidden the fact that her husband's marriage bed failed to satisfy her needs.

But Anne had never been that type. She'd been modest, and if she hadn't felt the true piety of a religious woman, she had at least been faithful in her prayers and church attendance. Her first marriage had been arranged when she was fifteen, and she had gone to her marriage bed as an unwakened child. Her husband, unwilling to bed a girl whose flow had not yet begun, had waited to consummate their union. And when she had finally become a woman, his own age and illness had prevented their coming together. Technically, she supposed, she was still a virgin.

A virgin. A virgin widow. Who would believe such a thing? And who wouldn't snicker behind their hands and whisper nasty jokes if they did believe?

She had always been afraid of men. Only one had ever stirred her blood. Anne remembered Brandon with a flood of sweet emotion. They had walked together in the apple orchard . . . They had held hands and exchanged kisses. They had promised . . . promised more than they could give. She had been reluctant to cuckold her decent, aging husband, and Brandon . . . Brandon was now wed to another and lived far away across the salt sea.

Sweet heaven help her! She had treasured Brandon's kisses, had spun marzipan dreams and hopes on them, but they had never ripped the woven fabric of her body and soul as the kiss of this wild Scot did.

Anne paused and stared up into the cold darkness. There was no moon, but the stars glittered through the velvet-black sky like scattered diamonds. She didn't remember ever seeing the stars glow with such dazzling splendor. She gazed at the vast sweep of heavens in awe, and as she watched, an incandescent spark flashed across the sky, followed by another and another.

"Bonny, aren't they?"

Anne jumped as Ross materialized out of the darkness beside her. "Ohhh."

"Hist, hinney, I'd not fright ye." He took hold of her arm. "You're cold as death."

"Let me go," she stammered. This time she would put up a struggle—would let him know she was no lightskirt who could be easily tumbled. She tried to pull away, but he held her as though she were anchored in solid rock. "Please . . ." she begged. Her lips formed the words, but she wasn't certain if she was begging him to set her free or to kiss her again. And if he kissed her here, when they were alone in the darkness, what must follow?

"Ye canna wander about these woods, chit. There are wild beasts and dangers ye know nothing about," he chided.

I know about you, she thought in desperation. None could be more dangerous than you. She clamped her teeth shut to keep them from chattering.

"Will ye walk back to camp, or must you be carried like a bag of grain?"

"I want to go home," she managed. The words came out muffled because her jaw was locked in place.

"Doubtless you shall when Sutherland has gotten ye with child. Your family will forgive you both and accept your marriage once there is no getting out of it."

Her jaw yielded. "I told you, I don't know any Sutherland. He's not my betrothed! This is all some horrible mistake."

"Aye, hinney, aye, and aye again. Say what ye will, but I need the money he'll pay me for your safe recovery."

"You're nothing but a common reiver! A mercenary!"

"Not by choice." Without further argument, he picked her up and slung her over one shoulder. Her pounding fists against his leather-clad back, her kicks against his chest, went as unheeded as her angry squawks of protest. He carried her back to the circle and deposited her at the door of the same caravan she'd been held prisoner in before.

From the firelight, Anne heard laughter and was certain they were all laughing at her.

"Into bed with you, wench," he said. "We have far to ride tomorrow. You may sleep easy. The gypsies are a moral lot—none will offer ye harm." He lowered her gently to the ground. Immediately she took two steps backward, out of reach of his arms.

"Colonial." The old woman's voice came from the darkness near the front of the wagon. "Come, share our meal with us. Bring the bride-to-be. She is lucky, and we would partake of that luck."

"No." Anne shook her head. "No . . . I'm tired."

"I will join you," Ross agreed. "Gladly."

"I am called Sara," the old gypsy said to Anne, shoving a battered tin plate at her. It was the same woman she'd seen hovering over her in the wagon.

Anne wanted to refuse the gypsy food, but the smell of bread and meat was irresistible. Her stomach growled in a most unladylike fashion. "Thank you," she murmured.

"You must taste it," Ross instructed. "Not to eat would be to insult our hosts."

Anne looked in vain for a fork or spoon, but there was none. As daintily as possible under the primitive conditions, she took a bit of the meat and put it into her mouth. It was sweet and juicy. She chewed and swallowed and quickly took another morsel. "It's good," she ventured, "but I don't recognize the flavor. What is it?"

The old woman's face folded into a mass of wrinkles as she grinned broadly. "Hedgehog," she proclaimed proudly. "Baked in a covering of clay under the coals of an open fire. We consider it a delicacy."

Anne choked on her mouthful. Horrified, she began to sputter. Ross slapped her hard on the back, and she swallowed with a gulp. "Oooh," she gasped.

"Just a bone," he put in hastily. "She needs something to wash it down." Sara offered a goatskin, and he lifted it to Anne's mouth. "Drink it," he whispered into her ear. "Drink, or I'll pour it down you."

Anne drank and sputtered as the strong liquor burned its way down her throat and hit the pit of her stomach with a jolt. The plate of food was still clutched in her trembling hands. Ross took it away and gently shoved her toward the *vardo* door.

"Many thanks, old mother," Ross said smoothly. "She'll finish inside. She is shy, my Anne, and not used to strangers."

"Modesty is becoming in a bride," Sara croaked. She turned away toward the fires and the laughter. Once more, sad gypsy music was beginning to filter through the night air.

Ross yanked open the door and gave Anne another push, this one not so gentle. "That was badly done," he scolded. "In a Mohawk camp, it would have cost you your scalp."

"Hedgehog," she whispered. "I can't eat hedgehog."

"Well, I sure as hell can." He crammed a piece into his mouth.

"You're horrible—all horrible," she cried. "Go

away and leave me alone." He reached for her, and she scrambled into the caravan and slammed the door behind her. His laughter burned her ears as she flung herself onto the bed and covered her head with a quilt.

Outside, she heard the notes of the gypsy violin and the rustle of wind through the dried branches of winter-bare trees. And she knew, although she could not see or hear him, that he was there . . . only a few feet away. He was waiting and listening, and Anne was afraid he could hear the uneven trip of her heart.

Chapter 4

Anne pretended she was sleeping when Sara entered the wagon hours later; she knew it was the old woman because of the strong scent of cinnamon that clung to the gypsy's hair and clothing. The door closed, and Anne heard a gentle sighing before her mattress sagged under Sara's weight. It was all Anne could do to keep from flinching when the woman rolled against her.

"Ye have an odd way of sleeping," Sara chuckled as she found a comfortable spot against Anne's back.

The sound was like the rustle of dried grass, and Anne suppressed a shiver. Her mouth felt parched; she held her breath and tried to lay perfectly still.

"Brides are always anxious," the gypsy continued in her thin, reedy voice. "I was anxious before my wedding night." She elbowed Anne's ribs and tittered. "Breathe, girl. You'll turn blue if ye don't. You're no more asleep than I am."

Bony toes poked the backs of Anne's legs. "I was anxious before all my wedding nights." Sara made a coarse sound with her lips. "You've a breme bridegroom for a *gorgio*."

"He's not my bridegroom," Anne burst out. "Why won't anyone believe me? He's a brigand—

42

a common thief. He stole me from my wedding to another man.''

Sara cackled with glee. ''As my first husband stole me. He carried me off in a sack from my mother's bed. Twelve I was, and already earning more than a grown woman at telling fortunes. I bit him and scratched his face so bad that he carried the scars to his grave—but he gave me three tall sons. We were well-matched for each other. Ahhh . . .'' she sighed wistfully, ''there was a bull of a man. Not so brawny as your Scot, but—''

Anne sat upright. ''Please,'' she interrupted. ''I'll pay you anything you ask if you'll help me escape.''

''—he had the black eyes of a fallen angel,'' the old woman said, ignoring Anne's plea. ''They hanged him at York for horse stealing, and my oldest son with him.'' She raised up on one elbow and stared at Anne.

Moonlight filtered through the cracks in the narrow walls to stripe the gypsy's shriveled face with silver and shadow. The air seemed suddenly still. Anne knotted her fingers together to keep them from trembling.

''Your man has a hangman's noose in his cards.'' Sara sat up and extended a gaunt hand. ''I'll read them for ye, Englishwoman, if ye cross my palm with silver.''

Anne drew her legs up and retreated to the far corner of the bed, near the wall. ''I hope they do hang him,'' she retorted. ''I want none of your fortune-telling. 'Tis witchcraft, and I—''

''Bite your tongue!'' Sara cried, making the sign to ward off evil. She mumbled something unintelligible in her own language. ''Are ye mad that you dare to wish for what ye don't want? Do ye not know your own power?''

Anne gasped. ''What is this nonsense about

power? If I had power would I be traded off to any husband my family picked for me? Would I be carried off like a stolen sheep?''

"Ssst," Sara hissed. "Ye truly do not know, do ye? Ahhh, *gorgio* girl, 'tis pity I feel for you. How can ye be so ignorant? How did ye come by the charm? 'Twas not bought for coin, I'll wager."

"My necklace?" Icy rivulets of fear trickled down Anne's spine. "What do you know of my necklace?" Her fingers closed around the ancient goldwork. The rectangular amulet bore strange patterns carved into its surface and was drilled with four tiny holes and one bigger one. A silver clasp suspended the piece to a chain around her neck. "It was a . . . a gift," she stammered.

"Who gave it to you?"

"A . . . a friend," Anne lied.

Sara chuckled. "Never try to fool a trickster. Blood to blood the power goes. 'Tis not Rom magic. The amulet comes from the old ones—the little dark people who raised the standing stones. Only those of the true blood can wear the charm. I am not the one to show you how to use the power. But this much I can tell you. The magic is real, and never, never wish for what you do not want with all your heart."

Anne remained crouched in the corner as the gypsy woman turned over without another word and went to sleep. A dozen questions rose in her mind, but she was afraid to voice them. Could Sara be a witch? How else could she know about the Eye of Mist?

Cameron Stewart, Lord Dunnkell, had given her the necklace when she was a child, telling her that it was magic. He'd been kind to her, so kind that she had believed the rumors about Lord Dunnkell and her mother to be just more ugly gossip. Hadn't her mother been linked romantically with every handsome man at court?

Barbara had ridiculed the amulet, calling it crude and tasteless—she'd wanted to sell it to the goldsmith. But Cameron, as he'd asked Anne to call him, had forbidden Barbara to dispose of the jewelry. "It belongs to the child," he'd said firmly. "And may the devil curse any others who touch it or plot to take it from her with the running French pox."

Normally a meek and biddable child, she had stubbornly defied her mother by refusing to give up the necklace. She'd worn it constantly hidden under her clothing, comforting herself by rubbing the amulet when she was afraid or lonely . . . even wishing on it. But nothing she'd wished for had ever come true, and after a while, she'd kept it close because it was the only thing in her life that never changed.

Servants came and went; even her nurse Janet left service to go and live with a married daughter. Barbara was constantly on the move, and she rarely had time to spend with her daughter or her husband. And Anne's father . . .

Anne pressed her cheek against the narrow boards of the wall. Her father . . . She swallowed the lump in her throat. All her life she'd believed Lord Langstone to be her father. He'd always been cold and distant to her, often severe, and she'd never guessed why. She'd thought that she was his only child—his heir—and she'd never been able to understand why he always seemed angry with her.

All those lonely childhood years . . . Times when she'd wished she could be Bess the dairymaid instead of Lady Anne . . . Bess and her six brothers and sisters had always seemed so happy, living in a one-room cottage with their merry father and laughing, plump mother.

Now, for the last year and a half, she knew why Lord Langstone had hated her—why she'd never been able to please him. She wasn't his daughter at all. Cameron Stewart was her real father. Lady Anne, the Marchioness of Scarbrough was an impostor—a bastard.

Cameron had broken the news to her before he left for the Colonies a year ago last summer. "You're a woman grown, Anne," he'd said, "and it's time you knew the truth."

"Did you love my mother, or was I an unfortunate accident?" she'd demanded tearfully.

"I've always loved you, lass," he'd replied. "Not being able to give you my name has been one of the saddest things in my life."

He'd told her more—told her that the necklace he'd given her when she was a child had been his mother's and that it had been handed down from mother to daughter for two thousand years. "It's called the Eye of Mist," he'd said. "It's made of Pictish gold. The legend says that whosoever possesses the Eye of Mist shall be cursed and blessed. The curse is that you will be taken from your family and friends to a far-off land. The blessing is that you will be granted one wish. Whatever you ask you shall have—even unto the power of life and death."

"I'm too old for a child's tale of magic," she'd replied.

"Nevertheless," he'd continued earnestly, "you must cherish the amulet and remember the legend. If you have a daughter, pass it on to her. It's the one thing I ask of you."

"You can't tell me you believe such superstitious nonsense?" she'd cried.

"It doesn't matter if I believe it, Anne. My

mother believed it, and I swore to her on her deathbed that I would pass it on to my true daughter." Anne remembered the strange expression that had passed over his face. "There's more I could tell you, lass, but this isn't the time. I want you to know that you'll be well provided for in my will. I've left you a fortune in—"

"I don't want your money," she'd said coldly. "There was a time when I needed you, but, as you say, I am a woman grown. I don't need you now."

She'd wept when he went away. She'd regretted her harsh words. She'd even ridden after him to London. But when she arrived there, she'd found that Cameron had sailed for America.

Later, she had confronted Barbara, demanding to know if Cameron was really her father. Barbara hadn't even had the dignity to try and deny it.

"Better Cameron Stewart than Langstone," Barbara had laughed brittlely. "That fop Langstone couldn't father a child—mine or anyone else's. A sponge has more backbone than his tool. He's useless between the sheets—always has been. It's why he claimed you as his heir. Your birth declared his virility to the world—or at least to those who didn't know what a soft sword he really was."

Anne was jerked back to the present by the old gypsy woman's loud snoring. Anne rolled her head around, trying to ease her stiff neck. All her muscles were cramped from sitting so long in one position. Gingerly, she crawled across the bed and climbed over Sara to stand on the floor.

She crept to the door and put her ear close to it, listening. The music had stopped. All was silent except for the hoot of an owl and the sound of the wind through the bare branches.

A plan began to form in Anne's mind. If she

could just reach the horses, she was certain she could bridle one and ride to the nearest village. Ross had been drinking earlier—doubtless he was passed out in some gypsy wench's arms.

Her fingers found the iron latch in the darkness of the *vardo*. Slowly, she lifted the bar and pushed the door open a crack. She blinked her eyes, trying to accustom them to the moonlight. The fire that had burned so brightly was now a blanket of scarlet coals. The other wagons were dark, shapeless lumps against the darker outline of the decrepit barn.

She opened the door and stepped down into the cold night, closing the door behind her. She listened intently. A woman's low giggle came from the nearest wagon. There was a creaking of wood, and the deeper voice of a man. Anne felt her face grow hot as she imagined the intimacies that must be taking place in that wagon between the man and woman. The thought that the man might be Ross came to her, and the heat in her face and neck grew more intense. Mentally, she chastised herself. What difference did it make to her if her kidnapper was quenching his lust with some gypsy jade? A slut and a rogue were well-matched, were they not?

Anne took a step, and dry leaves crunched under her foot. An owl hooted directly overhead, and Anne's heart leaped in her chest. Startled, she stared up as the dark form took wing. The owl swooped low over the wagon, his powerful wings carrying him as silently as mist. Anne gave a squeak of terror and turned to run. Something large and solid blocked her way.

"Going somewhere, hinney?"

Anne gasped as Ross's arms closed around her. She opened her mouth to scream, and he brought his head down and kissed her. His hand caught the back of her neck; his hard fingers twined in her hair. His other hand was low on the curve of her spine, crushing her against him. She could feel the heat of his powerful legs, his broad, muscled chest. Her eyes went wide in shock. Fear made her weak, and she clung to him to keep from falling . . . fear and something that was not fear . . . something she had never felt before.

She moaned deep in her throat as the tip of his tongue brushed her lower lip. The taste of his mouth was like stolen honey, forbidden and sweet, the sweetest thing she had ever tasted. She sighed, and somehow . . . somehow she was kissing him back.

Blood rushed to her head, drowning reason in the thunder of raw, unleashed passion. Her body molded to his, demanding, promising . . . Her tongue touched his, and she opened her mouth to take him within, reveling in the smell and taste of him, taking pleasure in the unfamiliar sensations that drove all reality from her mind. Her heart beat wildly; her breath came in deep, shuddering gasps.

"Hinney, hinney," he crooned in her ear. "Ah, hinney. What have I begun?"

His big, callused fingers touched her throat, stroking as lightly as the beat of a moth's wing, sending shivers of exquisite delight racing through her blood. He lowered his head and kissed the pulse in the hollow of her throat, and Anne felt a throbbing heat growing in her woman's secret place.

No one had ever made her feel like this before—not the hasty fumblings of her aged husband and not the awkward groping of half-grown boys she'd known before she'd wed. Not even Brandon's caresses had sparked a white-hot flame in her body like the scorching kisses of this wild barbarian.

She arched her back, wanting to be closer, ever closer, letting her hands run over his superbly muscled arms. Her breasts pushed against the rough gypsy clothing, aching with a need she had never dreamed she possessed. Her swollen nipples throbbed with a desire to be touched . . . suckled . . .

"Lass . . . lass," he moaned.

Anne could feel the swollen length of his manhood pressing against her, burning hot through the heavy wool of his belted plaid. His large, powerful hand spanned her hip possessively, cupping one buttock as his warm, moist mouth lingered over hers. His breath was sweet and clean; it tasted of mint. Boldly, Anne flicked the tip of her tongue across the surface of his square, perfect white teeth, savoring the delicious sensations that came with intimate exploration totally beyond her experience.

He pulled away to whisper in her ear. "Sweet Anne . . ." His husky voice was strained with emotion. "If we—"

The crashing of brush tore them apart. Anne's knees felt weak. She swayed and would have fallen if Ross hadn't steadied her with a sinewy arm. Wide-eyed and breathless, she stared at the rider on the lathered bay horse that burst into the circle of wagons.

A boy—a gypsy by his bright scarf and multi-colored vest—threw himself from the horse's saddle and ran shouting toward one of the wagons. Anne couldn't understand what he was saying, but within seconds men and women spilled from the wagons and began to harness their horses. Johnny Faa appeared fully dressed with an antique wheel-lock pistol stuck in his belt. He questioned the boy, then motioned urgently to Ross.

"Soldiers," Johnny Faa said in English. "Looking for a Scotsman and a woman. They searched the town and burned an Irish coppersmith's wagon. A man reported seeing gypsies pulling the pair from the Thames. You must go quickly, *gorgio*. If they find you here, my people will be in great danger."

"The map!" Ross demanded.

"The rings," the gypsy flung back.

Ross turned to where he'd left Anne standing beneath the bare limbs of a beech tree. "We've need of your rings, hinney."

Anne felt a flush of anger. Her mouth still stung from the pressure of his kiss, her body still trembled from his embrace—and he wanted her rings! "You'll not have them, you—you common thief," she retorted. Balling her fists behind her, she backed away from him. She blinked as the realization of what she'd let him do—of what she'd done to him—hit home. Shame fueled her fury. She whirled and ran toward the woods.

Ross caught her in six strides. "Don't be causing a fuss now, puss," he said calmly. He threw her over his shoulder and carried her, kicking, back to where the gypsy leader waited. When he reached Johnny Faa, Ross lowered her to the ground, captured her hand in his, and pulled off both her emerald and ruby rings.

The gypsy grinned and tucked the jewelry into an inner pocket in his vest. He took a rolled bit of leather from a waiting child and thrust it at Ross.

The Scot unrolled the map and glanced at it briefly, then nodded. "It's what I needed. Thank you." Ignoring Anne's struggles, he rolled the map tightly and tucked it inside his shirt, then grasped Johnny Faa's extended hand. "I'll not forget ye, and don't ye forget the Colonies."

"The Rom never forget. If it gets too hot for us here, we may cross your salt sea."

Dragging Anne after him, Ross strode quickly toward the spot where his stallion was tethered. "I can saddle him easier if I don't have to hold on to you," he said to her. "Can I trust you to stand still if I let you go?"

She nodded. He released her, and the minute he turned his back, she bolted for the forest again. This time she ran nearly a hundred yards into the darkness, tripping over fallen branches, scrambling through the underbrush. A brier jabbed into the palm of her hand, but she didn't stop to pull it out. Heart pounding, she ran as hard as she could in the direction of the dirt road.

Behind her, Anne could hear the gypsy wagons beginning to move. Without shouting, without even the crying of a single baby, the men and women hitched their *vardos* and drove off in different directions. As she glanced back over her shoulder, she saw a man's form kicking dirt over the fire. The glowing coals flared up for an instant and then went black.

Anne crouched down as Sara's wagon rolled within ten feet of her hiding place. The old woman was on the seat, cracking a whip over the back of her dapple-gray mare and urging the horse faster with threats in her own tongue. As soon as the *vardo* had passed, Anne got up and began to run, following the path of broken brush.

Off to the left, a dog barked. Anne stopped and turned toward the sound. A gunshot shattered the night, followed almost immediately by another. Anne screamed. "Here! Help me, I'm here!"

Through the trees, she could see a clearing in

the moonlight. Two figures on horseback detached themselves from the shadows and rode into the open. One raised his musket and fired. There was a flash from the weapon, and the second animal reared. The clouds obscuring the moon parted, and Anne could make out leather helmets. Soldiers! "Here!" she cried.

She ran toward them. The second man lifted his musket and fired. A branch exploded over Anne's head. She screamed and threw herself facedown on the ground. A man swore a crude oath. Another volley passed through the trees, and someone uttered a piercing cry.

Anne peered up through the tall grass. One of the soldiers was galloping toward her. Behind him ran a riderless horse. Terror gave her strength. She leaped up and fled back toward the gypsy campsite. Suddenly, ahead of her loomed another horse and rider. She screamed, realizing the animal was coming at her too fast for her to get out of the way.

"Down!" Ross shouted.

Anne dropped to her knees as the black stallion soared over her head. Too frightened to move, she looked back toward the oncoming soldier. Like ghostly knights of old, the two armed horsemen plunged headlong at each other. Seconds before the animals collided, Ross let loose an ungodly screech and swung low off the far side of his horse. The solder hacked at empty space with his sword, then gave a low groan as the apparition rose and knocked him from the saddle with one terrible blow.

Ross reined the black to a halt, spun, and galloped back, catching the soldier's mount before it could reach the place where Anne stood. Ross hit the ground on the balls of his feet, swooped her up, and deposited her in the saddle of the newly enlisted animal. Before she could protest, he was on the stallion again, leading her horse at a hard trot through the trees.

"Nooo," she said. "I can't—"

"Hist," he warned. He turned to fix her with a deadly stare. She couldn't see his eyes in the darkness, but she could feel them. "Not a word," he said softly. The tone of his voice raised the hair on the back of her neck. "These are fools who hunt us, and they'd as like shoot ye as me. Hold your tongue, woman, if you value your life."

Shivering with cold and fright, Anne clung to the saddle. Branches caught at her hair and tore her clothing until she lay low over the horse's neck. Gradually, the sounds of men and animals grew dim and the occasional shot was only a muffled echo in the distance.

They rode on through the forest for what seemed like hours, and then, when she was so weary she thought she would fall from the saddle, Ross reined up. He dismounted and led both animals into a deserted hut. One wall had fallen, leaving a gap high enough for a horse to pass through. He lifted her down from the horse and wrapped her in his woolen plaid. "I'll be right back," he murmured, tying the animals to a heavy beam. "There's a stream nearby. Ye must be thirsty."

She dozed without meaning to, and realized she'd drifted off when he touched her arm.

"Drink," he ordered.

The water was ice cold and tasted of fallen leaves. Eagerly, she swallowed, drinking every drop in the leather cup.

"What happened before," he said, "when we kissed . . ." He exhaled slowly. "It was a mistake, and it won't happen again. Ye need have no fear of me, hinney."

"Anne, my name is Anne," she said sleepily. She licked a drop of water from her upper lip.

"Anne, hinney . . . 'tis all the same. I've come to fetch ye for Sutherland. It was wrong of me to take advantage of ye."

"I didn't mean . . ." she began. Memories of what she'd done, of what she'd felt when they'd kissed, washed back over her, and she was ashamed.

"Nay, say no more. The blame was mine. You're a hot-blooded wench, and it's clear to me that you're as innocent as the morning dew. Ye belong to another, and he entrusted me with your care. I'll not break that trust again." He settled cross-legged in a corner and pulled her into his lap. "Sleep, little marchioness. I'll keep watch."

"Never," she answered hotly. "Let me go."

He chuckled, cradling her against his hard chest as easily as though she were a suckling babe.

She vowed silently to stay awake, to run as soon as he fell asleep, but he was warm and she was cold. Her eyelids felt as though they weighed a pound apiece. Her eyes burned, and her hand ached where she'd gotten the thorn in her palm. She fought to keep her eyes open, staring into the shadows where the horses stamped and blew softly through their lips. She let her eyes drift shut for just a minute, and when she opened them again, it was daylight.

Chapter 5

Edinburgh, Scotland

It was another rainy morning three weeks later when Anne sat astride Ross's black prancing stallion and stared up at the frightened face of Bruce Sutherland peering from the second-story window of a gray stone house in Old Town. Ignoring the gust of raw, bone-chilling air that struck her full in the face when she pushed aside her warm wrap, Anne leaned forward, unwilling to miss a single word her supposed betrothed had to say.

The distance to the pavement and the tossing of the great horse's head no longer troubled her. She gave no heed to the bits of foam blown from the nervous stallion's mouth or the sharp hammering of those deadly hooves against the ground. Instinctively, she knew that the man encircling her waist with one sinewy arm would not let her tumble from the horse—and if she did fall, she knew that those iron-shod hooves would dance around her as precisely and gently as an eagle placed her razor-tipped claws around her dewy hatchlings.

"Be gone from here," Sutherland hissed. His head swiveled as his bloodshot eyes searched the misty entrance to the narrow street. "Be gone, I say."

"Damn ye for a faithless bastard," Ross swore. "I've carried your bride up hill and down, across all of England, risking life and limb with the hounds at my back, and you have the gall to speak so! Come down out of that window, and I'll have the scalp from your head. Have ye no heed for your sweetheart?"

"Nay," Sutherland retorted. "How many times must I tell you, I've never laid eyes on the lady before. You've confused her with another. Now away with ye both, before you have the authorities on us."

"What have I been telling you?" Anne demanded, squirming around in the saddle to glare into Ross's face. "I told you I knew no Bruce Sutherland, didn't I? I—"

"Hist!" Ross commanded. The smile lines were gone from his handsome face, his features hardened to a smooth mask. His eyes were as cold as black polished stone. Only the slightest increase in tension in the muscles of the arm that held her betrayed Ross's apprehension.

"By whatever god you pray to, I'll have ye out of that window and down on your knees," Ross threatened. "Do ye deny you offered me a portion of her dowry to steal her away from the church and bring her safely to ye?"

The window slammed shut.

Ross drew his sword. "We'll see what tune your intended will sing when he feels the kiss of cold steel." He reined the black horse toward the iron-studded, oak door. "I'll have you out of there, Bruce Sutherland, if I have to burn you out," he bellowed.

The window opened a crack. "It's clear to me that you are a stranger to this land," Sutherland called down. "For that and Christian charity, I'll give you this warning. Patrols were searching the city far into the night. Even now, soldiers are massing at Edinburgh Castle. One hundred pounds silver is offered for the head of the giant outlaw on a black horse who kidnapped the Marchioness of Scarbrough from her wedding in London Town. I know not who you be or what your purpose, but I'd not be a stranger carrying a lady on a black horse in Edinburgh this day—not for all the kegs of whiskey in all the cellars in this city."

"You sent me!" Ross replied. "You hired me to fetch your Anne from the Church of Mary-le-Wood."

The window slammed once more, but not before Anne heard Sutherland say, "Not Mary-le-Wood, you fool. Saint Mary-le-Bow."

"I told you," Anne repeated. "I told you I wasn't—"

"Cease your caterwauling, woman, before I gag you," Ross said. Roughly, he wrapped the folds of the *breacan-feile* around her and pulled her tightly against him.

Anne seethed with unspoken ire. She wanted to strike him with her fists—to cause him physical pain. She'd never been so angry with anyone before, except when her stepfather, Langstone, had locked her up for refusing to wed Baron Murrane. Even then, she'd only wanted her freedom; she hadn't wished to cause anyone bodily harm. She'd never been that kind of person. What had this brute done to her to turn her as savage as he was?

For weeks she had slept in haystacks, ridden through rain and snow, eaten poached venison and stolen bread. Ross had robbed her of her jewelry and given her beautiful bridal gown to the gypsies. He'd laid hands upon her and kissed her in a most ungentlemanly way, causing her . . . causing her . . .

Vaguely, Anne was aware that Ross had urged his horse, Tusca, into a trot. They were riding away from Sutherland's house, but it didn't matter. She was lost in her own thoughts.

Ross had not kissed her again since that night the gypsy camp had been attacked by the soldiers. For days she had waited for him to take her in his arms again, but he hadn't, and the shame and disappointment had nearly been too great to bear. Even now, she remembered the feel of his mouth on hers . . . the touch of those big, scarred hands.

I wanted him to do more than kiss me, she admitted to herself. I wanted him to throw me down on the ground and have his way with me. I'm a widowed virgin who's never known a man's love, but I have needs . . . I have desires.

Anne bit her lower lip and clenched her eyelids together. The lump in her throat felt large enough to choke her. The agonizing memories were so vivid that she relived each sensation Ross had stirred in her body. Even to think about the kisses they had shared brought the heat rising in her loins again. Only pride had kept her from ripping off her clothes and offering herself to him. Only pride, or cowardice, had prevented her from seizing her own fate in her hands and proving that she was no different than her mother.

"You were wrong," she said. "Admit it. You stole the wrong woman." He didn't answer. Anne could hear the city awakening around them. A baby cried; a dog barked. She could smell oatcakes cooking. "You've made a mistake. You heard Sutherland. There's a death warrant out for you. Let me go, and try to save yourself while you can."

His deep voice was strained. "Ye really are this marchioness of whatever."

"I told you so."

"Aye, hinney, that ye did." He spoke to the horse in a strange language, and the animal broke into a trot.

"Admit it," she insisted. "You were wrong."

The thick wool wrapped around her muffled his reply. "I was wrong."

"I'm no good to you now," she said. "Let me go."

"And if I did, what would you do?"

"I'd wait long enough to give you time to escape, and then I'd tell someone who I was and demand to be taken to Edinburgh Castle."

"And what if ye started yelling the minute your feet touched the ground?"

"I'd not do that. I'm not a vengeful person. I've no wish to see you dead."

He sounded thoughtful. "If you went to this castle, what would they do to you?"

"Do to me?" Anne sighed in exasperation. "I'd be given proper clothing befitting my station . . . servants . . . food, I suppose. No one would do anything bad to me. It's your head they want to cut off. You're the criminal—not me."

"But later. What would happen to you later?"

"Someone would escort me back to London to my family."

"And they would force you to marry this Baron Murrane."

"Yes, I suppose they would. The contracts have been signed. I'd have to honor the agreement,"she admitted.

"But you don't want to marry him."

"What I want has nothing to do with it. Murrane is . . . is suitable. He is powerful enough to protect my fortune. He will—''

Ross reined the stallion up sharply. ''Fortune? You didn't tell me you had a fortune. You're a rich heiress, then?''

''I *did* tell you. You just didn't listen. Why do you think they are so determined to get me back? It certainly isn't out of love.''

''Ahtch, hinney, you're young to be so bitter.''

''Are you going to set me free or not?'' she demanded, ignoring his remark.

''No.''

''Why not?''

''Can't you guess?''

For the first time in days, fear lifted the hair on the back of her neck. Did he mean to kill her? Would some passerby find her lifeless, broken body in a dark alley? ''No,'' she stammered. ''I don't want to die.''

He sighed. ''Hist, sweeting. Have I given ye cause to believe I mean you harm? Have I put the smallest bruise on your soft skin a'purpose?''

She swallowed hard, thinking her bottom was covered with bruises from riding, but this was not the time to mention it.

''Have I?''

''No,'' she answered meekly.

''Then you insult my honor by asking me if I mean to kill you. God knows no jury would find me guilty for silencing your scolding tongue, but—''

''I'm no scold,'' she protested hotly.

''And I am no murderer of helpless women.''

Anne trembled. He was angry, really angry. She had spent enough time with Ross Campbell to know that the softer he spoke to her, the madder he was. ''What was I to think?'' she soothed.

"You've no good reason to hold me captive any longer. I'm of no use to you."

"Nay," he agreed, "but your fortune is."

The sun came out on their second day out of Edinburgh. Ross had ridden the stallion hard by night; by day they had hidden as they had done earlier in England when they were pressed by soldiers. Anne's supper had been cold, crumbly oatcakes, her only drink icy water from a rocky stream. Her bed had been the hard ground, and her only pillow Ross's arm.

She was angry with Ross. She'd been furious since they'd galloped out of Edinburgh. She'd not spoken to him for most of that first day, since it had become clear to her that he was no better than any other outlaw. He obviously meant to hold her for ransom.

She'd demanded to know where he was taking her, but he'd only chuckled and replied softly that she'd find out soon enough. This morning, as the big horse loped up the crest of a rise, giving her a view of miles of sun-sparkled countryside, she almost forgot to care where they were going.

This morning, Anne hardly felt the ache of her bones at all. The pain from stiff muscles and raw spots on her bottom had faded until she took no notice of them anymore. In some crazy, unexplainable way, she felt stronger—more alive than she'd ever felt in her life.

She parted the folds of the woolen *breacan-feile* and drew in great gulps of the clear, crisp air. The smoke and stench of Edinburgh's narrow, dirty streets had been left behind. Here, all was clean and open. On her right, a shimmering silver river flowed through a stretch of bare trees; ahead and to the left, rolling hills piled one upon another as far as the eye could see. The panorama was painted in shades of gray and brown and dull green, but the sky overhead was a glorious shade of blue, laced with fluffy white clouds.

The land was strangely empty. A few flocks of sheep tended by a lone shepherd and his dogs were the only life they had seen. "It must be beautiful in springtime," Anne said, breaking the silence between them.

"Aye, so my father always told me," Ross answered. "Purple heather, he said, and grass so green it hurt your eyes."

"I've been to Scotland, of course," Anne continued, "but I don't remember seeing anything like this." When she'd come as a child with Barbara, they'd ridden in a coach on main roads. Her memory retained only images of mudholes and a tree-lined lane with a great house surrounded by a stone wall at the end of that lane. She took another deep breath of air, so sweet and pure that she couldn't get enough of it. "I've heard there are no open fields in America—that it's all thick, tangled woods, too dark for the sun to ever reach the forest floor."

Ross laughed. "Aye, places are like that, but we do have fields—near the coast. Travel west as the crow flies for longer than what seems possible, cross rivers that were never meant to be crossed by men, and you'll come to an open plain that runs on into the sunset. There are herds of grazing animals there, bison and antelope and wild horses . . . herds that defy counting. And further still, the Indians say, are more mountains—mountains that reach up to the throne of God. I've seen the plain, but I've never seen those mountains—the big ones. I'd like to, though. I'd like to climb to the top of one and look for the ocean on the far side."

"Tall talk for a common outlaw," she scoffed.

"You'll end up under the headman's axe or hanging by the neck at some lonely crossroads as a warning to other brigands. Crows will pick your bones clean."

"Catch me first, said the rabbit."

"If we keep riding, we'll reach the sea. What then? How far can you run?"

"You're disappointed in me, hinney, I can tell."

She sniffed imperiously.

"I've no love of money for its own sake, sweeting. It's a purpose I have. Such as you be, you've no right to judge me. You were born with a silver spoon in your mouth, and folks have spread rose petals in your path ever since. Ye know nothing of the world, lass—nothing at all."

Ross leaned forward and patted the black horse on the neck. The animal responded by twitching his ears and lifting his feet higher. The stallion's ebony coat was filthy, and briers tangled his magnificent tail. The horse was thinner than he'd been when Anne first laid eyes on him in the church, but he'd lost none of his fire. The slightest sound would send ripples down his silken hide and set the beast to prancing. The barest nudge from Ross's knees would cause the stallion to quicken his speed.

Briefly, Anne regretted the loss of the soldier's horse they'd taken with them from the gypsy camp. He'd been unable to keep up with Ross's Tusca, and he'd gone lame some time in their second week of travel. Since then, the black stallion had carried them both, and if he felt the strain of the added weight, he'd given no sign of it.

"Don't tell me what I know or don't know," she responded. "You don't know me. And your being poor is no excuse to turn to crime." Unconsciously, she stiffened her body and leaned as far away from him as possible. "You've ruined me, you know. I'll be the talk of London. I'll be lucky if any suitable man will have me now that my reputation is in shreds."

"Aye," he agreed solemnly, "I can see where that would be a problem. Some dirty-minded creatures might think that you and I—"

"Exactly. Who wouldn't think that? A day, a night, perhaps, but weeks alone with a madman? Even reasonable people would have cause to gossip. I'll never be able to appear in public without my ordeal being mentioned."

"You must take part of the blame, lass. 'Twas you who told me that you were an heiress."

"You knew that I was a marchioness. What did you think? Did you suppose I was a butcher's daughter?"

"I thought you were Sutherland's woman."

"But you were wrong, weren't you?"

"Must ye harp on the one thing I've done wrong?"

"One thing? One thing? I can—"

"Hist, hist, mistress. Ye chatter on like an angry jay. You might have a little compassion for me, stuck with such a harridan for all these weeks. There are women who would have been kinder to me."

"Of certain," she cried. "Common strumpets—jades."

"Your constant talking makes my ears ache."

"Liar! I've not spoken to you for hours."

"It didn't seem that long to me."

"Very well, I shall be quiet . . . if you tell me where you are taking me."

Ross rolled his eyes heavenward. "For peace, I will do anything. I'm taking you to Castle Strathmar."

"Why? What's there? Will you send to my family for ransom from there? I don't—"

He lifted one wide palm in front of her mouth. "Silence I was promised, and silence I will have, one way or the other," he threatened.

Infuriated, Anne halted in midsentence and gritted her teeth to keep from saying something no lady should say. The arrogance of the man! Her breath came in strangled gulps and her head pounded as she tried to hold her temper.

Her earlier concern for his safety was wasted pity, she decided. Ross Campbell was a common outlaw and a kidnapper, and when Murrane's mercenaries caught up with him, he'd get no more than he deserved.

The horse's long legs covered mile after mile, and Anne rode in silence mile after mile, her resentment growing with each step. Images of castle dungeons formed in her mind. She had heard tales of women locked away for years in total darkness. The Highlands were known for cold and damp. What if she took ill? What if she wasted away in some rat-infested cell?

By the time Ross stopped to water the horse and give her time to tend to her personal needs, Anne was half in shock with fear. He swung down off the saddle and put his hands around her waist to lift her down, then paused when he saw her pale features.

"What's wrong, hinney?" he asked. "Ye look as though you've seen a ghost."

Anne opened her mouth to speak, then clamped it shut. To her shame, two fat tears rolled down her cheeks. Her lower lip trembled, and she sniffed, wiping away the tears with the back of her hand. "I . . . I spent .. five months," she managed, "five months locked in a tower room. I don't want to go in a dungeon. I hate rats."

Ross looked stunned. "What?"

She sniffed loudly. "Rats. I hate them."

"I can't promise you the castle doesn't have rats, but no one's going to lock you up," he promised. He helped her dismount and led her to a rock. "Sit," he ordered. "Now, what's all this about a tower?"

She looked up into his dark eyes. They seemed opaque, giving no hint of what he was thinking. She straightened her shoulders. "My stepfather wanted me to agree to marry Murrane and I wouldn't, so they held me prisoner for five months in one room."

"Bastard." Ross pulled her against him and kissed the top of her head. "Have I given ye reason to think I'd be so cruel?"

"No," she admitted. "But I . . ." He was holding her so tightly she could hear his heart beating. The anger drained away to be replaced with a warm feeling of security. Anne's heart began to pound faster. It felt so good to have him hold her like this. She tried to remember how much she hated him, how arrogant he was, how rotten, but her bones felt as though they were melting.

"Sweeting," he murmured. He rubbed her jawline with his thumb, then tilted her face up to his. "I'd never lock you in a cell, lass, and I'd kill any man who did." He brought his head down to within inches of her face. "Woman," he uttered softly, "woman, you—"

She silenced him in the only way she could, and his lips were as warm and sweet as she'd remembered. Her stomach felt as though she'd swallowed a handful of butterflies, and her mind swirled. God, but he tasted good. She slipped her arms around his neck. He groaned, and the sound sent chills down her back.

This time there was no hesitation. Her body

molded to his as easily as if she'd kissed this man a thousand times. Their tongues touched in a caress so tender that it brought tears to her eyes. And when at last they broke apart for air, Anne was trembling from her head to the soles of her feet.

Ross removed his plaid and spread it on the ground beside the rock. To Anne's relief, she saw that he was wearing a vest and short kilt underneath. He held out his arms to her. "I mean ye no harm, hinney. I swear it."

It seemed the most natural thing in the world to sit beside him, to cuddle her head against his shoulder, to raise her mouth to his to be kissed and kissed again. It seemed the sweetest thing in the world to hear his words of endearment, to touch his face, to run her fingers through his hair.

"Oh, Anne, what have I done," he said softly. "I was wrong to take ye from your wedding, but as God is my witness, I am not sorry."

"You're a good man," she whispered back. "I know you are . . . in spite of everything."

"Nay, not good . . . but not bad either."

"No, you are good." She moistened her lips and looked full into his face. "And a good man could never hold a helpless woman for ransom."

"Aye, you're right about that, lass. It's not a thing a decent man could be proud of."

"Then . . ." Her eyes misted over with moisture. "Then I judged you wrongly. You don't mean to hold me for a reward."

"Nay, hinney, I never meant to do that. When I thought you were Sutherland's sweetheart, that was different. I thought you wanted to be stolen. I did it for money, but I'd not take advantage of a woman."

A radiant smile broke across her face. "Then you're going to let me loose after all."

"Hell, no. I'm not going to let you loose. What ever gave ye that idea?"

Anne jumped to her feet and backed away. "You're not? Then what do you mean to do with me, you common ruffian?"

"Why, hinney, I thought you'd guessed. I mean to marry you myself."

Chapter 6

"You son of a bitch!" Anne scooped up a fist-sized rock and hurled it at Ross's head.

He threw up his arm to protect his face. "Ouch! Stop that, woman!" Her second rock drew blood as it bounced off his ear. "Damn it! Don't do that!" Ross dove for cover behind a boulder. "Stop, I say!"

"Marry me? Not bloody likely, you—you lying cur!" She threw another missile with skill born of hours of practice. "You rotten bastard!" she shrieked as anger boiled up within her. She'd let him kiss her again—no, worse than that, she'd kissed him, over and over. She'd actually begun to trust him, and now he'd shown his true colors. He cared no more for her than her family or any of the other men who flocked around her. All he wanted was her money.

Ross yelped as she scored another hit and his Scots bonnet went flying. "Not if my flesh were pulled off with hot pincers!" she shouted. "I'd not marry you to save my immortal soul!"

"Lady! Anne! Hinney! For the love of God, be careful! You'll hurt yourself!"

"You loathsome toad! Barbarian! I'd sooner marry a heathen Turk!"

He crouched low and covered his head with his

hands. "Think of your reputation," he shouted. "I'm saving ye from a life of shame."

"You're after my fortune, you depraved scum!"

Cautiously, he peered over the boulder at her. "Hinney," he called, "we must talk."

Anne dropped her last stone and ran toward the stallion. If she could just get up in the saddle, she had a chance to get away. "Whoa, whoa," she said to the horse. She'd never ridden astride alone—she wasn't even certain she could stay on the horse if she could mount, but she was too angry to worry about that. The stirrup was higher than she'd thought, but she managed to get one foot into it. Holding the reins in her hand, she tried to pull herself up, using the stirrup leather as a rope.

The stallion danced nervously and tossed his head. "Easy, easy boy," she murmured. She heaved herself upward and clung to the saddle as the horse began to walk.

"Damn it, woman, what do ye think you're doing?"

She glanced back over her shoulder, saw him running toward her, and gave a final heave that brought her up over the animal's withers. Heart pounding, she yanked on the reins and kicked the horse. "Gittup!" she yelled.

The stallion started trotting back the way they had come. "Woman!" Ross shouted.

Anne slapped the reins against the horse's neck. "Go! Go!" she begged.

Ross brought two fingers to his lips and gave a loud whistle. Tusca stopped short, and Anne slid forward on his neck. Ross whistled again, and the stallion turned back.

"No!" Anne screamed. "Stay away from me." Tusca snorted and began to paw the ground. He reared up, and Anne lost her precarious grip and tumbled off. She hit the ground so hard it knocked the wind out of her. When she opened her eyes, the Scot was leaning over her, glaring at her with those merciless black eyes.

"Are ye hurt?" he demanded, running his hands freely over her arms and legs. "That was a fool trick to try."

"Take your hands off me," she cried, rolling away from him and drawing her legs under her skirt. She pulled her knees up and hugged them against her. She was badly shaken, and fear was fast replacing her anger, but she wasn't about to have him pawing her.

"Ye didn't find my touch so loathsome a little while ago," he said gruffly. "A man would have to be a fool to believe you didn't enjoy it."

"You tricked me," she flung back. "I thought you cared for me."

His eyes narrowed. "What do ye want me to say? That I find ye desirable? You know that already. That I love ye?" He shook his head. "I've too much respect for you to whisper false words of love." He took her hand and pulled her to her feet. "At Strathmar, we'll be wed. That will save your honor and protect my neck from the hangman's noose or from the axe. My father tells me that half the brides in the Highlands were carried away by force in the old days. We'd not—"

"I don't want to marry you," she insisted. How could she ever have felt drawn to this man? Her own body had betrayed her, made her say and do things she'd never done before. "Nothing you can do to me will make me agree."

The image of Murrane's scarred face formed in her mind. Butcher of Sheriffmuir or not, at least he was a baron, a man of breeding. He'd had estates to take her to. Ross Campbell was nothing but an outlaw. "You're a common thief," she accused, "and mad as a bedlamite if you think you can save your skin by offering me marriage."

"If stealing a woman makes a man a thief, then I suppose ye can call me that. I've taken horses from the Seneca, and stolen back Delaware captives from the Onondaga. I've even lifted rifles and powder from the Frenchies up near Lake Ontario, but I'm not common—not by a far shot. For what it may mean to you, I've never deserted a friend in trouble, or lied to one, for that matter. At home in the Colonies, my father and I lay claim to enough land to put a dozen Londons in and still have room for Paris. I've killed men that needed killing, but I've never harmed a woman— not even the Iroquois women who deserved to be killed for their vicious torture of captives."

Anne put her hands on her hips and scowled at him. "You're talking nonsense. All your tall tales won't convince me. I'll have no part of you or your offer of marriage."

Ross retrieved his bonnet and put it on his head. "Ye have it all wrong, hinney," he said coldly. "I'm sorry for us both that it must come to this. I've no more wish to wed than you, and if I did choose a bride, it would be no dainty piece of English fluff." He folded his big, muscular arms across his chest. "I've made you no offer. I've only done you the courtesy of telling you what I intend to do."

Anne caught her lower lip in her teeth and blinked back the tears. "No," she repeated softly.

He motioned toward the horse. "Save your weeping, woman. Will ye, nill ye, by this time tomorrow, you shall be my wedded wife. And all the tears and all the rocks in Scotland won't alter that."

* * *

Strathmar was worse than Anne had imagined. The castle sat on a stony outcropping in the middle of a lake, or loch as Ross called it. For hours before they reached Strathmar, they had seen smoke from scattered crofts and an occasional herd of sheep or shaggy Highland cattle. The land looked poor to Anne; it was obvious to her that the rocky soil was ill-suited to crops. Trees were scarce and stunted. The few people she glimpsed seemed even wilder than the land.

A stone and wooden causeway led from the shore to Strathmar Castle, but the logs were rotting, and the stones slipping into the loch. Holes in the bridge were so wide and deep that Ross forced her to dismount and walk across. Wooden sections creaked and groaned under the weight of the stallion. Anne found herself clinging to Ross's hand, in spite of her reluctance to have anything to do with him.

Halfway down the span, at a spot where dirt had been dumped to fill in a sinkhole, the road had turned into a giant mud puddle. A skinny black sow and her six half-grown piglets wallowed in the foul-smelling slime.

Anne wrinkled her nose in disgust as she edged her way around the mud hole. "Who owns this castle, the Prince of Darkness?"

Ross grinned wryly. " 'Tis the ancestral home of the Earls of Strathmar of the clan Campbell. My father's cousin Robert Bruce held the title until he drowned three years past. First he spent all the silver, then he drank all the whiskey. When that was gone, he turned to ale in desperation. He tumbled into a barrel and drowned trying to scoop out the dregs."

"Your father's cousin? You're trying to tell me you're related to the new earl?"

"In a way of speaking. He's my daddy, Angus

Campbell. Lord Strathmar—the twelfth Earl of Strathmar.'' Ross's eyes twinkled with mischief. ''And that makes me the Master of Strathmar, the ancient and honorable title of the heir to this great estate.''

She snorted in derision. ''Master of Pigs, more likely. Need I say I'm not particularly impressed?''

He grinned at her. ''Me either. I've no need for such trumpery. At home, the Delaware call me Kuinishkuun Uipiitil—Tooth of the Panther. It's a title I earned, and one I wear proudly.''

Anne grimaced and scuffed her shoe to scrape pig dung off the sole. ''If your wilderness is such a paradise, why are you here? Why didn't you stay there with your Indians and your bears?''

''A question, lass, I've asked myself more than once since I set foot on this cursed island.'' The stallion kicked at a spotted shoat trotting down the causeway toward the mud puddle. Ross patted the horse's neck and whispered soothingly to him. ''Damned pigs,'' he muttered. In two strides, Ross caught up with Anne again. ''When my daddy left Strathmar, it was a thriving place. We thought there'd be a fortune connected to the title. I came over the water to fetch it home for him.''

''The title?''

''To the devil with the title. We had need of money, a lot of it. But instead of gold in the castle strongbox, I found unpaid bills. The sheriff wanted to throw me in debtors' prison. I met Sutherland in a tavern in Edinburgh. We'd both been taking a wee kiss of firewater . . . and you know the rest.''

She tilted her head and glared at him. ''So my life was ruined because two drunks met across a whiskey keg?''

"Harsh words, hinney. Harsh indeed for a lass about to be tossed to the likes of Murrane for his pleasure."

"Fitzhugh Murrane never lied to me. He never pretended to want me for anything more than what I could bring him."

"And you were so eager to share his marriage bed that you let them lock you in a tower for five months before you agreed to have him."

"What I wanted, and what passed between me and my family, are none of your affair. You stole me like I was a spare shift hanging on a clothesline. You're a thief, nothing more. I won't marry a thief. You can't make me."

"We'll see, said the crow."

Her gray eyes took on a pale glow of desperation. "You've got to listen to reason. If you let me go, I'll beg Murrane to drop the charges. I'll swear you never touched me. If you want, I'll lie and say you aren't the man who kidnapped me at all. I'll claim I never saw you before."

Ross frowned. "Nay, hinney. That's all well and good, but we know what your family thinks of your wishes. I never studied for the law, but this much I ken—if we are wed, you canna testify against me in a court of law. A wife canna bear witness against her lawful husband. That will prevent Murrane or anyone else from putting me to death on the kidnapping charge. Your fortune will get me back to the Maryland Colony."

"But I—"

Anne's argument was drowned out by an ear-splitting cacophony. Without warning a huge pack of fierce-looking hounds spilled out onto the castle side of the causeway and ran toward them in full cry. Anne gasped and shrank back against Ross.

Without hesitation, he seized her around the

waist and swung her up onto the stallion's back. Before she could protest, he yanked the horse's bridle off over his head, leaving her helpless to control the animal.

She suppressed a scream as three snarling dogs broke from the pack. The leader, an Irish wolfhound, was as big as a pony. Teeth bared, the wolfhound bore down upon Ross. The stallion reared and pawed the air with his front feet. Anne clung to the mane and watched in horror as Ross cracked the bridle reins like a whip and lunged toward the dogs. Uttering a cry as savage as that of the wolfhound, Ross snapped the leather over the dog's head.

The shaggy red beast dropped to a crouch and growled menacingly. "Down!" Ross ordered. He snaked the leather rein through the air to snap within inches of the wolfhound's nose. Another dog, hot on the leader's heels, thudded into the wolfhound and rolled aside with a strangled yelp. The third dog, a black and white mongrel missing one ear, circled left with raised hackles.

Ross snarled at him and lifted the bridle in warning. By the time the rest of the pack reached them, the wolfhound was whining and thumping its tail in submission. Ross dropped to one knee and called the red dog forward. The huge canine thrust its head against Ross's hand and panted good-naturedly. Anne let out her breath slowly in relief as Ross lowered his face to be thoroughly licked. When he stood up, the rest of the pack crowded around, eager for attention.

"They're your dogs, aren't they?" Anne cried.

"Nay, hinney, but dogs are dogs. They need only to be shown who's master."

Arrogant bastard, she thought hotly. With great effort, she resisted the urge to stick her tongue out at him like an angry child. He was infuriating. When she'd first seen the dogs running at them and thought they were in danger, she'd been afraid . . . for herself and for him. "Damn you to hell," she whispered.

"Atch! Mind that tongue, woman. You've an evil temper, certain."

She ground her teeth together in frustration. No one had ever accused her of being ill-tempered. She'd always been known for her sweet, gentle nature. Whatever she did, whatever she said when she was with Ross Campbell was his fault and none other. She glanced hopefully at the black and white cur. With luck, maybe the beast would take a bite out of the seat of Ross's kilt.

A man wearing the Campbell plaid hobbled down the causeway from the castle. "Who the hell do ye—" He broke off as he came near enough for his white-filmed eyes to focus on the intruders. "Master, 'tis ye. Welcome, sir." He began to shoo the yipping dogs away with his staff, and they scattered. One tumbled off the bridge, bobbed up in the water, and began to swim toward shore.

Anne stared at the graybeard. He was thin as a rail, with a rough, red complexion. His nose was wide and crooked, and his mouth boasted a single tooth in the front. Long snarled locks sprouted from under a Scots bonnet and fell to his shoulders. His exposed neck was as wrinkled as a turkey-cock's and as unwashed, she decided. The lines of gray showing above the folds of his plaid were undoubtedly dirt.

"Hurley." Ross nodded to the old man as he slipped the stallion's bridle back over his head. "Hurley is the steward here at Strathmar," he said to Anne.

"Since the first earl, no doubt," she replied.

She unpried her stiff fingers from the horse's mane and began to breathe normally again.

"Fie on the cursed lot o' ye," Hurley muttered to the dogs as he swung his staff one last time. He planted it solidly on the causeway and leaned against it. "Sheriff's been here twice lookin' for ye, sir. Thought maybe it might be him again."

"So you set the dogs on him?" Anne questioned.

Hurley puckered his lips and sucked his toothless mouth inward.

"This is Lady Anne," Ross said. "My bride-to-be." He lifted her down from the horse's back and set her on the bridge. "Have Greer fetch her water for bathing and find her something suitable to wear for the wedding. Is the dominie about?"

"Near enough," Hurley answered. "Mavis dropped another bastard, and he's come to make a Christian of it."

"We've no need of a clergyman," Anne insisted. "I'm the Marchioness of Scarbrough, and this man is a kidnapper. If you'll inform the authorities of my whereabouts, you'll be suitably rewarded. If you don't, you may find yourself hanging from the same gibbet as your master."

The old man gazed up at her with his bleary eyes and shrugged. "Save your breath, m'lady. I dinna ken your flothery English speech. Master Ross be the laird o' Strathmar. Do he bring a kye in a kirtle to this castle and say he will make her his bride, then Hurley Campbell will fetch the Good Book and the dominie. For three hundred years my family has served the Earls of Strathmar, and I'll nay be the one to break that trust."

"A cow in skirts would be a more fitting bride for such a pompous rogue!" she flung back. She continued to protest as they entered the gate to the castle and slogged through the mud of the outer bailey, threading their way among a flock of sheep and goats. The dogs trailed after them, barking and nipping at the animals and chasing several bedraggled roosters.

"Master of Strathmar," Anne intoned mockingly as they pushed aside a sway-backed pony and stepped around a large white sow. The pig sniffed at the stallion's tail, and the horse gave her a swift kick. Squealing, the pig dashed off through the middle of the sheep. They divided like the Red Sea and just as quickly closed ranks in the sow's wake.

A slovenly woman carrying a basket of wash turned away from the rough-looking clansmen she was arguing with and stared after the three. One of the men nodded to Ross; the others only watched with expressionless faces.

The gates to the inner bailey were missing altogether. A cart with one wheel blocked the wooden path that ran toward the crumbling stone keep. Chickens scratched in the great heap of manure and kitchen scraps, and a large white goose hissed at Anne as she walked by. Children stopped their games to gape, and a stout wench with a ragged shawl over her shoulders hurried out to meet them.

"Master," she called. She dropped the switch she'd been carrying in her right hand and wiped her palms on her greasy skirt. "Did we ken ye were coming, we'd have meat for dinner. Porridge'll have to fill yer belly now."

A tall, broad red-haired man with a brace of pistols thrust through his belt came around the corner carrying a keg on one shoulder. "Good day to ye, Cousin Ross," he boomed in thickly accented English "We were just about to breach this last keg of ale. In honor of Mavis's babe."

The woman snorted. "The bairn's yours, Rob

Campbell, and well ye know it. His hair's as red as yer own.''

"Bite your tongue, Greer. Red hair never named no man his kin in these parts,'' the giant replied good-naturedly. "Half the clan is rust-topped.''

"Half the clan ain't got a strawberry birthmark on their arse,'' Greer retorted. "The bairn's his, right enough, Master Ross. He don't want to own it, 'cause the dominie would haunt him and Mavis to the kirk.''

Ross grinned, accepting the easy manner of these low folk without question. "Breach the keg, Cousin Rob. We'll toast the bairn and my bride together. Greer, see m'lady up to the solar and find her something fitting to wear for her wedding.''

Anne drew herself up to her full height. "I said I—''

"Go with her and let her tend you proper.'' Ross turned his heathen gaze on Anne and threatened in soft tones. "Do ye cause trouble for this good woman, hinney, I vow I'll come up and bathe ye myself.''

The stout Greer took a tight grip on Anne's arm and hustled her into the keep.

The great hall was in no better condition than the bailey. The stone floor was covered with moldy rushes, and a great pile of hay was heaped at one end. More hounds lay around the room. Three benches were overturned and laid end to end to form an enclosure to hold a sheep in front of the fireplace.

The rushes crackled and sank beneath Anne's feet. She shuddered, imagining what vermin might make their home in the disgusting mess.

"This way, m'lady,'' Greer said, not unkindly. The maid's words, like those of Hurley and

Cousin Rob, were heavily burred and difficult for Anne to understand. "M'lady" came out sounding as though it rhymed with "batty." She thought of appealing to Greer for aid as she had to Hurley, but it seemed useless. She followed the serving woman up a flight of twisting open stairs to a leather-hung chamber.

To Anne's surprise, this room, although hopelessly old-fashioned, was at least clean. A wide bed, a straight-backed chair, and several benches were scattered around the chamber. Sheepskin rugs lay in front of the cold fireplace and beside the bed. The single window was shut and covered with another sheepskin, but she could see that it did contain glass panes. Beside the fireplace stood a battered copper caldron large enough to bathe a sheep in.

"I'll send a lad to build ye a fire," Greer said. She eyed Anne's tattered gypsy clothing. "There be ladies' things to fit ye. The late earl's granny was near yer size. Like her, ye look as though ye need a muckle bowl of gruel to fill out yer bones."

The woman left her alone. Weary, Anne curled up on the bed. The chamber was damp and chilly, so she pulled the thick sheepskins up over her. Without meaning to, she slept. She had no idea how long she had been asleep, but when she opened her eyes, there was a fire crackling on the hearth and a skinny youth was pouring a bucket of hot water into the brimming tub.

The boy bobbed his head respectfully when he saw Anne watching him. "Greer says tell ye to eat yer gruel afore it freezes," he mumbled.

Anne slid from the bed. Beside the fire was a low stool with a bowl of porridge, a mug of foamy milk, and a pile of butter-covered oatcakes. Hesitantly, she nibbled the bread. Finding it delicious, she banished all thoughts of what

Strathmar's kitchen must look like and devoured every bite of the plain, country food.

When she had finished the last swallow of milk, she undressed and stepped into the tub. The water was warm and deep enough to wash her hair in. Quickly, using a cake of yellow lye soap she found on the hearth, she scrubbed her body and her hair, rinsing off as best she could. Just as she was stepping out of the tub, Greer returned with an armful of clothing.

"These be auld things as I said afore," the maid told her. "But they will do better for your wedding than these." She scooped up Anne's ragged skirt and shift. "Here be a comb. Ye'll have to do yer own hair. I'm no lady's maid, but I can lace yer gown well enough. The master says be quick— the dominie's waiting below."

Anne stood like a statue while Greer dropped a soft, age-yellowed linen shift over her head. She tried not to weep as the serving woman helped her into the stiff, square-necked, rose velvet gown with full slashed sleeves and tight bodice.

"There be a cap with this, but like as not ye'll wish to go bareheaded." When Anne made no move to dress her own hair, Greer sighed loudly and took up the comb. "We'll do it plain," she said. "Men like the lassie's hair loose, and yers be as fair as summer wheat, all gold and brown together." She brought a lock of Anne's hair to her lips to feel the silkiness of it. "Yer hair's yer glory, m'lady, a crown as perty as any jeweled one."

Anne was numb inside and out. When she was small, she'd once seen a rook that had flown into her mother's orangery through an open window. The frightened bird had banged against the windows and ceiling in desperation until at last, exhausted, it had fallen to the floor and retreated into a corner. Ignoring Anne's pleas for the bird's release, Barbara had ordered one of the servants to bring a cat. The rook's eyes had been full of terror as it crouched, waiting to be eaten alive. Anne felt now as she'd imagined that bird had felt so many years ago. She was trapped. No matter what she did or said, Ross Campbell was determined to force her to go through with a marriage ceremony.

"Thank you," she said when Greer finished dressing her hair. "You may go." When she was alone, Anne went to the window and pushed aside the sheepskin. The rolling countryside spread out before her, cold and bright in the afternoon sun. For a long time she simply stared, not really seeing the sheep moving across the bare winter fields. "Damn it," she whispered. "I'm not a bird. I'm a woman. I can't be forced to wed my kidnapper."

"Hinney?"

Weak-kneed, she turned toward the deep male voice. She clasped her hands together to keep them from trembling. "Go to hell in a handbasket," she told him. "I'll not be your bride. I'd sooner jump from this window."

He laughed and strode toward her, his arms out to catch her, his black devil eyes daring her to try.

Chapter 7

Anne whirled and grabbed the first solid object she touched. Anger seared her breast as she hurled the porridge bowl at Ross. "No!" she screamed. "You can't make me marry you!" He ducked, and the bowl smashed against the fireplace.

"Hinney! No need to fash yourself. I told you, you're safe wi' me. I'd not hurt ye."

She threw the mug and it glanced off his head, drawing blood. "Oh!" she cried as her anger dissolved into fear. "I didn't mean—"

"Devil take ye," he muttered between clenched teeth. He fingered the cut and looked at his wet fingers. The amusement drained from his eyes. "I didna wish it to be this way between us." His words were low and precise. "Will ye walk or be carried?"

She shook her head. Her throat constricted as terror gripped her. She steeled herself for the blows of his massive fists. "No . . . I . . . I . . ."

"So be it, woman."

She gave a strangled cry as he strode toward her. She wanted to tell him that she was sorry— that she hadn't meant to hit him with the cup, only to frighten him. Her breath caught in her throat as his hands closed around her. She clenched her eyes shut and waited for the full force of his fury. Instead, he tossed her over one shoulder and started for the door. Her eyes snapped open in surprise, and a flood of relief washed over her.

"I take ye to your wedding, nay your funeral," he growled.

Anne shut her eyes again as Ross took the steep, winding stone steps of the tower so fast it made her dizzy. She could hear voices below. They grew louder, interspersed with rough laughter. She didn't open her eyes until he set her lightly on her feet.

"Cousin Malcolm," Ross said loudly, "this is my bride, Anne."

She stared wide-eyed at the stern man before her. The dominie was short and moon-faced, with fiery red hair streaked with gray. His clergyman's robe was open down the front, revealing a full belted Campbell plaid beneath. The man's eyes were pale blue and glowed with the fervor of a religious martyr. His mouth was hard and thin, his lips colorless.

"Are ye maid or widow?" the dominie demanded.

"I . . . I am betrothed to another," she stammered. "You cannot—"

"Maid or widow?" he repeated harshly.

She blinked. Did this sour little man believe that she could be forced to go through with a marriage ceremony against her will? It was impossible—it couldn't be happening.

Anne tried to speak, but her mouth was dry; her tongue felt as though it had swelled to twice its size. Her stomach was filled with butterflies. Her heart was beating so fast she thought it would burst from her chest; she couldn't seem to get enough air into her lungs. She swallowed and took a step backward, certain that she would shame herself by being sick down the front of her dress.

Frantically, she gazed around the great hall, seeking some means of escape. Dozens of wild-looking clansmen and women stood staring back at her. She couldn't imagine where they had all come from when the countryside had seemed so empty. But they were here, and they were real enough. Her nose wrinkled in disgust as she caught the heavy scent of damp wool, sheep, and unwashed human bodies. Unconsciously, she clasped her hand to her throat, and her fingers brushed the familiar, cool surface of her golden amulet.

A voice cried in her head, *Have courage. Would you have these barbarians scorn you for a coward?*

Heat rose in Anne's cheeks as her back stiffened and her chin rose a notch. She was English, after all. How dare these Scottish cattle thieves think they could terrorize her. "I am the Marchioness of Scarbrough," she said imperiously. "I have been brought here against my will, and I refuse to take part in this farce."

Ross chuckled, and she turned a frosty gaze on him. The swaggering bully! How dare he stand there with that self-satisfied grin!

Anne's eyes met his, and she felt her face grow even hotter. His sinewy arms were folded across his broad chest, his wide shoulders were thrown back, his head was held high, boasting that ridiculous Scots bonnet with those three eagle feathers. His thick, blue-black hair was long and flowing, hanging around those shoulders like some heathen god's. Golden rings flashed in his ears.

She ground her teeth together in frustration. The nerve of him! Even the bastard's widespread stance was insolent. From the toes of those high, soft leather moccasins up his muscular bare legs to the blue and green Campbell kilt cinched tightly around his narrow waist, he was the image of cocksure arrogance.

He winked at her.

Anne let out a burst of contained breath and balled her fists into tight balls in suppressed fury. *I wish I'd killed him with that cup instead of just putting a dent in his thick head,* she thought passionately.

"Maid or widow?" Malcolm Campbell barked.

"Widow, but—"

Ignoring her, the dominie turned to the bridegroom. "Do ye, Ross Campbell, take this woman to wife in holy wedlock, according t' the laws o' man and God?"

"He does," a male voice burred.

Anne glanced furtively to her left and saw the man Rob who'd been carrying the ale keg on his shoulder when she'd first entered the castle. Beside him, wearing a clean white apron, was Greer. "This isn't right," Anne protested hotly. "It's not legal."

"I do," Ross thundered. His booming voice reached to the far corners of the great hall and echoed back at them.

The clergyman turned his cold gaze on Anne. "Do ye, Anne, God-fearing widow, take Ross Campbell as your lawful husband, promising to obey and cherish him until hell freezes over?"

A wave of dizziness made her light-headed. She opened her mouth to utter a resounding *no* when Ross caught her around the middle and gave her a bearhug. "Ohhh," she gasped.

"She does," Ross said.

"By the power vested in me by God and Scotland, I declare that ye be man and wife." He closed his worn Bible with a snap and shrugged off his black robe. Greer caught it as it fell. A red-cheeked maid rushed forth to hand Malcolm a cup of ale. He downed it in one long gulp and wiped the foam off his mouth with the back of his hand.

"Good luck to ye," Rob Campbell said, slapping Ross on the back.

"Good beddin'!" called another red-haired man from the floor. "May she give ye a dozen stout lads."

Laughter and good-natured shouts from the assembled witnesses drowned out what Greer was whispering to the dominie. Two men rolled an ale keg from the kitchen while others carried in long crude tables. A woman's shrill laughter rang out. A grizzled piper began to play, and the swirling strains of the bagpipe echoed above the din.

Rob Campbell leaped into a circle of men, threw his hands over his head, and began to dance a wild Highland fling.

Anne stared dumbly at Ross. Surely he couldn't think this travesty would make her his wife. The cheers of the clansmen stung her like the lash of a whip.

"Kiss her!" a woman cried.

"A kiss! A kiss for the bride!" Clansmen and women alike began to clap in unison. "Aye, Cousin Ross! Give us a kiss!" they demanded.

The bridegroom grinned and pulled Anne into his arms. "Don't you da—" she began, but her protests were silenced by a sound and lengthy kiss. The onlookers screamed their approval.

Ross whispered in her ear. "Play the part, hinney. I'll nay do ye harm, I promise."

Before she realized what he was going to do, he swept her up in his arms. "First the wedding," he said loudly for the benefit of the witnesses, "and then the bedding."

"No," Anne gasped.

He kissed her again. "Trust me."

"Damn you," she hissed. "I'd sooner trust the devil."

"The bonny bride," he shouted, lifting her high, displaying her like a trophy to the crowd. Raucous cheers signaled their approval as he turned toward the stairs.

"No," she whispered frantically. "I'm not your wife."

Ignoring her protests, he carried her up the steep stone steps to the solar. "There are three score good men and women below who would disagree with ye on that, hinney," he said, slamming the door behind him and dropping her onto the center of the bed. "Take off your clothes. Be quick! We'll have witnesses here any minute."

"No," she whimpered. "No." She couldn't believe this was happening—she wouldn't let herself believe it. It had all been too fast. Maybe the awful clergyman wasn't a dominie at all. It was impossible that she could be wed to this colonial savage. Not really. She shook her head. "No." Spots danced before her eyes. She wasn't certain if she was going to faint or be sick. "I can't," she said, scooting to the far corner of the huge bed.

"You can leave the shift on, but the dress has to come off," he insisted. He swept off his bonnet and tossed it onto the floor, then began to unfasten his belt.

She bit her lip and shook her head again. Despite the heat of the roaring fire, she was trembling like an aspen leaf in a spring storm.

"The dress," he reminded her. He dropped onto a stool and pulled off one high, beaded moccasin.

Anne couldn't tear her gaze away from him. His coppery skin glowed golden in the firelight; his ebony brows were like slashes of midnight over those dark, slanted, heathen eyes. His wide nose and high cheekbones cast flickering shadows across the planes of his wickedly handsome face. He bent his head to tug at his other leather moccasin, and a mane of rippling crow-black hair fell forward over his high forehead, brushing the corners of his full, sensual mouth.

She drew in a deep ragged breath, and her nostrils flared as she caught the man-scent of him.

"Ye leave me no choice." He knelt and drew a hunting knife from the belt on the floor. Scowling, he stood up and shrugged off his plaid. Stark naked, he strode toward the bed, firelight glittering off the steel blade of his weapon.

Anne opened her mouth to scream, but no sound came out. For a heartbeat, Ross towered over her, then he lunged across the bed and caught her arm. Lifting her easily, he sliced through the lacings of her rose velvet gown. The dress parted, and he stuck the knife between his teeth and stripped the gown off her and tossed it to the floor. Ross gave a sharp tug on the ties that held her petticoats, making short work of them and her shoes, leaving her wearing only her shift and stockings. "Get between the sheets," he ordered gruffly.

Too frightened to protest, she did as she was told. He slid in beside her. She flinched as his bare thigh brushed her leg. Ross encircled her with an arm and yanked her against him as the chamber door burst open and a score of laughing men and women crowded into the room.

"Witness," cried Greer. "Let the dominie stand as witness." Someone shoved Malcolm Campbell to the front of the assembly. "Bear witness t' the bedding," Greer said.

"Aye," came Hurley's burred concurrence.

"Bear witness t' the master's bedding of the English widow. Let all who see remember."

Rob Campbell approached the bed. "Proof," he demanded. " 'Tis custom for the laird to show his bride."

Anne moaned low in her throat and hid her face against Ross's chest.

"We must see to witness," Malcolm called.

Ross lifted the edge of the quilt far enough to show his own state of undress and a glimpse of Anne's exposed leg. "You've seen all ye need to," he roared good-naturedly. "Away with ye now. Eat and drink. I'll join ye when I've finished this task."

"Aye," Greer said with a broad grin. "The lady is a widow. We've no need of stained sheets." She fixed Ross with a shrewd gaze. "Will ye take the lady with all her faults, be she barren or nay?"

"I take the lady," Ross replied solemnly. "I have seen her from withers to rump, and I take her as I see her."

"Do you, lady, take the Master of Strathmar with all his faults?" Malcolm demanded.

"What faults?" Ross retorted. The onlookers laughed heartily. "She takes me, don't ye, hinney?" He squeezed Anne tightly and she gasped again. "Aye." He grinned. "She takes me as I am. Now out with ye, afore I come down and drink the castle dry and leave no cup or bite of food for any of the rest of ye."

Still laughing, Rob turned and motioned toward the door. "Ye heard the laird. He's a task to finish, and one best completed alone."

Anne kept her eyes shut until she heard the last footstep and the thud of the heavy door closing. Then she let out her breath and opened her eyes.

It was done. Against her will, she had been wed to this giant barbarian. Now he would ravish her body, and nothing, not Church or law, would stop him. Tears pooled in her eyes. This way was not the way she had dreamed of losing her maidenhood.

"Do what you will to me," she whispered dryly. "I'll not fight you, but for mercy's sake be gentle, for I have never known a man."

Ross's angry bellow rattled the windowpanes. Swearing, he leaped from the bed and dashed the wine ewer and glasses off a low table and onto the floor. They shattered around his bare feet, but he paid no heed. "Could ye not trust me a little?" he roared. "Have I hurt a hair of your head since I took ye from London Town?" he demanded. "Sweet Jesus, but it twists my guts to see ye lying there whimpering like a whipped cur. Ye cut me deep, woman, if ye believe I could force myself on any wench, kitchen slut or lady wife." He seized the wooden stool and threw it hard against the hearth. "I had more respect for you when you split my head with that mug!"

Anne sat up, clutching the sheet over her breasts. "I thought—" she began.

"Hellfire and damnation! I know what you thought. But I gave you my word—I promised ye that I'd not hurt ye. I told ye the wedding was to save my life. Ye had no need to shame me before these people."

"But . . . but you married me," she stammered. The tears rolled freely down her cheeks.

"More fool I." Turning his back to her, he wrapped his plaid around his waist and threw a section over his shoulder. Buckling on his belt, he retrieved his knife from where it had fallen beside the bed and thrust it into its sheath. He raised his head, and his angry gaze raked over her with scorching contempt. "Look to your fortune, wife.

Your gold is in more danger from me than your cold thighs.''

"What was I supposed to think?" she protested. "A wife is a man's property to do with as he pleases. If Murrane had wed me, he'd have wasted no time in claiming his marital rights.''

Ross's eyes narrowed. "And ye think me no better than him.''

The unfairness of his accusations burned like fire. "You stole me," she reminded him. "You robbed me of my jewelry and dragged me across the whole of England on the back of a horse. You locked me in this tower and forced me to take part in a wedding ceremony conducted by a cretin, and now you blame me for not trusting you?''

"Aye, it's the earbobs and the rings, isn't it?" he said, and she knew he was deliberately refusing to answer her accusations. "Always we come back to your shiny baubles. If you be the great lady you claim—the great heiress—you can buy yourself more trinkets, can't ye?''

"Not now I can't," she threw back at him. "If we are truly wed, my money is yours to dole out to me as you please.''

He pulled on his moccasins and yanked the laces tight. "Let me cause you no more apprehension," he said between clenched teeth. "Once the warrant for my arrest has been canceled, I'll demand of you enough silver to see me and my horse safely back to the Colonies. After that, you can seek an annulment in the courts, or you can keep our marriage in name only—I care not what you do. I'll trouble ye no more." He stood and walked over to the bed. "Until then, we must play out this pretense of a marriage. I will share this chamber and your bed for the sake of the servants. But ye need have no fear for your body.

I'll not offend your tender sensibilities further by my lowly touch."

"You expect me to live in this pigsty until you leave for America?" Her own rising anger made her brave. He had frightened her half to death by cutting off her clothes and stripping himself naked in front of her. How dare he condemn her for thinking what any normal woman would think?

He arched a heavy brow. "Pigsty? I suppose it is by your standards. Live in it or set the servants to clean it. I'll not be here long enough to bother."

"You think they'd obey me?" she asked in amazement. The numbness in her mind was beginning to recede. He was angry with her, but it was clear he wasn't going to strike her with his fists, or subject her to a shameful rape. She swallowed a lump in her throat. "You give me leave to try?"

"Why not? You are mistress of the castle, aren't ye? You're the lady born. You should be good at giving orders to those below ye."

Anne stiffened. "I had the care of my husband's household. I have been taught the duties of my station."

"Well and well enough." He turned toward the door. "I think we've spent enough time together so that I can join the wedding celebration without losing face. I bid you good day and good night, madame. Don't wait up for me."

A hot retort rose to her lips, but she held it back, contenting herself with glaring at his broad back as it vanished through the doorway. He slammed the door behind him, and she turned over and buried her face in the pillow in frustration.

"Damn him," she cried. "Damn him to holy hell!" Through none of her fault, she was a prisoner once again. Would she never know a normal life? Never know what it was like to live in peace with a husband for whom she felt love and affection?

She rolled over onto her back and stared up at the ceiling. Cobwebs stretched from corner to corner and hung in dusty shreds. "Castle Strathmar!" she uttered in disgust. But with a man like Ross Campbell, what could she expect?

A man like Ross Campbell . . . Anne felt the familiar heat in her cheeks as she remembered the glimpse of him she'd had earlier. She'd seen naked men and boys before, of course—just none so breme and brawny. A curious flutter began in the pit of her stomach and traveled down to make her squirm on the linen sheets. She sighed. The man was well-equipped, there was no doubt of that.

Her mouth turned up in a mischievous smile. Ross Campbell had legs like tree trunks and a chest that . . . A giggle escaped her lips. His legs and chest were made as sweetly as God ever created a man, and his shoulders were too wide by half. That other part—she giggled again—that was enough to cause a maid to sigh.

My husband, she mused.

"No!" She swung her legs over the side of the bed and sat up. She was mad to even think such a thing. Ross Campbell was a hopeless barbarian—a savage. He was a common thief, hardly worth calling a man. He'd made it plain that it was only her money that he was after. He was no better than any of the other men who had held her captive—her stepfather, her first husband, her betrothed. No one cared for her, only for her fortune.

Absently, she rubbed the golden amulet on the chain around her neck. Cameron Stewart, the Earl of Dunnkell—her real father—had claimed to love her. He'd never asked anything of her, only that she forgive him for not being able to give her his name.

"Is this what you meant when you said the necklace carried a curse?" she whispered into the empty room. But he'd told her that the amulet carried a blessing as well. The thought lifted her spirits, and she went to the window, taking care not to step on any of the broken glass. "I wish you were here, Father," she murmured. "I could use some good advice."

She leaned her cheek against the cold windowpane and sighed. As much as she wished him to be here, he wasn't. He was far away in America.

"I'll have to work this problem out for myself," she said, "as I always have." From the hall below, she heard laughter and bagpipes, but here in the solar the only sounds were her own brave words echoing in her ears.

Chapter 8

Late morning sun cast a rainbow of soft colors across Anne's bedcover. She opened her eyes, shut them, and snuggled down into the feather-stuffed mattress. "Mmm," she murmured. Then realization hit home, and she sat bolt upright with a gasp. "Oh!" She yanked the blanket up to her chin as her gaze darted around the still chamber.

The only sound was the rustle of a mouse nibbling at the crumbs of Anne's oatcakes left from the day before. "Get out of here! Shoo!" The mouse dove down a hole beside the hearth.

Emboldened by her rout of the tiny rodent, Anne threw back the blanket and slid onto the icy floor in her bare feet. Memories of all that had happened yesterday flooded over her, and she sat back down on the bed with a jolt.

"Married," she said softly. "Married to Ross Campbell." She pursed her lips and let out her breath slowly. What was she to do? She glanced around the room, and her gaze lit on an old-fashioned powder-blue gown and undergarments lying across a hide-bound chest. Practically, she decided that any action on her part was best taken decently clothed.

Dressing herself, especially in the style of a hundred years earlier, was more difficult than she'd imagined, but eventually she managed. There were stiff shoes made of the same fabric as the dress, only a little too wide for her slender feet, and heavy silk stockings with black silk garters that tied above her knees. She couldn't tighten the bone stays properly because they fastened in the back, and the ties of the overgown gaped where she couldn't reach them, but at least she was covered. She found the comb and brush Greer had used on her hair the day before and made herself presentable.

Quieting her confused emotions was harder than smoothing the snarls in her long tresses. True, Ross had kept his word. He'd not forced her to yield her maidenhood to him in the night. In fact, he'd not even returned to the bedchamber, or if he had, she'd been sleeping too soundly to hear.

She blushed as images of their official bedding rose again before her. All those common people crowding into the room! It wasn't the first time she'd been subjugated to such embarrassment. Naturally, she had experienced the same thing with her wedding to her first husband, although the guests had been anything but common. The witnessing of the consummation was a vital part of the ceremony between a man and woman of high status—it prevented one or the other from declaring the marriage invalid at a later date.

Anne had little patience with her own timidity. She could excuse herself the first time—she'd been a frightened child of fifteen. Now she was a woman grown, and she should have been over her foolishness. Still, she had been horrified by the lewd jokes and innuendos.

The fact that Ross's bedding of her had been witnessed made her plight worse. Every living soul in the castle believed that she was his lawful wife. The question was, did she believe it? Could it be true? The thought that she might indeed be married to him, despite the irregularity of the ceremony, was hard to dispel.

"Am I?" she wondered aloud. "And if I am, how can I get out of it?" She folded her arms over her chest and hugged herself, letting her most daring thoughts slip off her tongue. "Do I want to get out of it?"

She nibbled at her lower lip and toyed with a yellowed rose on the wrinkled skirt of the taffeta overgown. Ross Campbell had assured her that all he wanted was to return to his wilderness in America. If he did . . . She sighed loudly. If she remained married to Ross, and he returned to the Colonies, she would be free to enjoy the gracious life she'd had since she'd become a widow. She could tend her flowers and read her books. She could come and go as she pleased without hindrance.

Truth to tell, she had enjoyed her widowhood. It had offered her peace and quiet—at least until her family had taken it into their minds to force her into another marriage.

Being the wife of a man thousands of miles away would have its advantages, she admitted to herself, but there would be disadvantages too. It would mean never knowing the joys of motherhood, of living a normal life with a husband. Would the freedom to come and go as she pleased be worth the price?

For an instant the image of a stark-naked Ross made her breath catch in her throat. Anne's stomach knotted as she remembered that brief glimpse of hard, bulging loins; that flat, muscular stomach; the dark mat of hair above his virile male organ. Her mouth went dry. He had been huge—

larger by far than any male she had ever seen. And his rod had not even been swollen with lust.

A fluttery feeling in her stomach made goose bumps rise on her arms and neck. What would he look like aroused? How could any normal woman accept such a—

Anne's reverie was broken by the loud click of the door latch. Startled, she looked up as Greer's plain face appeared in the doorway. The maid's hair was untidy, and her apron had a wet stain on it. Greer smelled of stale beer and cheese.

"Morning, m'lady." Greer's hands fell to her ample hips as she surveyed Anne from top to bottom. "I came to help ye dress, and I can see ye need me."

Through the open door, Anne could hear singing and laughter. "They're still at it," she said stiffly.

"M'lady? Oh, below. Aye." Greer unlaced the back of Anne's gown to get at the ties of the stays. "This needs redoing. Suck in." She yanked the strings tight and tied them. "Ye should have called me. I looked in earlier, but ye were sleeping." She began to redo the lacing on the gown. "Once the Campbells find reason to celebrate they're nay so anxious to go back to work. Like as not they'll drink and eat until the castle is as empty as a drum." She knelt by the front of Anne's gown and pulled the underskirt into place. "Will ye come down to break yer fast, or would ye rather I bring something up? There's more drunk than sober, I warn ye."

"And Ross Campbell's the drunkest of all, I suppose?"

Greer broke into a grin. "He's downed his share." She raised one eyebrow shrewdly. "If ye'd rather—"

"No," Anne said firmly. "I'll come down. Send

someone to clean this room and change the sheets. I want all that glass swept up before I cut myself.''

She had reached the top of the staircase when she heard the roar of male laughter, the sound of women screaming, and the unmistakable bellow of an enraged bull. Keeping one hand on the stone wall for support, she rushed halfway down the steps to see what was happening.

The great hall was in chaos. Tables were overturned, food was strewn across the rushes, and people were running in all directions. One half-grown boy was scrambling up the fireplace wall, and another clung to a bell cord six feet above the floor. Two women raced up the steps toward Anne, dragging a girl-child behind them.

At the far end of the hall, surrounded by barking dogs, was an enormous red bull with huge outspread horns. The wild-eyed beast lowered his shaggy head and pawed the floor. One ivory horn was stained scarlet, and at the bull's feet lay the still body of a spotted hound. By the hearth sprawled a second dog, his belly split open like a hog for butchering.

A dozen armed men circled the bull. They shouted and waved their weapon as one blue and green kilted clansman cracked a whip over the animal's head. To the left, closer to the foot of the stairs, Anne saw a woman bending over an injured man. Dark red blood ran from a gash in his arm. The woman was wailing loudly.

"How did this happen?" Anne demanded of the nearest wench. "Who let a bull into the hall?"

A slovenly black-haired woman grinned up at her. "Rob did it. Red Willy dared him to fetch Beelzebub into the hall and he did it." Her eyes flashed with excitement, "Beelzebub killed two of the dogs and horned Red Willy."

"He's a muckle breme bull, that one," added the second woman. "Too valuable to kill, and too mean to handle."

Suddenly, an Irish wolfhound lunged from the pack at the bull. Snarling, the dog sunk his teeth into the bull's right hindquarter. The bull twisted free, turned, and charged the wolfhound, catching him along the side with one horn and raking a bloody furrow in his side. The wolfhound let out a cry of pain and scrambled away out of the bull's reach.

The men surged forward to be stopped short when the bull wheeled to face them and began to paw the rushes angrily. A man raised a musket, but a second knocked it aside.

"Nay!" someone shouted.

"That bull's worth more than the dogs!" cried another.

A gray-haired woman pushed into the circle of men. "Shoot him, I say! He gored my Willy. Shoot him!"

Anne gripped the rough stone as her eyes scanned the hall. Where was Ross? There! She couldn't deny a rush of relief when she saw him safe beyond an overturned table.

A fierce brown dog ran at the bull, and the beast hooked the animal with his left horn and tossed it aside as easily as if it were a lady's lapdog.

The dog's dying yelp brought tears to Anne's eyes. She opened her mouth to demand that Ross order the bull's death when she saw her husband leap out from behind the table. To her horror, she saw that he was unarmed—not only weaponless, but stripped naked as well. Even his feet were bare. Certain that he'd gone as mad as the bull, Anne clamped her hand over her mouth and stifled the scream rising in her throat.

"Ha!" Ross shouted defiantly to the bull.

The circle of clansmen widened. One man let out a cheer. Another gave a burst of laughter, but it turned to a groan as the massive bull turned his bloodshot eyes toward the Master of Castle Strathmar.

"Holy Mary," the black-haired wench cried.

Foam spewed from the bull's nose and mouth. His chest rumbled as he let out a deep, earth-shaking bellow of rage. He lowered his head until his long tongue scraped the rushes. Muscles rippled beneath the shaggy red hide, and a burst of yellow liquid gushed down the bull's hind legs.

Anne gripped the precious fabric of her gown with clenched fingers as she caught the strong stench of sour urine. "Ross, don't," she whispered.

"Ha!" He taunted the bull, crouching in front of him, staring straight into the beast's eyes.

The bull charged.

Anne watched helplessly as the animal bore down upon her husband. Time seemed to crawl until the bull's thundering hooves carried him toward the raven-haired man as slowly as if she were seeing it all in a dream. A cry escaped her lips as the ivory horns dipped to pierce Ross's bare chest, but suddenly, inexplicably, Ross was no longer there.

Anne blinked, unable to believe her eyes. Ross wasn't crushed beneath the bull's feet, or ravaged on the tips of those terrible horns—he was firmly astride the bull's back, hands wound in the beast's long hair, powerful legs wrapped around the animal's sides.

Men and dogs scattered as the bull charged this way and that, tossing his head, twisting and bellowing in rage. Wooden tables snapped like twigs beneath his weight. Dogs howled and women screamed. Barrels and kegs flew into the air as the bull ripped through them. His hind legs slipped out from under him as he trod in the turmoil of spilled food, but he staggered up and attacked the fireplace wall. Still, the man clung to his back like a burr.

Anne heard Ross's whoop of laughter as the bull snapped the tip of one horn off against the stone wall of the hearth. Blood sprayed from the broken horn, streaking Ross's face with gore. Again, the dogs rushed forward, and the bull turned to challenge them. They broke rank as he ran the length of the hall and back again, coming to a stop in the center of the great hall.

If she hadn't been so frightened for Ross, Anne would have found pity for the bull. His breath was coming in great, shuddering gasps. Yellow foam streamed from his nose. His tongue lolled from his mouth, and his eyes were wide and terror-stricken.

Urged on by the men, the dogs closed in around the bull once more. Suddenly, Ross leaped from the animal's back and seized a horn in each hand. The bull struggled to throw him off. For long agonizing seconds they were evenly matched. Corded muscles strained along Ross's back as he threw every ounce of his strength against the tired beast. Veins bulged out on Ross's forehead as he braced his legs and attempted to wrench the bull's head to one side.

Heedless of her own safety, Anne pushed past the two women and ran down the steps toward him. He saw her and shouted a warning. Then, with a final surge of tenacity, he forced the broken horn up and back, and wrestled the bull to the floor.

Rob dashed forward with an open iron ring, thrust it through the bull's nostrils, and clamped it shut with an iron tool. A second man snapped a chain to the ring, and Ross let go of the bull and jumped back out of reach of the bloodstained horns.

The bull scrambled to his feet and stood trembling. His heavy panting was the only sound in the great hall. Even the dogs were silent. Then a woman began to cheer. In seconds, everyone was shouting. Rob led the subdued bull out of the hall as the clansmen surrounded Ross and raised him on their shoulders in triumph.

Someone found an intact keg and handed Ross a mug of foaming ale. He lifted it, drank, and poured the rest over his head. The clansmen and women roared their approval.

Anne turned and retraced her path up the steps. Halfway up, she turned and looked back. Ross was watching her.

He lifted his mug in salute. "To the bonny bride!" he shouted.

She ran the rest of the way up the stairs to her chamber.

He came to her bed that night.

She had known he would.

All day she had paced the floor of her chamber, too nervous to take more than a few swallows of milk and a mouthful of bread. Now she lay trembling on the far side of the mattress, her eyes shut tightly, her knees drawn up beneath her linen shift.

It was dark when he pushed open the chamber door. The single candle Greer had left had long since burned to a stub. Peat glowed on the hearth, filling the room with an earthy scent that permeated the damp corners and overpowered the musty smells of a place left too long unlived in. Humming to himself, Ross slid the bolt and began to sing loudly.

". . . Go take from me this gay mantle,
And bring to me a plaidy;
I care not for kith and kin,
I'll go with my gypsy laddie."

Unsteady on his feet, he knocked against a stool
and it went spinning across the room.

"Oh, come to my bed, says Johnny Faa,
Oh, come to my bed, my dearie;
I vow and swear by my bright sword,
Your lord shall nay come near ye."

Anne bit her lip to keep from whimpering with
fear. Ross was drunk. She couldn't miss the
strong stench of barley-bree that clung to his
breacan-feile. She was at his mercy, and her experience with drunken men had taught her that they
were seldom merciful.

"Hinney?" he called. His voice was deep and
rumbly. "Hinney? Be ye awake?"

She heard the rustle of wool as he dropped his
single garment to the floor and crawled between
the sheets. The bed sank under his weight.

Anne's heart hammered in her chest, and her
palms grew damp. Fear curled in the pit of her
stomach, igniting a spark of desire where she
should have felt only ice.

What was wrong with her? What Ross had done
before—stripping off his clothes and exposing his
naked body, leaping onto that bull in full view of
everyone—was barbaric. It proved he was as
much a beast as the creature he'd ridden into submission. Any decent lady would be disgusted—
revolted by the sheer savagery of the man.

But she wasn't . . .

"Hinney?" he repeated.

A lock of damp hair fell across her cheek. Anne

flinched. Somewhere, he had bathed. Though his kilt had smelled of whiskey, his squeaky-clean hair belied his drunken state. It felt like silk against her face. Black as midnight on a moonless night, smelling of heather. She stifled an urge to take that lock of hair between her fingers and rub it against her lips.

He chuckled softly, and she felt her skin grow hot, then cold. Her hands were burning up; her mouth was so dry that her tongue felt swollen. She could feel her blood pounding in her head.

"Anne."

That strange colonial accent gave her shivers. Where had he gotten that slow, lazy lilt to his speech? She had heard other Americans, but they hadn't sounded anything like Ross. His voice caressed her; it rolled off his tongue like warm honey.

He pressed his palm against her bare arm. Slowly, his hard fingers curled around her, searing her skin, sending her pulse racing. The spark in the pit of her stomach became a flame, and she could no longer hide her trembling.

"Hist, hinney," he murmured huskily. "I'd nay harm ye." He rolled over on his side, facing her, and she felt his warm breath on her skin.

She inhaled deeply, trying to clear her head, desperately fighting to keep her reason. Ross's breath smelled of wild mint. She wondered if his mouth would taste of it.

"Ye need not fear me, lass."

She found her tongue. "We . . . we had a bargain."

"Aye." He chuckled. "So we did."

Every square inch of her skin tingled. She could feel the texture of the linen sheet under her legs, the scratchy threads of her shift stretched tight over her breasts—a garment that had felt as soft as buttermilk when she'd dropped it over her head. Her breasts ached, her areolas were swollen, her nipples were as hard and erect as if she had run naked in the cold rain.

"I have never known a man."

"I gave ye my word."

She swallowed against the lump in her throat, trying to contain the need that tantalized her, the unfamiliar yearning that seemed so natural, so right. "I . . . I will hold you to it, colonial."

His fingers stroked her bare shoulder, sending rivulets of sweet sensation racing through her veins. "How can you be a widow if you've not known a man?" he asked.

"I . . . I was young," she stammered. It was hard to form the words when his fingers were doing such tantalizing things to her shoulder, to her throat. "I was young . . . and he was . . . was old."

"It must be a mortal sin to give a tender lass to one so old," he murmured. "Your mother—"

"My mother hates me," she said. "She always has." It would give her strength if she thought of Barbara—strength enough to fight her own body's betrayal of her will. "He was kind to me, my old husband."

Ross moved aside her golden amulet and brushed her throat with his lips. "And you never wanted to cheat on him? Never wanted to take a lover?"

She gave a tiny moan. The fire in her loins had brought with it a deep, sweet aching. Unable to lie still, she squirmed unconsciously, knotting her hands into fists so tight that her nails cut into her palms. "Do you think a woman incapable of honor?" Her breath came in ragged gulps.

"Nay." He kissed the hollow of her throat where the pulse beat close to the surface. "I've known women whose sense of honor would put men to shame." His warm hand cupped her breast.

She gasped with shock and pleasure. "No! Don't," she begged. "You promised . . ."

"Aye, I promised I would not take your maidenhood." His thumb teased her nipple, and she shuddered with delight. "I said nothing of giving mutual comfort."

Anne opened her mouth to protest, and he kissed her full on the lips. He did taste of mint, with only the faintest bite of whiskey. Not unpleasant . . . definitely not unpleasant . . . His strong arms tightened around her. She could feel his power, could tell how hard he was fighting to hold his desire in check.

Her mind spun as she was caught up in his slow, tender caress. She tried to pull away, but her body refused to obey. Her lips returned the warm pressure of his kiss; her fingers traced the chiseled lines of his beautiful face.

"Ah, hinney." His voice was strained and throaty. "It should be a mortal sin for a lass such as ye not to know love."

"Love has nothing to do with what we're about," she replied, pulling away. She was breathless with excitement, scared and bold at the same time. Another moment and she would have opened her legs for him. Reluctantly, she gathered her wits. How could she have been so stupid? Men talked of love when they meant lust. She had no doubt she would have liked his lovemaking, but she wasn't ready to give him that power over her—not yet. "You've the wiles of the devil, Ross Campbell," she accused, but the amusement in her tone took the sting from her words.

"Aye," he agreed, "and I'm a little drunk. I'd

not have made that mistake and frightened you away if I was cold sober.''

It was her turn to chuckle. She rose up on one elbow. ''We have a bargain. I'll not hold this against you if you keep your word.''

''You liked it.''

She blushed.

He chuckled. ''Admit it, hinney. A bed be not only for sleeping.''

She covered her face with her hands.

''Where is that brave wench that broke a cup on my skull?''

''I liked it when you touched me . . . when you kissed me,'' she answered softly.

''Good, ye had me worried. I've been without the warmth of a lass so long I was afraid I'd forgotten how.''

''I said I liked it—not you. I've had little experience with men. How do I know it wouldn't have felt the same with any gentleman?''

''At least I'm a gentleman now,'' he teased. ''I remember when you called me a common thief.''

''Don't put words in my mouth. I'd not call you a gentleman. Savage, perhaps, or colonial woodsman. It would cause a scandal if my friends knew I was here like this with someone like you.''

He beat his pillow into a lump and laid back on it with his hands behind his head. His thick hair fell down around his shoulders; it was nearly as long as her own. This time she couldn't resist running a strand between her fingers.

''We could hardly cause a scandal, being newly wed,'' he said.

''No wedding at all,'' she reminded him, ''and one I was forced into.''

''And one you'll pay to get out of.''

She sighed. ''You are the most exasperating

man. I'd not be shocked to learn you'd escaped from Bedlam.''

He grinned, and Anne's heart flip-flopped in her breast. Firelight illuminated his rugged features, making him seem younger, less threatening.

"You'll get your money," she said. "I'll send a message to my family telling them of our wedding and asking them to release my funds. Just tell me how much you want."

He named a sum. To her surprise, it was less than she'd expected. It didn't make sense. Nothing about Ross Campbell made sense. The memory of his close brush with death when he'd taunted the bull rose behind her eyelids. "Why did you do it?" she asked suddenly. "What made you take on that bull by yourself? Why didn't you just have him shot?"

"He was too good a breeding animal to be killed for meat. All he needed was ringing." He reached out and touched her amulet. "I never stole this from you, did I?"

"Not yet you haven't." His fingertips brushed her throat, and the warm sensations started again. She pulled back. "Why? Why did you make a spectacle of yourself? Was it necessary to strip yourself mother-naked?"

Ross chuckled. "Aye, hinney, it was. I tried to ride an elk once with my clothes on, and he hung me in a tree. Clothes get in your way. Bare skin is safer if you mean to ride a wild creature."

"Only a madman would try."

Ross scratched his shoulder lazily. "Would ye mind if I kissed you again? You're a bonny sight with your shift down around your breasts and your lips all soft and pouty."

"No more kissing," she said firmly.

He caught her hand and raised it to his mouth,

nibbled first the tip of one finger and then another until she went all shivery. "Not even a friendly kiss to seal a bargain?" he asked. Capturing her index finger between his sharp white teeth, he bit down teasingly.

She jerked her hand away. "No kissing," she repeated, "and no biting."

"You're an unforgiving lass, and that's certain."

"I'll get you your money, and you can be on your way back to America."

His expression hardened. "It's all I ever wanted from you."

She stared at him as he turned his back and pulled the covers to his neck. In minutes he was sleeping soundly while she lay awake wondering what she had refused, and if she would spend the rest of her life regretting her decision.

Chapter 9

Edinburgh, Scotland
April 1723

Cursing the pools of stagnant water that soaked his expensive German boots and added to the misery of his headcold, Colonel Fitzhugh Murrane, the Baron Murrane, followed his lieutenant deeper and deeper into the bowels of Edinburgh Castle.

Since his bride had been snatched from his grasp two months ago, Murrane's luck had turned sour. The story had spread through London in hours and to the far-flung counties within days. He had become an object of ridicule—the colonel who let a Scot outlaw rob him of his betrothed and make fools of his soldiers. The bandit's impossible leap off London Bridge into the Thames was still being discussed in taverns across the land.

A military man, Murrane had given more attention to his career than to his estates. He was no country squire. The Barons of Murrane had always put duty to the crown ahead of personal gain. As a result, he had inherited huge debts from his father, and he had continued to accrue bills for his own needs and for the maintenance of his private army. A man of his status had to

114

keep up appearances; blooded horses, fine weapons, even these imported German boots were necessary to the image he maintained.

Twice before he had shored up his crumbling finances by marrying heiresses. The first had been a hag twice his age—she'd lived only six months after their wedding. The second had been a sickly slut with a harelip. Murrane's mouth hardened as he remembered Agnes. She'd been six months pregnant when he'd come home unexpectedly to find her in the arms of his falconer. Both Agnes and her lover had taken a nasty tumble from the castle walls. Their bodies had lain in the dry moat until they were bloated and unrecognizable before he'd given the order to have them dragged out and buried in the pigsty.

He'd supposed his marriage to Anne Fielding, Lady Scarbrough, would be different. Not only rich, Anne was young and comely. He'd been assured that in spite of her mother's reputation, the daughter was pious and obedient. Damn her to a fiery hell! He'd even given serious thought to getting sons of her body to follow in his footsteps and inherit the barony. Now all those plans were ruined.

"Watch the steps, sir," the lieutenant said. "They're steep and slippery as grease."

A guard saluted and slid the bar on a low board and batten door studded with iron nails. Murrane's man took a lantern from a hook on the wall and led the way down the winding stone steps into the blackness of the lower dungeon.

Murrane sneezed again and wiped his nose on his coat sleeve. He swore foully as his left foot slipped and he was forced to catch himself against a rough wall.

"You all right, sir?"

"By the Pope's balls! Why did you put him

down here? Do you know what I paid for these boots? They'll be fit for nothing! This place smells worse than a battlefield in August.''

"Your orders, sir. The man's a cleric, a dominie. These heathen Scots put great store on a man like him. You said to keep him safe and out of sight.''

Murrane grunted. The cleric had fallen into his hands by sheer accident the day after he'd received word from Lord Langstone that the girl had been married. One of his foot soldiers had been drinking in a pub and had overheard the prisoner boasting about the wedding ceremony he'd performed for the Master of Castle Strathmar. An hour later, the loose-mouthed dominie had found himself a guest in Edinburgh Castle.

Brown, his lieutenant, had been thorough in his questioning. Murrane pursed his lips. John Brown had been born the son of a tanner. He climbed to his rank by wit and courage. Brown attended to all of his duties well. If he hadn't, he'd have been dismissed long ago. Brown had no family, no friends. His loyalty was unquestioned. It was an arrangement that Murrane found acceptable.

As if reading his mind, Brown spoke. "He was most cooperative, sir. He gave details of Strathmar's defenses, inner and outer walls, number of soldiers and cannon. Strathmore won't be easy to take, Lord Murrane. The castle is built on an island in a loch. There's a narrow causeway which can be cut by dropping three wooden bridges. And when you reach the outer wall, the stone is fifteen inches thick. He says the Campbell men are known to be fierce fighters.''

"Hmmpt. I've faced Campbells before. They're no better and no worse than any other Scot.''

The lieutenant grinned. "Right you are, sir. They piss themselves when they die like any other man. But this Master of Strathmar is no true Scot. He's a colonial.''

They reached the bottom of the staircase and turned left down a narrow corridor. The roof grew lower and lower, the walls closer together as they walked down the sloping passageway. It seemed to Murrane as though the weight of the castle was pressing down on him. It was hard to breathe, and the air tasted foul. Something scurried away from his feet and disappeared into the shadows. Murrane shuddered. Damn, but he hated rats!

John Brown stopped by a door. ''This is the cell, sir.'' He fumbled with the rusty iron bolt and opened the door, then ducked inside and held the lantern at arm's length.

Malcolm Campbell uncurled himself from his pile of damp straw and squinted against the light. He was naked; his face was battered and swollen, his hands devoid of fingernails on most of his fingers. He blinked and tried to stand, but his legs were too weak.

''You are the man who married Lady Scarbrough to this . . . this Ross Campbell?'' Murrane demanded.

The prisoner's pale blue eyes glowed with defiance. ''Aye,'' he croaked through broken lips. ''Wedded and bedded they be, according to the laws of God and man.''

''You witnessed the bedding?''

Malcolm grinned, a terrible smile of shattered teeth and blood-caked tongue. ''I and a score of others.''

''Was the lady forced? Did she protest the ceremony?''

The dominie tried to laugh, but it came out a choking gargle. ''If . . . if ye saw the bridegroom, ye'd not ask. He's twice the man ye be, and as beautiful as the Prince of Darkness.''

Brown raised a meaty fist to strike the prisoner, but Murrane stopped him.

"Don't bother," he said. He turned away, trying to control his seething fury. Anne had lain beneath the colonial dog while he pounded between her soft white thighs. She'd welcomed his rutting. Murrane felt sick to his stomach as a familiar pain knifed through his chest and radiated down his arm.

The whore! No better than her mother! He should have guessed. Murrane took a deep breath and turned back toward the shriveled cleric.

"If you want to leave here alive, you'll answer my questions without offering insults to your betters."

"Rot in hell, butcher of Sheriffmuir!" Malcolm Campbell flung back.

Murrane shrugged and walked out of the cell. Brown hurried after him. Murrane was silent until they reached the foot of the stairs.

"Send for another—" A violent fit of sneezing wracked Murrane. "Damn this cold," he complained. He coughed up a lump of phlegm and spit. "Another hundred men," he instructed. "Strathmar may be a tough nut to crack, but I have the time and the patience."

"Cannon, sir?"

Murrane nodded and started up the steps. The Lady Anne had been widowed once; a second time should be no shock to her. Murrane would have her fortune and put an end to the laughter at his expense before the month was out. And once they were legally wed . . . He smiled coldly. He'd lost two wives already—would a third cause undue gossip?

Murrane's fist struck the door twice before the guard opened it. Brown followed his master into the lighted corridor and hung the lantern back on its hook.

"What about the prisoner, sir?" the lieutenant asked.

"Kill him."

"You want the body disposed of in the usual way, sir?"

Murrane shrugged again. "Why not? The pigs don't mind." He dismissed the dominie from his mind and continued toward the upper levels of Edinburgh Castle and a hot breakfast.

Anne wiped her sweaty brow and stepped back to look at the interior of Strathmar's dairy with great satisfaction. No one who had seen the filthy dependency that morning would have believed that this clean, airy room was the same building!

The serving women had swept the birds' nests and cobwebs from the rafters, and they'd scoured the stone troughs with sand until they shone silver-white. Mavis, elevated from her position of castle whore to housekeeper, had scraped and scrubbed the wooden floor until she complained that it was cleaner than the table in her hut. Boys had coated the walls with whitewash, and Hurley had fitted real glass panes into the tiny windows.

"God almighty, Lady Anne," Jeanne protested. "I ain't never seen no diary this bonny. 'Tis only for the making of cheese and butter, not fer laying out the dead."

"This place looked as though the dead had been lying in it," Anne retorted. "No wonder the butter was rancid and the cheese tasted like old stockings." She looked down at her dirty hands with their broken fingernails and tried to keep a stern face. It was impossible; she began to laugh, and soon Mavis and Jeanne and the two boys were laughing with her.

The more Anne tried to control her amusement, the funnier it all seemed to her. "Lady Scarbrough," she gasped. "Marchioness of Scarbrough . . ." If my family could only see me, she thought. I look like a scullery maid. Her gaze dropped to her left shoe, one of the shapeless leather slippers she had borrowed from Jeanne—it was soaking wet, and cobwebs were gobbed on the toe. "I look worse," she managed between giggles. Tears of glee rolled down her cheeks as she dropped down on the stone steps and dissolved into peals of unrestrained laughter.

When she finally stopped, she looked up to see her grinning assistants staring at her as if she had suddenly taken leave of her senses. "Well," she said, affecting her great-lady tone. "What are you waiting for? You lads start moving the clean butter churns and the milk buckets back into the dairy. Jeanne, you may open the pipe and let the water in."

Despite Anne's approving smile, they jumped to obey her orders. Jeanne pulled a china plug, and cold water from the loch ran down the stone trough into the soapstone sink and out through a hole in the far wall. Outside the stone-walled building, a water wheel powered by a crude windmill creaked and groaned as the steady stream of water continued to gush through the dairy.

" 'Tis a miracle, lady," Jeanne cried. Her blue eyes widened in delight. "Lidikins, but 'tis easier than lugging buckets of water up from the lake!"

"And the dairy will keep cooler in summer. The milk won't sour so quickly," Anne said, wiping her hands on her homespun skirt. "You're in charge here," she reminded Jeanne. "No one is to enter without clean hands and clothing. You and the other girls are to tie your hair up and cover it with cloths. If I find so much as a fly in the butter or a hair in the cheese, there'll be hell to pay."

"Aye, m'lady," Jeanne replied. "Whatever ye say." The admiration in Jeanne's eyes told Anne that if she'd asked the wench to fly off the top of the west tower, she'd have attempted it without hesitation.

"Mavis." Anne turned her attention to the new housekeeper. New clothing and a decent cap hadn't altered her lush attributes a whit. Mavis's full breasts still strained the bosom of her dress, and her black hair continued to curl untidily around her sensuous face. Her half-closed eyelids and full pouting mouth always made the wench look to Anne as though she had just climbed out of bed . . . or was about to climb into one.

"Ma'am?"

"Go to the kitchen and tell cook to prepare pigeon pie tomorrow. The leftover lamb will do well enough for today, but I want fresh oatcakes for breakfast. Those we had today were fit only for the pigs."

"Geordie cooks what he pleases, lady." Mavis scratched her neck, and Anne made a mental note to order baths for all the castle servants on the first warm day.

"You tell him he'll cook what I say, or he can find other employment. And tell him that if he ever tries to serve donkey to the lord's table again, he'll rue the day he was born."

Mavis bobbed a curtsy and dashed off to follow her mistress's instructions.

Anne stepped into the pale April sunshine and squinted up at the sky. It was late afternoon, and still chilly. The sun felt good on her face after the long damp winter. She took a deep breath and rubbed the small of her back, not wanting to think about what the sun and wind must be doing to her once flawless complexion. She was tired, but it was a good tired.

She had risen at dawn that morning, breaking her fast in the great hall with only the servants for company. Ross had gotten up even earlier and had ridden out with Rob and two other clansmen to hunt for deer. Foodstores were running low, and they needed meat to break the monotony of fish and oat gruel. Winter food was always less appetizing than that in summer and fall, but Anne had never had such poor choices at table as she had in the weeks she'd been held at Castle Strathmar.

But if the high table was bare, at least the dishes and the board were clean. Anne had kept her promises to Ross. She'd sent word of her marriage to her mother and asked for money, and she'd turned the great hall of the castle from a pigsty to a presentable chamber.

The servants had been unwilling, at first, to give up their slovenly ways and do as she bid them. Ross had cured the malcontents by throwing three men and one cursing woman—Mavis—into the loch. After that, they had given Anne the respect due the Mistress of Strathmar.

She had attacked the castle filth with a vengeance. She'd ordered the servants to drag out the filthy rushes and burn them. The bare stone floors looked as though they hadn't been scrubbed in centuries; they were limed to kill insects in the crevices and then swept and washed down by the women. She had driven the dogs out of the great hall with a broom and forbidden anyone to bring them back until they were washed and brushed and free of fleas.

Anne frowned as she remembered the days it had taken to transform the kitchen into an acceptable place in which to prepare food. The pots and pans had been caked with grease; mice ran freely over the pewter and wooden trenchers. She had used the same broom she'd chased the dogs with to whack the cook around the ears when he'd been insolent.

The castle kitchen had boasted a well, an unfailing source of pure water for drinking and cooking, but generations of cooks had used that well as a place to throw broken bottles and pottery. It had required Ross's physical presence to get the cook's helper, Ian, to go down on a rope and clean out the well; a wheelbarrow had been needed to haul away the trash.

The week after that, she had set herself to ridding the inner bailey of livestock and poultry and having the garbage taken away from the kitchen door. Now, with the dairy in decent shape, she could begin to think of setting the rest of the castle in order.

Instead of following Mavis inside, Anne walked across the neatly swept stone path of the inner bailey. A young girl rocking a baby smiled at her, and she smiled back. Gradually, the people of the castle were beginning to accept and even like her, despite the fact that she was an Englishwoman who wanted to change the lazy customs of Strathmar. She paused for a moment and scanned the courtyard, making certain no chickens or pigs had found their way back in through the newly repaired gate, and then continued past two clansmen who doffed their bonnets respectfully, to the outer bailey and finally outside the walls.

Humming an old Scottish nursery rhyme to herself, Anne made her way to a sheltered spot among the rocks where she could sit out of the wind and watch the sunset over the water. The past weeks had seen great changes in Strathmar Castle, but even greater changes in the mistress.

Outwardly, nothing was different between her and Ross Campbell. He behaved gently to her in public and came to her bed each night. Once in her bed, he turned his back on her and went to sleep, ignoring her as completely as if she were part of the carved wooden headboard. When she woke in the morning, he was dressed and gone from the bedchamber.

He didn't interfere with her instructions to the servants—in fact, he made certain that her wishes were carried out. Neither did he offer her any unasked-for help. He spent his days in hunting and fishing, riding out with the clansmen to view the herds of cattle and sheep, and practicing archery. Evenings, he drank and took part in arm-wrestling contests with Rob and whatever men happened to be in the hall.

Ross had not kissed her again.

At first, she'd been relieved. Now, she wondered why he hadn't. After all, he did believe they were married.

She picked up a stone and tossed it into the water. Blue-green waves lapped against the rocks at her feet. Overhead, seagulls squawked and wheeled in great circles. Anne threw another stone.

They were married.

She sighed. Truth to tell, it mattered little whether a woman wanted to wed or not. Few women went willingly to the altar. She was as married to Ross Campbell as she would have been to Fitzhugh Murrane if Ross hadn't broken up the ceremony in the Church of Saint Mary-le-Wood. And Ross Campbell had wanted her for the same reason the other two men had valued her—because she was an heiress.

No matter how much she protested, she was the legal wife of this half-savage, colonial barbarian. And even though she knew he cared only for her wealth, she wasn't certain she wanted to be free of the marriage.

Anne pitched another stone. She'd been married once to an old man; she'd nearly been married to another, not as old, but ugly and brutal. Now she found herself tied to a young, virile devil with the face of a fallen angel.

Ross Campbell was a reckless fool, but he was more courageous than any man she had ever known. He had a fiery temper, but he wasn't vicious. He had the strength of will to control that temper. He held her captive, yet he'd not used his position to shame her in any way. Ross Campbell had wooed her with soft words and a softer touch.

If a woman had to be governed by a husband, why not a man who caused her heart to quicken and her palms to grow moist? No, Anne decided wistfully as she threw another stone, the duties of the marriage bed would never be formidable with such a husband to serve. A woman would have to be stupid to want to be rid of him, wouldn't she?

She drew her knees up and hugged them against her chest. Marriage was an arrangement that had little or nothing to do with love. She'd been a child with her head full of dreams to believe that she could ever have more than a satisfactory agreement with a husband.

She'd believed once that she was in love with Robert Wescott, Viscount Brandon, but he'd married someone else. She'd almost made the same mistake again, almost offered her heart to Ross Campbell. Thank God he'd reminded her that it was her money he wanted, not her.

Anne had always been practical, and she'd been shrewd enough to know that she was not so pretty or graceful as to be desired for herself. Hadn't her mother told her that many times? "If you were a farmer's daughter, you'd be a spinster to your dying day," Barbara had shouted. "No man wants a skinny armful of bones with big eyes and a stuttering tongue."

Eventually she'd lost her coltish look and gained enough weight in the right places to claim a woman's shape. Her face had grown to match her eyes, and her speech had gained confidence, but Anne would never deceive herself that she was a beautiful woman. It was enough to have intelligence and the patience to accept what life offered.

Would she be a fool to let a man like Ross go because of foolish pride? Still, she mused, he would be difficult to shape into a proper husband.

If there were so many things right with Ross, there were just as many things wrong. First and foremost, she could never agree to live in the Colonies. Scotland was bad enough! If there was any chance of them staying together as man and wife, Ross must come to London, or at least to her estates in Kent or Sussex. Second, he must shed his uncivilized manners and learn to behave as a gentleman. No English courtier ever arm-wrestled with the castle blacksmith, and he certainly never stripped off his clothing to ride a wild bull in public. He would have to learn to eat with a fork and to cover his legs with fashionable breeches and hose. He must wear a shirt and coat instead of a plaid, and get rid of that terrible Campbell bonnet with the eagle feathers in it.

She was a lady, gently bred. She expected to spend her evenings at plays, or balls, or listening to find music. She wanted silk hangings on her bed and delicacies on her table. She liked to read poetry and discuss politics. She enjoyed wearing the latest fashions and expensive jewelry. Ross would have to learn to buy her exquisite gems as gifts instead of stealing what she had.

In return for those sacrifices, she could give him all the money he needed. She was rich enough to buy anything he wanted—horses, land, titles. If he would—

Her thoughts were interrupted by the baying of the hounds. She jumped up and ran toward the causeway. On the far side she saw several figures on horseback. She shaded her eyes with her hand and made out Ross's black stallion. There was no mistaking horse or rider. The big wolfhound had already reached them; it had stopped bellowing and was circling the horses, giving a friendly bark.

Ross and the hunting party! If he'd returned this early, he must have gotten lucky and brought down a deer. Anne started to run down the causeway to greet him, then stopped short and looked down at her dirty clothing. Not only was she a complete mess, but she was wearing an old skirt and bodice of Greer's.

"Halloo!" Mavis leaned from the wall and waved to the men.

Anne looked up at her. Mavis's cap was off and her long black hair was blowing in the wind. Her sleeves were pushed back and her shift open to expose the tops of her full breasts. Anne sniffed. Mavis always looked as though someone had put her in a sack and shaken her, but it didn't seem to matter—the man flocked around her just the same.

Greer ran past her down the causeway, followed by Jeanne and another girl. The horsemen had seen them and were shouting something.

Anne was certain the hunters must have gotten a deer. To hell with how she looked, she thought boldly. Ripping off her headscarf, she hurried after them, eager to share in the excitement. Her scarf was as filthy as her skirt and shoes, but what did it matter? Ross would be all sweaty and smelling of horse. If she could tolerate him, he should be able to put up with her.

Ross spotted her and put his heels into the stallion's sides. He trotted down the causeway toward her and called her name. "Anne! Anne!" he shouted.

"Did you get a—" She broke off as he leaped down from the saddle and caught her in his arms and gave her a hearty kiss.

"Good news, hinney," he exclaimed, motioning back toward the others. "We have guests."

Anne turned to look. To her horror, she saw that there were more riders on the way, and behind them came a two-wheeled cart drawn by white horses. No, not horses—mules. "Guests?" she repeated. "But who would be—" She looked down at her stained skirt and shoes, and her hands flew to her disheveled hair. "Guests coming here?"

"Aye, sweet," he said with a grin. "Come especially to see you."

Anne watched speechless as a flaxen-haired woman was assisted from the cart. No, she thought, no. It can't possibly be.

"Will ye just stand there like a stone?" Ross demanded. "Or will ye go down and bid welcome to your lady mother?"

Chapter 10

Lady Langstone wrinkled her nose in disgust as she surveyed the muddy causeway and lifted her wide hoop skirts, revealing the tips of jeweled, high-heeled slippers. One shapely ankle flashed as she tapped her right toe impatiently. "Roger, Roger," she fumed, "this simply won't do. My slippers will be ruined if I have to walk."

Anne came to a halt a few yards from her mother and sank into a graceful curtsy. "Lady Langstone," she murmured. Her mouth was dry, her heart beating irregularly. The last thing in the world she'd expected when she'd sent the message was for Barbara to come herself!

"Good God!" Anne's mother pushed back the ermine-lined hood of her velvet cape and covered her delicately painted lips with a beringed hand. "By the sacred wounds of Christ! I vow, Roger! Come and see! This ragged slut is the mirror image of our little Anne."

Anne gritted her teeth as the beginnings of a throbbing headache gripped her temple in an unrelenting vise. Any suppressed hope she'd had of mercy had vanished when her mother opened her mouth. Nothing had changed between them—Barbara intended to be as cruel as ever. "Barbara . . . Roger, it's me." She rose and extended her dirty hand. "Forgive my disgraceful appearance, and welcome to Castle Strathmar."

She forced herself to raise her head proudly. She'd spent a lifetime trembling before this woman—she'd not give her the satisfaction of doing so today.

Barbara avoided meeting Anne's direct gaze and turned to motion her escort, Roger Martin, closer. "Come, dear," she called, "and greet my errant child."

Anne's fingers tightened on her skirts. She clung desperately to the rough wool, afraid that if she lessened her grip, Barbara would see her trepidation. She'd provide no show for her mother's latest lackey. Roger was the do-nothing third son of Lord Montclaire, and a good ten years her mother's junior.

She's as beautiful as ever, Anne's castigating inner voice cried. *Beautiful, as you will never be.* Anne raised her fingers to clasp her amulet and blocked out the voice. The smooth surface of the golden charm felt warm to her touch and gave her strength. She smiled woodenly and stiffened her spine. If it was war Barbara wanted, this time Anne would defend herself.

Lady Langstone tucked her arm through the bewigged gentleman's and whispered in his ear. Roger laughed, and she slapped him playfully. "You naughty boy," she teased.

My esteemed lady mother, Anne seethed. Trust her to come dressed in her finest. Barbara's fashionable French gown was a deep mulberry satin with a square decolletage; her underskirt was pearl velvet shot with gold thread and hemmed with seed pearls. Both of her hands were weighed down with rings, and glowing tear-shaped pearls the size of olives dangled from her ears. Barbara's golden hair was pulled away from her oval face to fall forward in one flawless curl over her shoulder. Fingerless mitts covered her hands, allowing her perfectly manicured and shapely fingers to be seen.

Barbara's thick lashes fluttered as she made a pretense of noticing her daughter once more. She bestowed a dazzling smile. "Anne, darling, I can't believe my eyes. I mistook you for a serving wench in that dreadful costume."

The pain in Anne's head intensified until it seemed as though her mother's face was hidden by a red mist. "Lady Langstone," she said precisely, "may I present my husband, the Master of Strathmar. Sir, may I make known to you my mother, Lady Langstone."

Barbara extended her hand to be kissed. "No need for such formality, you silly chit," she cooed. "This marvelous gentleman and I have already met on the castle road."

Anne felt Ross's strong arm go around her waist, and tears of gratitude clouded her vision. Ross wasn't intimidated by her mother—he wouldn't add to her own shame by letting Barbara know that their marriage was a farce. Unconsciously, Anne molded her hip and shoulder to lean against Ross's solid frame.

Barbara cleared her throat and glanced down at her waiting hand. His bronzed features immobile, Ross stood as still as a statue. A hint of color tinted Barbara's cheekbones as she withdrew her hand, unkissed.

Anne clutched Ross's fingers gratefully. His clasp tightened around hers, and she blinked to keep her tears from falling. He really is a good man, she thought—rascal, bandit, or savage, he really is.

"Hmmm, yes, of course," Barbara murmured. Her sweet demeanor vanished as her eyes flicked to her daughter. Barbara's scorching blue gaze began at Anne's scuffed toes and traveled up over her borrowed gown and stained bodice to her bright red cheeks. "How dreadful you look, child—but then you always had the most awful complexion." The tip of her tongue showed between tiny, perfectly shaped teeth. "Where did you get those . . . those rags—from a goose girl?" She made a delicate moue. "Your hair looks as though something has been"—she cut her eyes at Roger and giggled—"nesting in it."

"I've been supervising the cleaning of the dairy," Anne replied flatly. "What would you have me wear—court dress?"

"I expect you to remember your station." Barbara's features hardened to rose marble. "You've caused us all a great deal of concern, not to mention financial hardship."

Anne didn't give an inch. "Did you bring the money I requested? It is mine. I am of age, and I am legally married."

Barbara flushed. "This is hardly the place to discuss private matters. Am I to be invited in, or am I to remain here all night?"

Ross stepped to the center of the causeway and stood there arrogantly, fists on his hips, moccasined feet spread wide. His heathen dark eyes sparkled with humor as his gaze flicked from Anne's mother to the powdered gentleman beside her.

Anne tried to keep from laughing as she imagined how a man like Roger Martin must appear to Ross Campbell. Roger's lavender, pleated-velvet coat and flowered satin waistcoat might cause envy at a royal ball, but here at this wild Scottish castle, Roger's curled periwig, his jeweled buttons, his wide lace garters, and his high-heeled red shoes with purple satin roses on the toes looked ridiculous.

"Ye must come in, of course, Lady Langstone," Ross said in his deepest Scottish brogue. "Your coming was a shock to Anne. Be ye welcome at Castle Strathmar, both ye and the laddie."

"Lady Barbara," Barbara corrected coyly as she favored Ross with one of her most endearing smiles.

She sees past the rough kilt to the man beneath, Anne thought shrewdly. If I'm not careful, she'll have Ross in her bed before dawn.

"When people call me Lady Langstone, I always think of my husband's late mother," Barbara continued. "She was old and shriveled, and I hope I do not favor her yet."

"Lady Barbara then," Ross agreed. He motioned toward the castle. "Come. We've fresh venison for supper, and it's best we get the two of ye safe inside before the dogs take Master Roger for a pheasant and drag him off into the heather to eat."

Later that evening, Anne sat at the high table between Roger and Ross and pushed her slice of roast venison around her plate with an ivory fork. She couldn't have eaten a bite of the juicy meat if her life depended on it.

Ross's table manners were somewhat less than elegant. Ignoring the knife and fork at his place, he ate with his fingers—using a huge knife he'd pulled from his belt to stab anything he wished from the serving platters. His appetite was unbelievable. It was all she could do to keep her eyes off his plate as he devoured enough meat and bread and vegetables to feed four ordinary men.

Not that Ross's fingers weren't clean. Between bites, he dipped them in his wine goblet and dried them daintily on the table cover. Roger's eyes were as wide as shoe buttons, and he emitted a small sound every time Ross reached for another helping of food. Barbara seemed to be the only person at the table who was indifferent to Ross's eating habits.

A piper entered the hall and took up a position before the high table. Anne forced herself to listen to the music and tried to ignore her mother's laughter and whispered innuendos.

It was impossible for Anne not to be miserable. Too late, she'd bathed and changed into one of the old-fashioned gowns Greer had provided from a seemingly unending source. But the damage was already done—Barbara had seen her at her worst, and she'd never let her forget it. Her mother had assured her that she'd brought some of Anne's own clothes with her, but Anne had received none of them yet.

Barbara was quartered in the only decent chamber, the solar, while Anne was crammed into Greer's small room. God only knew where Ross had ordered Roger housed—Anne hoped it wasn't the pigsty. The gentleman's sour face had left small doubt that he was unhappy with his accommodations, and Anne knew that Roger would delight in spreading tales of her poor marriage throughout the court.

Her mother simpered and leaned close to Ross. Her neckline was shockingly low, giving him a clear view of her ample bosom down to her rouged nipples. "You're outrageous," she teased. "How my daughter's managed to keep you hidden from us all this time is a mystery." She batted her lashes up at him. "We never guessed Anne had a secret lover."

Anne stiffened. No wonder her mother had accepted Ross so easily—she believed that the abduction was arranged beforehand. She hoped Ross would go along with the misunderstanding. Being kidnapped by a lover was much more acceptable in Barbara's world than being stolen by a mercenary Scottish reiver. If the worst happened—if Ross took Anne's money and left her—she could always convince her mother that she'd tired of him.

Barbara speared a chunk of venison and popped it coquettishly into her red-painted mouth. "You look a lusty man," she said to Ross. "Too much man for my shy little Anne."

"We suit each other well enough," Ross murmured, glancing affectionately at his bride. Deliberately, he covered her trembling hand with his rock-hard one. "Anne has a side to her a mother would nay be expected to know."

Anne bit her quivering lower lip and flashed him a look of gratitude. Suddenly, her mood lightened. What did it matter if mice ran over her mother when she slept, or if she soiled her velvet slippers with goose droppings? Hadn't she sold her only child to the highest bidder without considering her feelings? When had Barbara ever thought of anyone or anything but herself?

You've never been a real mother to me, Anne thought vehemently. I've had neither mother nor father because of you. When will I learn to stop trying to earn your approval? She sighed and took a sip of the sweet Dutch wine Barbara had brought with them. If you're not too comfortable, Mother, and the food is unappetizing, you won't stay long, and I can get back to convincing Ross that it would be advantageous to him to remain married to me.

Roger mumbled something inane, and Anne replied in kind. She drained her goblet and held it up for Greer to pour another cupful. Her head felt a little fuzzy, but Anne didn't care. She would need wine to get through this unending meal.

Barbara had told her earlier that she had sent a messenger to Baron Murrane telling of the marriage. "Langstone was furious at your deception," she'd said, "and I doubt that Fitzhugh will be any happier."

Damn Murrane and her stepfather, Anne thought as she finished her third goblet of wine. She cared not a whit for either of them. She would have Ross Campbell, or she'd let him return to America without her. So long as she remained legally married to him, no one—not even King George himself—could force her to wed anyone else.

Barbara leaned against Ross's shoulder and whispered to him again. She stroked his arm with her scarlet-tipped fingernails.

Anne couldn't hear what she was saying, but she could guess. Either Barbara was ridiculing her awkward daughter or inviting her son-in-law to come to her bed that night. Anne felt as though as iron band were tightening around her chest. How dare Barbara be so brazen? She had her own plaything with her. Ross belonged to—

Anne's bottom tooth clinked on her empty wine goblet. She gripped the pewter tightly, wanting to bounce it off her mother's head. He's mine! she wanted to shout. Take your hands off him! But the years of learning to keep silent had left their mark. Anne's throat constricted and her stomach churned, but she sat mute, unable to lash out, unable to voice her anguish.

Barbara moistened her full lower lip with a wet tongue and cooed. "Is there nothing"—her lacquered fingertips dropped from Ross's arm to his naked thigh and began inching upward beneath the heavy wool of his kilt in slow, sensuous circles—"about me," she continued lustily, "that you find particularly—" Barbara's seductive whisper turned to a sudden shriek of outrage as Ross sprang to his feet, seized a huge crockery pitcher of ale from Greer's hands, and dumped it over Barbara's head.

Roger leaped up in protest. Anne sat frozen in her seat, unable to believe her eyes.

Barbara screeched as her hair fell over her face and one ale-soaked, yellow false curl came loose and dropped into her bowl of soup. Her eye makeup ran in black streaks down her cheeks. "How dare you?" she screamed. "How . . . how . . ." The piper blew a sour note, and Greer snickered. Barbara dropped back into her chair and began to wail.

Ross turned to Anne and made a show of offering his arm. "Hinney?" She rose imperiously and took his arm.

"Why did you do it?" Anne asked when they were halfway up the curving stairs and out of sight of those in the hall. She was unsteady on her feet and clung to him.

Ross grinned. "No disrespect to your lady mother," he answered, "but she was in desperate need of cooling off."

Anne giggled. "It's the most wonderfulous thing anybody ever did for me." Happiness bubbled up inside her so that she was all warm and mellow. "The most wonder-ful-ous," she repeated.

He took her by both arms and turned her so that he could see her face. "Anne? Be ye all right?"

She blinked and gave him a slow, lopsided smile. "I'm the best."

"You're tipsy, lass."

She sucked on her top lip. It felt numb. Her head was definitely spinning, but Ross was very close, and she felt safe. "I'm not," she protested. "I'm happy . . . happy because Barbara has . . ." She took a deep breath, raised on tiptoe, and slipped her arms around his neck. "I think I'm in love with you," she said.

"Are ye now?" He chuckled as he caught her up in his arms and climbed the remainder of the staircase. "Did ye drain the keg, sweeting?"

She shook her head. It was hard to talk when her lips were numb and Ross smelled so good. She laid her head against his chest. "You're nice to me," she admitted. "I don't want you to go away—ever." She sighed heavily. "I want you to stay with me and be my hus-husband."

He made a gruff sound deep in his throat. "Where are ye sleeping, hinney?"

"Greer. Greer's room. I'm sleeping in Greer's chamber, and Greer's sleeping in . . . I don't know where Greer's sleeping, Ross. Am I supposed to remember?"

Ross carried her easily up another twisting flight of ever-narrowing steps to the chamber at the top of the tower and shouldered open the low door. The only light in the room came from an arrow slit in the massive stone walls. Anne blinked to accustom her eyes to the semidarkness and smiled as he lowered her onto a low, sheepskin-draped bed. She locked her hands behind his neck and refused to let go. "I mean it," she said. "I do want you for my husband."

Ross kissed her cheek. "That isn't part of our bargain, sweeting," he answered. He loosened her arms from his neck and sat on the bed beside her. "Not that I don't appreciate the offer, but

I've no need for a wife . . . at least not a wife like
you.''

"Hmmpt.'' She pouted and brushed his mouth
with her finger. "I thought you liked me.''

"Aye, but I do.'' His voice dropped to a husky
whisper. "I find ye the loveliest lass I've seen in
all of Britain. It's just that we come from different
worlds, love. Ye know nothing of mine, and what
I know of yours, I've wee use for.''

She pushed herself up on her elbows and kissed
him. For a second, she felt him hesitate, then his
mouth melted against hers, and he pressed her
back against the bed. Anne's lips parted, and she
sucked gently against his tongue. Ross groaned,
and his kiss deepened.

"You see,'' she murmured. "I like you very
well indeed.'' She rubbed her cheek against his
and threaded her fingers through his hair. "All
of you is very . . . very . . . nice.''

He chuckled and nuzzled her throat. "And
what do ye like best about me?''

"I like your thighs—I mean your eyes.'' She
giggled. "You have eyes like a fallen angel.'' His
hand had dropped to the bodice of her gown. She
could feel the heat of his palm through the layers
of clothing, and she squirmed up a little so that
his palm cupped her breast. She looked up into
the dark, ebony pools of his eyes, and suddenly
it was hard to breathe.

Moonlight spilling through the arrow slit reflected off the planes of Ross's high cheekbones
and accentuated the strong line of his chin. He's
beautiful, she thought, the most beautiful man
I've ever known. A lock of his hair fell forward,
and she caught it between her teeth and tugged
gently.

"Dinna begin what ye canna finish,'' he said.

"Don't go,'' she begged. "I want you here with

me . . . I want you . . ." She inhaled with a ragged breath. Ross's nearness was as heady as the wine she had drunk at supper. She knew she was asking him for what no lady should ever ask—but it didn't matter. A hunger deep within her cried to be filled. Just once, she thought, just once, I want to know what it's like to be loved by a man like this.

"Hinney."

She strained against him, offering her mouth to be kissed, her body to be caressed. "Please . . ." she whispered. "Stay with me." She covered his hand with hers and pressed his palm harder against her aching breast. "Kiss me . . . here . . ."

"Aye . . . hinney." His warm mouth was moist against her throat as he lifted her against him to unlace the back of her gown and then her stays. He kissed her bare shoulder, and Anne felt the embrace of cool night air against her skin when he pulled her linen chemise over her head.

"My bonny, wee Anne," he rasped as he laid her back against the sheepskins. "You're beautiful." He fumbled with the strings of her old-fashioned barrel pad, then broke them when they knotted, and tossed the garment away.

Joy spiraled down to coil in the pit of Anne's belly. He was lying—she knew he was lying—but she didn't care. The words were so sweet to her ears. Hesitantly, she caught his head between her hands and pulled him down to her naked breasts.

"Anne," he whispered.

Her senses reeled as she savored the sensations of his face pressed so intimately against her. His hair was a cascade of raw silk, tickling, caressing . . . His breath was warm as his lips parted and his wet tongue flicked out to taste her skin. She moaned softly and arched against him, stroking the rippling muscles of his neck.

"Woman, ye would tempt the devil."

His fingers cupped her breast, and she sighed with pleasure, a sigh that became a startled "Ohhh" when Ross's mouth covered the bud of her left breast and he suckled the nipple until it became a hard, erect peak.

She dug her fingernails into his bare shoulder where the folds of his *breacan-feile* had fallen away and buried her face in his hair. The pulsing in her loins had become a live flame, and she forgot who she was and who he was. Nothing mattered but the throbbing pleasure, the bittersweet anguish of wanting him.

She drew in a deep, shuddering breath as he teased her right breast with the nub of a callused thumb and caressed her exposed midriff with his lean fingers. Her head spun, and the room fell away. She was floating on a moonbeam, and the heat of her fever brought whispered words of love to her tongue. "Ross . . . Ross . . ."

Her throat constricted as his fingers moved with tantalizing slowness down over her flat stomach to stroke the curls below. He nuzzled lower, letting his tongue trail a line of searing kisses down to her navel and then still lower. She whimpered as his fingers delved ever so lightly into the moistness between her thighs.

"Oh!" Desire flooded her veins, turning her bones to water.

"Darling," he whispered thickly. The sound of his voice made her shiver with joy. He ran a hand down her stockinged leg and raised her knee to nibble at the spot where her garter was tied.

Slowly, he rolled her stocking down, kissing each inch of her leg in turn, until his hot breath tickled her instep.

"What are you doing?" she began. "No man . . ." But then he'd begun on the other stocking, and his free hand was doing delicious things to her inner thigh. This time, he didn't stop when he reached the spot where her garter had been. His flicking tongue teased the place where his fingers had traced invisible circles of excitement.

"I want to taste you," he whispered. "Let me taste you, sweeting . . . all of you." He raised his head and stared at her with luminous eyes. Her protests died on her lips, and, heart pounding, she fell back against the pillow.

"Sweet Anne . . ."

Tremors of pleasure fanned the flames of her passion as Ross parted her legs and pressed hot, wet kisses against her woman's mound. "No," she protested. "I . . . can't . . . you can't . . ." But the fire in her blood burned back the last of her restraint, and she opened to him like a flower to the rain.

She moaned as she felt the seeking caress of his hard, hot tongue. He caught her hips in his hands and raised her up off the bed. His searing tongue flicked and tantalized until she cried out for release, and when he plunged deep within her wet folds, she felt her body convulse and shatter into a thousand shards of crystal teardrops. Each teardrop pulsed with joy as it tumbled through a rainbow of color and sound. And when the pieces that had once been Anne fell to earth, Ross was there to catch them and rock them against his chest until they melted once more into a living, breathing woman.

She snuggled against him, unable to speak, unwilling to break the spell of ecstasy. I love you, she cried silently. I love you.

He held her without speaking. His lips brushed the corners of her mouth and her eyelids with butterfly-soft kisses, and when he pressed his mouth to hers it was with great tenderness. Finally, after what seemed to Anne like hours, he laid her down and covered her with warm sheepskins.

"Stay with me," she murmured sleepily.

"Nay, lass. I fear 'tis nay safe."

"But you . . . you . . ." She knew what she wanted to say, but her lips wouldn't form the words correctly. She was so sleepy and it seemed too much effort to open her eyes. "What if I have . . . a baby? Will you still go away?"

He chuckled. "From tonight?"

"It could happen." She tried to raise her head from the pillow, but the room was spinning. "Why . . . why not? We did . . . we did do it . . . didn't we?"

He laughed again and leaned over her to kiss her forehead. "Good night, my innocent."

"I don't . . ." She waited for him to explain, to say something more. "I was . . . was wrong," she admitted. "I don't care if you did steal my earrings. I want you to be my . . . be my . . . Ross, are you listening to me?" But when she opened her eyes, she was alone in the tower chamber, and only the cold moonlight shining on her discarded garter told her that she'd not dreamed it all.

Chapter 11

Sunlight touched Anne's face. She yawned and stretched, then froze as she remembered some of what had happened the night before. A slow smile began at the corners of her mouth and spread across her face.

Naked, she rose from bed and went to the arrow slit in the tower wall. She had to stand on tiptoe to peer out at the ground far below.

With tentative fingers, she stroked the surface of the heavy blocks of stone. The window was high and deep, wider at the inside of the room, and narrow on the outside so that an archer might shoot out at enemies with the least amount of danger to himself.

The gray stone windowsill had warmed where the sun's rays streamed across it. My life is like this window, Anne mused, but opposite. All that I knew was narrow and confined, but my window to the world has opened outward. Before her planned wedding to Murrane, she had watched life through a narrow slit in thick stone walls. Now the passageway had opened so that if she tried hard enough, she could slip through to the sunlight outside.

Ignoring the cold morning air on her bare skin, she scrambled up to kneel on the rough stone and looked out. At the far end of the loch, hills rose

144

out of the water to vanish in mist, an ethereal blanket that covered much of the lake and framed the countryside in soft walls of velvet gray. Anne inhaled deeply of the fresh air, and her eyes twinkled as she smelled heather and the pleasant damp scent of water washing against the lake grass and the rocks at the foot of the tower.

"Dinna jump."

She turned toward his teasing voice and smiled when she saw him standing in the doorway, and Ross thought the sight of her in the sunlight, garbed in nothing but her soft brown hair falling around her shoulders, was the bonniest thing he'd ever seen.

"Ross," she murmured, her voice husky with invitation.

Atch, so that was the way of it, was it? He smiled back at her, and she stretched and ran her fingers through her hair. His heart skipped a beat, and he felt the warmth grow in his loins. "Wee Anne . . ." he murmured. There was more of woman and less of girl about her this day than he had seen before. "I wanted to see ye before ye went down to the others . . . to be certain ye understood about . . ."

She held out her hands to him, and he crossed the room and took her in his arms. She fit like an arrow fits the bow—like the bark of a canoe fit the frame, and she smelled of soap, and rose petals, and woman.

Anne raised her heart-shaped face to be kissed, and he knew he was lost. The hunter in him tensed to flee, but the man brought his mouth down to hers and drank of her sweet offering. "Anne."

He caught her around the waist and lifted her up, letting his eyes take in the curves of high, firm breasts, creamy thighs and the soft brown curls between them. His throat constricted as he brushed the nub of one rose-tinted breast with his lips and brought her close to him.

Anne wrapped her bare legs around his waist and smothered his face with kisses. She tangled her fingers in his hair and whispered his name as no woman had ever said it before.

The tight aching beneath his kilt intensified as he remembered the wet woman-taste of her and the sound of her cries of pleasure in the night. "Anne," he growled. And then he was pushing her back against the heaped sheepskins of the bed and crushing her mouth with his.

The texture of her tongue as it twined and thrust against his, the warm honey taste of her mouth, the satin smoothness of her bare skin against his ignited a fire that only she could quench. She bucked and moaned beneath him, scratching his skin with her nails. Her head was thrown back, with her golden-brown hair tumbled around her shoulders; her gray-green eyes were heavy with passion.

His fingers splayed across the curve of her hipbone, then slid lower to gauge her readiness to accept him. He murmured her name again, fighting his raging desire to possess her completely, desperately holding back to give her time to catch up.

She arched her hips against him and lifted her love-swollen breast to be kissed and sucked. "Love me," she cried urgently. "I want you."

She shuddered with arousal as he used his fingers to ease the pathway. She was so small—so tight. The thought drove him mad with longing. He could wait no longer. Cushioning his weight on his arms, he plunged into that sweet, hot, mystery.

Anne's eyes widened, and she bit her lip

against the pain. He felt the tear of tender flesh, and then he was in. Slowly he withdrew, kissing her and fondling her breasts to excite her again. The pulsating urgency of his own need boiled within him, and he thrust in deeply.

Tears filled her eyes, but the pain vanished to be replaced with a sparkling wonder. She began to move again, under him, with him . . . hesitantly, instinctively. Then, too soon, he reached the apex of his own rapture, and his desire exploded in a firestorm of blinding ecstasy.

He rolled away and pulled her against him as his breath came in great shuddering gulps. "That, hinney," he gasped, when he could speak again, "is the stuff of making bairns . . . nay what we were about last night."

She cuddled against him, making a soft whimpering sound deep in her throat.

"Did I hurt ye? It has to be that way for a woman the first time. But it will never be that way again."

She hid her face in his chest. "I thought . . . I thought last night . . . After what we . . . what you . . ."

"Nay, sweeting, that was but love play. This is the real work." He chuckled and lifted a damp tendril of her wheat-colored hair. "I fear we've made an end to your maidenhood."

She hid her face again. "I didn't know it would be so nice," she whispered. "No wonder Mavis has made it her life's work."

" 'Twill be better next time, hinney."

She caught his hand and nibbled the tip of his index finger. To his surprise, he felt a wave of new desire flood his veins.

"Did I please you?" she asked quietly.

Please me? he thought. How to tell her that his joy went beyond the physical pleasure she had given him? What words would convey to her how he really felt? What could he say that would make her understand how deeply his feelings for her ran? He was not a man to whom such words came easily.

"Did I?" Anne repeated.

"Aye, but it shames me that I couldna do as much for you." Her tongue darted the length of his thumb, and he shivered with pleasure.

"When can we try it again?"

He laughed. "With a lass, it is always *now*, but with a man, ye maun have a wee bit of patience." He cupped her small, rounded buttocks possessively. Anne was a beautiful, desirable woman . . . but she was more than that. The word *love* surfaced in his mind, and he pushed it away to answer lightly, "If you keep pestering me like this, 'twill be sooner than usual."

She giggled, a warm, soft sound that caused a bubble of happiness to form in his chest. "We are truly man and wife now, are we not?"

"Aye, lassie, that we be." He'd answered what she wanted to hear . . . but was it a lie? Was she truly his wife now? Had their coming together—starting with his fool's mistake in stealing the wrong woman—been part of his fate? The Indians believed that a man's future was written in the stars on the day he was born, and that a man was never whole until he found the woman who was meant for him. His Scottish heritage scoffed at such superstitious Indian nonsense, but his Delaware blood whispered that it was so, that this was the woman he'd searched half a lifetime and crossed an ocean to find.

"Do you remember what I said to you last night?" Anne asked. Her gray eyes were large and luminous. Her smile twisted his guts and made him want to promise things he knew he'd regret.

"The part about my being wonderful, or the part about you liking my thighs best?"

She drew small circles on his chest with her finger. "Not that," she protested. "The part where I said I wanted you for my husband . . . my true husband."

Ross sat up. Suddenly the room that had been so cool had become stifling. The stone walls of the tower seemed to press in around him until he found it hard to breathe. He wished he could answer her in his mother's tongue—the English words would sound harsh. He'd cut off his right arm to keep from hurting Anne, but it would be crueler still to let her believe something that could never be. "I'm honored, hinney," he replied gruffly, "but my life isn't here—it's in America. All of this . . ." He motioned. "I've no use for it."

"Not this godforsaken castle in Scotland, but England. I've money, Ross, more money than you know. If you stay with me, you can have whatever you want."

He sighed heavily and rose from the bed. "Aye, the money for my passage home." He retrieved his plaid and wrapped it around him. "Did your mother bring the amount ye asked for with her?"

Anne's hopeful expression faded. "I don't know. She's greedy—she and my stepfather would like to consider all that's mine as theirs. Barbara won't give up gold easily." She drew a sheepskin over her bare breasts. "She's a hard woman, Ross. You're one of the few who have ever stood up to her." She swallowed. "Can't we fight her together? Can't we try to make our marriage work?" She moistened her lips with her tongue. "Don't you owe me that much?"

He turned away from her, unable to look into that small, hurt face as pain knifed through him. "Anne," he began, "ye knew from the start that ours would be a marriage in name only." He was a hunter who loved the excitement of the hunt—but he'd never taken joy in the kill. He'd brought down animals, and men when he had to, but it came hard to him. And when he had to, he made the kill quick and merciful. Better to hurt Anne's pride a little now than to ruin her life by dragging her into a world she'd never accept.

"I didn't change the rules," she cried. "You did."

He whirled on her. "Nay, lass. If the bargain was broken, we broke it together—each with our eyes wide open."

"I don't want an annulment, at least not now . . . not yet. We could try, Ross."

He shook his head. "Nay. In this I will not weaken. My father waits for me in the Colonies. Even though I've failed him, I'll not leave him to wait in vain. I'll go home and tell him so." He shrugged. "I care for you, hinney, more than I realized, but I dinna fit the coat of the man ye want. Have your annulment or not, as ye please, but I sail on the first possible ship."

"And what happened here . . ." Tears rolled down her pale cheeks, and each tear was a steel-tipped arrow through his flesh. "It means nothing?"

Did she believe that—that it was only lust between them? Her angry words cut deep, and he struck back. "We both wanted it, hinney. We both took enjoyment from it. Can't ye leave it at that?"

"Damn you!" she shouted at him. "Damn you to hell, Ross Campbell!"

He turned and strode from the tower room with her angry words flying around him. His mouth hardened as he reached the flight of stairs. It was time he left this hunting ground. It was not his place, and he was ill at ease here. He'd go back where he belonged, where the copper-skinned girls moved like deer through the autumn woods, where he knew his own mind.

For a few seconds, he thought of Anne, of showing her the forest that ran west forever, of paddling down a rocky stream with her in twilight, of making love to her beside a crackling campfire with only the stars for a canopy. He shook his head. "Nay, not the Lady Anne," he murmured. Anne was made for silks and satin, for strings of pearls and royal masquerades. Anne was English through and through, and he was . . . He laughed. What was he? Not Scot, and not Indian . . . he was something else. And whatever he was, there was no room in his life for a woman like Anne.

He knew in his mind that he'd made the right decision. The question was, would his heart? Or would he spend the rest of his life wishing he'd kept Anne by him—no matter the cost.

Two hours later, Anne—properly dressed with Greer's assistance—descended to the great hall in search of her mother. Ross had already ridden out on his stallion; Greer had informed her mistress of that fact as she brushed Anne's hair and braided it into matronly loops. She'd also whispered the news that the young English gentleman had wasted no time in making Mavis's acquaintance.

Anne paused at the foot of the stairs; the great hall was empty except for two people. Mavis and Roger were seated next to each other at the far end of the high table. Anne nodded a greeting to Roger and ignored Mavis. The housekeeper was giggling and popping wine-soaked bread and cold venison into Roger's mouth. There would be time enough for Anne to remind Mavis of her proper duties in the castle when Roger had departed—now Anne had more important matters to attend to.

"Barbara's in a foul mood this morning," Roger called. "She went out. I think she may be looking for your husband."

"No doubt," Anne replied. Her eyes scanned the room as she walked. There were no dogs in evidence, and someone had cleaned away the spilled ale and dirty dishes from the night before. Something I taught them must have sunk in, she thought. Head high, she crossed the immense room and proceeded through the arch toward the outer bailey.

Her anger at Ross had receded, and she had no regrets for what had happened between them in the castle tower. Thoughts of their intimacy brought heat to her cheeks and a slow, curving smile to her lips. She sighed. Ross's lovemaking had been marvelous. She wondered if he had left her with child.

I'd like a child, she thought. If I had a child, I'd never be lonely again.

She stopped in the cool shadows of the thick stone arch and fingered her golden amulet. Ross Campbell was exasperating, but he was the best thing that had ever happened to her! She'd be damned to hell if she'd give up on him without a fight.

It had been a mistake to shower him with calf-eyed declarations of love. A twinge of uneasiness plagued her composure. She'd known all along that what Ross cared for was her fortune. Why did she persist in expecting more?

Ross was kind and gentle to her. He'd shown

her passion that she'd only dreamed of before. He was strong enough to stand against Barbara and Murrane, and he made her laugh. Only a silly woman would let such a husband go because she'd been the one to fall head over heels in love, because she believed in storybook romances.

The money was the key. As soon as he got it, he'd be on his way back to America. If Anne could delay him by not giving him the passage fee, she would have longer to try and convince him that life in England as her husband could be very pleasant.

Barbara's scream broke through Anne's reverie and brought her to the inner bailey on the run. She stopped short as she caught sight of her mother and began to laugh.

Barbara stood shrieking atop an ale barrel and waved her arms frantically at the large white goose below. Emitting angry hissing noises, the goose spread her wings and snaked her long neck up to snap at Barbara's ankles.

"Help! Help me!" Barbara cried.

Anne picked her way through the mud and animal droppings. "What are you doing to that poor goose?" she demanded.

"Me? Me? What am I doing to the goose?" Barbara's voice hovered on the brink of hysteria. She grabbed at the skirt of her flowered satin gown and tried to lift it out of reach of the goose's sharp bill. The hem was muddied with something Anne suspected was more than just dirt, and there was a great tear in her violet silk petticoat. One of her pink satin shoes lay a short distance from the ale barrel in a puddle of rainwater.

"Where is my husband?" Anne asked. "Did you see him this morning?"

"The goose, girl! Do something about this horrid creature!"

"Did you talk with Ross this morning?"

"No! No, he was gone from the table when I came down. I was coming out to look for him when this *thing* ran at me. Get it away!"

Anne looked around the bailey. It was deserted, if you didn't count the sow and her piglets near the outer gate. Anne crossed to the wall and came back with a broom.

"Did you bring my money, Mother?"

Barbara swore an oath that would set a sailor's whore to blushing. "I'll rip out every hair on your head when I get down from here," she threatened.

"Did you bring my money?"

"I brought your damned money. Now drive off this monster, or call a servant to kill it."

Anne struggled to keep a serious expression as the goose beat her wings against the ground and made another leap at Barbara's skirts. "You must have gone near her nest. She's sitting on eggs. Geese are very defensive about their nests."

"Get rid of it, you blithering jade!"

Anne's gaze lit on the pearl earrings her mother was wearing. "How kind of you to bring me my jewelry as well as the money." She held out her hand. "Give them over." She had lost her other pair of pearl earrings to the gypsies, and she was not about to give up these.

"My pearls?" her mother asked.

"Scarbrough gave them to me as a wedding gift." Anne insisted. "There's not another pair just like them in the kingdom. I'll take them now if you don't mind."

"How dare you talk to your mother like that? I should hope I'd taught you better manners. You're no better than that colonial clod you've—"

"Spare me the performance. I've seen them all

before. Now, give me my pearls before I call Roger Martin out here to see just how ridiculous you look. I'm certain he'd spread a pretty tale about this at court."

"Take them!" Barbara muttered furiously as she ripped the earrings out of her ears and threw them at Anne. "Take them and welcome. They'll not do you justice anyway, you mewing little mouse."

Anne caught the earrings in the air and calmly fastened them in her ears. She'd seen them on Barbara when she'd arrived, and it had galled her then that she'd not had the nerve to demand her mother give them up. "Very well," she said, raising the broom to drive off the goose, "I'll—"

Dogs began to bark in the outer bailey. "What—" Ignoring Barbara's protests, Anne turned toward the racket.

"Mistress! Mistress! Come quick!" Jeanne called, running through the outer gateway. "Ye maun come at once."

Leaving Barbara at the mercy of the incensed goose, Anne hurried after the serving girl.

"A man has come from Edinburgh Town," Jeanne cried excitedly. "He demands to see the master, but he's rode out no one knows where. Hurley says ye maun come and hear."

Hurley and a small knot of clansmen were gathered in the outer bailey. As they saw Anne coming, the circle widened to include her. The steward nodded respectfully. "Mistress, this be Cousin Archie Campbell of Edinburgh."

The stranger tugged at a forelock of sandy-blond hair. "Mistress Strathmar," he mumbled.

"Archie is a guard in Edinburgh Castle," Hurley explained, "and he comes to us wi' sad news. Our dominie, Malcolm Campbell, is dead."

Anne waited without speaking. It was clear to

her that the man's distress went far beyond the untimely death of the cleric.

"Murdered," Rob Campbell said. Anne had not noticed him among the group of burly kilt-clad men. "Foully murdered." He nudged the guard. "Tell the lady what ye told us."

Archie removed his bonnet and twisted it between his scarred hands. "I work in the castle," he began. "It's nay work I favor, but I've a wife and six bairns to—"

Rob elbowed him. "Never mind that," he ordered. "Tell her about the dominie."

"Malcolm Campbell was brought to the dungeon on the orders of Baron Murrane. He was tortured and put to death by the baron's will. Even now, Murrane marches the Strathmar road with two hundred English soldiers. He's sworn to kill Ross Campbell and take ye back, lady."

Anne's knees went weak. She stared at him in disbelief. "Why would you risk your own life to come and tell us this?"

Archie's protruding Adam's apple bobbed up and down. "The dominie promised me salvation. He swore to fix things with the Almighty for my sins if I come in time to warn your master." Archie's sunburned face flushed deeper red. "Some of what I tell ye came from the dominie's lips, some I heard with my own ears. The number of English soldiers I saw with my own eyes." He took a deep breath and let it out slow. "I done things in my life I ain't proud of, lady, but I'd have no part of murdering a dominie. And I'd be a bigger fool to risk my chance at heaven to help an English lord murder a Scotsman."

"How far behind ye be they?" Rob asked.

"An hour's march, maybe. Maybe closer. My horse threw a shoe, and I had to run the last two miles. As God is my witness, lady, Baron Murrane is coming—and he's coming for you."

Hurley looked around at the crumbling castle walls. "Strathmar canna stand against an army, mistress. A herd of sheep could climb these walls. If the butcher of Sheriffmuir comes against us with steel and shot, he'll run the loch red with Campbell blood."

Anne tried to curb the waves of cold fear that washed over her. "If I went out to Baron Murrane . . ." she began in desperation. "If I surrendered myself to him? One of you could warn Ross. He would have time to get away."

"Give yerself to such a monster?" Hurley scowled. "Nay, lady, you're no good to him so long as the master lives."

"I could try and reason with him—offer to get an annulment of my marriage to Ross."

"A Scots annulment," Rob scoffed. "That's the only annulment he'll be wanting. A dead husband is the quickest way to claim an heiress."

"Nothing will stop Murrane from sacking Strathmar and murdering all within who give allegiance to the master," Hurley said.

"Then you must all flee," Anne said. "Take anything of value you can carry and run into the hills. My mother is here and Roger Martin. Murrane won't dare harm them, or me if I'm with them."

"Run before English dogs?" a clansman grumbled. "I'd sooner give them a taste of my claymore."

"Aye," another man shouted. "We'll drive them back to Edinburgh with—"

"She speaks common sense," Hurley disagreed. "There are women and bairns to think of. Once Strathmar was a name to be reckoned with, but no more."

"As your mistress, I order you to go," Anne repeated. Her voice trembled, but she stood firm. "I've brought this trouble on you, and I'd not have a drop of blood shed for my sake."

"Aye, there's sense from an English mouth," Rob said. "There be time to fight, and time to run away to fight again. We've short notice. Look to your families. Bruce, alert the herders. Gray, Cullen! Take horses and ride out to search for the master. I'll see to the servants." He halted long enough to give Anne an admiring look. "God keep ye, lady, you're a brave lass and that's certain—brave enough to be Scot and nay English."

"Ye heard him," Hurley shouted. "I want Strathmar as empty as an ale keg on New Year's morning when Murrane crosses the causeway."

Rob hesitated. "Lady, come with me," he offered. "I'll see ye safe into the hills with Jeanne and Greer."

Reluctantly, Anne shook her head. "No, I can't. None of you will be safe so long as Murrane seeks me. Go quickly. I'll be all right."

The men scattered to begin the retreat, leaving Anne standing alone in the muddy courtyard. Hurry! she wanted to urge Gray and Cullen. Find Ross and tell him that his life is in danger. For the love of God, find him and tell him to run!

She knew she should go back into the castle herself, but she couldn't resist walking to the outer gate and looking toward the far end of the causeway. If only . . .

And then, like an image summoned from a dream, she saw the outline of a dark horse and rider galloping toward the bridge. "Ross!" she cried. Without thinking, she ran down the causeway toward him.

Chapter 12

Ross reined in his stallion hard when he recognized the woman in the apple-green gown dashing toward him down the causeway. The horse reared and pawed the air. One powerful front leg was stained to the knee with human blood, and the scent maddened the animal. Ross leaned in the stirrups, throwing his weight forward, loosened the reins a fraction, and spoke to the horse in Delaware. Nostrils flared, neck arched, Tusca rocked and danced sideways as yellow foam sprayed from his open mouth.

"Easy boy," Ross murmured in English. He patted the stallion's damp neck and tightened his knees. "She's a friend," he said, "she belongs to us."

Small wonder if the horse was nervous, Ross thought. They'd ridden through a straggly grove of trees straight into the arms of a four-man scouting party. The stallion had barely missed being hamstrung when one soldier slashed the animal's left hind leg with a sword.

Ross kept his gaze on Anne as she skirted the mud holes and broken planks. Absently, he rubbed his right arm. He'd taken a lead slug—a flesh wound only, but the damned thing had bled like fury. The bullet had ripped through his *breacan-feile* and glanced off his silver brooch to

159

bury itself in his outer arm. When he found a few minutes, he'd have to dig it out, but time was something he was lacking. All too soon Murrane's army would come charging over that hill.

Anne was close enough now that he could make out the frightened expression on her face. Ross's tight mouth relaxed a notch—the castle was already warned. If they had the sense God gave an opossum, the men and women of Strathmar would light out as if their bonnets were full of wasps.

Ross's eyes caught the first flash of blue-green as a group burst from the outer gate and started down the causeway, driving pigs and goats ahead of them. He grinned. Trust his kinsmen to be shrewd enough not to leave Murrane's soldiers anything to eat. Black smoke began to curl from the area of the great hall. If he guessed correctly, the Campbells were burning everything they couldn't chase or carry.

He wiped his forehead, and his palm came away dripping blood. Ross fingered the furrow in his scalp and winced. At least that bullet hadn't lodged in his thick skull. The slug had sliced an angled path that nearly cost him his feathered bonnet and left a neat round hole in the back. If the twice-cursed scratch didn't stop bleeding soon, it would stain the wool. God knew where he'd find another bonnet in the Colonies!

"Ross!"

Anne's cry of anguish made his throat constrict. Damned if she didn't love him!

"Ross! Murrane's coming to kill you! You've got to run!" She stopped short, breasts heaving, nearly out of breath. "A messenger," she gasped. "We've had a messenger from Edinburgh. Murrane's bringing two hundred soldiers to murder you."

The stallion rolled his eyes and pawed the wood planks beneath his night-black hooves. He laid his ears flat and sent muscles rippling beneath his sweat-streaked hide. A nickering rumble started in his deep, wide chest and gained strength until it came out as an angry squeal.

Anne eyed the stallion with respect and stepped away from him. "Please, there's no time!" she continued. "Hurley says—" She broke off, and her eyes widened. "Ross! You're hurt."

His mouth went dry.

Murrane's scouting party lay on the heather behind him. The road to the sea was open ahead, and he had good horseflesh under him. There was no earthly reason for him to delay a minute. Murrane wanted Anne's fortune—he'd do her no harm. She was as safe in the baron's arms as she'd be in the Tower of London, surrounded by King Geordie's palace guard.

"Ross, you're bleeding!"

His gaze flicked over her, branding the memory of every line and curve of her, every curl, onto his soul. Sunlight sparkling off the surface of the loch lit her wheat-gold hair with fairy dust. Her lips were as red as ripening cranberries, her enormous eyes echoed the gray-green of the deep, cold water. Anne was such a little thing, he thought, such a wee lass to capture his heart in a noose and pull it tight. And he knew that when he kicked his heels into Tusca's sleek sides, he'd never set eyes on her again in this life.

Unless I take her with me . . .

"Ross!" she cried frantically. "Are you deaf? Can't you understand what I'm saying? You've got to flee for your life. Murrane's army will be here any minute!"

His Scots logic bade him turn and ride like the wind, told him that any rational man would put

Strathmar and this Englishwoman behind him for good.

But his fierce Indian blood seared away reason, and he leaned from the saddle and seized her in his arms.

"What are you doing?" she screamed, striking out at him with her fists. "Put me down! What are you doing?"

"Taking ye wi' me," he answered. He pulled hard on the reins, and the stallion reared again. Ross raised his left hand to salute Rob Campbell, galloping down the bridge on a bay horse with Jeanne clinging to his waist.

"No!" Anne screamed. "You can't!"

"I was promised a ransom," he growled into her ear. "And no man or woman shall cheat me of it." He gasped as her fist struck his bad arm. "Be still, hinney," he threatened, wheeling the horse in a tight circle. He leaned forward with Anne held tightly against his chest and dug in his heels. Tusca shot forward like a bolt from a crossbow, and they thundered down the rocky path away from the Edinburgh road toward the open sea.

Murrane's second cannon volley shattered the inner bailey gate. His lieutenant, John Brown, led the charge across the empty courtyard—an enclosure guarded by a single barking mongrel and one lame donkey.

A mercenary in the front rank ran the dog through with a pike. Baron Murrane shot the donkey.

The English soldiers swarmed over the castle, overturning furniture, slashing moldy tapestries, and thundering up and down the stairs.

Beet-red with frustration, Murrane deposited himself in a chair at the high table in the great hall and ordered beer. Two of the soldiers found an intact keg in the kitchen cellars and carried the ale up to the great hall. ''Leave it,'' Murrane ordered.

When no drinking vessels could be found, a uniformed orderly ran back to Murrane's pack train at the end of the causeway and returned with a tin mug. He poured ale for the baron with trembling hands, placed the mug carefully in front of his master, then leaped back before Murrane could deliver an accustomed blow to his head.

''The castle is empty, by God,'' Murrane fumed. He drank long and deep of the coarse ale and wiped off the foam with the back of his hand.

Brown hurried down the curving stone steps. ''We've found them, m'lord,'' he said.

''Don't just stand there, you fool!'' Murrane snapped. ''Bring them here. And I'll have the balls of any man that harms a hair on Lady Anne's head.''

He took another swig of the ale and wrinkled his nose. By the sacred wounds of Christ, it was foul stuff! These Scots lived like pigs, he decided. He slammed the mug down on the scarred table and rubbed his aching arm.

He'd suffered mild chest pains when Brown had reported the four dead soldiers in the road. Then, later, when those hairy-arsed milkmaids who dared to call themselves fighting men had lost one of his cannons over the edge of the causeway, he'd thought the pain would knock him out of the saddle. A French cannon! Worth more than a hundred men and the horses under them! Murrane ground his teeth together in seething fury.

Brown had said the loch was too deep to recover the cannon without rebuilding the causeway and bringing experienced seamen and engineers to the site.

Murrane cursed the soldier who'd caused the accident—cursed him back to the day he'd dropped from his mother's womb. He'd put a bullet between the man's eyes and kicked him over the side after the cannon, but he took small satisfaction in his revenge. It would take a fortune to replace the gun, whereas soldiers were to be had for a handful of coppers on any street corner.

He swore again into his ale. Five men and a cannon Ross Campbell had cost him—six men if you counted the clodskull who'd managed to fall off his horse and break his neck on the road from Edinburgh. Murrane massaged his arm; the pain had receded to a dull ache. He drained the mug and motioned for the orderly to pour him another cup.

Men didn't appreciate good health when they had it, he mused. A bad heart had plagued his father. For most of his seventy-six years his sire had moaned and pissed about his chest pain— then the old fool had been stabbed to death in his bed by a drunken whore.

Murrane leaned back and propped his spurred boots on a bench. He'd given up strong drink and rich food on his doctor's advice, anything more was in the Lord's hands. He'd not spend his days coddling himself. He was a soldier, by God, not some sniveling, lace-drawered Jack of Dandy.

He straightened in his chair as he heard the sounds of a woman weeping. That would be his dear, sweet Anne. Murrane's eyes narrowed to slits. Damn her for a wanton slut! He'd give her reason to weep when he had her lover's hide peeled like an orange and his codpiece tanned for a tobacco pouch.

Protesting loudly, the small group, surrounded by armed soldiers, moved toward the high table. Murrane counted nearly a dozen, mostly liveried servants. He was surprised—Strathmar looked too poor to support a proper staff.

"Fitzhugh? By the king's royal arse, is that you, Fitzhugh Murrane?" A lady in a scarlet gown pushed to the front. "What's the meaning of this outrage?" She spun and slapped a crying maid-servant soundly across the cheek. "Shut up," she commanded.

Murrane leaped to his feet. He knew that voice—it belonged to his bride's mother. "Lady Langstone?"

Lady Langstone's blue eyes spit flame as she continued to castigate him. "You? You're the one who attacked the castle? Are you stark, raving mad?"

With a sinking feeling, Murrane realized Anne was not among the prisoners. He recognized the foppish gentleman behind Lady Langstone as Lord Montclaire's third son. Murrane signaled, and the foot soldier holding Roger Martin's arms behind his back released him.

Roger dusted off his coat and moved to stand alongside Anne's mother. "My father will want to know the meaning of this," he said haughtily. "By what right am I assaulted by common soldiers?"

"Where's Anne?" Murrane demanded.

"Where indeed?" the lady flung back.

Murrane's chest grew tight. "I want Ross Campbell!" he roared. "I want them both. Where are they?"

She didn't flinch. "These are my people," she insisted shrilly. "*Mine*—all but this one wailing slut." She indicated the maid she'd slapped earlier. "Mavis. You'll not touch her—Roger has taken her under his protection. Treat us with the respect we deserve, and I'll be more willing to answer your questions. Unless, of course, you're planning on murdering Roger and me and all our servants. Have you forgotten the position my husband, Lord Langstone, holds? It won't be the same as doing away with Scots peasants. You'll have to kill us all, you know, and then you'll never keep it quiet. Some of your people will talk, and you'll be facing charges before the—"

"Shut up!" Murrane shouted. How dare she speak to him like this? He wanted to order her thrown down a well—or have her tongue ripped out. He forced himself to smile ingratiatingly. "To the contrary, Lady Langstone, you were never in any danger from me." Sweat beaded on his forehead, and his fingers ached to tighten around her throat. "I came here to rescue your daughter from the hands of a vicious bandit. I'd no idea you were in residence."

Her mouth puckered. "You came to steal her back from her husband."

"Not her husband at all," Murrane lied glibly. "You've been deceived, m'lady. They aren't legally married. The cleric who performed the ceremony was a fake. Anne and I were formally betrothed. If anyone can claim her, it's I. This has all been a foul plot to rob us of the Lady Anne and—"

"And her fortune," Lady Langstone finished for him.

"I see we understand each other."

She shrugged. "Perhaps. But you've forgotten we're in Scotland. Here, it is only necessary for a couple to declare in public that they are man and wife for a marriage to be recognized. Your tale of a false cleric means nothing. Anne is wed. Unless . . ." Lady Langstone fluttered her thick eyelashes. "Unless an accident should befall Ross Campbell . . ."

Murrane fixed her with a glare. "Where are they?"

She spread her scarlet-tipped fingers gracefully. "According to the servants, they're on their way to take ship for the American Colonies."

Murrane's stomach lurched. "How did they know I was coming? Who warned them?" He knotted his hands into tight fists. "You permitted your daughter to go with him?"

She laughed. "Permitted? Hardly. That colonial's made as much of a fool of me as he has of you."

Murrane turned away, unable to look into Lady Langstone's face any longer without planting his fist in the center of her painted mouth. He picked up his mug and drained it to the dregs. "I'll find them," he swore softly. "I'll find them if I have to follow them to hell." He sank into the chair again.

Mavis tugged on Roger's sleeve, and he tilted his head to listen to what she had to say. Then he nodded and smiled. "Baron Murrane."

"What is it?" Murrane snarled, holding out his mug to be refilled.

Roger Martin's smile grew even wider. "The girl says not to drink the ale."

"And why the hell not?" Murrane demanded.

Roger snickered. "She says the steward, Hurley Campbell, left it especially for your pleasure."

"And? And?"

"And she says it is common practice for the Campbells to serve their enemies beer that—" He broke off delicately. "I'd not wish to say, actually." Roger glanced at Lady Langstone. "Not with a lady present."

"Out with it man!" Murrane roared. "Am I poisoned?"

Roger whispered in Lady Langstone's ear, and

she began to giggle. "Hardly poisoned, Murrane," she murmured with amusement, "unless Scottish piss contains enough venom to do in an English baron."

Murrane gave a strangled cry and hurled the tin cup against the hearth as the lady's unsuppressed laughter burned his ears and contorted his features with rage.

Four days later in a tiny village along the rocky Scottish coast, Ross held tightly to Anne's wrist as the final barrels of water and provisions were loaded aboard the brigantine *Laird's Bounty*. His stallion, Tusca, was already below, nervously pawing the deck in his close, dark quarters. Ross could hear the animal's frantic whinnies across the water.

Anne planted both feet stubbornly on the dock. "I won't go with you. How many times do I have to tell you? You can't take me to America against my will."

"Aye, hinney, so you've told me." Ross pulled her out of the way as two pigtailed tars staggered by with a heavy, coffin-shaped wooden box. As they lowered the crate into the longboat to be rowed out to the ship, one corner of the box struck the edge of the dock. Wood splintered, and Ross caught sight of musket barrels in the crate.

The bosun cursed and boxed the nearest sailor alongside his ear. "Gently, ye maggot-brained swabs!"

Two other sailors came down the dock with a similar box. With the aid of the first two men, the second crate went into the longboat without mishap. The small boat was nearly loaded; when the sailors delivered the cargo to the ship and rowed back to the dock again, it would be time for the passengers to board.

Ross's gaze scanned the *Laird's Bounty* from bow to stern, taking in her scarred masts and gunwales, the three light cannon visible on the aft side of the brigantine, and the weathered figurehead of a unicorn that had long since lost its gilding. The ship was well-seasoned; the crew and captain as lean and battle-hardened as the worn deck. Bound from Glasgow to Jamaica and Philadelphia, the *Laird's Bounty* had no honest reason to be docked in Saile. Ross smiled. It was obvious to him that the brigantine was a smuggler's vessel, carrying untaxed goods to the Colonies.

Luck was with them. If he could have picked a ship weeks ago, he'd couldn't have chosen better than this fast, well-armed brigantine. He and Anne were the only passengers, and the ship rode high in the water. Whatever contraband she carried, the *Laird's Bounty* wasn't weighed down with heavy cargo—she would lift her skirts and fly across the ocean to the American Colonies.

He glanced down at Anne. She was still furious with him for taking her from Strathmar. What would she say when she learned he'd promised her pearl earrings to the captain for passage to America?

The lie he'd told her grated on his nerves as a poor-fitting saddle rubbed a horse. Lying wasn't in his nature—it came hard to him, but harder still to tell Anne that he'd carried her off because the thought of living without her was too bleak to contemplate.

Anne and he were wrong together.

He shut his eyes against the glare of the bright sunlight reflecting off the waves, and for an instant, another woman's face filled his mind, and a rush of emotion flooded over him. Nibeeshu Meekwon—Moonfeather of the Shawnee . . .

He'd been in love with her for years. At least he'd believed he loved her . . .

Moonfeather. Fiercely independent, so beautiful she took his breath away whenever he saw her. The daughter of a Shawnee peace woman, Moonfeather shared with him the legacy of a Scottish father. Unlike him, she had rejected her white blood, and she had refused his offer of marriage because he was not Indian enough—choosing instead a Shawnee warrior not worthy of her.

Nibeeshu Meekwon was the image of the woman he'd always thought would stand beside him in times of trouble and of joy. She was what he pictured as the mother of his children. She could shoot an arrow as straight and sure as he could; she could run a canoe through rapids and track game over the stoniest ground.

Nibeeshu Meekwon had grown up in a Shawnee Indian village, but the Shawnee way of life was much like the one his own Delaware mother had given him. The Shawnee and the Delaware were cousins; they shared a similar language, songs, dances, and religious beliefs. He and Moonfeather had played the same games as children, and had both been rocked to sleep in *ambi'-sons*, cradleboards, hung from tree branches when they were babies. Their mothers had baked the same good corncakes, and in early spring, when the sap ran in the sugar maples, they had made maple candy by pouring boiled sap onto the snow.

His mother and Moonfeather's mother had belonged to different clans, but they had been linked by kinship ties too complicated for him to unravel. His mother had taken him to visit in the Shawnee village when he was a boy, and Moonfeather and her mother had come to his father's trading post every spring.

He and Moonfeather had swum, and fished, and explored underground caverns together. Once, they had been hunting a deer when they were surprised by two enemy Seneca warriors. Together, they had killed one brave and wounded the other, escaping to relate a tale of adventure that no one else would believe.

Nibeeshu Meekwon . . . He'd not given up hope of having her, even after she'd wed. Sometimes he thought that she was the reason he'd never married himself. As long as he was free, there was a chance that they could someday . . .

Ross chuckled to himself and opened his eyes to look at Anne again. She was about as far from a Shawnee squaw as a man could get. Oh, she was as small and neat as Moonfeather, and she was beautiful in an English way. She had the same heart-shaped face and expressive hands that moved when she talked. Her complexion was much fairer than Moonfeather's, but he had always favored copper-skinned lasses. Anne's eyes were gray and ever-changing. Sometimes they picked up the blue of the sky. When they'd made love in the castle tower, he could have sworn they'd been sea-green. Moonfeather's eyes were as black as obsidian.

Two beautiful women, lovely in face and form, but as different as earth and sky . . .

Anne would be lost a hundred paces from the back door of his trading post. She would be fearful of every snap of a branch and the moan of the winter wind through the endless forest.

Far from being able to hunt down an animal, skin it and cook it for dinner, Anne would be horrified by his normal diet of wild game and Indian maize. She would be helpless around a campfire, and unable to preserve meat for the winter or do any of the woman's tasks necessary for survival in the wilderness.

Without servants, Anne would have to learn how to dress and bathe herself, how to do her own hair, and how to sew her own clothes.

It was impossible to conceive.

She would hate his way of life. She would come to hate him if she didn't hate him already.

He had lied to Anne when he told her he took her for the money. He had wronged her when he carried her off against her will from Castle Strathmar. He could still undo those wrongs.

He could leave her here in Saile. She was a gentlewoman. Someone would care for her until her family came for her.

Ross's jaw tightened as he remembered the shameful way Anne's mother spoke to her, the way she ridiculed everything Anne did. The Lady Langstone would come for her daughter gladly, and she would hand Anne over to that pig of an English baron, Murrane.

Anne would have the life she was born for: servants, precious jewels, silk gowns, palaces. But the price would be dear. All Anne's wealth could not buy her dignity or a man who would love and cherish her for her own sake.

Would she be happier in his unspoiled wilderness? Would she believe him if he told her he'd taken her because he loved her?

"Damn you to everlasting hell, Ross Campbell!" Anne cried. "Don't you hear a word I'm saying to you?"

Startled from his thoughts, he focused on her and the fact that she was kicking him in the shins and pounding his good arm with her free fist.

"I won't get on that boat, I tell you!" she insisted. "This is a smuggler. The captain and crew are no better than pirates. Don't you see what they're doing? There's no dock master here. They're carrying muskets on board. There are no stamps on the boxes. It's all illegal.''

Ross forced himself to keep his features immobile. "Do ye think so, hinney?"

"Think so? I know so! I won't go to America with you, and I certainly won't go on a pirate ship. If we get on that boat, we're as guilty as they are. We'll all be arrested and hanged."

"Pirates, ye say?"

"As good as."

He released her wrist and she stepped back out of his arm's reach. "Ye wish to stay here and marry Murrane?"

"Yes . . . I mean no," she stammered.

He moved toward her, and she backed away down the dock. "Yes, ye want Murrane in your bed, or nay, ye do not. Which is it, hinney?"

"No. I don't want Murrane." She took another step backward.

"Then ye've made what I'm about to do all the easier," he declared with a grin.

Anne stopped short, suddenly realizing that she'd reached the end of the dock and there was nowhere to run. She let out a startled squeal and tried to duck past him.

He caught her, lifted her up, and tossed her in the arms of a bare-chested sailor in the longboat below. "Catch her," Ross warned. "If you let her jump overboard, you'll have to swim after her. Ross leaped into the stern of the boat, picked up a set of oars, and began to row.

Anne screamed and began pounding the hapless seaman with both fists. The bosun laughed and bent his back to another pair of oars, joining in heartily when Ross began to sing in a deep, rich voice:

"Oh, how do ye love the ship, my dear?
And how do ye love the sea?
And how do ye love the brave sailor lads
That wait upon thee and me?"

Chapter 13

*The Caribbean
June 1723*

Anne pushed open the hatchway, and a gust of wind and rain struck her so hard that it knocked her halfway down the steps. Blinded by the onrush of water, she clung to the ladder and tried to get her footing on the slippery surface as the hatch banged back and forth above her.

Ross's angry voice rang out over the howl of the hurricane winds. "Get ye below, Anne! Are ye mad?"

"I'm not going to die down there like a rat in a hole," she shouted back. "I want to be on deck!"

"You'd be washed overboard in minutes. Get back to the cabin." He yanked the hatch shut behind him, descended the ladder, and lifted her in his strong arms. "Are ye hurt, Anne?"

"No. I'm . . . I'm all right." Her teeth were chattering from the icy water, and her left knee felt numb where she'd struck it on the step. She was scared half out of her wits, but she'd not admit it to him. She wanted to be out of this dark hole, up where she could breathe.

He cupped her chin gently in his hand and lifted it to stare into her face. It was too dark for her to see more than the outline of his head.

Anne's heart was pounding. "Please . . ." she began.

"Ye'll nay die, lass," he rumbled. "I swear to ye. It's a bad storm, but the ship is sound. The captain knows his business. Now, go back to the cabin. Ye'll be safe there. They need me on deck. In weather like this, it takes three men to hold the ship's wheel, and each man's strength will only allow him an hour or two at the post. I maun take my turn like the rest, Anne."

"You're lying to me," she cried. The deck quivered under her feet, and they swayed to and fro with the pounding of the waves. Again and again, the ship rose on a swell and then dove to dash against the black, rolling water. With each buffet, Anne felt the *Laird's Bounty* creak and groan as ribs and planks strained beneath the weight of the angry sea.

He leaned close to her ear. "If the ship begins to break up, I'll come for ye, hinney. I swear it— on my immortal soul."

She shrank away from him. "When a godless man speaks of his soul, I know we're in trouble."

Ross shook his head. "Nay, never godless. I may not see him as ye do, but I have my own faith." He pushed her back along the narrow passageway to the captain's cabin. "Stay here, Anne," he ordered. "Tie yourself to the bunk if ye have to—but think no more of dying. 'Tis bad luck."

Ross pulled the low wooden door closed behind him, and Anne was left alone in the dimly lit interior of the cabin. The deck tilted under her feet, and she slammed against the wall hard enough to bruise her arm. Shakily, she made her way back to the bunk and sat down.

She supposed that it was night—the hurricane had lashed them for more than twelve hours. At noon, the skies had darkened as though it were twilight, and the gray swirling clouds had sunk lower and lower until they enveloped the top of the foremast. The wind had changed direction. In minutes, the temperature had dropped, and the gusts had ceased to snap the sails; instead, the force of the wind billowed them to taut walls of canvas.

Ross had ordered her below deck, but not before she'd seen the strain on Captain Gordon's face or the naked fear in the sailors' eyes. She'd known then that this was more than a storm at sea. Now, the harsh whisper of the wizened ship's cook came back to haunt her.

"Hurricane."

Hurricane. Even behind the sheltered walls of her London existence, she'd heard of the fury of these terrifying New World winds that flattened houses and forests and swept ships from the surface of the ocean like pieces from a chessboard.

Anne shivered. She curled into a ball and drew a blanket up over her, trying to still her chattering teeth. Overwhelming fear rose in her mind as she imagined the *Laird's Bounty* breaking apart, or diving deep into the black sea, never to rise again. She covered her ears with her hands and shut her eyes, trying to blot out the sounds of the ship's agony.

She wouldn't think about the storm.

Ross's image flickered behind her closed eyelids, and her breathing slowed to near normal.

Ross had promised her she wouldn't die.

Her mouth tightened. Nonsense. He couldn't stop the wind or keep the ship from sinking. He was telling her what she wanted to hear, soothing her as if she were a frightened child with nightmares.

Anne rubbed the smooth surface of her golden

amulet between her fingers. It was silly, but Ross's promise comforted her—like this charm her father had given her. Ross had said he'd come for her if the ship were in real danger.

She believed him.

Of all the men she knew in the world, Ross Campbell was the last she should have chosen. He was uncivilized, a barbarian. He'd kidnapped her, not once but twice. He'd forced her into a marriage against her will. And he'd done it all for her money.

How could she possibly trust him?

She counted off in her mind the people she'd known and trusted, the ones who had never betrayed her. Her childhood nurse; Scarbrough, her dead husband; Robert Wescott, Viscount Brandon, whom she called Brandon; Cameron Stewart, her real father. So few? Anne's eyes snapped open. And Leah. A rush of warm emotion brought moisture to Anne's clenched eyes. Yes, definitely Leah, Brandon's exotic wife . . .

Anne's lips curled in a faint smile as she remembered the beautiful Shawnee Indian girl Brandon had brought back with him from America. Anne had believed herself desperately in love with Brandon, and she'd expected to despise his new wife. Instead, she'd found a friend.

Anne chuckled as she thought of Leah. It was as outrageous an idea that she and Leah might have become friends as it was that she trusted Ross Campbell.

Leah was everything that she herself was not. The Indian girl was tough and hot-tempered; she considered herself the equal of any man, no matter his rank or title. She could ride, and shoot a bow and arrow, and defend herself with a knife as well as any London cutpurse. She had the courage of a lion—Brandon had said that Leah had

defied an enraged war party and her entire tribe
to save him from burning at the stake in an Indian
village.

Leah, with her strange Scottish accent, her lilting Indian tongue. She walked with the grace of
a leopard, and her slanted, obsidian eyes drew
men like bees to honey.

"Words like winter snowflakes . . ." Leah had
quoted that from Homer's *Iliad* one day when
Anne had taken her out to view the sights of London. The words had come back again and again
to echo in Anne's mind. Leah's tongue was as
sharp as her wit. They had shared a love of books
and learning, as well as the love of the same man.

Leah was an enigma to Anne. She was a savage, as wild in her way as Ross Campbell, yet a
savage who could quote Homer and Milton as
easily as an Oxford scholar. The abandoned love-
child of a Scottish nobleman, Leah was like no
other woman Anne had ever met.

Anne took a deep breath as she realized that
Leah's irregular birth was yet another link bind-
ing them.

"We are both half Scottish, and both born out
of wedlock," she whispered into the empty cabin.
"Both bastards."

Anne clutched her amulet tightly. The knowl-
edge of her shameful parentage played heavily on
her own mind, but it had never bothered Leah.
What was it the Indian girl had said about bastards?

"Among our people, there is no word for bastard. A child takes the clan of the mother, and
since every babe knows his own mother, no child
can be illegitimate. A child is a gift of God. How
can His gifts be shameful?"

A simple belief, Anne thought, held by a child-
like race of people. The tightness in her bosom

eased. "Would that it were true," she murmured.

Part of her inner self had cried for joy when Cameron told her that he was her true father, but another part had withered in shame. As Cameron's daughter she was not entitled to the rank she held in society. Her mother had made a match for her with the Marquis of Scarbrough; if her husband had known she was born on the wrong side of the blanket, he might have taken her for a mistress but never as his wife.

"All my life has been a lie," Anne whispered. She should have hated Cameron, but it was impossible. The loving friend of her childhood would not become a villain in her heart. She could readily blame her mother, but not Cameron. For if the charming Scottish lord was not her father, Langstone must be, and she could find no affection in her memory for her mother's husband.

"I did not invent the lie, but I must continue it." She sighed. Her shameful birth was a secret, and a secret it must remain. So long as the world believed her to be the lawful heir of the Earl of Langstone and the rightful widow of Lord Scarbrough, she would be received in the best homes. She would remain a member of the nobility. She could dine or dance with the Crown Prince of England did it please her—and she had.

A drop of water splashed on her forehead, and she looked up to see a dark line of seepage running across the deck above her. Her gaze followed the leak to its source—a minute crack in the planks above one of the cabin portholes. She swallowed the lump in her throat and shivered. For a short time she had forgotten the hurricane, but now . . .

Anne rubbed her arms and tried to think. If the ship did go down she would swim. Brandon had taught her to swim in a castle moat when she was a child. *Fool*, a voice sounded in her mind, *your petticoats will drag you down.*

"Then they must go!" Resolutely, Anne began to divest herself of her layers of clothing, first the gown, then the underskirt, not stopping until she wore only her stockings, a corset, and a simple linen shift. Undressing without a maid was difficult but not impossible—she'd done it since they'd begun this accursed voyage.

Damn Ross Campbell for bringing her here to die. Anne kicked at her pile of discarded clothing. She'd not drown! She'd survive to spite him!

He'd used her priceless pearl earrings to procure passage to America for the two of them and his horse. Captain Gordon had even given up his cabin so that she might make the voyage in comfort. Where the captain slept and where Ross slept she didn't know or care. She and Ross had not lived as man and wife since they'd left Castle Strathmar.

A pity. She was angry—nay, she was furious with him. She hated him. But yet . . . Anne nibbled on her lower lip and sighed. He did trouble her dreams with his great brawny shoulders and his lean, hard thighs.

I am like my mother, she thought—a shameless hussy. If I could make him return me to England, I'd still have him as a husband. The memory of their lovemaking in the tower at Strathmar was bittersweet, but it was an opium that cried out to her for more.

If he had shared this cabin, I would have given him my body in a week's time, she admitted. Even now, her mouth grew dry as she remembered the feel of his strong hands on her hips, the taste of his mouth.

A curious sensation warmed her loins, and she

blushed as she realized that the forbidden thoughts of their shared lust had caused a moistness between her thighs. "I am wanton," she murmured, then laughed aloud as she realized what she had said. "I desire my own lawful husband—surely that cannot be a great sin."

Still, desires of the flesh could not make right what was wrong between them. Even Scarbrough had asked her permission before transporting her to London or to the country. He'd never hauled her off like a sack of stolen flour to a New World inhabited by wild animals and wilder natives.

Ross cared only for her money, not for her. She must remember that. And if he would not take her home to England voluntarily, then she must find her own way. As wife to the Master of Strathmar—tumbled-down ruin that it was—she could not be forced to wed another. She would be free to live out her days in comfort, going where and when she pleased, taking orders from no man.

If she did not drown within the hour . . .

Anne's reverie was shattered by the sound of the cabin door slamming open. She whirled to see Ross filling the doorway with his massive frame. His clothes were soaked to the skin, and his midnight hair had come loose to hang around his shoulders in a wet, tangled mane. A single drop of water glistened on his lower lip.

Anne's first instinct was to throw herself into his arms and lick that drop away with the tip of her tongue. She tensed to spring into action, then froze as the reason for his appearance formed in her mind. "We're sinking," she gasped. Anxiously, her gray eyes scanned his face for the awful truth. "We're going to die, aren't we?"

"Nay, hinney." Ross's copper-bronzed skin was stretched taut over his chiseled features, and his black eyes were unreadable. He held out his hand to her. "We be halfway through the storm. The eye of the hurricane will be passing over us in minutes."

She opened her mouth to speak, but her tongue seemed too thick to utter the words. Sliding off the bunk, she swallowed and took a hesitant step in his direction. "The eye?" she managed huskily. "What does that mean?" Fear distorted her voice until it sounded like the rasp of an old woman to her ears.

Ross took two strides and enfolded her in his arms, crushing her against him until she could feel the pounding of his heart. " 'Tis like a wheel," he grated. "The storm be shaped like a wheel with a hub. When that hub passes over us, like as not the sun will shine and the sea will calm." He tilted up her chin to cover her mouth with his own.

His kiss was hot and demanding, and his hard fingers dug into her arms as they slid to their knees on the rolling deck. Anne shut her eyes and savored the tremors of pleasure that made her limbs weak and her head spin. She was kissing him back, welcoming the thrust of his tongue and the heady scent of salt and wind and water that radiated from Ross's wet skin and clothing enveloping them both.

The crash of the waves against the ship faded before the throb of her own blood, and her fear drained away. She threaded her fingers through his thick hair and pulled his head down to nuzzle against her breast.

"Ah, hinney," he groaned. "I've missed ye so. Wanted ye . . . lain awake nights with sweat pouring off me, aching to touch ye like this . . ." His big fingers tugged at the ties of her corset, and the tight garment came loose.

Her hands dropped to his belt, then lower. Anne's breath caught in her throat as she felt the heat of his huge, swollen manhood through the wet folds of his kilt. She slipped her fingers beneath the garment and clasped his silken-smooth shaft in her hand. Ross moaned and pushed her shift off one shoulder, gently lifting her breast free and stroking the nipple teasingly with the pad of his thumb. He caressed her ear with his lips, then laid a fiery trail of hot kisses to the nape of her neck.

Anne cried out with joy as sweet desire spread from her breast to her loins. Breathing heavily, she pushed him backward to the deck and raised his shirt, letting her hands trace the hard curves of his chest. She kissed his damp skin above his belt and laid her cheek against him as her fingers explored his muscular body.

Around them, the hurricane raged, but Anne no longer feared it. Ross's nearness, the taste of his skin, the pressure of his hands caressing her, the scent of his virile manhood . . . they made the angry sea a far-off dream. This man was her only reality—this man and the white-hot yearning that possessed her.

"Anne," he gasped. Stripping away his kilt, he claimed her mouth again, branding her with the heat of his own blazing passion. "I want ye, Anne. I want to fill ye with my love, to make ye part of me."

She trembled with anticipation as the pounding need in her veins drove her almost mad with wanting him. "Yes," she murmured, "yes." And then he was pressing her back against the deck. Wet and ready for him, she opened her thighs to receive his great, tumescent member.

And it seemed to her that they were no longer carried on the storm, but they were the storm, rising and falling, caught in the crest of wind and wave, glorying in the power of their creation.

Time and space were lost to her.

And later, when she opened her eyes and stared into Ross's incandescent ones, she did not try to speak. There were no words to express her feeling of bright, blithe rapture.

"Hinney." He grinned down at her.

She shut her eyes. "Mmm?"

"Hinney, you . . ." He trailed off and chuckled. "Lass, lass, ye pass understanding."

"Mmm." She snuggled against his shoulder.

"Ye canna sleep now, wife. Have ye forgotten the storm?" He rose, pulling her up with him and snatching a blanket off the bunk, wrapping it around her shift-clad body. "I'm taking ye on deck, sweeting. The eye is passing over now, but when it—"

"The storm is over?" Anne blinked, realizing that the crashing of the waves had stopped. Sunlight spilled through the cabin windows. "It's finished."

He shook his head. "Nay. Would that it had. When the eye has passed, we'll be hit again from the storm, but this time from another direction." He donned his kilt and recovered the knife that had fallen from his sheath and slid away across the polished deck. "I mean to tie ye to the mast, to keep ye from being washed overboard."

She began to shiver. "But you said—"

"I said ye were safer below." His mouth firmed, and his loving eyes narrowed with resolve. "Now I say different." He brushed her lips with his. "I will stay close. If the ship begins to break up, I'll cut ye loose."

"And Tusca? What of Tusca?" Her eyes clouded with moisture as she thought of the beautiful stallion trapped below in the hold. "We can't leave him down there to—"

Ross caught her arm roughly. "I canna help him." Anne was speechless as he shepherded her out of the cabin and up on deck. Captain Gordon was shouting commands; the sailors were too busy clearing fallen yards and tangled sails to pay Anne and Ross notice as he led her to the foremast and wrapped her waist with stout rope.

Anne stared up at the blue sky. It was inconceivable to her that the storm would return with full fury, when the winds had died and all around them the foamy waves were tinged with sparkling sunlight.

"God save ye, mistress."

Anne turned her head to see the captain coming toward her. He was a little man, whip-thin, and burned as dark as tanned leather by the sun and salt of a seaman's life. She could not guess his age—he could have been thirty or sixty—but his hair was gray and his pale eyes were old beyond his years.

"Pray for us," Captain Gordon said in a thick Scottish burr. "She is a breme ship and I love her like a bridegroom loves his bonny bride. She rode a hurricane off Jamaica that took eleven ships to the briny deep, and wi' God's help, she'll ride this one. But if she falters, ye maun make your peace with the Almighty, for we are leagues from land, and no man born of woman could survive in such a sea." He motioned to his second-in-command. "Mr. Thomas, secure that spritsail."

Thomas ordered two sailors to the bow to carry out the task, and Captain Gordon continued on toward the bridge without waiting for an answer from Anne.

"He's a good man," Ross murmured to her. "He'll see us through this if anyone can."

"I still think he looks like a pirate," she replied. "They all look like pirates."

Ross shaded his eyes with his hand and pointed toward the horizon. "Look there, hinney. See those clouds. It's coming."

In the time it took to harness a team of four to a coach, the sky had darkened overhead, and the first gusts of wind began to billow the sails. Anne's pulse quickened as the temperature dropped and the light began to fade.

The waves grew higher. Ross leaned close and spoke above the wind. "I'll keep ye safe, hinney. I promise."

Ross's words were something solid for Anne to cling to when the storm hit them full force, churning the blue-green water to a boiling caldron, and the howling wind ripped at the sails with dragon teeth and nails. Waves crashed across the deck, snapping rails and tearing loose cannon. Driving rain blinded her, and she clenched her eyes against the stinging salt.

Icy ocean water soaked her to the waist. Anne's teeth chattered until she grew too numb to feel the cold. In desperation, she clutched her amulet and tried to pray, but fear had frozen her mind as well as her flesh, and she could only murmur a nursery prayer. And then she lost consciousness.

"Hinney. Hinney."

Anne shook her head. She was sleepy . . . so sleepy. She was dreaming of a yule log in the great fireplace in Scarbrough's country house. The flames from the hearth were warm, and she was sipping brandy. She choked as fiery liquor filled her mouth and trickled down her throat.

"Sip it, hinney. Easy."

Ross's voice. What was he doing in— She

choked again and sputtered, opening her eyes. For a minute she couldn't remember where she was, and then she saw the porthole over the bunk. The captain's cabin. She was on a ship in the Caribbean. "No," she protested. "No more."

"Take a little," Ross insisted. " 'Twill warm your insides."

She sipped the rum, then gasped as the alcohol seared a path to the pit of her stomach. She coughed and covered her hands with her face. "The storm . . ."

"Over."

Anne's fingers brushed the rough wool of a blanket. She realized she was lying on the bunk, and she was wrapped in a blanket. "It's over?" she asked dumbly.

"Aye. Ye gave me a fright, lass. When I went to untie ye from the mast, ye hung there like a dead man on a gallows, pale as whey." He rubbed her hair with a towel. "Ye've no fever, but you've been unconscious for hours."

The rum felt warm in her stomach, and her eyelids seemed made of lead. "I'm sleepy," she said, "and I want to go home. Take me home."

"I am," Ross said. "I'm taking ye to our home."

Anne's eyes snapped open. "I want to go home to England," she cried, "to a place where—"

"Nay," he answered gruffly. "Where I go, ye go. I'll not give ye to the sea, or to any man. Ye be mine, Anne—as much a part of me as my right arm." He leaned over her to kiss her, and she turned her head away.

"No. You can't treat me like this. I won't have it."

"I love you," he said hoarsely. "I canna give ye up."

"Me or my money?"

His eyes narrowed in anger. "Does it matter? If ye canna read my heart by now, I'll waste no words in trying to convince ye."

"I can read you," she flung back. "That's the problem. I know what you want from me!"

He rose to his feet, glaring down at her. "Do ye now?"

"Yes. You've made it plain enough."

He shrugged. "Have it your way then, Anne. But ye shall never see England again. Resign yourself to it."

"Resign yourself to hell!" She grabbed the flask of rum off the bunk and threw it at his head. He ducked and caught the flask with one hand.

Tears ran down her cheeks.

"Save yourself the trouble," he said. "Ye be my wife, and where I go, you go."

"Better wife to the devil," she sobbed.

"Perhaps, but he'll have to kill me first if he wishes to wed ye." With hard eyes he turned away and left her weeping her heartbreak into the empty cabin.

Chapter 14

Maryland Colony
August 1723

The forest towered over them, brown and green and full of life. To her left, Anne could hear the chattering of a squirrel; to her right, the ringing *kuk-kuh-kukkuk* of a pileated woodpecker. As she rode, she kept a sharp eye in the woodpecker's direction, hoping to catch another glimpse of the large red-crested bird.

Anne was mounted behind Ross on Tusca's broad back. They had been riding into the wilderness for weeks, ever since the *Laird's Bounty* had limped into port in some godforsaken village in the Carolinas. They had ridden through swamp and meadow, crossed broad rivers and dense thickets, rarely catching sight of another human. Together, they had suffered rain and beating sun and the stifling heat of steaming hot nights when buzzing insects tormented them until they could not sleep.

But the discomforts of the journey had been dispelled by each day's new experiences and new sights. She and Ross had swum in clean rivers and roasted fish over an open campfire. They had made love beneath the hanging branches of a willow tree and watched the sun come up over the horizon, all orange and pink and rose. They had found shelter from a storm beneath an overhang of rock where thick moss and wildflowers grew, and had witnessed a brilliantly hued rainbow when the heavens cleared. They had seen a fox vixen and her tiny cubs and watched a quail chick hatch from a shell. She and Ross had laughed together and teased each other, and told things they had never told another.

"He came to this land when it was really wild," Ross had explained one evening, speaking of his father, Angus Campbell. "He went among the Shawnee, the Delaware, the Fox, and the Iroquois and learned to speak their tongues. He lived with them and took their daughters as wives. My mother brought him fifty thousand acres as her dowry. Wait until ye see it, hinney. It's bonny country, I vow. He built his trading post at a spot on the Mesawmi River in a gap between two mountains."

Ross threw another stick on the fire and put his arm protectively around her, and they listened in silence to the wolves howling on the far side of the river. Then Ross kissed the top of her head and continued. "Although my mother claimed all the land—"

"What was her name?" she interrupted, suddenly wondering what kind of woman had mothered such a man-child.

"Among the People, it's considered bad luck to speak of the dead by name."

"Surely you don't believe such superstitious nonsense?"

"Whether I do or not means nothing, lassie. My mother believed, and I maun honor her memory." He stretched out his long legs. "My mother claimed the land as hunting ground," he said. "The Delaware and Shawnee dinna own land as the English do. All land belongs to Him above. Men and women merely have use of it. But my father was a Scotsman and canny. He drew up a treaty with the tribes and paid a token to all who would put their fingerprint in red paint to the elk hide—even babes made their mark. Paying the fee beggared him for years, but he was an honest trader, and in time he prospered. For years, he was the only white man for weeks' travel. But . . ." Ross sighed. "Times change, sweeting. English and French soldiers, German settlers, other traders, other tribes. Times change, and the man who canna or willna change with them must vanish like the woods bison."

"What of your mother?"

"She died, and my 'little mother,' her sister, died too, of a child's disease—measles." For the briefest flicker of time, Anne saw the pain on his face. Then his features smoothed and he smiled down at her. "Surely ye had the measles when ye were a babe, did ye not?" She nodded. "Aye, and so did I," he went on. "My Scots blood made little of the sickness, so my father said. I was not even abed the space of a day and night. But Daddy lost his wives, and another son, and two small daughters. For years, he lived alone. A few years back he took another wife, but so far they've nay been blessed with children. he's stuck with me for an heir."

"You claim the land? Regardless of your mother's beliefs?"

Ross chuckled. "Aye, hinney. The Scots half of me lays claim to every foot of it—to every tree, and rock, and blade of grass. To every drop of sparkling water that runs down from the high places or falls from the clouds." He exhaled softly. "The Indians call it Wanishish-eyun—Thou Art

Fair." He grinned. "Daddy and most everybody else call it Fort Campbell."

Ross went on to explain that when he was grown, he'd been concerned that other white men would claim the land if they didn't have English title to it. He'd traveled to the coast to secure the documents and found that he was too late by nearly sixty years. King Charles had awarded the land to a favorite after the Restoration—Fort Campbell stood on ground that belonged to an English nobleman who had never set foot in America.

"The rest I've told ye before," Ross had concluded. "I went to Scotland hoping to get the money to buy Wanishish-eyun, and ended up with you."

She'd been disturbed by his remark, but not so angry that they hadn't ended the evening in each other's arms.

Anne had buried her resentment at his kidnapping, her deep hurt that she was valuable to him only because of her fortune—buried it beneath the day-to-day living. Since childhood, it had been her way to accept graciously what happened to her. She was a woman. It was her place to bow before her parents' wishes and before those of her husband. She did not forget the pain, but she hid it, and wished that things could be different between them. She would have given ten years of her life if only Ross loved her for herself, because, in spite of everything, she loved him.

That her love was illogical and impossible meant nothing—she adored Ross Campbell. She felt about him as she had never felt about another human being. She wanted to be with him, to touch him, to see his face when she opened her eyes in the morning, to feel his hard body over her at night.

But she had not told him of her love. She'd not shame herself by offering her undying love when she knew he didn't return her feeling.

She pleased him physically; of that she was certain. Even in her inexperience, it was plain that they both found joy in their lovemaking. Ross was an exciting, thoughtful lover. He cared for more than his own pleasure; he wanted hers as well. He wooed her as romantically as any court gallant—picking wildflowers for her, and even singing love songs to her as they rode.

A woman of less sense would have been deceived, would have accepted Ross's devotion as an honest declaration of love. But she knew all too well what she was. No man would want her if she were poor, especially a man like Ross who could have any woman he desired.

He could have her money and welcome to it. She had more than enough. So long as he left her enough to live as a gentlewoman, it would not matter.

But once he had the price of his land, he wouldn't need her anymore. Then she would ask him to let her return home to England, and if he refused, she would find a way to get there on her own. A husband could control his wife's finances, but he couldn't take everything. Certain monies were hers as long as she lived.

This time with Ross was something she would remember all her life. She would enjoy every day, every passionate night. She would love him without reservation, and she would hide her secret heartache.

Anne laid her cheek against Ross's broad back and closed her eyes. The smells of the forest filled her brain and crept under her skin. The crackle of dried leaves and the snap of twigs under the stallion's hooves gave off a rich, musty scent. Evergreen branches brushed against her skirt. She opened her eyes, broke off a handful of needles, and lifted them to her nose, inhaling the sharp bite of cedar.

She had never realized how peaceful a forest could be, or how the majesty of trees and sky could make you feel as though you were in a great cathedral. Unconsciously, she tightened her grip on Ross's waist. He looked back over his shoulder and smiled at her.

"We're almost home, hinney," he said. Her eyes widened in surprise, and he chuckled. "Did ye think we meant to ride forever?"

"It seemed like it," she admitted. She leaned around his solid bulk, trying to see if the forest ahead looked any different.

"We've been riding over Wanishish-eyun since our noon meal," he explained. "The fort is just ahead, no more than a mile as the crow flies. Lord, but Daddy will give ye a fine welcome. He's been after me to marry for years. He wants grandchildren."

Anne did not answer. When her courses had come a few days before, she'd hidden her disappointment. She, too, wanted Ross's child. Now, the thought that he might want a son was frightening. If she gave birth to a child while she was here in America, would he let her take it back to England with her? What if he refused? Better to be barren than to have a babe and have it taken away from her.

Their magical time together had ended, she realized with a jolt. The arrival at Fort Campbell and the meeting with Ross's father would mean the end of her courtship. She was a stranger, an Englishwoman, and she would have no friends here in the wilderness. Uneasy, she fingered her amulet.

"Ye need have no fear," Ross murmured, as though he'd read her mind. "I'll keep ye safe from harm. And in time, ye shall come to love Wanishish-eyun as I do. I promise ye."

Anne bit back the angry words that threatened to spill out. Promises! Promises came easy to men . . . and what defense did she have if Ross failed to keep his promises?

Ross read the hostility in her eyes, and it shocked him. Once more, he wondered if he'd been wrong to bring Anne to the Colonies against her will.

Nay! he argued with his conscience. What choice did I have? If I'd left her behind in Scotland, her family would have turned her over to that slime, Murrane.

He fixed his gaze on Tusca's twitching black ears. The stallion had picked up his pace. Even after the weeks of carrying double, the animal still had a reserve of blazing stamina. The horse knew he was nearing home and his stable.

Ross's mouth firmed. 'Twas no use to pretend he'd brought sweet English Anne to America to save her from ill use. He'd brought her because she was a fire in his gut—because even the thought of the endless forests and dark rivers of his homeland seemed a prison without her near him. She would come to love the wilderness— who could not?

But if she didn't? What then? Ross's throat constricted. He would make Anne love his world. There was no other solution.

She was uneasy now, he knew that. Whenever she took comfort in her amulet, he knew she was afraid or apprehensive. The gypsies had said her necklace was a powerful charm. A totem, his mother's people would have called it.

Anne's golden amulet was unusual, but not so

rare that he hadn't seen another like it when he was a child. Moonfeather—the girl he'd meant to marry when he was grown—had worn one. Moonfeather's amulet had been a different shape, triangular, almost like an arrowhead, but it had been gold too, he was certain of it. And both charms bore incised decoration. More than once, he'd meant to question Anne at length about her necklace, but each time he'd been unable to form the words.

Ross chuckled softly and patted the big horse's neck. I'm more my mother's son than I care to admit, Ross thought. To question another person about his totem was the worst possible display of bad taste. Even a nursing child knew better. An amulet was a personal link with the spirit world, and a polite person wouldn't admit that he even noticed a totem being worn by another.

Tusca topped the ridge and broke into a downhill trot through the ancient oak trees. This section of woods had never been cut; if Ross had his way, they never would. The five thousand acres that made up Wanishish-eyun would be a sanctuary for the Delaware and the Shawnee, no matter how many whites moved west. And if he made any money when he took over the business from his father, he'd use that money to buy more land from the English. Indian titles meant nothing to the Europeans, but most English didn't know he was half Delaware. He'd use their own rules against them and hold whatever land he could as the Creator had made it.

Ross wondered what Anne would think of his house—Angus's house, really. His father had started the house as a twenty-first birthday present, and the edifice had taken four years to build. His father had brought German stonecutters and masons at great expense, along with carpenters and other workmen.

And he had never wanted it until now, never expected to have need of it. If he had wed Moonfeather or some other almond-eyed Indian beauty, the house would have been a joke. His wife would have been more comfortable in a wigwam or a simple log cabin.

The answer was so simple it amazed him. This was Anne's house. It had been from the first. Hadn't his mother always told him that all things were foreordained, that past and future were one? He chuckled again and reined in Tusca to point out the twin granite chimneys rising through the trees in the valley below.

"See there, hinney, 'tis your house." She made a small sound of surprise, and he tightened his knees around the stallion. Eagerly, Tusca leaped forward into a canter.

The plastered and whitewashed stone house rose two and a half stories from the knee-high grass. It had five bays and was gable-ended, with a slate roof and massive end chimneys; the house was so similar to some Scottish manor houses it could have been whisked to the wilderness by magic. The massive front door was four inches of solid oak, studded with iron nails; the lovely twelve-pane windows boasted both inner and outer shutters on both floors.

Seven-foot-high stone walls extended ten yards from each end of the house, then ran back to form a half-acre walled garden with an iron gate at the far end. At the rear of the house, Angus Campbell's shrewd Scots mind and a lifetime of living on the frontier prevailed. An attached battlemented projection formed a three-story, twenty-four-foot square tower with no outside door, with a natural spring in the cellar level and narrow slits through the granite walls for windows on the second and third stories.

Ross dismounted and lifted Anne down from the saddle, keeping her in his arms. "The house my father calls Heatherfield, but I give it to ye as a bride's gift, hinney. Ye may name it whatever ye wish."

Anne stared at the house in wonder. "It's . . . it's beautiful," she murmured. "I didn't think . . ."

"Did ye expect me to bring ye to a cave?" Ross lifted the latch and stepped carefully around a rabbit nest on the doorsill. Shouldering the heavy door, he carried her inside. "Welcome home, Anne," he said gruffly.

The only light in the hall parlor came from the open door. In the dimness, Ross could see the wide staircase with its carved cherry balustrade, dusty but intact, and the four paneled doors leading off the hall. " 'Tis dark, I know, but when we open the inner doors and window shutters—" he began.

Anne kissed him and hugged his neck, squirming to be put down. "No," she cried. "It's a lovely, lovely house! I never thought—"

"Ye did believe I meant to bring ye to a cave."

Anne's feet touched the floor, and she ran to open the first door on the left. Her features froze as she saw the empty room. There was no furniture at all—none. As she took a hesitant step into the shadowy parlor, a mouse scampered past, and she gasped. "Oh!"

"I'll open the outer shutters," Ross offered. " 'Tis a bonny house, but nothing in size to what you're used to in England." He hurried out, leaving her standing on the dusty hardwood floor.

Anne heard the squeak of boards and hinges, and a little more light filtered into the room. Ross returned and slid the heavy iron bars, opening the paneled inner shutters and folding them back against the window enclosures. Light flooded into the spacious parlor, revealing the raised paneling and built-in cupboards along the fireplace wall. "It's all beautiful," she said, running a finger along the dusty granite mantel. "It's a wonderful house, Ross."

"Aye, so think I, but ye could probably set it down in a corner of your home in—"

"It is a beautiful house," she repeated, "and as you say, this is not England. Pray, husband, show me the rest."

Proudly, he took her from room to room. She tried to hide her dismay at the lack of furnishings. There was nothing—not a chair or table, not even a bed.

"What do ye think?" he asked when they reached the master bedchamber with its wide windows overlooking the green valley.

Anne stepped around the mangy bearskin that lay in the center of the room. "A magnificent view," she agreed sweetly. The fireplace was smaller than the one she had seen in the first parlor, directly below, but the cherry paneling was expertly fitted, and the wainscoting below the white plastered walls on the other three sides of the room gleamed in the sunlight. "A room as lovely as any I have ever lived in." She eyed the bearskin surreptitiously for any sign of movement.

Ross was not deceived. "Ye think the house too small and mean for a lady such as yourself."

"No," she protested. "The house is—" She took a deep breath. "Where is the furniture? Is it in storage?"

Ross's eyes narrowed. "I thought ye'd notice. There is none. The money ran out before Daddy could buy any. But I'll get ye some if it means so much to ye."

Anne's lower lip quivered. "How can you expect me to live in a house without any furniture? Am I to sleep and eat on the floor?"

His copper tan deepened. "I thought I'd fetch us some cooking utensils and skins from the trading post."

Her mouth gaped open. "Skins? You want me to sleep on skins? And the servants? Are they to cook over a campfire? Are they . . ." She trailed off, feeling suddenly foolish. "There are no servants, are there? You expect me to cook and sew and milk the cows."

"Nay," he answered quickly. "No milking. We've no cows to milk."

"No cows. No poultry either, I suppose."

Ross shook his head.

She covered her face with her hands as the awful truth became clear. Ross was a savage, and he expected her to live like one too.

"Now, hinney, don't take on so," he soothed.

Anger gave her sudden courage. "Don't take on!" she flared. "I'm kidnapped, carried across the ocean, nearly drowned in a hurricane, and now you expect me to live without furniture? I won't do it! I won't!" she shouted. "Kill me if you want to, but I won't live like this. I want to go home!" She rubbed at her eyes as they clouded with tears. "I want . . ." She gasped. "I . . . want . . . to . . ."

Ross's arms closed around her. "Shhh, shhh, hinney," he murmured. "You'll have your furniture, I promise ye." He kissed her hair, and her forehead, and her neck. "Shhh, darling, dinna cry. I canna bear it if ye cry." He tilted her head up and kissed her full on the mouth. "You're tired and hungry. Ye need rest. This be all strange to ye." He kissed her again. "Let me take ye to the fort, hinney. It's only a mile away, down the valley, beyond the trees. You'll feel better tomorrow, I promise."

They reached Fort Campbell at dusk. The rambling log structure was built on a hillside overlooking a river crossing and was surrounded by a log palisade with watchtowers at the four corners and a water-filled moat around the outside of the walls. Spiked logs, crisscrossed to form an impenetrable barrier, circled the moat.

"Is your father expecting a war?" Anne asked.

Ross grinned. "Always." He rose in the saddle and pulled the rope of a bronze bell that hung from a post at the foot of the hill. Before the bell had stopped ringing, a pack of hounds burst from the open gate and ran toward them.

"Not more dogs," Anne muttered under her breath.

Ross laughed. "They might lick you to death, but other than that, they're harmless." He twisted in the saddle and caught her with one arm, lowering her to the ground.

"No," she protested. "I—" She broke off as an inhuman cry cut the still evening air. She whirled to see a painted and feathered Indian on a white horse appear in the gateway.

Ross stiffened in the saddle and screamed an answering war cry. He yanked back on the reins and Tusca reared, baring his teeth. Ross raised his rifle in defiance and reined the stallion into a tight circle, then gave another chilling whoop.

Anne stared in horror as the stranger echoed Ross's challenge and galloped down the hill toward him, brandishing his own weapon. Clods of earth flew from the horses' hooves as the two animals thundered toward each other. Ross let out another war cry and threw himself from the saddle seconds before they collided. Tusca veered to the left, barely missing the Indian who vaulted from his own mount, rolled, and leaped to his feet to face Ross.

Screaming a Shawnee war whoop, the buckskinned warrior threw aside his rifle and pulled a knife. Ross tossed his own weapon to the ground and retrieved a blade from the sheath at his waist.

"No!" Anne cried, running toward them. "Don't!"

Crouching, the two circled each other. Anne could see now that Ross towered over the smaller man, but the Indian was quicker, and Anne's blood ran cold as his burnished steel knife flashed in the fading twilight. He lunged toward Ross, and Ross grabbed him in a bearhug. Anne screamed and then came to an abrupt halt and blinked to make certain her eyes weren't lying to her.

Ross Campbell was roaring with laughter—and he was enthusiastically kissing his painted opponent.

Chapter 15

Anne stared in disbelief at Ross and the Indian girl—for it was obvious to her now that this fierce warrior was clearly female. "What are you doing?" she demanded. "Ross? Do you know this—"

"Aye. I know her well enough." He held the laughing woman at arm's length and grinned at Anne. "Wife, meet the lass I almost married, Nibeeshu Meekwon—Leah Moonfeather Stewart."

"Nay," the stranger replied with a lilting Highland burr. "I am wed to an *Englishmanake*." She gave Ross a mischievous smile. "I be Leah Moonfeather Wescott, now." She tilted her beautiful heart-shaped face and covered her mouth with her fingertips, suppressing a soft giggle. "Lady Brandon, do ye please, Ross Campbell."

Anne's eyes widened. There was a ringing in her ears, and she felt as though she were going to faint. Surely she had heard wrong. The woman had not said her name was . . . "Leah?" she murmured. It was impossible, but the woman looked like her friend. "Leah?"

The Indian squaw spun around and fixed her intense gaze on Anne. Instantly, she flung herself forward and seized Anne's hands. "Anne! Sister. What do ye do here?" Understanding dawned over her dirty, paint-smeared face, and she glanced back at Ross. "Ye be wed? Truly? Ye and my Anne?" Still grinning proudly, Ross nodded. "Aiyee," Leah exclaimed, "can it be so?"

"Leah?" Anne repeated. She'd not expected to meet Brandon's American wife here. They'd gone back to the Colonies two years ago, and she'd not heard from them. To find the only friend she had in this vast new land was impossible to believe. And to find Leah in the arms of her husband was insane. Confused, Anne looked from Leah to Ross and back again. The last time she'd seen Leah they'd returned from a day of sightseeing by coach in London; Leah had been dressed in an exquisite hooped gown. She'd been gloved and jeweled, and her hair had been fashionably dressed. Anne had known Brandon's bride was an Indian native, of course, but she'd not seen her in skins and paint and feathers. Anne was shocked almost beyond speech.

Leah tugged at Anne's hand. "It be so good to see ye, Anne," she exclaimed. "Ye have been in my thoughts often." Her gaze dropped to Anne's amulet, and she waited expectantly. "Have ye never thought of me?" she asked.

Anne drew in a ragged breath. Leah's huge dark eyes revealed an anxiousness absent in her speech. Anne was at a loss as to what was expected of her. "Yes," she admitted slowly. "I did think of you . . . and of Brandon. Is he here?"

A ripple of disappointment passed over Leah's copper-tinted face. "Nay," she replied. "Brandon be not here. He is at the plantation—at King's Gift near Annapolis." She released Anne's hand and glanced back at Ross. "They make harvest of tobacco in this moon. We have an agreement, Brandon and me. In winter, we are together in his English house beside the Chesapeake; in spring and summer, I return to my people with the children."

Ross's deep voice questioned lightly, "You are married and have children?"

"Ye knew of Kitate?" Leah said. She stepped back away from Anne. "And ye ken the death of my first husband."

"Aye," Ross answered.

Anne suddenly felt as though she had invaded the privacy of two strangers. Heat rose in her cheeks. "I didn't know you and Leah were friends," she stammered. "Did you have to attack each other like Mongols? Couldn't you just have said *hello?*"

Ross didn't seem to hear her. "I heard your husband had been killed," he told Leah, "but I didn't know ye had remarried—"

"An *Englishmanake,*" Leah finished for him. She brought the palms of her hands together and raised them until the tops of her fingers brushed her lips. " 'Tis a long story," she confided, "and one to be told over a late-night campfire." She turned back to Anne. "If Ross Campbell is your husband, ye have picked a good man. Do not let him tease ye. We were children together."

"More than that," Ross insisted. He walked to Anne's side and put his arm around her shoulders. "I asked Moonfeather to marry me."

"He was sixteen," Leah said.

"I asked you again when I was twenty," he reminded her, "and again when—"

"And I said no." Leah smiled shyly at Anne. "I did not wish to wed a white man."

"Ye turned me down for not being Indian enough, and then you go and marry an Englishman!" Ross grimaced. "An Englishman. I'm hurt, Moonfeather. Deeply hurt." His words were teasing, but his eyes revealed more to Anne than he wanted to admit.

Leah shrugged daintily. "Ye must content yourself with being my friend, Ross Campbell." She picked up her fallen knife from the dust, cleaned it on her fringed legging, and slid it into the sheath. "And if ye did not know that I had wed, ye betrayed our love by choosing an Englishwoman instead of me—did ye not?" She giggled softly. "Enough. I be wed and content. Ye be the same, unless I am less a peace woman than I think." She smiled at Anne once more. "As this one's wife, do ye need to ask why I was reluctant to put my hand in his?"

"No," Anne said firmly. "I don't. I was somewhat reluctant myself." Unfamiliar feelings rose to trouble her, feelings that smacked of jealousy and anger. The trouble was, she wasn't certain she wanted to be angry with either of them. She took a deep breath. Beneath the dirt and blue and yellow streaks of paint, Leah was a breathtakingly beautiful woman, with her flawless complexion, high cheekbones, and dark curving brows—more attractive even than Anne remembered her from England. "You spoke of children," Anne reminded Leah. "In England you told me of Kitate from your first marriage, but do you and Brandon—"

Leah beamed with motherly pride. "A little daughter," she confided, "with eyes as blue as her father's. She is inside the trading post. She sleeps now, but ye must admire her come morning."

Ross caught the reins of the horses and together they walked up the hill toward the enclosure. "It's quiet," he said. "Where is everyone?"

"Angus was thrown off a horse this morning. Nothing is broken, but he is making life unpleasant for his woman. John Red Shirt has gone downriver with his family to trade, and Mary's mother, Ruth, is visiting her other grandchildren across the Ohio. Your father will be glad to hold you in his arms. He does not say so, but I know he feared for you so far away in Scotland.''

"You didn't come alone?" he questioned.

"Nay, Ross, I have an escort, but there is no need for you to make such a fierce face. I be a peace woman now. None will harm me or mine—not even the Iroquois. I can travel where and when I wish."

"Why—"

Leah frowned. "Later. First you must take your bride to your father. We will eat together, and laugh and talk."

"Aye. I've been around the whites so long I've almost forgotten Indian custom." Ross tightened his grip on Anne's shoulder. "It's not polite to come right to the point with my mother's people, hinney," he explained. "First we talk about everything under the sun, then we get down to business."

Leah laughed. "A civilized custom, ye must agree."

"Daddy fell off a horse, you say?"

"Aye. A half-broke colt he bought off a Dutchman. Mary warned him to leave the training to you, but ye know Angus."

"Mary is my father's Indian wife," Ross said. "You'll like her."

They entered the log palisade with the dogs following close behind. A small Indian boy appeared from behind the gate, bow and arrow in hand. The arrow was drawn and leveled at Ross's chest.

"Nay," Leah called. " 'Tis no need for that. This is an old friend. Come Kitate, and meet Ross

Campbell and my friend Anne." She motioned to the boy. Cautiously, he moved toward the three of them. Leah smiled at him. "Ross, this be my son, Kitate. He is part of the escort I told ye of."

Ross nodded to the boy. Ross's features remained serious as he made a fist with his right hand and placed that fist over his heart. "Greetings, Kitate. It eases my heart that the peace woman has such a guard to protect her."

The child lowered his bow and offered a shy smile as he repeated the formal greeting. "My mother speaks of you," he said solemnly. "You helped her kill the bear."

Ross chuckled. "A long time ago, little warrior." He glanced at Anne. "May I present my wife, Anne. Anne, this is Moonface's oldest son, Kitate."

"Kitate," Anne murmured. "Is there a younger son?"

Leah laughed softly. "Not yet, but Brandon has hope."

Above them, on the palisade walk, Anne noticed two more painted Indian men armed with muskets. Nervously, she looked at Ross to see if he had seen them.

"They are my cousins, Niipan and Liiuan," Leah explained. She waved to the guards, and they waved back. "They keep watch for Angus tonight. Ye need have no fear, it be only a precaution," she said soothingly to Anne. "Those who do not sleep with one ear open sometimes sleep longer than they plan." She motioned to the horses. "Take them for us, Kitate."

The boys eyes narrowed.

"It is all right," Leah assured him. "These are friends. Make certain that the black has grain and water. He has come a long way."

"That he has," Ross agreed. He led them toward the two-story log structure that stood in the center of the fort.

Night was falling fast, but Anne could see that there were no windows on the first floor, and only a narrow, low door in the center. A well stood a few feet from the door. "This place looks more like a fortress than a store," she said. "I thought your father sold goods to the Indians."

"More trading than selling," Ross answered. "And there's none done inside the house. Friendlies—friendly Indians—are invited into the post. The others do their dealing outside the walls. He rarely allows whites inside, French or British. Daddy prefers to keep his defenses secret." He caught her hand and followed Leah inside. "Watch your step," he warned.

Anne squinted to see in the darkness. The doorway was more of a tunnel than an entrance. A second door opened another six feet inside. Ross pulled her hard to the right, and she gasped as the floor vanished where she would have stepped if he hadn't pulled her away.

"Murder hole," Ross said. " 'Course it won't murder anyone. Step there, and you'll slide into the cellar. Mary's mother kept forgetting, so we had to put a pile of hay down there to keep her from breaking her neck."

"Are you attacked often here?" Anne asked. What kind of place had Ross brought her to? A shiver passed up her spine. "Are we in danger?"

"Daddy didn't live to have white hair without being cautious," Ross answered. He sounded amused, but Anne found little about this place amusing.

Ross led her on through a room that smelled of black powder and musty skins. The walls were piled high with things she couldn't make out in the darkness.

"This is where we store most of our trade goods," he explained. "Cloth, knives, scissors, needles, salt. Daddy keeps some food stock for white folk, but most of his customers are Indian."

Keeping close behind, she followed him up a flight of stairs, through another thick wooden door, and into a large room. One wall was dominated by a huge stone fireplace. There was a long table with benches, and chairs hanging on hooks along the walls. Animal-skin rugs lay on the wide plank floors. From the high peaked ceiling hung an assortment of strange items, interspersed with baskets and all manner of what could only be Indian weapons. The wall opposite the fireplace was an arsenal of muskets, rifles, and pistols. Shot bags, powder horns, knives, and bows and arrows hung in orderly rows from one end of the room to the other.

A smiling Indian woman with a round face rose from her sewing to greet them. She wore an English-style skirt and bodice of rough homespun, a white cap over her long braids, and beaded moccasins. "Ross!" she cried in a heavily accented lisping voice. "Well to come home!" She threw herself at him. "Angus! Angus! It be our Ross."

Anne's attention was riveted on the mountain of a man stretched out on a crude bed beside the fireplace. One leg was wrapped and bandaged from knee to toe, but it didn't stop him from coming up off the bed with a roar. Using a musket as a crutch, he lunged toward Ross and the woman. Leah grabbed Anne and pulled her clear of the bearded man's charge.

"Ross!" he bellowed. "Ross!"

Ross let go of Mary and braced himself for his father's engulfing hug. "Daddy!" he exclaimed. Tears ran down the older man's face as they held each other, and Angus pounded his son on the back with blows that would have felled a buffalo. Somewhere in the midst of the shouting and confusion, a crow fluttered down from the overhead beams and landed on Ross's head.

"What in God's name . . ." Anne began.

"Ignore the crow, it's Angus's pet. He wants you to make a fuss. Neither he nor Ross has ever grown up. They are like two bear cubs growling and swatting at one another."

The crow spun off into the air as Angus continued to hug and slap Ross. Leah raised her hand, and the crow lit on her wrist. "This be Henry," she said to Anne. "He talks but—"

"Hellfire. Hellfire," the bird squawked.

The two men turned toward Anne and Leah. "Daddy, I brought home a bride. Ye'll like my Anne, I promise ye—though she be English, and as much trouble as any Delaware squaw." He grinned at Anne. "Hinney, meet my daddy, Angus Campbell."

Flustered, feeling foolish, Anne dipped a graceful curtsy. "Lord Strathmar." The earl was as unlikely a father-in-law as she had ever expected. He was as tall and broad shouldered as Ross. She could not guess his age, but his face was as weathered as the foremast of the *Laird's Bounty*. Lord Strathmar's nose had been broken and healed crookedly, and he bore a scar down one side of his face. His thick hair was as white as a swan, cut off straight at his shoulders and held off his face with a leather thong. His mustache was long and drooping, and his long white beard was braided into thick plaits. A Scots bonnet in Campbell blue and green perched on the back of his head, but other than that, he was garbed all in fringed buckskins. And his eyes . . . Anne took in a deep breath. His eyes were the milky white of opals.

"Aye," Leah whispered. "He is."

"What's that?" Angus shouted. "What are ye sayin' of me? Did ye tell her that I was blind? What is she, simple, that she can't ken that herself? Come over here, lassie, and let an old man see for himself." His voice was much like Ross's, but thickened by time, and bore the heavy burr of a youth spent in Scotland. "Come, I say!" he ordered. "And let me hear no more of Lord Strathmar. Angus Campbell I was born, and Angus I'll die."

Ross gestured to her. "It's all right, hinney. He's all bark and no bite."

"No bite, am I?" the old man growled. "Damn ye, lass, I've waited too long for grandsons to eat ye for supper. Come here so that these fingers can tell me what ye look like."

Holding her breath, Anne crossed the room, stopping within arm's length of Ross's father.

Ross caught her hand and squeezed it. "Be brave," he warned. "Didna I tell ye I was half wolverine the first time we met? Well, lass, this be the wolverine that sired me."

"Sir," Anne managed. "It is an honor to meet you."

Angus laughed loud enough to shake the rafters and raised a beefy, callused hand. Anne trembled but stood firm, letting him trace the outline of her features with a gnarled finger. Surprisingly, Angus's touch was gentle.

"Hmmph," the old man grumbled. "Ye've brought home a wee lass no bigger than Moonfeather. If ye had to pick an English bride, couldn't ye ha' found one brawny enough to carry a deer?" His hand slid down Anne's shoulder to test her biceps. "Scrawny as a chicken," he declared, "but bonny. I'd trust ye to find a pretty one—no neat trick among the English. What color is your hair, wee Annie? Nay yellow, is it?"

"Brown, sir," she answered shyly. "Just brown."

"Just brown," he mocked with a snort. "The Delaware tongue has a dozen names for brown. Be it the brown of muddy water, the brown of dry grass, the brown of earth? What color is your hair, wench?"

"Honey-brown," Ross said, "and soft as duckling down."

"Well, then, honey-brown lass, a welcome to ye. And the sooner ye give me grandsons, the more welcome ye shall be." His head snapped around to face Ross. "Did ye pull it off, son? Did ye bring home enough gold to buy the land?"

"Hist, Daddy," Ross replied. "Time and time enough for such talk. I'm home and home to stay, and ye still be the Earl of Strathmar. Tomorrow will be soon enough for all of that. For now, we are half starved, and I smell Mary's rabbit stew and corncakes. Can we eat and share a nip or two of good Scotch whiskey?"

"Aye, lad, so we can," Angus agreed heartily. "So we can."

Hours later, Ross rose from the bed he shared with Anne and pulled on his kilt. Moonfeather was waiting for him outside under the starry August sky. Together they walked to the wall, and she called to her cousins to come down from their posts.

"We will keep watch until sunrise," she said in Shawnee. "Fill your bellies and sleep. Tomorrow we begin our return journey to the camp." As silently as shadows the young Shawnee braves obeyed, climbing down the ladders and passing near enough to touch Ross without seeming to notice him.

"Peace to you," he murmured in the Algonquian tongue shared by both the Shawnee and the Delaware.

"And to you," Niipan replied. His brother Liiuan only grunted.

"They dinna trust ye, Ross," Moonfeather whispered when the warriors had entered the trading post. "They didna think much of ye when ye were a bairn either."

"They never forgave me for killing that bear," he said.

"Who killed the bear?" she teased.

"Ye helped," he admitted. "Ye be bold enough—for a Shawnee."

"And ye boast as much as any Delaware."

They climbed to one of the watchtowers and stood a long time without talking, listening to the sounds of the forest around them. The moist night air felt good on Ross's bare chest, and Moonfeather's faint scent brought back old memories. As much as he loved Anne, he knew he would always have a place in his heart for this woman. As sweetheart or sister he wasn't certain, he only knew that the tie between them was strong. He inhaled deeply and let the smell of pine forest and river fill his head.

"It's good to be home," he said, "and good to see you." When she didn't answer, he knew his fears were right. "Ye didna come to trade."

Her sigh was audible. "Ahuttch. There is trouble."

"The Iroquois?" When he'd left for Scotland, a peace treaty had been signed between the Shawnee and the Seneca, but a treaty could be broken with the flight of a single arrow. If any of the five tribes of the Iroquois Nation went to war against the Shawnee, the frontier could go up in flames.

"Nay, *jai-nai-nah*," she answered softly.

He leaned against the wall and stared out at the black void of the Mesawmi River. Moonfeather had called him brother. Aye, it was better that way. A tightness eased in his chest, and he smiled at her in the darkness. "I do love my Anne," he said. "She told me about her friend in London, but I didn't realize it was you."

"There is more than ye ken between us, but as glad as I be to see Anne, it is a bad time for her to be here at the edge of Shawnee territory."

"If not the Iroquois, then who?"

"Roquette."

Ross's shoulders stiffened. "The hair buyer?" Roquette was a Frenchman who traded guns for English scalps, then sold the scalps to the French across the Canadian border.

"Roquette has been spreading rumors among the tribes. He denies that he sells scalps to the French and says that the English general in Philadelphia pays for Indian scalps. A German family was killed at Blue Mountain, and their cabin burned. An English priest is missing. He crossed the Juniatta River and vanished like smoke. It may be that he drowned, or that a bear ate him, but the English blame the Shawnee. They say the priest was murdered. I do not think my people killed him. He was mad, and ye ken the Shawnee never do harm to those who are in the protection of the spirits, but . . ." She shrugged. "In these times, who can tell?"

"Could the Iroquois raiders have killed the German settlers?"

She made a small sound with her lips. "I canna say. Shawnee arrows were found at the burned cabin, and marks in the ashes that were said to be the tracks of Shawnee moccasins. The English soldiers are certain the Shawnee are to blame. They marched against Seeg-o-nah's band. Two women and a child were killed.''

"When did this happen?" It had been quiet for so long here on the Mesawmi that he'd thought it safe to bring Anne. If the Shawnee went to war against the British, Fort Campbell would be in danger. "Surely the Shawnee don't put stock in what Roquette says."

Moonfeather shook her head. "Seeg-o-nah's people were murdered last month. It is hard to reason with a father holding a dead child. Many hear what they wish to hear. There is bad blood between the Shawnee and the English."

"Who's for war?"

"Matiassu. Ye ken that he be a war chief. The sachem, Tuk-o-see-yah, called for us to keep the peace, so Matiassu took his followers and left the tribe. He's gathered other young men around him. Matiassu's always hated the English."

"But you are the Shawnee peace woman. Won't he listen to you?"

"Nay, Ross," she answered sadly. "Matiassu wanted me to marry him three years ago. When I took Brandon to husband instead of him, he turned against me. He hates me. I can do nothing with him."

"Has a High Council been called?"

"Aye. The Shawnee and the Delaware will come. Tuk-o-see-yah asks that ye come and speak for the English and against the French. Roquette will be there, and he will urge other men to take up the war trail. He claims to be our friend, but he brings whiskey as well as guns and powder. The Shawnee respect you, and ye be Delaware by your mother's blood."

Ross nodded. "I'll come, of course. I was afraid

it was something like this." Anne would take it hard that they'd only just arrived and now he'd have to leave her here and go up into Shawnee country for God only knew how long. "When do we leave?"

"At first light."

"I'll wake Anne and tell her."

"Aye, tell her to make ready."

"Anne? She's staying here at Fort Campbell with my father."

"Nay, *jai-nai-nah*, 'tis nay so easy. Ye maun bring your English bride. All men bring their women when they come to council. To leave Anne behind when other warriors bring their families would be viewed as suspicious. Roquette would surely say that it proves ye mean deceit. She is my blood-sister and your wife. I would not risk her life any more than I would risk Kitate's or my wee Cami's, but she must come if your mission is to have any chance of success."

"By the wounds of Christ, Moonfeather, ye do set the world on end when ye come calling."

She laughed softly. "And ye, my old friend, ye be known for your meek and gentle manner."

"Would anyone dispute it?"

"Nay, Ross Campbell, no one would dare."

Chapter 16

A nne knelt in the painted birchbark canoe and watched as Ross, stripped to the waist and wearing only his kilt and plaid Scots bonnet, dug his paddle into the water and thrust the vessel forward with each stroke. Muscles rippled under his tanned skin as he repeated the motion over and over. His black hair, so dark and shiny that it seemed to glow with an inner brilliance, fell loose over his neck and back. Anne was so close to him that she could have reached out and touched him, but she didn't. She was content to watch him and listen to the Indian song he joined the others in chanting as the two canoes made their way upriver.

Behind her, one of the two Shawnee warriors manned the other paddle. Leah—Moonfeather, as Ross called her—had introduced the Shawnee braves to her, but since they were identical twins, Anne wasn't certain if it was Niipan or his brother, Liiuan. Leah, the other brave, and Leah's children were in the first canoe ahead. Leah paddled as skillfully as the men, even with her baby daughter, Cami, strapped to her back on an Indian cradleboard.

Glancing down at a water stain on her leather dress, Anne unconsciously began to brush at the spot. When she realized what she was doing, she smiled at her own foolishness. Skin clothing was meant to be worn in all sorts of weather; the doeskin would dry without being harmed. It was the reason that Ross had asked Mary to loan her a dress and moccasins.

At first, she had felt as though she were naked in the Indian clothing. Worn uncorseted, without even a shift or petticoat, the simple garment seemed indecent. Now, on the third day of their journey, Anne had to admit that the dress was comfortable, and the soft leather moccasins were perfect for a canoe, even if they were a little large.

"I'll give you a pair of mine when we reach the camp," Leah had offered. "Our feet are the same size."

Still singing, Ross glanced back over his shoulder at her and winked. The blue and yellow stripes on his face made him look even more of a barbarian, but Anne couldn't resist winking back at him.

She was happy.

She hadn't realized that she was happy until Leah had asked her this morning. The two women had gone off alone to wash their hair using sweet-smelling ground herbs that Leah had brought with her for soap. Together, they'd knelt by the side of the river, laughing and talking as easily as if they were careless girls. Leah's baby, Cami, was propped up against the side of the tree in her cradleboard, her bright, blueberry eyes fixed on the path of a yellow and black butterfly.

"Ross loves you," Leah said, slipping naked into the river to bathe.

"He says so," she answered. Suddenly the talk had turned serious, and she'd been at a loss as to how she should respond. She was no longer jealous of Leah and Ross, at least she hoped she wasn't, but she didn't wish to discuss her fears of inadequacy with a woman who seemed to have all the skills that she lacked.

"It be a fine thing to be loved by such a man. Be ye happy, Anne?"

She opened her mouth to spill out all the pent-up anger—to tell her friend how Ross had stolen her, and how he'd carried her off across the ocean without so much as a by-your-leave. But the words hadn't come. "Yes," she found herself answering. "Yes, I think I am." She fingered her amulet thoughtfully. "I shouldn't be. There are many things I want, things I need, but . . ." She sighed. All her life she'd kept her wants to herself, accepting what others told her she must do without complaint. It was a hard habit to break. "He is a rough, wild man . . . but I love him too," she admitted.

"Then ye must change him to be what ye need," Leah replied.

"Change him? It would be easier to carve granite with a wooden spoon."

Now, as she watched Ross take stroke after stroke, as she gazed at the water trailing off the tip of the paddle in clear blue-green drops, she wondered if it might be possible to soften her husband's heathen ways. England, she realized with a flood of emotion, was a lost cause. Looking at Ross with his eagle feathers in his bonnet and his Indian paint, she knew that England and even harsh Scotland were too small for such a man. He belonged here in this untamed new land where the forest ran on forever and the rivers were so clean they seemed made of liquid glass.

I do love him, she thought fiercely. No matter why he took me to wife . . . no matter why he brought me to America. I do love him. Was there a possibility that he could bend, that she could bend, until their hands touched?

Ross's painted face had been hard to accept. "You look like an Indian!" she'd exclaimed when she'd first seen him wearing it the morning they'd left his father's trading post. He'd awakened her before dawn and told her that it was urgent they go north into Shawnee Country to a meeting of the High Council.

"We travel with a peace woman," he replied. "Moonfeather is a very important person among the tribes. No one, not even an enemy tribesman, will attack a peace woman or her party. This paint identifies me as part of the peace mission. It will do more to protect us in these woods than a company of British soldiers."

"I don't understand," she said, staring at his face. Without the Scottish bonnet and kilt, he could have passed as full Indian. He looked as savage as the two braves pulling the canoes down to the landing. "What is a peace woman," she demanded, "and how can a mere woman have such standing with the savages?"

"Fie, hinney. 'Tis hard to explain in English. A peace woman is a sort of spiritual leader."

"Like a minister?" she suggested.

"Aye, and nay." He grinned at her. "Partly, but also part ambassador, and part witch. A woman—and it maun always be a woman—is born to the role. Moonfeather's mother and great-grandmother were peace women. Settling disputes among the tribes is their most important duty. Ye may find it hard to believe, but this little lass has the power to send the Shawnee and the Delaware on the war trail—or to hold them back."

She watched Leah walking down the riverbank with her two small children. It was still hard for her to believe that her beautiful young friend was a political leader. "Then why does Leah need you or this . . . this . . . council?"

"Aye, darlin'. High Council. Very special, very rare. This is a time for the People to be harvesting their corn. If they don't put up their crops for winter, they risk starving before spring. That the tribes would send their leaders to pow-wow now means the situation is serious."

"If Leah is a peace woman, as you call it, can't she just tell them not to fight?"

"Aye, she could try. Most would listen, but a few might not. An Indian is the most contrary human being God ever created—it's why the English can't understand them, and why the two cultures will never be able to live side by side without strife. In England, a man listens to his betters. He heeds his pastor, his squire, the lord above him, his king, and finally—if he's a decent sort—his God. A Shawnee talks straight to God. Oh, he allows a few men or women to dress themselves up fancy and style themselves chiefs, but when the time comes for a decision, every brave and squaw heeds his own conscience. They can't be led or driven unless it pleases them." Ross had raised that dark compelling gaze to lock with hers. "Free People they call themselves, and free they be—more independent than the wind."

More independent than the wind . . . Ross's words rose in her mind again. They described him perfectly. Whenever she thought she'd come to understand her husband, he did something shocking and completely unexpected.

Anne smiled as she remembered Ross at the campfire the night before with Leah's little daughter on his knee. He'd sung a silly nursery rhyme to her and plopped his bonnet down over her eyes to make her laugh. Ross's hands had been gentle, his voice soft as he played with the toddler. And after the night meal, it had been Ross's arms the baby had fallen asleep in.

He'll make a good father, Anne thought. And she wondered what a child of Ross's would look like . . . and how it would feel in her arms. She glanced over at the baby in the other canoe. Cami's sweet, round face was shaded from the sun by the overhang at the top of the cradleboard. Her eyes were closed in sleep, and one chubby hand hung limp.

Kitate noticed her staring at his sister and offered a shy smile. Anne smiled back and made a rocking motion with her arms. "Her doll?" she called. Beaming, he retrieved the toy from the bottom of the canoe and held it up.

Anne nodded. She's been afraid the baby had dropped it overboard. The doll was Cami's prize possession. Leah had sewn it of deerskin and stuffed it with sweet-smelling cedar bark, attaching two tiny black braids made from a horse's mane. The doll had a round head, and arms and legs, but no face. Leah had explained that Indian dolls were made without features. It seemed a strange idea to Anne, but Cami didn't notice the lack of eyes or a nose. At night, she wouldn't go to sleep without the doll clutched tightly to her bosom.

Ross paused in mid-stroke and pointed with the blade of his paddle. Ahead of them, Anne saw two deer swimming across the river. They reached the far side, scrambled up a muddy bank, and disappeared into the forest. They were the first deer Anne had seen all day. They were so beautiful, she was afraid that one of the men might shoot them, but the men merely watched, as captivated by the sight as she was.

In the last few miles the river had become gradually wider, and jagged boulders jutted out of the water. A swifter current made the paddling harder. The trees on either bank were a tangled mass of twisted logs and branches, and the water had turned from blue-green to muddy brown and frothy white.

"There was flooding here in the spring," Ross said. "There's been no rain for days, so we're in no danger, but this water runs fierce in bad weather."

Though it was only midafternoon, to Anne's surprise, Leah steered her canoe toward the shore. Ross followed with the second canoe. He leaped into the shallow, fast-running water and steadied the fragile boat for Anne and the Shawnee to get out.

"There are rapids ahead," Ross said, helping Anne onto the bank. "We'll unload the canoes and portage inland for a few miles."

"We're leaving the boats?" she asked.

He handed her a pack and showed her how to fasten it over her shoulders with leather ties. "Nay. "We'll carry them on our backs. We return to the river above the falls.

Ross and the brave hoisted the birchbark canoe over their heads. Leah and the second man did the same with their canoe. Kitate motioned to Anne. "Follow me," he said in soft, lisping English. "We walk ahead."

Grateful for the chance to stretch her legs, Anne adjusted her pack and followed the boy into the deep, still forest.

Murrane leaned over the starboard railing of the three-masted sailing ship, *Cumberland*, and spat into the flat sea. "Twenty-two days," he fumed. "Twenty-two days we've laid off the godforsaken coast! How long must we sit here rotting in the sun?" He rubbed at his aching arm and tried to ignore the tight squeezing sensation in his chest.

The captain drew a deep puff on his long-stemmed clay pipe and shrugged. "Twenty-two days, Lord Murrane. It's not so bad. The winds were favorable from Dover. We crossed without losing a single man to sickness."

"Hellfire and damnation! I should have been in the Maryland Colony weeks ago. I'd not have chosen the *Cumberland* if Lord Langstone hadn't assured me you were a competent master."

"No captain can command the winds, m'lord." He pointed toward the far horizon. "Virginia lies forty-five leagues east. We need easterly winds to run the Virginia Capes into the Chesapeake."

"Sir." John Brown came from the stern and handed over a silver flask.

Murrane unfastened the cap and drank deeply of the fiery rum. It burned his throat and brought tears to his eyes, but it dulled the gnawing pain in his chest.

His old misery had come back to haunt him when the ship had become becalmed three weeks ago. Damn but the waiting came hard to him! He'd expected to be in Annapolis and have the matter settled by now.

In his cabin was a letter of introduction from Anne's father, Lord Langstone, to the Maryland Royal Governor, explaining that Langstone's daughter, and Murrane's betrothed, had been spirited away to America by that scoundrel Campbell. Gathering men and supplies for the voyage had taken longer than he'd expected, and the expense was like to beggar him. He'd recoup it all when he had the bitch in his hands, but for now, the burden weighed heavily on him. He'd had to borrow against lands he no longer owned.

If he didn't get Anne's money, he'd be ruined. If . . . He refused to think about the alternatives.

Ross Campbell had made a fool of him—he and the slut together. Now they would pay the price.

"Pray for a change in the wind," the captain mouthed piously. "We stand for the bay when He grants us an easterly."

Murrane took another drink, then shoved the empty flask at his lieutenant. Ignoring the captain, he stalked across the deck and went below where the mulatto wench he'd purchased in the Canaries waited for his pleasure.

A smile crossed his scarred face as he descended the ship's ladder. The trull was young and ripe, the way he liked them. He'd paid top coin for a virgin, and even with the marks he'd left on her back, the captain had assured him he'd take the woman off his hands at double the price when they reached the Colonies.

Murrane laughed as the tightness in his chest became a tightness in his groin. The rum drummed in his ears, and his organ swelled as he imagined the girl's screams when he threw her facedown and entered her.

He slid the bolt on the cabin door and tried to push it open. Something heavy held it back, and he cursed and threw his shoulder against the door. "What the—"

The girl's body fell forward onto the deck. Her lifeless head rolled back like a broken doll. Murrane gasped and turned her over with his foot. A fork protruded from the woman's throat. Murrane backed away as he saw the tide of blood that covered her naked breasts and soaked her curly black hair.

"John!" he shouted. "John!" He staggered against the wall and thought of the bright, shiny golden guineas he'd paid for her living flesh, coin lost forever because the stupid wench had committed suicide. "John!" He backed away from the cabin door as the familiar pain knifed through his chest and radiated down his arm again.

Anne could hear the roar of the waterfalls as they launched the canoes again in late afternoon. This time, she was to ride in Leah's canoe—Kitate had begged her to trade places with him so that he could travel with Ross and Liiuan. "*Manake,*" he'd whispered to her, "just us men."

Kitate was a sweet child, solemn without being sullen, and mature for his six years. His skin was a light copper color, his eyes as dark and innocent as a fawn's. He'd spent the portage time pointing out trees and birds and telling her their names in Algonquian.

A movement in the trees on the left bank caught her attention, and she shaded her eyes with her hand, hoping to catch sight of another deer. "Look," she said to Leah. "Is that—"

A chilling whoop rolled across the water. Before Anne could react, a feathered shaft thudded into Cami's cradleboard. The baby screamed in pain, and blood sprayed over Anne's face. Leah moaned and sank to one side as musket balls broke the water around them.

Liiuan toppled from the other canoe with an arrow through his chest. Anne couldn't see Kitate, but Ross had a musket in his hands and was taking aim at an Indian on the far bank. Ross squeezed the trigger, and his target tumbled from a tree branch into the river.

An explosion directly behind her head deafened Anne. She whirled around to see Niipan frantically reloading his smoking musket. Ahead of them, a howling Indian—his face painted black and his head shaved except for a cock's comb down the center—plunged toward them through chest-deep water, an upraised hatchet in his hand. Anne's breath caught in her throat as she saw the glazed look in the man's eyes.

Numb with fear, she pried the canoe paddle from Leah's limp hands and swung it with all her might, striking the painted warrior on the side of the head. He fell backward with a groan and slid under the surface of the river.

Niipan fired again and shouted an order to her in Algonquian. "What?" she screamed. "I don't understand!" Arrows were flying like hail around her head. Tears streaked her face as the baby's terrified shrieks turned her blood to ice. Every instinct urged her to help the injured child, but Anne was afraid that if she moved forward, she'd overturn the canoe.

Niipan shoved a pistol into her hand. "Shoot!" he commanded. He picked up his paddle and with powerful strokes turned the canoe, letting the current aid him as he drove the boat back downriver—in the direction they had come earlier.

Another painted face appeared in the trees. Anne pointed the pistol with shaking hands and fired. The man let out a yell, and she dropped the empty weapon in her lap and began to paddle as best she could.

Two braves ran from the forest and waded into the river. Ross shot the first man through the heart with Liiuan's musket; the second he wounded with his own pistol. A war whoop sounded on his left, and he twisted around to face the attack with an empty weapon. Kitate pushed back the bundles under which he'd taken shelter and rose from the bottom of the canoe, bow in hand. Notching an arrow, he sent the shaft winging into the enemy brave's thigh. The warrior yelled, but kept coming.

Ross's heart was pounding as he caught a

glimpse of Anne's canoe in midstream. Moon-feather was down, but Niipan and Anne seemed unhurt. With a cry to match those of the attacking braves, Ross leaped from the canoe into the river. He shoved the boat toward deeper water, then, grasping his musket by the barrel and swinging it like a club, he waded to meet the wounded man.

The brave went down like a felled tree, but another took his place. Ross struck him in the pit of his stomach with the musket butt. The warrior aimed his pistol point-blank at Ross's chest and pulled the trigger. Ross braced for the blow, but the wet flintlock misfired, and Ross's return stroke brained him.

A musket ball cut a furrow along Ross's arm. He felt a brief sting of pain before a killing rage numbed everything but the urge to strike out at the enemy. Seizing the dying warrior in his hands and using him as a human shield, Ross charged out of the shallows and up onto the riverbank. An arrow lodged in his arm, and he snapped it off, then dropped to one knee and began to reload his musket.

A brave shouted a challenge and ran down the bluff toward him swinging a spiked war club. One side of the man's face was painted black, the other yellow. Ross caught an acrid whiff of bear grease as the screaming warrior bore down upon him.

Ross's eyes never left the man's face as his fingers went through the routine of loading: dump a measure of black powder into the barrel, position patch over the muzzle, seat a lead ball in the patch, ram it down with the wooden ramrod, and load the frizzen pan with powder. There was no time to lift the loaded musket to his shoulder; the Indian had already raised his club to deliver the death blow. Ross fired from the waist, and the man flew backward with a bloody hole in his belly.

Anne's scream cut through Ross's trance. He spun around to see a brave poised on a rock ahead of her canoe. A second enemy warrior was wading out toward the rock, his musket held high over his head. Ross plunged back into the river. Kitate called to him. The boy was trying desperately to bring the canoe back, but the current was too strong. It spun around, then tipped over when a musket ball struck the boy's paddle.

"Kitate!" Anne cried.

The boy's head bobbed up in the river, and the man on the rock took aim at him. Ross's shot caught the attacker full in the chest, and he toppled into the water.

"Kitate! Here!" Anne held her paddle out to him, oblivious to the second brave swimming toward her on the far side of the canoe.

"Niipan!" Ross yelled. "Behind you!" He dove in and swam in their direction. He was closing the distance between them when a great weight slammed into his head, and suddenly the river, the sky, and Anne's pale face dissolved into blackness. The last thing he heard was Anne's scream.

"Ross!"

Niipan hurled his knife at the enemy brave. It lodged in the man's throat. Thrashing, he went under and didn't come up.

"Ross!" Anne cried again. Blood was streaming from his head as he tumbled over in the current. "Ross!" Near exhaustion, Kitate seized the tip of her paddle, and she pulled him to the edge of the canoe. Niipan thrust the canoe out of the current toward the far bank.

As soon as the boat scraped bottom, Niipan leaped out, gathered Moonfeather and the baby in his arms, and carried her up the bank into the trees. Anne scrambled out and ran along the shore, trying to keep sight of Ross.

"*Maata!*" Kitate ran after her and seized her hand. "No!" he shouted. "No! We must go! Quick!"

"I can't leave Ross," she insisted. "He's hurt."

A shot ricocheted over their heads. "Come!" the child insisted. "It be death to stay."

"Go on without me!" Stubbornly, Kitate tugged at her hand. "I can't leave . . ." An icy grip tightened around Anne's chest as she realized that she could no longer see him. "Nooo," she cried.

"Please!" the boy begged.

Another shot plowed through the trees from the other side of the river. Waves of despair flooded over Anne as she turned and followed the child into the forest.

Once the trees sheltered them from enemy fire, Kitate began to run parallel to the river. Branches whipped Anne's face and tangled in her hair and clothing as she ran after him. They rounded a huge oak and crossed a narrow path. "Come," he hissed. "The falls. We must reach the falls before Ross goes over."

Terror lent wings to Anne's feet as they sped along the twisting game trail. Her breath came in ragged gasps and her legs felt as though they were made of lead. Still Kitate ran and she pounded along after him, the metallic taste of fear strong in her mouth. She could hear the roar of the falls growing stronger by the moment. Then he ducked to the right. She followed him, tripped over a tree root, and tumbled down a muddy bank into the edge of the misty river.

Anne pushed herself up on her hands. Kitate was scrambling across the slippery rocks toward the edge of the waterfall. Spray rose twenty feet in the air, and the roar of the boiling water was like constant thunder in her ears. Her eyes searching the white water for Ross's body, Anne stripped off her moccasins and ran barefoot over the rocks to the boy. He was shouting and pointing to a spot just out of reach.

"Ross!" Anne caught sight of his head bobbing in the churning water. One hand gripped a rock. His bonnet was gone. His hair streamed around his blood-streaked face like dark seaweed.

Kitate lunged for Ross's hand, and his foot slipped. Anne grabbed hold of the child's vest and pulled him back to safety just as Ross lost his grip on the moss-covered rock. For a heartbeat, his gaze locked with hers and his lips formed her name. Then the swift current swept him over the falls.

Chapter 17

Anne found her way to the bottom of the falls, climbing down, sliding over the loose rocks as fast as she could . . . despite that she knew Ross's broken body was all that awaited her. If she could find it . . .

Kitate had gone back along the river searching for his mother and sister and Niipan. Anne had tried to prevent the boy from leaving her. She'd told him it was too dangerous—the war party that had attacked them was still nearby and might strike again at any moment. Kitate had nodded solemnly, then melted into the forest.

One moment she was reasoning with him, and the next she was alone at the brink of the cataract. She'd tried to find Kitate, but the woods were so thick that she realized she'd be lost as soon as she was out of earshot of the falls. So she'd returned to the river to search for Ross.

Below the waterfalls, the river spilled out into a deep, wide tarn before rushing through a rocky channel to form whitewater rapids. The base of the cascade was a tumble of strewn boulders and foaming water. Mist rose above the water's surface, distorting Anne's vision as she crept close to the edge searching for the one thing she dreaded to find.

He was floating there, facedown, at the edge of

the pool in the shallows. Heedlessly, she plunged in and swam back to the bank with his body. He was heavy, much too heavy for her to pull up on shore. Somehow, she did. She dragged him up the slight incline, and water gushed from his mouth. Hope surged through her. She rolled him onto his back and shook him, crying out his name desperately. "Ross. Ross."

His beautiful, dark eyes were open and fixed; his tanned complexion had taken on a ghastly shade of blue. The bullet wound along the side of his head had ceased to bleed.

He wasn't breathing.

"Don't do this to me," she sobbed. "Don't die on me, you great barbarian half-breed." She wound her fingers in his hair and lifted his head. Only traces of the paint he had worn remained. Tenderly, she kissed each spot, letting her tears run down his cold, pale cheeks. "Oh, Ross, don't leave me. I don't want to live if you leave me."

For an instant, she thought she saw a flicker of life. She laid her face against his bare chest, listening for the beat of his heart. There was nothing. "My darling," she murmured. Pain greater than any she had ever known twisted her insides. She raised his limp hand to her cheek and kissed his palm.

"You've given me more happiness than I dreamed possible," she whispered. "Feathers, and paint, and absurd Scot's bonnet . . . I'd not trade one night with you to be Queen of England."

She bent over him and kissed his cool, unyielding lips as memories of the first time she'd ever seen him swept over her.

Ross had ridden into the church and carried her off in a whirlwind. She'd hated him . . . and fought with him before she'd come to love him.

"You made me feel!" she said fervently. "I walked though my life half asleep, and you made me wake and laugh and cry. You gave me hope."

If she closed her eyes, she could hear him singing, could hear the poignant notes of gypsy violins in the moonlight and the crash of the waves against the *Laird's Bounty* when they'd almost drowned in the hurricane.

"Please, God," she whispered, "don't take him like this."

Panic took hold of her, and she began to tremble. *He's dead*, a voice in her head intoned. *Dead.*

"No!" she screamed. "I won't let him be dead! I won't." Using all her strength, she rolled him onto his side and pounded on his back with her fists. More water ran from his mouth, but still Ross showed no signs of life. "Wake up!" she insisted. "Wake up, damn you! I won't let you get away this easily. I won't."

She released him, and he fell forward heavily and lay facedown on the grass. Anne threw herself across his back and sobbed dry sobs of futile desperation. Unconsciously, her fingers tightened around her golden amulet. If only the magic were real, she thought. If only I could wish breath into him and . . .

"Make him live," she whispered. "If love means anything . . . if there is a God or magic under heaven, please, give him back to me."

"Ye maun say the words."

Startled, Anne looked up to see Leah standing a few feet away from her. Niipan was holding the baby; Kitate stood behind him at the edge of the trees. Leah was pale and leaning on a bow for support, but she was walking under her own power. "You're alive—" she began.

"Nay!" the Indian girl cried. "There is no time

for talk! The Eye of Mist. Use it! Call upon it. Save him. Now!''

Bewildered, Anne's gaze flicked from her friend to her amulet. ''How could you know—''

''Ye have a wish. Use it!''

Suddenly, Anne seemed to feel a throbbing heat from the golden charm. A blessing and a curse, her father had said. *''Whatever you ask you shall have—even unto the power of life and death.''* The burning surged through her fingers and gave her strength.

''I call upon the Eye of Mist,'' Anne whispered. ''If this is God's blessing and not the devil's work, my wish is that Ross Campbell will live.'' She glanced up at Leah, and hope faded. The man beneath her seemed no more alive than he had before.

''Give him your breath,'' Leah urged. ''Breathe life into his mouth. Do it!''

As though in a trance, knowing it was useless, Anne raised Ross's head and blew air into his mouth.

''Again!'' Leah commanded.

It was easier to obey than admit that he was lost to her. Again, she puffed air through his cold lips.

A shudder ran through his body.

Anne inhaled as deeply as she could and blew in.

Ross coughed, and his eyes closed.

Leah grabbed one shoulder and motioned Anne to take the other. They raised him to a sitting position, and Leah weeping openly, slapped him on the back.

Ross groaned, leaned forward, and choked up what seemed like a bucket of river water. Anne was shaking and laughing all at once as he coughed and gasped and began to curse the men who had attacked them.

When he could stand, he opened his arms and Anne went into them. "Ye be safe?" he asked hoarsely.

She clung to him and touched his face with trembling fingers. "I had the sense not to go over the falls." He hugged her against him so tightly she couldn't breathe. But it didn't matter—she could hear the powerful throbbing of his heart. Questions filled her mind, but she pushed them back. She didn't care how he was alive. He was, and that was what mattered.

Then, almost at the same instant, they remembered Moonfeather's injury. Anne tore herself away from Ross and went to her friend's side. "You were hurt," she said. "And the baby—"

"Cami's neck was only grazed by the arrow," Leah replied. "She lost blood, but her wound does not even have to be sewn. Her cradleboard stopped the arrow from going too deeply into my back. My own injury be slight."

"Slight?" Anne stared at her friend in disbelief. "But you were unconscious."

A flush crept up to tint Leah's cheekbones. "Aye. I have shame to be so weak," she admitted. "Niipan stopped the bleeding."

Anne took the baby from the Indian brave's arms. Cami's dress was stained with blood, but the gouge on her neck had crusted over and didn't seem serious. The toddler put her arms around Anne's neck and gurgled merrily.

Niipan handed Ross a musket and powderhorn. The brave said something to him in Algonquian, and Ross nodded as he slung the weapons over his back.

"What of Liiuan?" Anne asked.

Leah frowned. "He is gone, my sister. The

Shawnee do not speak of the dead by name. We looked for his body, but could not find it. The village is only a half day's march. We maun go quickly before we are attacked again. Men will come back to search for my cousin—to bring him home for burial. But it be nay safe here. We maun go.''

Anne looked at Ross, and he nodded. "What she says is true, hinney. I don't know why they didn't stay and finish us off. With Indians, there's no telling. But the best thing for us to do is get clear of here fast."

"You told me we were safe," she said. "You told me that no one would attack a peace woman and her party." She wanted to stay close to Ross—to hold his hand, to touch him and keep touching him to be certain she wasn't dreaming. "Leah is hurt. You're hurt." The wound on Ross's head was seeping blood.

"We're alive," he answered, "although I admit I feel like I've been kicked half to death by a horse." He rubbed at the swelling on his head. "And as to who attacked us—"

"They used Seneca arrows," Leah said softly, pulling an arrow from her waist. "I took this from Cami's cradleboard." She held the feathered shaft up for them to see. The wood was stained with dark spots. "But this"—she lifted a bow—"this bow is Shawnee."

Niipan spat on the ground. "Matiassu," he uttered with contempt.

"The men I faced dressed as Iroquois," Ross agreed, "but they weren't Seneca or any other member of the Five Nations."

Leah's eyes narrowed. "Matiassu. Only he would dare." She looked meaningfully at Ross. "He cannot show his face at the High Council now."

"Nay," Ross replied. "He and his men will be outcast."

"I don't understand," Anne said. "Who is this Matiassu, and why would he attack us if he's Shawnee?"

"He is my enemy," Leah answered. "Once, he wanted to be my husband, but now he hates me. He leads a band of warriors who break the peace, and he trades with Roquette the hair buyer. Matiassu would have come to High Council to argue for war. It may be that the people would have listened to his words—men are ever ready to kill each other. But Matiassu could not wait. He wanted me dead. He broke the greatest of Shawnee laws—he killed the brother of Niipan. Shawnee does not kill Shawnee. Now he will be—as you say—outlaw, and every man's hand will be raised against him."

"If he's an outlaw, why didn't he kill us all? Then no one could have testified against him."

"He probably thought Moonfeather and I were dead," Ross said. "It could be that he didna want to risk any more of his men trying to kill you and Niipan and the boy. Matiassu could have been killed or wounded. He could have been frightened by an owl. God knows, Anne. He's Shawnee. There's no saying why he'd do a thing or not do it."

"But you didn't see him. You can't be certain it was Matiassu."

"Aye," Leah agreed. "What ye say is true. But if Matiassu does not come to council, then he shows his guilt."

Anne caught her arm. "Before, when Ross was . . . unconscious. How did you know the name of my necklace? Did Ross tell you about it? How did you know about the legend that goes with it?" She still was not certain what had happened on the riverbank. She'd thought Ross was dead, and now he was alive and giving orders. She wondered if . . . It was too much to try and understand. This she could ask. "Leah?"

The Indian girl smiled and reached for the cord around her neck. Tugging on it, she pulled an amulet from under the bodice of her dress. It shone yellow gold in the sunlight.

Anne stared in disbelief. The charm looked like her own.

"See," Leah continued softly. She drew the necklace over her head and held it against Anne's. The two pieces fitted together perfectly. "Don't you understand?" she said. "They are the same. Both be parts of the Eye of Mist given to us by our father, Cameron Stewart, when we were bairns. I be your friend, Anne, but I be more. We are blood sisters."

Sisters. Leah's words echoed in Anne's brain in the hours that followed. They marched by night, silent and quick. There was no opportunity for speech, but Anne needed none. She needed only to try and sort out all that had happened that day. How many times had Leah called her sister? Yet, never had she realized that the term was anything more than a symbol of their friendship.

Leah's statement that they were blood sisters was impossible to believe—but more impossible to deny. Cameron Stewart . . . he was the link that bound them together. Their blood father.

Anne had known that Cameron had spent seven years in America—Barbara had mentioned it many times. She'd seen Indian articles that Cameron had brought back with him. But she'd never thought of him fathering a child in the wilderness. And even if she'd known he had, it was inconceivable that her friend Leah might be that child.

The amulet had been solid proof. Leah's charm was triangular shaped, her own rectangular, but the incised decoration was the same, and the golden amulets fitted together as though they were one. As she and Leah had fitted together . . . Even in England, Anne had recognized that Leah was a friend to be found only once in a lifetime. That a friend might be a longed-for sister was a blessing she'd not thought to receive.

I've never had anything that counted, Anne marveled over and over. I never had a family. Now I have a sister and a father.

Cameron was in Annapolis. Leah had told her so in the brief moments before they'd begun the walk to the Shawnee village. If she and Ross had docked in Annapolis, she might have seen him.

There were so many questions she wanted to ask, so many voids to be filled . . .

Leah had explained that Cameron had come to America with her and Brandon. He'd wanted to be near Leah and Cami, to be part of their family.

"Brandon makes a planter of wheat," Leah had said. "Our father works beside him in the fields. You would not know him as a court gallant—he looks much younger. Brandon swears Cameron has lost two stone and ten years. The riding and plain food are good for him. He will be so full of joy to see ye, Anne. He talks of ye often."

A father. Tears filled her eyes as she thought of what it must mean to have a real father—not a man such as her mother's husband, Langstone, had been to her. Even as a child she'd known Lord Langstone despised her; she simply hadn't known why.

A sister, a father, and a husband. The curious tickling in her throat had made her want to

laugh—to dance. She had a family. The knowl-
edge straightened her shoulders and gave
strength to her legs and back so that she hardly
felt the weight of little Cami in her cradleboard.

To hell with England! To hell with the past!
Books and silk gowns, music and art—she could
forgo it all if she could keep these three people in
her life.

But it was too good to be true.

Her own doubts and fears scratched at the windows of her house of cards. Fairy-tale endings
were only for children's stories—not for such as
she.

. . . *Plain as dirt and timid as a scullery maid.* Barbara's hurting words surfaced to taunt her in the
depths of the shadowy forest. Not only her mother's rebukes but those of others . . .

Ugly.

Slow-witted.

If she were mine, I'd drown her.

Biddable. It's all one can say about her.

Would a man such as Ross keep her to wife
when he could have any woman he wanted?
Would Cameron want to acknowledge her when
he had Leah? Why did Leah bother with her at
all?

Anne put her hands over her ears to drown out
the hateful voices, but it didn't help. The words
came from within her own mind—there was no
running from them.

She did not complain during the long hours of
walking from the falls to the Shawnee village. She
did not mention the mosquitoes that bit her, or
the thorns that drew blood on her legs and arms.
She did not ask to stop and rest when her breath
came in gasps and sweat ran down her neck to
dampen her dress and cause her tangled hair to
stick to her skin.

She was so weary when they reached the Indian camp that she fell asleep within minutes of being shown into a hut. Vaguely, she was conscious of Ross cradling her head in his lap and wiping her face with something cool and wet. Then she knew nothing more than the deep sleep of utter exhaustion.

She awakened to the smell of bread baking.

Kitate brought her water and corncakes still hot from the stone, and a stout Indian woman he introduced as Amookas offered Anne a bowl of delicious stew and a horn spoon to eat it with.

"Auntie say you be more than honored guest," Kitate said shyly. "She say you family." Grinning, he ducked out of the hut, leaving Anne alone with the strange woman.

"The food is good," Anne said hesitantly. Amookas grunted and crouched, watching her.

When she had finished every bite and drained the water gourd, the woman motioned for Anne to follow her. Amookas led her out into the warm summer twilight. Immediately, Anne felt dozens of pairs of eyes on her. She forced herself to smile as she looked around at the curious Shawnee.

Most of the people staring at her were women and children. There were dogs and horses, and a few turkeys scratching around the bark houses. Anne saw only two men; they were old and white-haired. Shockingly, the small children were all naked, and most of the women wore only short skirts, leaving their breasts completely exposed. Anne's face grew hot, and she knew she was blushing. She kept her eyes down, trying not to stare back as Amookas led her through the scattered huts to the river.

"Wash," the Indian woman ordered briskly.

Anne waded into the river and obeyed as best

she could without soap and without removing her dress. When she was finished, Amookas signaled her from the water and directed her to a low stone and mud hut sunk into the ground. There was a fire pit full of round stones directly in front of the low door.

"Take off clothes," Amookas said.

"Why?"

"No talk. Take off clothes."

Before Anne could protest, two giggling women appeared and began to tug at her gown. To her dismay, they drew the skin dress over her head and shoved her inside the hut in less than a minute. One of the girls followed, taking Anne's hand and leading her to a seat along one wall.

It was dark and steamy inside the hut. Hot rocks filled the center of the small room. The girl poured water from a container over the rocks to make even more steam, and Anne struggled to breathe.

"No have fear," the Indian girl said over the hissing of the rocks. "Make clean. Good."

They sat in the dark room until Anne thought her skin was boiled; then the girl grabbed her hand again and pulled her outside. Amookas and the other Indian woman were waiting. Anne tried to cover her nakedness with her hands, but the women pushed her down the bank into the river.

Anne gasped. After the steam house, the cool river water felt like ice. The heat followed by the cold water left her stunned, and she offered little protest as the women dragged her out and repeated the whole process again.

It was pitch dark when Anne was allowed out of the river for the last time, rubbed dry with soft skins by her attendants, and wrapped in a cloak of white otter. They combed her hair and spread it around her shoulders, then, laughing and talking among themselves in the Indian tongue, escorted her back to the hut where she'd slept. Leah was waiting for her with Cami in her arms.

"Leah," Anne cried.

Leah laughed, a sound like the tinkling of bells. "Have they cooked thee, older sister? How do ye feel?"

Anne took a deep breath and settled onto a skin rug, trying to keep herself modestly covered with the cloak. "I think I lost my clothes somewhere."

"Aye, but these be better." Leah held out a white fringed gown decorated with beautiful quill and beadwork. "Fitting for the sister of a peace woman," she murmured. "Ye have met our Amookas. She be the sister of my mother—aunt to thee and to me."

Anne nodded, too confused to try and sort out Shawnee rules of kinship. Better to have the stern Indian squaw as aunt than enemy. Suddenly she smiled. "If we are sisters, then Cami is my niece."

"You are auntie, or"—Leah chuckled—"or little mother."

Anne smoothed the deerskin dress over her hips. It had been worked so thin that it was as soft and light as velvet. "This is beautiful," she said. Her eyes widened. "Your wound. Does it trouble you? Where is Ross? Did the council—"

Leah held up a hand in the firelight. "Nay. Too many questions. My wound will heal." A look of sadness came over her face. "If Amookas was stern, blame her not. He that died on the river, brother of Niipan, was her beloved son."

"Amookas is the mother of Niipan and Li— Oh . . . I'm sorry. I didn't mean to break the rule about not talking about—"

"Brandon says it be silly superstition. Do not blame yourself. Our ways be strange to thee, sister. As to your other questions, Ross speaks with

Tuk-o-see-yah, the sachem. The council waits for other men to come. And Matiassu has not shown his face.''

''So we must wait.''

''Aye.'' Leah pulled Anne's amulet forward so that it hung over the fringed neckline of the deer-skin gown. ''My cousin Niipan is much taken with you. He calls you Meshepeshe-Equiwa, Mountain Lion Woman. The people whisper of your bravery to one another. I have much pride of you.''

''Me?'' Anne was almost too astonished to reply. ''But I didn't do anything brave. I was terrified when we were attacked.''

''Bravery lies in deeds, Meshepeshe-Equiwa, not in fears.'' She smiled. ''Did you nay kill the enemy with your bare hands? Did ye nay put a magic spell upon them to drive them away when we were helpless and at their mercy? Did ye nay call upon the Eye of Mist to bring Ross back from the fangs of the Dark Warrior of Death?''

It was Anne's turn to laugh. ''Hardly. I nearly swooned when the arrows started flying around us. And as for Ross's drowning . . .'' She trailed off. ''Ross . . .'' Anne clasped her hands to-gether. ''What did happen on the riverbank?''

Leah sighed and leaned close, taking Anne's hand. Points of flame from the tiny fire reflected in her dark, soulful eyes. ''I know only what our father told us of the Eye of Mist,'' she answered softly. ''I know only that once my Brandon seemed lost to me and I called upon the power of the amulet to save him. I know only that Brandon lives and Ross lives.'' She squeezed Anne's hand. ''Some things are not to be questioned. Be thank-ful and cherish your man. Remember, the magic of the amulet only works once.''

Anne raised her gaze to lock with Leah's. ''For

a woman like you, I can believe in magic. For me, it comes hard."

Leah shook her head. "Ye be strong and wise. What more could ye ask?"

Anne flushed and cast her eyes down. "Sometimes," she confided, "many times, I would wish to be beautiful. So beautiful that men's eyes would follow me when I passed . . . as beautiful as you are."

Leah's eyes narrowed in concern. "Ye really do not know, do ye?" She turned away and took down a skin bag from a hook on the wall. Carefully she unwrapped an oval mirror set in silver and held it out. "Ye look, but ye dinna see," she said. "Now truly look."

With trembling hands, Anne stared into her own face in the mirror.

"See, my English friend," Leah pronounced in her soft, lilting accent. "There be a beautiful woman."

As Leah spoke, it seemed to Anne that a transformation took place in the silver looking glass. Old cobwebs fell away from her inner vision, and her pulse quickened as she realized the truth of her sister's words. She really was seeing the reflection of a beautiful woman in the mirror.

"Who has blinded ye, sister, that ye dinna realize your own worth?" Leah demanded. "I know the English value their women as little as they do honor, but ye be a woman of great wealth and power."

Anne continued to stare into the mirror, and secret joy bubbled up inside her as Leah's words sunk deeply into her consciousness. "My mother," she whispered breathlessly. "My mother, Barbara, told me that she was ashamed of me."

"Aiyee. Can it be so? How could a mother—"

Anne made a low sound of derision. "If you

knew Barbara, you wouldn't have to ask." She lowered the mirror with trembling hands and gazed into the fire. "I remember once, when I was very small. Barbara had been away for a long time. I wanted to see her so badly, but when I threw my arms around her, she pushed me away and scolded me for wrinkling her dress," she murmured. "I was ashamed and . . ." The awful scene played out behind her closed eyelids as though it had happened yesterday.

The flickering fire, the warm darkness surrounding the two women, the danger that they had shared and survived together, made it easy for Anne to tell Leah things that she had never shared with another human being. All the grief and anger, the shame and fear of her childhood came spilling out. Anne talked for hours without stopping until her voice grew hoarse, and Leah listened.

"I have great sorrow for this mother of yours," Leah said at last. The sound of her voice told Anne that her sister had wept with her. "She may be beautiful on the outside of her skin, but inside she is twisted and ugly."

Relief made Anne giddy. "You're right. I can see now that Barbara failed me. I never failed her." Anne hugged herself and rocked back and forth. "I don't hate her anymore—I don't think I feel anything for her. When I was little, I used to think God would strike me dead in my sleep for thinking awful thoughts about Barbara. I'd have nightmares, and I'd wake screaming. It made the servants angry, and they'd pinch me or shake me." She shivered. "I never woke Mother with my crying—she always slept too far away to be troubled by a worthless girl-child."

Leah clasped Anne's hand. "Among the Shawnee, a female baby is welcomed. We know that the woman is the heart of a family. She will choose the father of her own children, she will give wisdom to her people, and she will care for the old ones when they grow weak. A strong daughter is a mother's greatest possession.''

"My father—my stepfather, Lord Langstone, wanted a son to carry on his title. My mother bore him no other children. Later, she said that he was unable to father a babe. He was always harsh to me, and I never knew why until a few years ago."

"There was no love between your mother and this lord?"

"Barbara loves only her own mirror." Anne swallowed the lump in her throat. "That and the contents of Langstone's treasure house. She's a vain, deceitful creature without a conscience."

"Ye must feel pity for her. What will she have in her old age? When her face wrinkles and her yellow hair turns white? Will she have a daughter to sit by her feet and listen to her stories? Will she have laughing grandchildren to sing to her? Nay. This English Barbara will have her bright gems, but their fire will give no heat. And the men who flocked after her will laugh behind their hands and call her harlot."

"I tried to be what she wanted me to be," Anne insisted, "but I never could."

"When I met ye in England, ye were a widow. Tell me of your first marriage."

"I begged Barbara not to make me marry Scarbrough," she began. "I was only fifteen and still more child than woman. I'd not even begun my monthly courses . . ." The telling eased Anne's heart so that the words tumbled over each other. She found herself relating all that had happened to her as Scarbrough's wife—even how she had been attracted to Brandon, the man who was now

Leah's husband. She told of her genuine sorrow at the marquis's death and her time as a widow.

Finally, she shared with Leah how her mother and Langstone had imprisoned her in the tower and forced her to nearly become the bride of the Baron Murrane. "I'd be his wife now, if Ross hadn't kidnapped me from the church in London."

Leah was indignant. "He took ye against your will? He forced ye to wed with him?"

"Yes," she admitted uneasily, "but—"

"Nay! Ross has treated ye no better than the rest. He brought ye across the sea to America when ye didna wish to come?" Leah's dark eyes glittered with emotion. "Ptahh! He is the son of a Delaware woman—he should know better."

Anne shrugged. "Perhaps it was the curse of the necklace—perhaps Ross was as helpless as I was."

"Ross Campbell is never helpless." Leah rose and paced the wigwam angrily. "He knew what he did was wrong. He did so because he is a man who has never had his lead rope jerked tight. Always," she exclaimed, "always he has had his way. Angus would have taught a wolf better manners than he taught Ross when Ross was a child. That one he let have his way. So long as his son could run faster, ride harder than any man—so long as he could hit every target he shot at and never show fear, there was nothing he could not have by putting out his hand and taking it."

"What does it matter now?" Anne asked quietly. "I love him. He's the best thing that ever happened to me."

"Aye, this one has love for him also—infuriating though he may be. Nay, do not bristle with jealousy." Leah chuckled in the shadows. "I dinna love your willful giant as ye do—I love him like a brother." Leah moved into the firelight again, and her expression grew stern. "Ye are to blame for his wrongs as well, Anne. Ye must not give in to him. Ye must make him respect you—make him see that ye canna be ruled by a man. Ye can walk beside him as an equal, but never behind him as a slave walks."

Anne buried her face in her hands. "I don't know what I want. I thought I wanted to go back to England, but I don't. I can't bear the idea of never seeing Ross again. I realize he married me for my money but—"

"Nay! That be fool's talk. Selfish he may be. Hardheaded as Linimuus the elk. But he would never take a wife for gold. Ross is a man of honor."

"You're wrong. He told me so himself."

"I dinna believe it. If he said the words, then he doesna ken his own heart and mind."

"You may have been his friend for a long time, Leah, but I think I know him better than you do."

The Indian girl shook her head. "A breme man is Ross Campbell—one who needs taming by a strong woman. But ye hold his heart in your hands, my sister. Nothing he could do would change what I read in his eyes when he looks at ye. And nothing ye can say will make me change my mind."

Anne fingered her golden amulet. "If I'd known before that the magic was real, I'd have asked for Ross to love me for myself, not my fortune." She shook her head. "But that's foolish talk, for if I'd used up my wish, I couldn't have used it to save his life." Her voice grew thin. "He was dead—wasn't he, Leah?"

Her sister shrugged and spread her hands palms up. "Who can say?"

Anne stood and stretched her stiff back. "The thing is—I don't care anymore why Ross married me. I only want to keep him. He can have all my money. I want to stay with him and give him children. I want us to grow old together." She exhaled slowly and exposed her deepest fear. "But I'm still afraid I won't be able to hold him."

"Aye," Leah replied. "There be a danger that ye willna keep him—not if ye let him run over you. Ye must demand the respect of a man. It is not you, sister, but Ross who should worry. He has wronged you. Let him lie awake at night and wonder if ye will stay by him and bear his children."

"I don't know . . . I don't know if I can be as strong as you want me to be. When he was washed over the falls, I didn't want to go on living." Gooseflesh raised on her neck and arms as she remembered the terrible moment when she'd realized she couldn't reach Ross in time. She sighed. "I'm so confused. I don't know what to think or do."

"It might help if ye went to our father in Annapolis." Leah's voice was soothing. "He is a wise man. It could be that he will help ye find a path ye can walk that will let ye keep Ross by your side without being dominated by him."

"What is this about being dominated?" Ross pushed aside the entrance covering and bent to enter the wigwam. "Leah." His gaze passed over her to fix on Anne. "God, woman, ye are a sight for sore eyes. Have the Shawnee treated ye well?"

"She is my sister," Leah flung back. "Would they do less for the sister of a peace woman?" She glanced toward Anne. "I go now, but this much I remind ye of. Ye be a child no longer. Those who hurt ye in the past have only as much power now as ye give them." She smiled. "Walk proud, and bow your head for no man." With a parting nod to Ross, she left the wigwam.

"Who put a thorn under her saddle?" Ross asked as he dropped onto the bearskin rug beside Anne. "Ah, I'm so tired I could sleep for a week." He reached for a cold corncake left in the bottom of a bowl. "I've been smoking the pipe with the sachem, but I don't know what good it's done." He devoured the bread. "I'm proud of ye, Anne," he said. "Back there, on the river, you—" His voice broke and he inhaled deeply. "Ye saved my life." He caught her hand and pulled her down to him. "I came near to drowning. When I opened my eyes and saw you, I thought you were an angel."

"You had a head injury," she reminded him stiffly. Leah's words lingered in her mind. She had let Ross have his way too long. He'd come to expect it.

"Lucky for me I've a skull of stone," he said, rubbing at his head wound gingerly. "It hurts like hell, but I'll never die of it."

"A few inches deeper . . ."

He laughed. "A few hours sooner and that war party would never have caught us." He kissed the top of her head and yawned. "Roquette isn't here yet. We both need sleep, sweeting. Tomorrow's going to be a long, long day."

Anne lay down beside him and fitted her body next to his. In minutes, Ross's even breathing told her that he was asleep, but her mind was still racing. She tried to sort out all that had happened and to come to some decision. She was still mulling it over in her mind when the first coral rays of dawn spilled over the eastern treetops.

Chapter 18

Ross slept as Anne left the wigwam in mid-morning. She had snatched a few short periods of sleep before the stir of the village beckoned.

Everywhere, families were rising and going about their daily routine. Anne saw no sign that the Shawnee feared attack, or that they were alarmed by the death of one of the peace party delegates. Children ran back and forth, women knelt by the river dipping water into copper vessels, and men strode forth in twos and threes into the surrounding forest.

In front of one of the huts, Anne saw the woman, Amookas, sitting with Leah's Cami on her lap. Anne approached them cautiously. The baby saw her and threw up her arms. Her bright blue eyes twinkled merrily, and a dimple appeared in the center of her left cheek as she ran to Anne as fast as her chubby legs would carry her.

Anne stooped to be near the little girl's height. "Hello, Cami," she said. The toddler giggled, and Anne lifted her up, anxiously inspecting her to see if she had recovered from her injury without serious harm. Someone had bandaged the arrow wound with clean linen. Her hair and skin were sweet-smelling and still faintly damp, telling Anne

that Cami'd been bathed only minutes ago. Anne
hugged her gently and kissed her silky dark hair.

"The child is well," Amookas said in heavily
accented English.

Cami wiggled to be free. Anne stood her on her
feet, and the baby trotted after a brown puppy.
Amookas signaled Anne to join her.

"Dinna have afraid."

Amookas's eyes were red-rimmed from weeping, and Anne was reminded that Leah had said
the older woman had lost a son in the river battle.
Anne wanted to offer her sympathy, but she
wasn't certain what she could say that wouldn't
break some Indian custom. "I'm sorry," she murmured, "for your loss."

Amookas nodded. For an instant Anne could
read the deep sorrow etched in the squaw's gaze.
She opened her clenched hands, and Anne
flinched as she saw that two joints were missing
from the woman's littlest finger on her left hand.
The raw end of the open wound was covered with
pitch, but it was clear to Anne that the loss was
fresh. "Oh," Anne gasped.

Amookas looked down at her mutilated hand.
"My husband cradles the body of his dead son. I
cradle a live child. My heart weeps, but the child's
warm flesh gives me hope." She sighed. "Niipan
say that you fight beside him like a forest demon.
A mother thanks you. If you had not courage, it
might be that both of my hands would bleed with
sorrow."

Shaken by the thought that Amookas might
have cut off part of her own finger, Anne mumbled something inane and turned and fled back to
the wigwam.

Ross opened his eyes and sat up as she came
in.

"That woman—Amookas. I think she cut off her

own finger!" she cried. "I don't understand these people! I don't belong here—I never will." She felt sick to her stomach. Her head ached, and her palms were sweating. For some unexplainable reason, Amookas's mutilated finger seemed more horrifying than the deaths on the river. "It's senseless and savage."

Ross rose to his feet and enfolded her in his arms. He didn't try to make excuses or explain away her fears. "Ye've had a bad time, hinney," he said. "Ye need food and rest."

"Leave me alone. I won't be calmed like a tired horse." Her eyes burned, and she was afraid she would start to cry.

"Shhh," he murmured. "It will be all right, Anne. I promise. We'll have this council, and there won't be any war, and we'll go home and make babies."

"I don't want to make babies," she protested. "I don't want to go back to Fort Campbell. I want to see my father. I have to see him, can't you understand? It's all so . . ." Against her will, she began to weep. "I don't know who I am anymore. I've got to go to Annapolis and talk to Cameron."

"Don't cry, hinney." He rocked her against him. "If it will make ye happy, I'll take ye to him. I promise ye. When this matter with Roquette and Matiassu is settled, we'll go and visit your father in Annapolis."

The tears flowed down her cheeks, and he held her against him until exhaustion overcame her and she slept in his arms. Sometime in late afternoon, she woke just long enough to drink water and eat a little meat. Then she slept again until the following morning.

* * *

It was midafternoon when Ross led Anne through the deep forest to a pool beside a waterfall. "Ye can bathe here in perfect privacy," he assured her.

"You are here," she reminded him.

He grinned wickedly. "Aye, lass, I am."

"I don't like this place. I never want to see another waterfall again." She glanced around nervously. "Isn't there a war party out there somewhere? What makes you think they won't come and scalp us while we're bathing?"

Ross laughed. "Nay, hinney, not here. This is an enchanted pool. The Shawnee call it the Place of the Maiden's Kiss. No harm can come to us here. Only those wi' loving hearts can find this place. To the evil, it's invisible."

Anne's eyes narrowed in disbelief. "A magic pool," she said sarcastically. "Invisible. I vow, Ross, you are as superstitious as the Indians are."

He waved a hand, encompassing the pristine glade, the blue-green sparking water of the pool, and the breathtaking wall of white water tumbling thirty feet to feed it. Sunshine filtered through the thick trees overhead, causing drops of water to form a thousand rainbows in the air. The moss around the brink of the pool was thick and cushiony, as soft as a Turkish carpet, and the air resounded with the musical sounds of bird calls. "How can ye see all this and deny the magic?"

Her resolve softened, and she sank to the grass. "It is beautiful here," she admitted, "but I hardly think we're invisible."

Ross picked a handful of violets and dropped them into her lap. "It was a war party that spun the sorcery," he said. "As the story goes, enemy braves chased a Shawnee girl to the brink of the falls. Rather than be captured, she leaped to her death. Her body was found the following day by the man who was to be her husband. He carried her from the water and kissed her." Ross knelt in front of Anne and brushed her lips with his. "Like this," he whispered.

Anne's heart skipped a beat, but she turned her face away from him. "No. I don't want to . . ."

He drew back, his features immobile. "It's only a story. The Great Spirit, who is a grandmother, Inu-msi-ila-fe-wanu, saw the lovers and took pity on the man. She couldn't bring the dead girl back to life as a woman, but she did have the power to change them both into hawks. Together they flew high above the trees and off into the heavens. This pool was formed by Inu-msi-ila-fe-wanu in memory of their love."

Anne raised her eyes to his. I do love him, she thought as her heartbeat quickened, but what's wrong between us won't be mended by the act of making love. She looked down at her lap and began to pick up the violets, one by one. "It's a good story," she said stiffly.

"What's wrong, Anne?"

She wound the flowers into a lover's knot and tied them to the neckline of her laced deerskin gown. "Everything . . . and nothing."

"Are ye with child?"

"No." She shook her head. If she had been pregnant with his babe, it might have made her mind easier. If she carried Ross's child, he would stand by her—she was certain of that. Leah had said that Ross loved her for herself, not her fortune, but it was hard to believe.

"The Shawnee play on an eagle-bone flute for the women they love. I could play the bagpipes for ye, but it would frighten the crows for miles around." He unwrapped a bundle he'd brought with him and offered her a handful of blackberries, a leg of rabbit, and a corncake. "There's honey water to drink." He produced a gourd with a corncob stopper in the top. "No cups—we'll have to share."

"I don't mind." Anne nibbled at the broiled meat and found it tender and well-seasoned. To her surprise, she was hungry, even though they'd eaten with Leah at noon.

Ross finished off the rest of the rabbit, four corncakes, and the berries. Then he stretched out on the grass. Anne noticed that although he'd insisted they were in no danger, he'd brought a musket, a flintlock pistol, and an axe, and kept them close by. "Moonfeather doesn't believe Roquette will show up," he said. "Two other Shawnee chiefs and one Delaware have sent council members to the circle, but they won't meet until Liiuan's been given a proper sendoff and buried."

Ross pulled his hat off his head and dropped it onto the grass. "The scouting party that brought back Liiuan's body found my bonnet, but they didn't find any other bodies. Whoever attacked us carried off their dead."

Anne sipped from the gourd bottle and handed it back to Ross. He drank deeply and recorked it.

"This must seem like a lot of confusion to ye," he said, "but if I can help prevent a war between the Indians and the British, I must. Fort Campbell—Wanishish-eyun—stands because the tribes let it stand. If they turned on us, we'd not last the turning of the moon. Daddy's spent a lifetime on that land, and I mean to spend ours there. I no more want to see the Indians drive us out than I'd want some highborn English lord to do the same. It's my land, Anne, and I'll fight for it with the last drop of my blood."

"And mine?"

His face clouded, and he rose to his feet. "We

came here for pleasure, not to argue." He offered her his hand. "Will ye swim with me, bonny Anne?"

"Only swim?"

"Aye. If ye wish it." He hesitated, then withdrew his hand when she didn't take it. This time, she glimpsed the hurt in his eyes. He stripped off his vest and let it fall carelessly to the ground. "When have I ever forced ye?"

Ashamed, she shook her head. "Never."

He turned away and left her aching as he pulled away his kilt and kicked off his moccasins. His muscles rippled under the bronzed skin on his back and thighs as he walked naked to the edge of the pool and dove in. Trembling, she untied the laces at the front of her gown and slid the dress up over her head. The air on her bare skin did nothing to cool the heat in her loins. Desire rose to tempt her, and she forced it back. Only swim, she had insisted.

Anne's cheeks burned as she watched Ross break the surface of the water just short of the falls. His hair had come loose from its leather thong, and it lay over his broad shoulders like wet silk. His eyes were on her, devouring, caressing, daring her . . .

A scarlet bird flew over the pool, its red wings bright against the blue water. She realized that she had never seen such vivid colors as here in this hidden spot. Even the tree leaves seemed greener, so many shades of green that it hurt her eyes to look at them.

"Are ye afraid?" he challenged. "To swim with me?" Water ran down the contours of Ross's superbly muscled chest.

Anne's breathing quickened. She raised her hands over her head and dove into the clear, cool water, letting herself glide down and down until she touched the clean sand bottom. When she surfaced to breathe, she found herself in the circle of his arms.

For a long time, they gazed into each other's eyes, and then she forgot her pride and raised her mouth to his. His arms tightened around her as their lips brushed with teasing ardor. Ross caught her lower lip and nibbled gently, sending tremors of excitement through her.

She closed her eyes and sighed as he slid his hands down to cradle her buttocks, all the while outlining her lips with the tip of his warm, wet tongue. Her fingers twined in his thick, dark hair as he kissed her closed eyelids and the corners of her mouth with exquisite sensitivity.

Trembling, Anne ran her hand down his cheek, tracing the bones of his face with her fingertips and wrapping her legs around his waist. The heat of him seared her, and she moved against him, reveling in the sweet sensations that made her bones and muscles feel as though they had turned to water.

Ross suckled the tip of her finger and lowered his head to kiss the pulse at her wrist. His hands were moving possessively over her hips and buttocks, his fingers fondling her in places that no other man had ever dared touch. Anne moaned with delight as desire stabbed through her. She arched backward, letting her hair touch the water, raising her breasts for his kiss. Instead, he nibbled her neck and the top of her shoulder.

"Kiss my breasts," she whispered huskily. "Please." The cool water had made her nipples hard, and they ached for his touch.

He nuzzled the hollow of her throat and cupped her left breast with his hand. His dark eyes were luminous and filled with love as his gaze met hers. "Sweet Anne," he murmured as his hot fingertips teased her nipple to a swollen nub of yearning.

She drew in a shuddering breath and moaned with pleasure as his lips closed over her nipple. With tantalizing slowness he circled it with his tongue, then drew it gently into his mouth. His right hand caressed her spine and moved to warm her neck with the heat of his callused palm.

She stroked his heavily muscled arm and let her hand rest on his corded neck. "I love you, Ross Campbell," she whispered.

"And I you," he replied.

They kissed again, blending mouth against mouth as the intensity of her passion flamed higher and higher and the sweet aching in her loins had become a pulsating demand. The heat of his body permeated hers until she no longer felt the cool water. She pressed against him, wanting him as she had never wanted him before, and moved her hand to clasp his swollen member.

"I don't want to swim," she murmured huskily. "I want to love you."

"And I want you," he answered, grasping her by the hips. "I want—"

The rolling echo of a musket shot shattered their moment of passion. Anne's gray eyes dilated with fear as she realized what she'd heard.

Ross's shoulders stiffened.

Two more shots sounded.

"That came from the village," Ross said. "Come." He turned and swam to the edge of the pool. "Hurry," he urged. It took him only seconds to wrap the kilt around his waist and snatch up his weapons. Anne scrambled to pull the deerskin dress over her wet body. "There's a cave behind the waterfall," he told her. "Hide there. Don't come out for anyone until I call you."

"No," she flung back. "I'm going with you."

"Like hell you are."

"I am."

"You're my wife," he snapped. "You'll do as I say."

"Because I'm your wife, I'm going with you."

"I've no time for games, woman. Now get into that cave. You'll be safe there."

"And you?" Her fingers closed on his arm. "Can you promise me you'll be safe?"

"Aye, hinney. Safe as a rabbit in a brier thicket." He started for the edge of the woods, and she followed close on his heels.

He whirled on her, his features contorted with anger. "I told ye to stay."

"And I told you I'm coming." She met his black glare with an unwavering stubbornness. "If there's danger, I want to be with you. A man who has no more sense than to go over a falls needs someone with a level head behind him.

Ross swore under his breath and primed and cocked his flintlock pistol. "Take this then," he muttered between clenched teeth, "but, by God, ye'd best not stumble and shoot me in the back."

Anne clutched the pistol grimly. "If I ever shoot you, Ross Campbell, it will be straight on. I'd not want to miss the expression on your face when I pulled the trigger."

Chapter 19

Ross approached the Shawnee camp with caution, keeping Anne well behind him. He was still angry that she hadn't obeyed him and stayed in the hollow behind the falls. Whoever the hell had decided to start shooting in the village could damned well have waited another quarter hour. He hadn't meant to make love to Anne, not after she'd been so cold toward him. But just being close to her in the water, feeling her soft, sweet body next to his . . . It was enough to drive a man mad. God, but he loved her . . . exasperating or not!

He glanced over his shoulder to be certain that she was still following and that the pistol he'd put in her hands was pointed away from him and toward the ground. She was there, trudging along with the determination of a soldier, her lovely heart-shaped face set in a worried frown and her mouth pursed tight. His little English wife had courage—he'd give her that. The woods were new to her, and the Shawnee were enough to keep anyone from a good night's sleep, but Anne hadn't faltered. She'd pulled her weight during the fight on the river, and she looked ready to take on Matiassu's war party single-handedly here and now.

He circled the village and came in from the direction of the east cornfield. Using the mature corn as cover, they could get close to the trouble before anyone knew they were there. At the edge of the field, just beyond the closest wigwam, he motioned Anne to get down.

"Put your face in the dirt and stay here," he ordered. "Don't move, and don't shoot unless you're in danger. But don't let anyone close enough to take that pistol away from ye." He didn't give her any instructions as to what she should do if the shooting started and he didn't come back. If that happened, Anne would be on her own. For the first time since the battle on the river, he was sorry he hadn't left her at Fort Campbell.

To his relief, she did as she was told. He got down on his hands and knees and crept forward. Using the wigwams to screen his approach, he crawled around the first one, then got to his feet and dashed to the second. There he checked the powder in the frizzen pan on his musket and peered around the wigwam.

Roquette stood in the center of the dance ground. There was no mistaking his long yellow hair and beard, or the white and red French military coat he wore. Two other white men were with him. One was a half-breed by the name of Charley Sacre; the other was a stranger to Ross. There were six Indian braves, Menominee by the look of them, and they were all heavily armed. The whole party was back to back, hackles raised, muskets leveled and ready to fight for their lives. Roquette was arguing with someone, but Ross couldn't see who.

Slowly, Ross moved out onto the edge of the dance ground. "Afternoon, Roquette," he called.

The Frenchman's head snapped around. "What are you doing here, you Scots bastard?"

"Looking after my interests, same as ye." Ross walked forward, keeping his hammer back and his finger on the hair trigger of his flintlock. Scattered around the outside of the dance ground were taut-faced Shawnee with bloodlust in their eyes. He caught sight of one or two women, but most were men—all holding muskets or drawn bows. The Shawnee looked as primed for battle as Roquette and his followers.

"I came here to the High Council in good faith," Roquette shouted. His English was accented, but clear enough for Ross to understand him plainly. "That son of a bitch Mackenzie tried to kill me."

Ross glanced to his left and saw Amookas's husband, Alex Mackenzie, leaning on a crutch with a flintlock musket in his hands. Alex was Liiuan and Niipan's father and the man who'd acted as father to Moonfeather since she was a child. The grizzled old Scotsman had been one-legged ever since Ross had known him, but it had never slowed him down. A gunsmith and crack shot, Alex had made his home among the Shawnee for over twenty years. Ross couldn't understand why Roquette was still breathing if Alex Mackenzie wanted him dead badly enough to fire on him.

"I wouldna ha' missed the devil if Moonfeather hadn't spoiled my aim," Alex grumbled. "Drop yer gun, Roquette. I'll fight ye wi' tomahawks or knives. I'll fight ye barehanded, do ye dare stand against a mon!" The Scotsman's voice was thick with the burr of the Highlands. His narrowed eyes and grim expression left no doubt in Ross's mind that he was dead serious about killing the Frenchman.

"Ye best lower your weapons," Ross suggested

to Roquette. "If the shooting starts, not one of ye will see sunset."

"Mackenzie started this," Roquette said. "Tell him to put his gun down."

Alex spat on the ground. "Ye murdered my son."

"I don't know what you're talking about, you crazy old fool!" the Frenchman shouted.

"Ye and Matiassu are in this together," Alex retorted. "He may ha' pulled the trigger, but ye be the one who's paying him for scalps."

"Liar," Roquette flung back.

Moonfeather moved into Ross's line of vision. She raised her empty hands and stepped away from Alex. "Put down your guns," she called to Roquette in English. "I give ye my word that ye willna be harmed here."

"A half-breed squaw's word is not good enough," Roquette snapped.

Ross stiffened. He wanted to hurl himself at the Frenchman and beat him to his knees for the insult he'd offered Moonfeather. Roquette knew that she was a peace woman, and he knew that she carried the burden of her tribe's honor as well as her own, yet he dared to speak to her this way. Ross glanced at her—she was still watching Roquette—and her composure left no doubt as to who possessed the strongest will. Roquette's face was twisted in fear and anger, Moonfeather's expression gave no hint that she had even heard his foolish taunt. Ross's rage receded to a manageable level as Moonfeather's voice rang out in clear melodious French.

"A half-breed squaw's hand was good enough to save your life."

To Ross's surprise, Roquette's face flushed. Ross wouldn't have believed the French renegade had enough humanity left in him to feel shame.

"If you will not accept the word of a Shawnee peace woman, will you accept mine?" A tall, imposing figure wearing a wolfskin cape complete with head and bared teeth came from Tuk-o-see-yah's wigwam. He straightened to his full height and raked the scene with dark, smoldering eyes. The wolf's head fitted over the man's like a tight-fitting cap. Mica chips had been sewn into the eyesockets of the headdress. The mica glittered in the sunlight, making it appear as though the Indian possessed a second pair of ghostly eyes. Beneath the wolfhide, his wide, muscular chest was bare except for a necklace of mountain lion claws. He carried no weapons other than the skinning knife on his belt, and the fringes of his rawhide leggings were decorated with silver bells.

Ross heard a woman behind him murmur, "Wolf's Shadow."

"Wolf's Shadow," another brave repeated. "It is the shaman."

Ross waited until the medicine man's gaze met his own, and Ross nodded. He'd heard plenty about the Shawnee shaman, but he'd never seen him. Wolf's Shadow was the stuff legends were made of—a man dedicated to welding the Shawnee and Delaware into a single nation. Both a spiritual and a political leader, he traveled among the tribes from the Great Lakes to the Chesapeake. Ross hadn't realized Wolf's Shadow would be attending the High Council.

The shaman nodded back, then turned his attention to the Frenchman and his men. "If the word of Wolf's Shadow means anything to you," he began in perfect, precise English, "then lower your weapons and let us settle this as men—not as animals." He repeated himself in French, and again in the Menominee dialect.

Muttering to his companions, Roquette turned

his musket barrel toward the ground. The others followed suit.

"Now you must do the same," Wolf's Shadow ordered the Shawnee in their own language. When they obeyed, he waved toward a shady spot beneath the trees. "Come." He switched to English. "We talk."

Niipan and two Shawnee braves closed around Alex and coaxed him away from the dance ground toward his wigwam. Alex glowered and grumbled, but he handed his musket to his son as he stooped to enter his house.

Anne appeared at Ross's side. "Does this mean there isn't going to be a fight?"

"I thought I told ye to stay where it was safe," he said to her.

Moonfeather walked quickly across the hard-packed ground to her sister. "That was a bad situation," she said. "Uncle Alex tried to blow Roquette's head off. He blames him for Matiassu's actions, and he's probably right."

Ross frowned. "We heard more than one shot."

"Aye." Leah sighed "Alex fired and Roquette fired back. I'm not sure who shot the last time. I should have let Alex kill him, but the peace of the council can't be broken."

"Matiassu broke it," Ross said.

"Maybe. Probably. Tuk-o-see-yah thinks so. He's decreed that Matiassu has the turning of one moon to come in and explain himself. If he doesn't, he's declared an outlaw—dead to his people and fair game for anyone to kill." She glanced at Anne. "Dinna worry. I think the shooting be over for the day. Roquette willna swing anyone to his way of thinking. He'll bluster a wee bit to save face, but I dinna think he'll want to spend the night here."

"A good thing Wolf's Shadow was in camp," Ross put in. "When did he arrive?"

"Sometime in the night. He's been with Tuk-o-see-yah all day. Amookas told me he'd come in, but I wasn't invited to their smoke, so I didn't get a chance to talk to him." Moonfeather glanced at Anne. "Wolf's Shadow is a great shaman—a medicine man."

Anne's brow furrowed. "You mean he's some sort of physician?"

"Aye, but he be more than that. They saw he can read men's minds. He is a good man. Very mysterious—very powerful. The Shawnee will listen to his words."

Ross took his pistol out of Anne's hands and eased down the hammer. "We'll have to join the council members, hinney," he said. "Go back to the wigwam and wait for me. You'll be safe there."

She looked uncertain.

Moonfeather touched her sister's arm. "Go," she agreed. "We will be all right. Roquette be evil—nay stupid."

Ross flashed Anne a smile. "Maybe we can finish what we started a little later."

Anne's eyes twinkled. "If you think you'll be up to it," she murmured huskily.

His throat constricted as he remembered how good she'd felt pressed against him. "To the wigwam, woman," he teased, thrusting the pistol into his belt. "I'll join ye as soon as I can." He waited until Anne entered the hut, then followed Moonfeather to the council circle.

It was evening when Leah returned to the wigwam where Anne waited. Earlier, Kitate had brought Anne something to eat. She'd thought she was too worried to have much appetite, but she'd finished every bite of the hot bread and squirrel stew.

Leah smiled at her. "All be well, sister."

"Where's Ross?" Anne rose anxiously to her feet.

"He will be with ye soon. He makes arrangements for your journey to the coast. At dawn, ye leave for Annapolis and our father's house. The Delaware will go with ye as escort, so that ye need have no fear of another attack by Matiassu." Leah sank down on the bearskin beside her and added another log to the fire. "There will be no High Council. Matiassu's treachery has shamed those who would speak for him. His ally, Roquette, is on his way north out of Shawnee hunting ground. Wolf's Shadow travels with him to prove our good faith."

"How can you be certain that it was Matiassu who attacked us on the river? Maybe it really was Iroquois."

Leah shook her head. "Nay. Once, long ago, Matiassu tried the same trick with Seneca arrows—the Seneca are a tribe of the Iroquois Five Nations and our old enemies. I discovered what Matiassu had done, but I did not reveal his perfidy to my people. That was a mistake. Now he has done it again."

"But if he knew that you had caught him before, wouldn't he—"

Leah's eyes narrowed. "He thought that I would be killed. A dead woman accuses no one."

"If the council won't talk, does that mean peace or war?" Anne put out her hand to the warmth of the fire. It seemed like a dream that she should be sitting here in an Indian wigwam in the middle of the American wilderness talking to her sister as calmly as if they were sharing high tea in Scarbrough's London mansion.

"I think we maun have peace—at least through the winter. When spring comes . . ." Leah shrugged. "Who can say?"

"Are you coming with us to Annapolis?" As much as she wanted to see her father and talk with him, the thought of being parted from Leah was alarming.

"Nay. Later I will come—after harvest. When the geese fly south to the Chesapeake, then I return to my husband with my little ones. He will be surprised when he sees how much the two of them have grown."

Anne clasped Leah's hand. "It pains me to say good-bye to you. There is so much I want to ask you. When will we be together again?"

"Wait for me in Annapolis. My Brandon makes much of your Christmas. Stay with us and share the festivities."

Anne nibbled at her lower lip. "I . . . I don't know. I want to see Cameron, but I cannot invite myself to stay with him indefinitely. And Ross may not—"

"Ross has a house and a store in Annapolis." Leah cut her eyes at her sister. "He didna tell ye, did he? That one!" she scoffed. "He wouldna think it was important. Many years ago, before Angus went west and built his trading post on the Mesawmi River, he owned a small plantation on the bay. In the town, he has the place of selling and a dock. Angus's wife—not Ross's mother but Angus's first wife—was a merchant's daughter. From this woman came the Annapolis land. No one lives in the plantation house, but it be . . . Nay!" she declared. "We be sisters. Ye maun go to Brandon and stay with him."

"With Brandon?" Old memories welled up in Anne's mind. Once she had believed that she loved Brandon. Could she think of him now as a friend . . . as her brother-in-law? "Ross—"

"Not what Ross wishes, Anne—what ye wish."

Brandon would welcome them, Anne was certain of it. She had been a guest at his mother's home before, and he had stayed with her family. "Would there be room for us—"

Leah laughed. "Aye, elder sister. Brandon builds a palace by the bay. There would be room for half my tribe to sleep. He may not even be there. Brandon's father has plantations in Virginia also, and Brandon travels to see that they are well cared for. Ye and Ross maun go and make our home your own. Our father lives only a mile away."

"I think I would like that," Anne replied honestly. "And I will wait for you to come. I want my marriage with Ross to work . . . but there are still problems between us. I need a sister."

"It is good to need," Leah said. "But remember that ye have much to give. Ye be a strong woman, Anne. It makes my heart glad that my children will know ye and come to love ye also." She rose to her feet. "I do not like good-byes. I will say to ye, safe journey. May the Creator guide your footsteps and keep ye until we meet again." She unwrapped a small roll of rabbit skin and handed a tiny pair of beaded moccasins to Anne.

"Ohhh," Anne gasped. They were exact miniatures of the moccasins Leah had given her when they reached the Shawnee village, the ones she was wearing now. "They're beautiful. But why . . . these are for a baby. I'm not with child." I wish I was, she thought. She cradled the exquisite white leather shoes in her hand.

Leah laughed. "Watch the moon, sister. It may be that ye will need these before ye think." She hugged Anne tightly and hurried out into the night.

Puzzled, Anne stared after her. True, she had never had a child, but surely she would be the first to know if she were to have a baby. She'd not missed a showing of blood. In the last few weeks, her stomach had troubled her and she'd had periods of dizziness, but women who were with child lost their appetites. It certainly hadn't happened to her—if anything, she was hungry all the time. Even the strange foods of the Indians had tasted delicious. Leah might be a wise woman among the Shawnee, but she didn't know everything. Perhaps, Anne decided, her sister had given her the baby shoes in the hopes that she would get with child.

The thought that she might be barren chilled her. How terrible it would be in old age to have no one. If she gave Ross children, it would be more reason for him to want to keep her. In time, she told herself. They had only been wed since early spring. Many women took a year or two to swell with the first child.

Her musing was broken by the high, poignant notes of an eagle-bone flute. She started to rise, but the unearthly music held her transfixed. Tears filled her eyes as she listened, knowing that it could only be Ross courting her according to the Shawnee custom.

At last, when the flute was silent, she went to the entrance of the wigwam. There, on a white deerskin, lay her pearl earrings—the ones Ross had given to the captain for the price of their passage.

"I dinna think I'll be able to find Johnny Faa's band of gypsies and recover your rings or your other earrings," Ross said from the darkness. "Will these do for an apology? Leah's right. I haven't treated you like a man should treat the woman he loves."

Anne dashed away her tears with the back of her hand. Too full of emotion to talk, she grabbed his hand and held it.

"I feared they'd been lost in the river," he said sheepishly. "I'd sewn them inside a pocket in my bonnet. Lucky for me the Shawnee found it washed up on the shore."

She sniffed. "How . . . how did you get them back from Captain Gordon?"

"I promised him double our passage fee the next time he docks in Annapolis."

"And where was this money to come from?"

Ross grinned. "I did marry a rich wife."

She laughed with him as she fastened the pearls in her ears.

"Come with me, hinney."

Without question, she followed him through the darkened village to a secluded spot on the riverbank a few hundred yards from camp. There they slipped out of their clothing and swam together in the cool, fast-flowing water.

The night was very dark. Heavy clouds covered the moon and hung so low they brushed the treetops. Not a single star pierced the velvet heavens with flickering radiance. A single drum sounded from the camp, and with it came the low, repetitive reverberation of joined voices rising and falling with an ancient tribal chant.

Neither Ross nor Anne spoke. It was enough to hold each other and let the current carry away their differences. At last, when the rumble of thunder broke through their shared enchantment with the night, they waded from the river and walked naked through the fog back to their wigwam.

The warmth of the coals in the fire pit drew

Anne and freed her from her self-imposed silence. "Are we really going to Annapolis in the morning?" she asked, holding out her hands to the tiny flame. "Truly?" She folded her deerskin gown and laid it aside. Ross's gaze burned her naked skin, but she felt no shame—only pride. She smiled at him with her eyes.

"Aye, sweeting, we are. If ye want to see your father, I'll take ye." His deep voice was husky. "I have wronged ye, Anne. I ken that now. Moonfeather told me what ye did for me by the falls. She said ye called upon your amulet to save my life."

Thunder rolled across the sky, and Anne sensed a change in the wind. A puff of damp air rippled the deerskin at the entrance to the wigwam. The fire sparked. "You don't believe in magic," Anne answered breathlessly. She could smell the rain coming. Her skin prickled.

"Nay, Anne, I dinna, but I believe in you. It matters not if the magic be real or not. What matters is that despite what I've done to you, ye love me." He held out his arms, and she went to him. His kiss was long and sweet and tender. "Ye mean the world to me, hinney, but if ye want to go back to England, I'll help you."

She clung to him as lightning arced across the heavens. "You'd do that for me?"

"Aye. Do ye wish it?"

"And if I want to stay here in the Colonies—if I want to be your true wife?"

The first drops of rain pelted against the wigwam. The flames in the fire pit hissed as smoke spiraled upward toward the hole in the ceiling.

"Oh, God, woman." He kissed her again, harder.

Her knees went weak as she melted against him. The rain assaulted the wigwam in sheets, and the wind tore at the bark covering as the storm grew closer. Anne's head was filled with the musty odor of wet leaves and the virile man-scent of Ross's skin and hair.

He kissed her again, letting his tongue brush her teasingly—not demanding but asking.

She trembled in his arms. "Stop kissing me," she protested weakly. "I can't think." She pushed herself to arm's length. "If I stay," she warned him, "you must treat me differently. I'll not be dragged about like a sack of raw wool. I want respect from you, Ross. I want you to treat me like you do Leah."

He crushed her against him and nuzzled her neck. "Not exactly as I do Moonfeather, I hope." He cupped her chin in his hand and tilted her face up so that he could stare into her eyes. "I love ye, Anne," he whispered. "Can ye ever forgive me for the way I've treated ye?"

A crash of thunder nearly deafened her. Lightning flashed so brightly she could see it through the walls. "Forgiving is easy," she said above the rain. "It's the forgetting that comes hard. Give me time."

"I don't want to lose ye, but I can't give up Wanishish-eyun. Do ye think ye could learn to love it as I do? I'm nay a man for towns and tight breeches. Maybe I expected too much of you—that ye should do all the giving—but I won't lie to you to keep ye. I canna live in England, and I canna live a gentleman's life along the coast either."

He does love me, she thought—he really loves me. Is it enough? Can we be happy together? Can I forget the past? Her heart was beating so hard she thought it would break, and her chest felt tight. "I don't expect you to go back to England," she whispered. "I think I could learn to love this new land as you do . . . but . . ."

"But what?" he pulled her down gently, and they knelt, facing each other on the bearskin rug.

"I'm not sure I can live at Fort Campbell. I . . ." She covered her face with her hands. "I can't tell you what I want, Ross, because I'm not sure myself. After I've seen my father . . . after I've thought all this out . . . maybe then . . ."

He planted soft kisses in her hair. "If it's time ye want, it's time ye shall have. So long as ye love me, darling, we'll work things out. It will be all right, I promise ye."

"I never knew what love was until I met you," she said shyly. His hands were warm against her bare skin, and delicious sensations ran up and down her spine. She smiled up at him in the firelight. "I want you now," she admitted. "Love me, Ross. Push away the doubts and the shadows."

"Ah, hinney," he murmured.

Anne gazed at him wide-eyed. He was so beautiful, this great man of hers. Trembling, she laid her hand on his bare thigh. The muscles were taut under her exploring fingers. Excitement made her light-headed.

"I want to touch you . . . all of you."

They kissed again, a long, slow kiss that made Anne's blood race. She took his hand in hers and brought it to her breast, shivering with delight when he caressed her.

"I do love you so much," she said. The storm tore at the wigwam, but here with Ross she was safe from the wind and the rain . . . safe as she had never felt before.

"And I you." He trailed hot, damp kisses down her bare shoulder, and leaned close to whisper in her ear, telling her what wonderful, wicked ways he meant to make love to her.

She laughed and arched against him, catching a bit of skin on his chest between her teeth and nipping gently, letting her tongue graze his slightly salty skin, savoring the taste and texture of him. "If you do that," she dared, "I may—" Then she squealed as he growled and rolled her over, seizing her wrists and pinning her down against the thick, soft rug.

"Ye be my prisoner," he teased, "and I shall take my pleasure of ye, English wench."

She struggled against him, playfully raising her knee to rub against his swollen shaft. He groaned. "Two can play this game," she said.

Ross lowered his weight onto her, bracing himself with one arm to keep from hurting her, and their mouths met. Anne strained against him, reveling in the sensation of his body pressed against hers.

"When do we have to leave for Annapolis?" she murmured innocently as she stroked his tumescent member. He was hard and ready.

"At dawn." He drew in a deep breath and moaned with pleasure. "Witch." He kissed her again deeply, filling her mouth with his tongue, moving his body over hers until she whimpered with desire. "Or the next day," he whispered. "Or the next."

"Mmm." Anne sighed, wrapping her arms around his neck and pulling him closer. "Then let's not waste a moment."

He threaded his fingers through her hair and stared into her eyes. "Nay," he agreed hoarsely. "Not a minute. For once, hinney, ye share my thoughts exactly."

Then they were kissing again, and his hands were doing wonderful things to the most intimate parts of her body. The sensations of his skin rubbing hers, of the delicious heat growing in her loins, of soft, silky bearskin beneath her were heightened by the awesome power of the storm that raged around them.

"Now," she murmured. "Now."

"Aye, darling," he answered, "for it would kill me to wait longer."

And then he thrust into her, and she cried out with intense pleasure. Stroke for stroke she met him, giving and receiving, until their naked bodies glistened in the firelight with a light film of moisture and their breath came in ragged gasps. Anne felt her spirit spiraling upward like the smoke from their fire pit climbing toward the sky. She clung to Ross as their shared passion peaked and then exploded in a climax of soul-shattering rapture.

Slowly, Anne became aware of the rain and the wind and the now-distant sounds of thunder. Ross leaned over her and nibbled her lips, then cradled her against his chest, whispering sweet words of love.

Her fingers brushed her amulet, and she wondered again at the magic that had brought her so far to this unexpected happiness.

And then their mouths were locked together again, and nothing mattered to Anne but Ross and their precious night of love.

Chapter 20

Annapolis, Maryland
October 1723

Fitzhugh Murrane cleared his throat for the second time. He'd been standing in the Royal Governor's private parlor for the better part of an hour, and no one had brought him a chair or offered him refreshment. His patience was fast fading, and one side of his jaw throbbed from a broken tooth. "Governor Calvert—"

Charles Calvert frowned and reached for a quill pen. "This is distasteful business, Lord Murrane, and it couldn't have come at a more inconvenient time." The governor pushed Murrane's warrant and letter from Anne's father aside. He dipped his quill in ink and scrawled his signature across a document bearing his own seal. He pursed his lips. "You are unknown to us, and Ross Campbell—one should properly say the Master of Strathmar, according to these papers—is a citizen of standing in the colony. Your allegations of a runaway wife—"

"Kidnapped!" Murrane interrupted. "My wife was kidnapped."

Governor Calvert spread his raised fingers. "Whichever." The Black Forest clock on the mantel chimed twelve noon, and Calvert stood up. "We will issue orders that the Master of Strathmar be summoned for questioning, and that inquiries be made about Lady Anne." The governor stroked his chin thoughtfully. He was a pleasant-looking man of medium height and even features, and his soft voice conveyed the authority of a man born to unquestioned power. "These charges of murder and"—he sniffed—"kidnapping are quite serious. We will certainly give your petition sincere consideration, but London and these alleged events are many months and a great distance away."

Murrane leaned over the front of the governor's desk. "I have a warrant for Campbell's arrest for murder and kidnapping," he rasped. "I have a letter from my wife's father, the Earl of Langstone, stating that Lady Anne was taken against her will. What more do you need?"

Charles Calvert yawned politely, covering his mouth with a lace handkerchief. "Pardon me, Lord Murrane, but this has been a dreadfully long day, and I have the customs agent waiting in my antechamber. I've been here since seven, and I want my dinner."

Murrane scowled. "This was a courtesy visit. I have the legal authority, and I have the men to arrest Campbell myself."

The governor's expression hardened. "Indeed you do not, sir. You have exactly the authority here that I permit you to exercise. I am His Majesty's Royal Governor, and I answer to no one but King George. You will do well to remember that." He lifted a silver bell from the desk and rang it twice. Immediately, a door opened on the left, and the governor's secretary, James Crew, appeared.

"Governor Calvert. You rang, sir?" The secretary wore a wine coat and vest, and buff breeches. His wig was neatly styled and tied in the back with a wine-colored silk ribbon.

"Crew." The governor smiled politely. "Kindly show the baron out." He glanced at Murrane. "On the evening of Tuesday next, there will be a ball in honor of my birthday. Tell Crew where you are staying, and he will arrange for my carriage to pick you up at eight. Most people of consequence in Annapolis will be present, and it may be that we can hear word of your missing lady." He offered a curt nod of dismissal. "Do nothing without my leave, sir, or you shall rue the day you first set foot on Maryland soil."

Murrane's face swelled with engorged blood as he walked stiffly from the parlor and descended the wide staircase. "I'm at the White Swan," he muttered to the governor's secretary.

"Very good, sir." Crew waved to a male servant to open the door for the baron.

Swearing under his breath, Murrane shouldered past the liveried footmen and hurried out onto the crowded street. John Brown was leaning against the brick building, arms folded over his chest, eyes nearly closed. He leaped to attention and fell into step behind his employer.

Murrane ignored Brown and stalked across the dusty square in the direction of the White Swan Inn. An oxcart lumbered past, bearing two hogsheads of tobacco to the harbor. The near ox raised its tail and dropped a wet glob of greenish-black manure into the street, splattering Murrane's shoe. Murrane cursed and shook his fist at the driver.

The farmer made a rude gesture and offered a

comment on the lineage of Murrane's mother. A woman selling dippers of milk from an open bucket laughed. The oxen kept walking.

Murrane cast a scornful glance around the square. "Annapolis," he scoffed. The capital of the Maryland Colony was little more than a village of surly plowmen who didn't know how to show respect for their betters. "Weeks we've cooled our heels waiting, and now this puffed-up governor says he will give my petition serious consideration!"

"Trouble is, sir, nobody knows exactly where Campbell's fort is. West, they say. There ain't no roads, an' it's all wild Indian territory. One man wasn't certain Fort Campbell was in the Maryland Territory. He thought it might be on Pennsylvania land, or even Virginia."

"To hell with them. I don't care where it is. Find me someone who can guide us there. I'll deal with Ross Campbell and my dear wife when I catch up with them."

A shaggy cur with golden eyes growled at Murrane, and he kicked it in the ribs. The dog yipped, ducked under a farm wagon, and fled down an alley.

The rutted street was thick with horsemen, carts, and wagons. Merchants and Indians vied for position as they dodged sedan chairs and boisterous sailors with seabags over their shoulders. Men called to each other across the thoroughfare, and dogs barked above the clang of a blacksmith's hammer on steel.

Red and gold autumn leaves swirled on the salt-tinged breeze; everywhere tramping feet stirred the dust and blackened the faces of the passersby. Three British soldiers in uniform swaggered by—one reeking of rum, although it was only midday.

The wind caught the skirts of a half-grown girl herding a flock of sheep uphill away from the harbor and lifted her petticoats to show a glimpse of bare knee. The soldiers hooted, and the girl blushed and waved her shepherd's staff to hurry the docile animals.

"Capital of the colony," Murrane grumbled. "The futterin' town smells like a cattle fair."

A broad-faced black woman in a mobcap and golden hoop earrings was doing a brisk business selling fresh baked gingerbread from a tray suspended by a strap around her neck. "Hot gingercakes!" she cried. "Hot and spicy. Just from the oven. Gingercakes!" A bearded man in buckskins tossed her a penny and began to stuff the sweet into his mouth. Seagulls swooped down to snatch up the fallen crumbs.

"Soft crabs!" cried a street vendor, pushing a wheelbarrow full of fish and crabs so fresh that they were still wiggling. "Buy my fish," he cried. "Fresh fish! Soft crabs! This morning's catch!"

Murrane reached the far side of the square and glared at his lieutenant. "Hire a guide to take us into the wilderness no later than Thursday. I'm tired of your excuses. I'll not be made a fool of by these colonials. Anne is my property. I'll have her back and Campbell dead before snow flies."

John Brown kept silent.

Murrane spat out a mouthful of dust. Brown better have the sense to hold his tongue, he thought. Whether Anne was his legal wife or his betrothed was a fine point. The marriage contract had been signed, the church service that Ross Campbell had interrupted was only a formality.

The sign of the White Swan loomed ahead. Murrane wondered if the innkeeper would have fresh beef for dinner. He could have sworn the stringy duck that was served last night had died of old age. "I'll take my meal in the private room," he said to Brown. "See to it that the men are served peas and salt pork. I'll not pay for them to eat like gentlemen." The cost of keeping English mercenaries in Annapolis was staggering. "Oh, and Brown . . ."

"Sir?"

"See to it that someone brushes my brown coat and smooths the wrinkles out of it. I've been invited to the governor's birthday ball."

Cameron Stewart, Earl of Dunnkell, led the way to the plantation stables. "You'll appreciate this mare, Ross," he said. "She has Turk blood. I've bred her to one of Brandon's stallions. If I get a filly out of her, I mean to have it trained for Leah's daughter, Cami. By the time the filly has been properly schooled, the girl will be old enough to ride her."

Anne stood in the shade of a beech tree and watched as her father and Ross admired the chestnut mare. To her surprise, the two men had struck up an instant friendship. They shared a love of horses, horse racing, and good whiskey.

In the days since she and Ross had arrived on the coast, all her apprehensions about meeting Cameron again had proved formless. As Leah had promised, their father had been overjoyed to see her and Ross.

They had gone to King's Gift as Leah had told them. Brandon had been leaving on important business for his father when they'd arrived. He'd made them welcome and instructed the servants to give them anything they asked for during their stay. "I'll be back in a few weeks," he'd said.

"I'd give a hundred pounds to glimpse Cameron's face when he sees Anne."

She had been delighted with Leah and Brandon's palatial home, and had altered some of her opinions about the primitive living conditions in the Maryland Colony.

The homes of the gentry were smaller than the great mansions of England, but the lifestyles of the people here—rich and commonfolk alike—seemed infinitely better. Even the black slaves were better dressed and healthier-looking than London's poor. The water was clean and fit to drink. There were no open sewers full of dead animals and stagnant water in Annapolis. Everywhere Anne looked, she saw prosperous, hardworking citizens and rich fields full of fat cattle.

Cameron's nearby manor house, Gentleman's Folly, would do credit to any earl in England. The furnishings were beautifully crafted; the walls were hung with fine paintings and the paper in his hall parlor was handpainted in France. Silver and china graced his tables—tables that groaned under a remarkable variety of excellent meats and fruits and vegetables. Venison and goose, roast beef and ham, were cooked as well as any Anne had been served at the best tables in London. Gentleman's Folly was hardly a backwater farm—it was a magnificent home.

"I've wronged you, Anne," Cameron had said on the first night they'd come to see him. "You suffered for the fleshly pleasures I shared with your mother. I can't give you back your lost years of childhood, but whatever I can do for you now, I will. God knows I'm rich enough."

"It's not money I want of you," Anne replied. For months she had wondered what she would say to her father when she saw him. She'd rehearsed conversations in her mind and had lain awake nights thinking of the right words. But now that she was actually here, the words didn't matter. She and her father fitted together as naturally as a hand and glove.

I can see Leah in him, she thought. They both have the ability to make me feel good about myself just by being near me. Her father had a wonderful sense of humor and an easy manner.

"I wish I'd known who you were when I was a child," she admitted to him. "Barbara always . . ." She trailed off awkwardly, not willing to reveal her mother's faults to him.

Genuine regret filled Cameron's blue eyes. "I know Barbara as well as anyone," he said. "I didn't want to leave you with her, but she laughed when I suggested that you come to live with me. 'Utterly preposterous,' I believe that was her reaction. And of course my idea *was* impossible. I was wed to Margaret then, and Barbara was married to Langstone." His eyes clouded with moisture. "I gave her money," he said. "I'm certain she never told you, but I always made an allowance for your expenses."

"Would you have married her if you'd been free?" Anne asked.

He shrugged. "Honestly? I can't say. At one time your mother was . . ." Cameron sighed. "Probably not."

"Are you two of a kind?" Anne demanded. "Barbara was never content with one man. And you, obviously . . ."

The barb struck home, and Cameron flinched. "You have a little of your mother in you," he said. "It's no secret that I've loved many women, but . . . Had I had a real marriage, Anne, it might have been different."

Cameron Stewart was finally free of the marriage of convenience his parents had made for him when he was sixteen and the lady was thirty.

He indicated the portrait of a richly gowned, plain-faced woman hanging in the hall parlor of his manor house. "Margaret's gone, God rest her soul. She fell off a horse and broke her neck only weeks after I sailed from England. A pity. She was a good woman. There was never love between us, but we were always friends. Margaret had health problems. She wanted a child desperately, but our bairns were stillborn. Once it became clear that she couldn't bear living children and that trying would kill her, we went our separate ways. She had her own interests, and she closed her eyes to mine."

"And now you are a rich widower," Anne said.

"Aye. I am." Cameron flashed a charming grin. "And the lassies of Annapolis—young and old— are buzzing around me like flies around a cherry tart."

Anne wasn't able to suppress her amusement. Lord Dunnkell—her father—was an extremely handsome man. His russet hair was tinged with gray, but his blue eyes glowed with youthful vigor. He was tanned and lithe, with a lean belly and a spring to his step. "You are impossible, Cameron," she teased. He'd asked her to call him by his Christian name.

"I'd not soil your reputation, Anne," he explained. "Are ye any less my flesh and blood if the world knows you as Langstone's heir? You'll inherit his fortune as well as your mother's. Ross made a canny choice—even for a Scot—when he took you to wife."

"It was a mistake," Anne said. "He took the wrong bride."

"And I'm certain that will make for a good tale to tell your grandchildren," Cameron flung back. Then he said seriously, "I never thought to have both my girls near me in my old age. All my life I've enjoyed the finer things in life. Now, all I want is to play at being a farmer. I want to see crops grow, and I want to be part of my children's and grandchildren's lives." He took her hand. "Can you forgive me, Anne? Can you give me a second chance at being a father?"

It was all she could do to keep from crying. When Cameron had told her in England two years ago that he was her real father, she'd been angry and hurt. Now all the bitterness was gone, and what remained was her own desire for a father. "I can try," she managed.

"I've treated you badly." Cameron had admitted. "Maybe I can make up for it in the future."

"Anne."

Her father's voice brought her back to the present, and she smiled at him. A black groom was leading the chestnut mare in a circle at a trot. The animal's darker-colored mane and tail had been brushed and combed to a high shine. Her ears were erect, her eyes wide and intelligent.

"What do you think?" Cameron asked. "Will she throw magnificent foals?"

Anne nodded. "She's beautiful."

Cameron gave instructions to the groom, and he and Ross joined her. "I want you to see the orchard I'm starting on the far side of the slaves' quarters," her father said. "Apples and cherries. I've gotten some really nice stock from a friend, Mistress O'Hara. You'll be meeting her tomorrow night at the birthday ball I'm throwing for Charles Calvert, our Royal Governor. He's been away on government business—that's why you haven't met him already." He grinned boyishly. "You'll love Kati O'Hara—she's a widow, but she runs her own plantation. She grows the best tobacco for miles around."

"Kati, is it?" Ross teased. "Methinks your father willna be a widower long."

"Nay," Cameron protested. "Kati and I are just friends. I've been a married man most of my life. I intend to spend the rest single."

"Do ye believe him, Anne?" Ross asked.

"I'll reserve my opinion until after I've seen Mistress O'Hara."

The following night, Anne made her entrance at the governor's birthday ball on her father's arm. She swept down the wide staircase at Gentleman's Folly wearing an exquisite borrowed gown of pink satin and Irish lace. The bodice of the dress dipped fashionably low, making a perfect frame for Anne's golden amulet.

Cameron paused on the bottom step. "You'll be the most beautiful woman here tonight," he said proudly.

"It's Leah's gown," Anne replied.

"Nay, lass," Ross rumbled behind them. "It be the woman in the dress."

Brandon had been unable to return for his father-in-law's party, but he'd sent orders that Anne and Ross were to make free with any clothing they could find in the house, and he'd hired Annapolis's finest mantua maker to do any necessary alterations.

Ross's coat was powder-blue velvet over a matching vest and white shirt. The craggy planes of his tanned face were accented by the frothy white stock at his throat, and Anne's heart skipped a beat every time she looked at him. His doeskin breeches fitted over his muscular thighs without a wrinkle, and his black leather shoes bore crystal rosettes.

"Your sister's husband be a bit of a fop, wouldn't ye say?" Ross whispered to Anne, when Cameron finally left off introducing them to his friends and went to greet a newly arriving guest. "I feel like a badger in a trap. A man's legs were meant to breathe."

Anne chuckled. "I like your legs in breeches," she murmured behind her fan as she nodded to a bewigged matron.

"Take ye for a feather-heeled jade," he exclaimed. "Do ye say ye dinna like my kilt?"

"I didn't say that at all." She tapped him playfully with the ivory fan. "Be good, Ross. You promised me you'd be on your best behavior." Excitement bubbled up inside her as the first strains of music drifted from the great hall. Already a few couples had begun to gather there. "Oh," she whispered. "The musicians are playing a country dance. Do you know how to dance, Ross?"

"Aye," he confided, "I can. But these dances be too tame. What say I get them to play a Highland fling or . . ." His black eyes sparkled with mischief. "Or maybe a Shawnee stomp."

"Don't you dare," she began. Anne was saved from further teasing by Cameron and the lady he was escorting toward them. "Look," she whispered. "It's Father, and unless I miss my guess, that is his dear friend, Mistress O'Hara."

Kati O'Hara smiled and offered her hands to Anne. She was tall and well-rounded with dark auburn hair and green eyes—a pretty, freckled woman half Cameron's age. "I'm Kati," she said.

"Cameron hasn't stopped talking about you since you arrived in Annapolis. Any friend of his . . ." She arched a dark eyebrow meaningfully. "Welcome to Maryland, Anne. I do hope we'll be friends."

Anne squeezed Kati's hands. "I think we will," she answered. "This is my husband, Ross Campbell, Master of Strathmar." To her surprise, Ross took one of the plump redhead's gloved hands and lifted it to his lips.

"Mistress O'Hara," he said.

Kati gave Ross a long look and laughed—a deep, merry sound. "I can see why you grabbed this one," she said to Anne. "What I'd be knowin' is—does he have any brothers?"

"Enough of that talk, me foine girl," Cameron teased with a feigned Irish accent. "Would ye care to dance, Mistress O'Hara? I think that is a Sir Roger de Coverley starting now."

"Aye, that I would," she agreed. "Is that an invitation—or merely an inquiry?"

"Ye see what I'm forced to put up with?" Cameron tucked his arm firmly through Kati's and led her toward the music.

Anne tapped the floor with the toe of her satin slipper. "Ross . . ."

"Ye want to dance too?"

She nodded hopefully.

"I'd rather take ye upstairs and find a dark room."

Her throat constricted.

"I think you're the most beautiful woman I've ever laid eyes on, Anne Campbell. I want to rip that dress off you and make hot, wet love to you." His fingers scorched her skin as he made small circles on the underside of her forearm. "I want you now," he said huskily.

Anne spread her fan and raised it to cover her face, trying to hide the blush she could feel spreading across her cheeks. The thought of doing just what Ross suggested was exciting, and a bubbling sensation ran up and down her spine.

"Well, woman? What say ye?" Ross leaned close and brushed her lips with his own. "Shall we have our own celebration?"

"Later." It was hard to breathe with his eyes on her . . . with him standing so close he was crushing the hoops under her gown.

"Later," he repeated sensually. Then he winked at her. "Fie on ye. 'Tis a typical woman's answer." He sighed dramatically. "Well, I suppose if we canna make love, then we must dance. M'lady?" He bowed gracefully and offered her his hand.

Anne curtsied and took it.

For nearly an hour, they danced every set. The room grew so warm that servants threw open the windows to let in the night breeze and brought chilled sherbets for all the guests. As the music swirled around them, Anne laughed and enjoyed every step. Twice she danced with her father, and Ross danced with Mistress O'Hara. Cameron was an excellent partner, but Ross was amazing. Country reel or stately minuet, he never hesitated, never missed a graceful bow or turn.

Anne's heart was full to overflowing. Whenever their fingers touched, her pulse quickened. He's my husband, and we've never danced together before, she thought. Just that once . . . when we were with the gypsies. But she'd hated him then and feared him too—so that time didn't count.

When the musicians stopped to rest, Ross

pulled her close. "We can still find a place to hide," he whispered in her ear. She laughed.

The tinkling notes of a harpsichord were coming from the parlor across the hall. "Ladies, gentlemen," Cameron said loudly. "You must all come into the next room. Mistress O'Hara has consented to play for us first. If you remember what I told you last year, you're all expected to sing, or dance, or recite. Any cowards will pay a forfeit—said forfeit to be decided by"—he flashed a grin at Anne—"the Lady Anne."

The brightly gowned ladies and their escorts assembled around the harpsichord. Kati introduced Anne and Ross to several guests they hadn't met earlier, then began to play the delicate instrument again.

"This is your last chance," Ross murmured, nuzzling Anne's neck. "I'll hold them off while you run."

She covered her lips with her fan and suppressed a giggle. "Be good," she reminded him.

"Lord Dunnkell," someone called. "Governor Calvert and his party have arrived."

"Excuse me," Cameron said. "I must greet his excellency. Carry on." He took Anne's hand. "Come with me, my dear. I want you to meet our governor. He's quite an interesting man."

"I'll be right back," she murmured to Ross.

Cameron led her from the room. "Are you enjoying yourself, Anne?" he asked.

"Oh, yes," she replied, "it's a wonderful party. Your friends are all—" She suddenly froze and stared at the man standing by the door in the hall parlor—the man she'd never expected to see again. Bile rose in her throat. "No!" She gasped. "Not you, here . . . it can't be."

Cameron didn't notice. He stepped forward and

offered his hand to the governor. ''Your excellency,'' he said. ''We're so happy to—''

''That's her!'' Murrane cried, shoving past Governor Calvert and jabbing a thick, scarred finger directly at Anne. ''Seize that woman! She's my wife.''

Chapter 21

✧✧✧✧✧

"**N**o!" Anne cried. "That's a lie! He's not my husband." Murrane lunged toward her. She whirled and dashed into the great hall where the musicians were preparing to begin playing again.

Her father stepped into Murrane's path. "What do you—" Murrane's fist slammed into Cameron's jaw and Cameron went down. Murrane ran after Anne and caught her shoulder. Screaming, she tore free from his grasp.

For an instant, he stared down at the handful of pink satin in his hand, then his hooded eyes gleamed as he leered at her exposed bosom. "Enough of this," he growled. "Where do you intend to run now, you faithless slut?"

Sheer terror gave her courage. Ignoring her ripped dress, she ran between an elegantly dressed tobacco planter and his wife to the polished Irish hunt table standing along the far wall of the room and seized a silver punch cup. With unerring accuracy, she hurled it at Murrane's head. "Don't come near me, you bastard. I'll kill you if you come near me!"

Murrane gasped as the cup struck him squarely above his right eye and drew blood. "You'll die for that, bitch," he muttered.

"Who are you?" the planter demanded, thrusting himself forward. "How dare you come—" Murrane turned a black look of contempt and unvoiced threat on him, and the planter pulled his wife away. "This is not our affair . . ." he mumbled.

Anne threw a second cup—it bounced off his chin. "Not if I get you first!" she shouted. "Ross! Help me!" Murrane's twisted expression mocked her. She shuddered with revulsion, her mouth tasted of ashes. If he touches me I'll vomit, she thought, backing against the table.

Murrane charged her. The planter's wife screamed.

"No!" Anne cried. Grabbing the long-handled sterling dipper, she smashed it against his forehead.

Stunned, he staggered back. Anne ducked under his arm and ran back toward the hall parlor, holding her ruined dress up over her breasts. As she crossed the threshold, she saw a soldier's body flying through the air. The blue-coated figure hit the staircase, slid down, and sprawled unconscious at the foot of the steps.

Two more of the governor's guards hung on to Ross's arms. Men and women were shouting and craning their necks to see into the hall. A ship's officer in a red coat stood protectively in front of the governor with drawn sword. Her father sat in the middle of the floor with a dazed expression on his face, blood trickling from the corner of his mouth.

"Cease this at once!" Governor Calvert roared.

Ross twisted and dropped to one knee, coming up so fast that his movements were little more than a blur. There was a crack as he slammed the guards' heads together, then he had Anne by the arm and half lifted, half shoved her to the staircase. Suddenly all she could see was the taut wall made by the back of Ross's torn coat, and a glimpse of steel. Somehow, Ross was holding one of the soldier's swords as he backed up the steps with Anne behind him.

"Hist, now," Ross cautioned. "Dinna come too close if ye wish to see the light of morning." He was breathing hard and his burr was so thick Anne could hardly understand his words. Candlelight reflected off Ross's naked rapier as he moved it slowly back and forth.

"You see, Calvert!" There was no mistaking Murrane's grating voice. "Here is your honest citizen. He's a criminal with a price on his head."

"Put down your weapon, Strathmar," the governor commanded. "I have soldiers outside. You can't escape."

"'Tis a bonny night to try," Ross answered lightly.

"Fitzhugh Murrane is a lying, murdering bastard!" Anne cried. "He's not my husband! He never was!"

The soldier at the bottom of the steps groaned and opened his eyes. He got up on his hands and knees and crawled toward his fallen sword. Murrane was quicker. He grabbed the weapon and advanced on Ross.

"Is this how you colonials uphold the king's justice?" Murrane shouted. "To let an outlaw make fools of the Royal Governor and his escort?"

"Back," Ross hissed to Anne. "Give me room."

"Enough." Cameron was on his feet. He shouted to someone in the doorway. That man threw a loaded pistol to Cameron, and he leveled it point blank at Murrane's chest. "Put down your sword. There'll be no more violence in my home.

We can settle this like men—not beasts. Do you agree, your Excellency?''

"I'll not put myself at his mercy," Murrane snarled. "Tell Campbell to surrender."

Cameron's voice grew soft and dangerous. "Hold your tongue, sir," he said coldly to Murrane. "You are the one who came into my home and struck me down without reason. Ye are the stranger making accusations ye cannot prove."

"All of you! Surrender your weapons at once," the governor ordered. "I have a dozen soldiers outside to enforce my peace."

Cameron glanced at Ross. "What his Excellency says is true. You must put down your sword as well. Further violence will only prejudice the case against you and put Lady Anne's life in danger."

"I'll not give her over to this hellhound," Ross replied heatedly. "Anne is my wife—not his. All he'll have of mine is six inches of steel through his black heart."

"Surrender, Master Strathmar," Governor Calvert declared, "or be shot. I give you my word that the lady will be held in protective custody until the right of this matter is discovered."

"You can't arrest me," Anne protested hotly. "I've done nothing wrong."

"I am a longtime friend of Lady Langstone, Lady Anne's mother," Cameron said, ignoring Anne's outburst. "With your permission, Governor, I will take responsibility for her safety."

"No!" Murrane growled. "She's mine. I have the marriage contract. Anne is my legal wife. Regardless of her immoral conduct, I'll take her back."

Anne's gray eyes darkened to slate, and she trembled with anger. "I don't need anyone to take responsibility for me, and I'd sooner hang than go ten steps with that foul dogsbody," she said.

"I am of legal age and sound mind. Do you think me such a fool that I don't know my own husband?"

Governor Calvert smoothed the wrinkles from his plum-colored coat. "Lord Dunnkell is well known to us. The Lady Anne may remain here at Gentleman's Folly during the investigation." The governor pursed his lips. "Providing, of course, that you can assure us, sir, that there will be some respectable lady to chaperone—"

"I am a married woman," Anne insisted. "I need no—"

"I will be happy to assist Lord Dunnkell," Kati O'Hara interrupted. "If that's all right with you?" She glanced at Cameron. He nodded. "I will stay here with Lady Anne, or she is welcome in my home."

"I said—" Anne began.

"Quiet, woman," Ross snapped.

"Remember to whom you're speaking," Cameron reminded Anne sharply. "Governor Calvert's word is law here."

"That's settled," Governor Calvert said. "Lord Murrane, Strathmar, put down your weapons." He pointed to Ross. "You are under arrest, sir, for breaking the peace. You will be held in the jail until I've reached a decision on the right of this affair." He frowned. "Clearly, Lady Anne seems to have two husbands. We may be far from England here, but we are English citizens, and we do live by English law."

"She is my wife," Murrane muttered stubbornly as he lowered his sword.

"Lying pig!" Anne spat.

"Strathmar." The governor's voice rang with authority.

"Please," Anne implored Ross. "I don't want you shot. You must do as the governor says."

He glanced at her over his shoulder. "For ye, Anne," he said. He half turned and offered her his weapon, hilt first. "The only one I've ever surrendered to."

"That's better," Cameron said. He returned the pistol to its owner. "Now we can— Look out!"

Anne screamed as Murrane lunged forward and drove his sword into Ross's midsection. Instantly, Cameron was on Murrane, knocking the weapon from his hand as soon as Murrane withdrew his bloody sword.

Ross's face turned the color of whey as he slumped back, clutching his side. Blood seeped between his fingers. Anne dropped the sword, and it slid down the steps. "Daddy was right," Ross managed. "He said never . . . never give up . . ." He gritted his teeth against the pain.

Two planters pinned a struggling Murrane to the floor. Cameron rose and grabbed Ross as he slumped forward, only half conscious.

"Ross . . ." Anne cried. The room was spinning around her. Suddenly she couldn't breathe, and waves of nausea swept over her. "Damn you," she muttered between clenched teeth. "Don't you dare die on me."

Cameron lowered Ross to the floor, and Anne lost sight of him as men gathered around. She gripped the banister and tried to keep from fainting. Curious faces stared at her, and women pointed.

"Two husbands—did you hear the governor?" a woman's shrill voice quipped.

"The deceitful jade. Look at her," said another.

A firm arm locked around her waist. "Let me take you upstairs," Kati O'Hara said.

"No," Anne protested. "I must know how—"

"He'll be all right," Kati said. "It's a flesh wound. Men can lose a lot of blood without dy-

ing—believe me, I know." She tugged at Anne.
"Come. It's better if we don't provide a—"

"I won't leave him," Anne said stubbornly.

"Your father will look after him," Kati said quietly. Anne's eyes widened. "Yes, I know who you are. Cameron told me. Come, you'll be safe here."

"I don't want to be safe!" Anne argued. "I want to be with Ross. He needs—"

Cameron stood up and came partway up the stairs. He threw her a compassionate look. "Go with Kati," he said to Anne. "I'll see that Ross is seen by a physician. The wound isn't fatal."

Anne shook her head. Tears clouded her vision, and she was certain that if she let go of the banister, she'd be unable to stand. "You're lying to me," she said. "He's dying, isn't he?"

Cameron shook his head. "Nay, lass, he won't die of this." He motioned to Kati and turned back to direct the men around Ross. "Handle him gently. He's sore wounded—he's not a sack of oats."

"Come," Kati urged. "It's best if we go."

Reluctantly, Anne let Kati take her upstairs to a bedchamber. An anxious maid followed close on their heels.

Once the three women were in the room, Kati settled Anne onto the bed and waved to the servant. "Bring cold water and a cloth for Lady Anne's head—and a glass of brandy."

"I don't want anything to drink," Anne murmured. "It's not fair. Why was Ross arrested and not Murrane? Murrane is—"

"The brandy's for me," Kati said, "and apparently this Murrane is a very wealthy and powerful man. Therefore his excellency put Ross under arrest." She stroked Anne's hair soothingly. "It means nothing. Governor Calvert is a fair man. Ross will be heard.''

Anne buried her face in her hands. ''He has to be. They can't—'' She felt suddenly nauseous again. ''I . . . I think I'm going to be sick,'' she admitted.

''There, there,'' Kati soothed, unfastening the laces of Anne's torn gown. ''Let's get this dress off you.'' She removed the gown, then loosened Anne's corset so that she could breathe easier, and pulled a coverlet up over her. ''Trust Cameron,'' she said. ''He will let nothing happen to your husband.''

''He already has,'' Anne said fiercely. ''He let him be run through with a sword. If Ross dies . . . If he dies, I'll kill Murrane myself.''

Kati chuckled. ''Your father didn't tell me you were such a fiery little hothead. A sweet lady, he said.''

The maid brought water and the glass of brandy. Kati downed the liquor in three swallows. Anne breathed deeply, trying to gain control of her protesting stomach. The black girl gave Anne some of the cool water, and she took it sip by sip.

''That's it,'' Kati said, ''relax. Jassi,'' she said to the maid, ''bolt the door, please. Bolt it and sit in front of it. We need no prying eyes or ears from curious neighbors.''

''Murrane isn't my husband,'' Anne said. Waves of nausea were still making her lightheaded. She clenched her fists so hard that her nails cut into her palms, and she shut her eyes.

''Thank God for that,'' Kati proclaimed, ''for poorer husband material I've seldom seen.'' She rubbed Anne's forehead. ''You've no need for such carrying on in your condition—it's bad for the baby.''

Anne's eyes snapped open. "What? I'm not with child."

"No?" Kati's voice couldn't conceal her amusement. "You could have fooled me." She laid a palm on Anne's belly. "You're sick to your stomach, aren't you? And I'll wager your breasts are tender."

"Yes," Anne admitted. "I'm nauseous, but this is evening—not morning. Women in the family way have morning sickness."

Kati scoffed. "Where have you been living your life, girl—in a sealed jar? You've the look of one bearing to me. Unless you and that great braw of a man have been living like holy saints." She cut her eyes at Anne. "I didn't think so. I know I wouldn't if I were you."

Anne's heartbeat quickened as a ray of hope pierced her utter desolation. Could it be true? Was she going to have Ross's child? "I can't be," she said, meeting Kati's honest green-eyed gaze with her own. "I haven't missed my flow."

"Mmm," Kati mused. "You certainly look . . . Has it been different . . . less?"

"Yes, it has, but—"

"I've heard of women who bleed for a few months. You've been through a lot from what your father says. Best you take it easy if you want to carry this babe to term."

"Ross is my husband," Anne said with a note of desperation in her voice. "If I am . . . if I am with child, it's his. I won't go anywhere with Murrane—I don't care what your governor says. I'd rather be dead."

Kati went to the window. "They're bringing a carriage around for Strathmar. There's a physician in the town. They must be taking him there." Kati motioned to the maid. "Jassi, your master is going with Lady Anne's husband."

"Which one, Miss Kati?"

"Strathmar." Kati suppressed a smile. "Her only husband. I want you to go downstairs and speak to the musicians. Can you do that?"

"Yes'm."

"Good. Tell them that Lord Dunnkell won't need them anymore tonight. They may leave a bill. Also, I want you to find Sterling Comegys and ask him to see to the guests' departure. He will know what to do."

When the black girl was gone, Kati turned back to Anne. "I don't know your Ross Campbell," she said, "but I know Cameron Stewart. If you're his daughter, you're a good judge of men. I'll say a prayer for your Ross . . . and for you." She blew out the candle by the bed. "Try and get some rest. Your father is an influential man, and he's a friend of Governor Calvert. If anything can be done for your husband, Cameron is the one to do it."

"Pray God, he can," Anne murmured. "For if judgment goes against us, or if Ross's wound turns bad, I don't think I could go on living."

"So I've heard other women say," Kati replied softly, "but saying is easier than doing. And if you do carry Strathmar's babe, you have more reason than not for living."

It was nearly noon the following day when Cameron's servant drove Anne and her father to the Annapolis jail. Again, at Cameron's insistence, Anne was richly gowned in another of Leah's dresses, and adorned with magnificent jewelry from her father's personal collection.

"If Ross is put on trial, we want to impress the good citizens of Annapolis that you are a genteel lady of high birth. Most men are easily deceived," Cameron said wryly. "They welcome anything that confirms their rigid opinions. You must appear too pure and sweet to have run from a lawful husband into the arms of a lover. And if you are innocent, then it follows that the Master of Strathmar must also be."

Anne leaned forward on the carriage seat and chewed her lower lip. The fingers of her left hand unconsciously rubbed her amulet.

"I see you kept the gift I gave you as a child," her father said lightly. "It was my mother's, and her mother's before that."

Puzzled, Anne glanced at him.

"The necklace. Of course, there are two other pieces. I separated it, years ago."

"Oh . . . yes." She gripped the charm tightly. "Did you know . . ."

"Of the legend?" He patted her right hand. "My mother told me stories, of course . . ." Cameron sighed and gazed directly into her eyes. "I'm a practical man, well educated. I always prided myself on my intelligence." His eyes twinkled. "Would a sophisticated man, such as myself, believe in fairy tales? Perhaps I do . . . perhaps not."

He looked down at Anne's hand. Heavy rings adorned each of her fingers: diamonds, rubies, and a flawless emerald. "You must keep the rings," he said, "as a payment on gifts owed."

She raised her gaze to meet his. "You owe me nothing."

He sighed. "I've been a selfish man, Anne, but I suffered for it. Not one of your birthdays ever passed that I did not grieve for you, not a Christmas or a May Day that I didn't wish to have you with me. I sent your mother money, of course, but I was afraid to be too open about giving you gifts. There was talk when you were born. Your mother and I . . ." He flushed. "We were not as discreet as we might have been."

"Barbara was never discreet about her . . . friends."

"I didn't give you the necklace to hurt you—ye must know that. My mother entrusted it to me and made me promise to give it to my true daughter. It had been in her family for so many centuries. By giving it to you, I claimed you as my daughter, at least in my own mind. I only hope it hasn't brought you too much unhappiness."

"Didn't I . . ." No, she hadn't told Cameron about what had happened with Ross on the riverbank. It was something so personal that she wasn't certain she ever could. Did the necklace contain real power? Had the amulet brought her husband back from death?

Troubled, Anne looked away at the sturdy frame houses along this wide dirt street. In one yard, a little dark-haired boy, too young for breeches, ran after a puppy. She swallowed against the thrill that rose in her throat. Did she truly carry Ross's babe? If it was a boy, would he look like this adorable child? The puppy had allowed itself to be captured. Now, boy and dog were being carried back to the house by a laughing maid.

Cameron squeezed her hand again. "Don't worry, child. He will be fine. I told you this morning. The loss of so much blood is always frightening, but your husband is as strong as an ox. Governor Calvert was furious with Murrane. He fined him one hundred pounds sterling and confined him to his ship. Neither Murrane nor any of his men are permitted to set foot on the dock until the governor hands down a decision." Cameron called to the driver. "Pull over here. We can walk around the corner."

The coachman reined in the matched pair of black horses. Cameron waved him to remain in his seat, pushed down the folding carriage step, and assisted Anne from the vehicle. He nodded to a passing merchant and tucked his arm through his daughter's.

"Smile to the passersby," Cameron whispered. "Let them all see you've nothing to be ashamed of. Mistress Colby." He removed his three-cornered hat and nodded to the elderly woman going by in a pony cart. "How is your husband's gout?"

Anne flashed her a demure smile.

"Herbert's well . . . Thank you, Lord . . . Lord Dunnkell," Mistress Colby replied, plainly flustered. Her small white dog yapped at them and scrambled up on the cart seat as the fat brown pony ambled by.

Cameron leaned close to Anne. "Good girl. My mother would be as proud of you as I am. She was a strong woman, Anne, and she admired steel in other women." He nodded to a spare man in black coming toward them with a seaman's rolling gait. "Captain Taylor. A good day to you, sir."

"Lord Dunnkell." The captain removed his hat and bowed to Anne as he walked past.

"I wish I could have known her . . . your mother," Anne said.

"You're very like her," her father answered with a waver in his voice. "You've her hair and eyes, but the similarity goes deeper. She was a tiny woman, but she once put King William of Orange in his place when he tried to take advantage of her widowhood. He sent her an apology and this ruby ring to make amends." Cameron chuckled and indicated the ring on Anne's little finger. "Mother said she'd rather have a respite on her taxes than the apology, but she kept the ring. We were so poor that one Christmas we ate oat porridge for dinner at the high table—but mother wouldn't sell the ring. She said it gave us dignity." His blue eyes twinkled. "Dignity is what we're showing the masses today, my dear."

"You were in desperate conditions, yet she never sold the amulet?" Anne asked.

Cameron shook his head. "Nay, lass. She'd have sold me sooner. She never felt the Eye of Mist belonged to her—I think maybe it was the other way around." He stopped in front of a small brick house. "This is the jailer's home. I've already gotten permission for us to visit the prisoner. Prepare yourself, Anne, a jail is a jail. There are no gentlemen's cells here."

Beyond the house was another building. A mastiff chained beside the outside steps growled as they walked by. Cameron knocked on the door, and it was opened by a burly red-haired man named Tom Pate.

The guard peered around suspiciously. "Lord Dunnkell?"

"And the Lady Anne to see Strathmar." Cameron glared at Tom. "This visit has been approved," he said sternly. He glanced with contempt at the man's stocking cap. "Where are your manners?"

The guard flushed beet-red and snatched off his hat. "This way, sir, yer ladyship." He led them into a sparse room, through a doorway, and down a flight of wooden stairs. As he descended the steps, the guard took a lit lantern from a hook on the wall. "Mind yer step, it's steep," he warned.

Anne blinked to accustom her eyes to the darkness on the cellar level. It was cooler here, and damp. The jail reeked of stale beer and urine, and the ceiling and walls were thick with cobwebs. Anne shuddered. She hated spiders.

Brick walls broken by thick wooden doors rose

out of the dirt floor. The jailer held the lantern high, and Anne could make out a square hole in the nearest wooden door barely larger than a man's hand and covered with an iron grate. Anne jumped as a man scraped a tin cup across the inside of the barred peephole.

"Where the hell's my dinner, Tom?" the prisoner demanded. He followed his question with a string of foul profanity that scorched Anne's ears.

"Shut up, Wills. They's a lady out here." The guard looked at Anne. "Don't pay no attention to him, ma'am. He don't know no better—he's a pirate."

Wills slammed the cup against the grate again. "Ye ain't gettin' no dinner," the jailer shouted. "Ye're hangin' at dusk, and we ain't wastin' no meat on a hanged man." The second cell was empty, and the door stood ajar. Tom led them to the third door and unlocked it with a large iron key. "The lady can go in, but ye must stay out here," he explained apologetically. "Rules of the jail, sir. I don't make 'em, but I lose my job if I don't keep 'em." He raised the lantern again.

Anne shuddered as she saw Ross lying on a pile of straw in the far corner of the dirt-floored cell. A bloody bandage was wrapped tightly around his middle. His face was bruised and swollen, his hair loose and tangled with bits of straw. "Oh, Ross," she cried aloud. She pushed past the guard and ran to her husband. "What have they done to you?"

"Anne?" Ross demanded, rising unsteadily to his feet. "What do ye do here?" He shaded his eyes against the light. "Damn it, Cameron. She's no business here."

Anne threw her arms around him. "I belong wherever you are," she said loudly, pressing herself against him. "I was so frightened." Ross was as unyielding as the brick walls; Anne could feel the anger emanating from him. "Darling," she said with false sweetness. "Have you no kiss for your wife?"

Ross's features were immobile in the flickering lantern light, but she sensed his bewilderment at her unnatural behavior. She lifted her face expectantly.

"Kiss me," she hissed. When he lowered his head to do so, he put one hand on her waist. Smiling up at him, Anne slid a knife from the folds of her full ruffled sleeve and passed it into his hand. "Because I love you," she murmured.

"Dearest Anne." Ross's fingers locked around the hilt of the knife. "I canna tell ye how much this means to me."

He released her. Heart pounding, she backed away a few steps. "I can guess," she said breathlessly. She brought her fingers to her lips and blew him a silent kiss as tears filled her eyes.

Chapter 22

❦

"Time's up," the jailer said, returning down the wooden stairs. "I ain't supposed to let ye stay in there long." He looked apologetically at Cameron, standing near the cell's open doorway, and scratched the back of his dirty neck. "It's the rules, m'lord."

Cameron flipped him a silver shilling. "I'd ask no honest man to break his trust, Tom Pate, but I would take it as a personal favor if you'd leave the lantern and return to the top of the stairs."

"I couldn't do thet . . ." Warily, the guard hefted the weight of the silver. " 'Tis against—"

Cameron smiled with Stewart charm. "Use your head, Tom. The stairs are the only way out of the prison. I give you my word as a gentleman that I have no intention of helping this man to escape. There are muskets in the guard room above. If you stand in the doorway with a gun, you won't harm anyone by allowing us a little privacy—and you'll be the richer."

The redhead frowned.

"Two minutes. And I'll lock the cell door when we leave. What harm can it do?"

"Two minutes, then," Tom said reluctantly, "but I swear to ye—lord or no lord—if ye try any tricks, I'll blow ye to Judgment Day."

Cameron waited until he heard Tom's heavy

footsteps on the stairs, then he entered Ross's cell. "Campbell." His voice was low and angry. "What did she give ye?"

Anne and Ross came to the open doorway of the cell together. "Nothing," Anne lied. Her knees felt weak, and she could hear her blood pulsing in her head. "I just—"

"Never try to fox an old fox." Cameron's face was hard in the lantern light, and Anne's gaze dropped to the floor. "I told ye to leave this to me. Governor Calvert will allow me to stand bond for Ross. I'll have him out of this cell in twenty-four hours—legally. Where is your sense, girl? This is no time for your reckless heroics."

"Anne has no business here at all." Ross's voice grated with exhaustion. "Send her to my father at Fort Campbell. She'll be safe from Murrane there."

Anne clung to Ross's arm. "No. I won't leave him," she said stubbornly. She'd known that bringing him the knife was risky, but she couldn't bear the thought of him helpless in prison.

"Fie, Anne. Did ye ever stop to think that if the guard had caught you, you'd be a prisoner in the next cell?" Cameron glanced warily toward the stairs. "Ye must put your trust in me, Ross. I'll deal with the governor. I know an excellent barrister in Williamsburg. We'll bring this to trial if need be. We'll prove your innocence and Murrane's perfidy. If we don't, Anne will never be able to hold her head up in decent society, and you'll spend the rest of your life as a wanted outlaw."

"To hell with decent society," Anne whispered hotly. "We'll go west. No one will find us there. Murrane is too rich and powerful for us to receive justice from the court here in the Maryland Colony." It was true, she thought. Nothing mattered but Ross's safety. She didn't care about her old life—she didn't even care if he'd married her for her money. All she wanted was for them to be together—and if she had to live like an Indian squaw to have Ross, then she'd put on paint and feathers and learn to chew bearhides.

"If I take Anne into the Ohio Country, none will touch us—of that ye can be certain," Ross said. He tightened his arm around her. "I believe ye mean us well, Cameron, but—"

Anne heard a stranger's insistent voice from the room above, then candlelight glowed at the top of the steep stairway. "You've another visitor, Master Campbell," Tom yelled down. "I can't let him in until the others leave."

"Do you know who it is?" Cameron asked.

Ross shook his head. "Nay. Unless it be someone who works for me at the store."

Cameron took hold of Ross's arm. "I'll go to the governor now," he promised. "Do nothing you'll regret. Remember, if ye escape from here, you'll become the criminal they say you are. And if you did get away—then what? Ye might be content to live as an Indian in the backwoods, but Anne never will. When ye carried her off from that church, you plucked an English rose, not a wildflower. My daughter loves you with all her heart, but she needs books and music, the companionship of other women of her class. She needs her family. Don't force her into a life of hardship that will stifle her spirit, lad."

"I'll go where you go and live as you live, Ross," Anne said passionately. "Don't worry about me. I'll learn to be the wife you need."

"Listen to her," Cameron said with pride in his voice. "You're a strong man, Ross Campbell and used to doing things your way. Mayhap it's time you learned to bend a little. Force Anne to bend too far to your ways, and she'll snap like an oak sapling in high wind. She might well run off with you now—but what of the years to come? The two of ye can make a life here in America if you'll have the patience and courage to work this out sensibly. And common sense says ye must be released from this jail legally.''

Ross's eyes narrowed. ''I want your promise that you won't let Murrane touch her—no matter what,'' he demanded fiercely of Cameron.

''She's my daughter.'' Stewart blue eyes locked with eyes of Campbell black.

''Swear,'' Ross demanded.

''Aye. I do so swear,'' Cameron answered softly. ''On my mother's soul, and on my hope of salvation. Murrane shall not have her.''

''Your time is up, Lord Dunnkell,'' the jailer called.

''Not yet,'' Anne pleaded. Ross was weak from loss of blood, and the thought of leaving him here in this awful place was almost more than she could bear. ''I can't go yet. Please ask the jailer for a little more time.''

''Don't worry about him,'' her father said. ''It will be all right. Have faith, child.'' He turned and walked through the darkness.

''Where's the lady?'' Tom asked as Cameron ascended the steps. A small, thick man in a powdered wig and gentleman's attire stood behind the jailer. ''Solicitor Andrew Freeman to see the prisoner, sir. He can't go down until the lady comes up.''

''I'm certain Master Freeman won't mind, will you?'' Cameron passed Tom another coin. ''Lady Anne is concerned for her husband's health, and rightly so. She will be along directly.''

The solicitor nodded to Cameron and went down the stairs, candlestick in hand.

"Wait," Tom insisted. "I said—"

"Don't trouble yourself," Cameron soothed. "You know Master Freeman. He handles Governor Calvert's personal affairs from time to time. Surely you don't believe him a conspirator in an escape plot."

"No, but rules is—"

"Aye, and ye have done your job admirably. I intend to praise you to the governor myself." Cameron beamed at the jailer. "I'm on my way to see him now. I'm certain . . ." Cameron kept up a running conversation as the guard unlocked the front door and let him out.

Below in the prison, Andrew Freeman greeted Ross nervously. "Good day, Master Strathmar."

"Not the best place to conduct business, is it?" Ross asked lightly. He introduced Anne, explaining that Freeman had acted as solicitor for the family for many years. "I have the greatest trust in Andrew," he added.

"You can imagine how distressed I was when I heard that you were incarcerated, Master Strathmar." He cleared his throat. "I received a letter from my brother's firm in London yesterday, sir, concerning the land purchase."

Ross nodded. "Aye." He looked down at Anne. "Before I set sail for Scotland, we instructed Andrew to make contact with the Englishman who claimed Wanishish-eyun and begin negotiations to buy the land from him." He sighed. "At that time, Daddy and I were certain that we'd have the money from his earldom to pay for it."

Freeman looked uncomfortable. "We did find out who owned the land grant, sir, but we haven't been able to inquire about purchasing it." He glanced at Anne. "Did you wish me to give you my full report here, sir? In front of the lady . . ."

Ross grinned for the first time since Anne had arrived at the prison. "Aye, man, get on with it. She is my wife—I have no secrets from her."

"Well . . ." Andrew Freeman drew himself up importantly and adjusted his wire spectacles. "Finding the lawful owner required time but no real skill. It seems the land grant has remained in one family since the time of the Restoration. The problem is that the present owner . . . well . . ." Freeman made a droll sound in his throat. "It seems the man we were hunting for is dead, and the new heir is missing. He left his title to a nephew, but all else—part and parcel—went to his young widow."

"And? And? Get on with it. How can the lady be missing?"

"I'm not certain, sir. Rather, I do know why she's missing. It's quite the talk of London. Naturally, if no one can find her, we can't find her either. And if we can't find her, it's impossible to inquire about purchasing the land grant."

"Who is this lady?" Anne asked. "I know a good many people of quality. Perhaps she is an acquaintance of mine."

Freeman rocked forward on the balls of his small feet and handed Ross a packet of papers. "We are searching for the Marchioness of Scarbrough, widow of the late marquis." The solicitor leaned closer. "All we could learn of the poor Lady Anne was that she'd been kidnapped at her own wedding last winter and has never been heard of since."

Anne was stunned. "You're not serious," she said. "If this is some sort of jest, I find your humor quite—"

"Madam," Freeman replied indignantly, "it is not my habit to make light of my duties."

"Nay," Ross agreed. His dark gaze flicked from

Freeman to Anne and back to the solicitor. "Andrew is a serious man. Are ye certain of what ye say, man? The land that Fort Campbell is built on belonged to the late Lord Scarbrough?"

"It did. He left it, as I said . . ." The solicitor scowled at Anne. "He left the property to his widow, the Lady Anne, born Anne Fielding of Langstone."

Anne stepped back away from Ross and clasped her amulet. It wasn't possible. She'd heard Henry speak of a land grant in America but . . . She swallowed to ease the tightening of her throat as butterflies fluttered in the pit of her stomach. "I . . . I didn't know," she whispered, feeling suddenly giddy.

"Is this missing lady of legal age?" Ross asked.

"Yes, sir."

"Then it is with this mysterious Lady Anne that I must conduct my business."

Freeman pushed his glasses higher on his nose. "Most assuredly, Master Strathmar."

"That's all I need to know, Andrew," Ross said. "Thank you for your prompt attention to the matter."

Freeman looked puzzled. "Do you wish us to continue the search for the missing lady?"

Ross smiled. "Nay, that will not be necessary. When this nonsense with Baron Murrane is settled, I'll be in to talk with you. But ye may consider that your search was most successful."

Anne didn't speak again until Andrew Freeman was gone. "I can't believe it," she murmured. "How could I be the owner of Fort Campbell? I never knew it existed until you took me there. I—"

"All this time," Ross interrupted. "Yours from your dead husband." He took her hands and pulled her close. "Mayhap 'tis more magic, hinney. But magic or nay, 'tis a muckle weight off my shoulders. And a man could do worse than have a witch for a wife.''

His touch sent thrills up and down her spine. ''And a woman could do worse than have a feathered barbarian for a husband,'' she said softly, and her heart filled with love for him as she tilted her face up to meet his tender kiss.

Three days later, Anne stood beside Ross's bed and watched out the window as the physician drove away down the tree-lined lane of Brandon and Leah's house. ''The doctor is right, you know,'' she said. ''You do have a dangerous wound. You must rest if it's going to heal properly.''

Ross tucked his hands behind his head and lay back against the heaped pillows. ''Ye make me feel like a babe, fussing over me. I've been run through with a sword before.''

''This time you lost a lot of blood, and Dr. Johnson says there is infection.''

''Aye. And what did he suggest? He wanted to bleed me more.'' Ross grimaced. ''I've no faith in your English physicians. If Leah were here, she'd make me a poultice that would draw out the poison.''

''Well, she isn't here, and you'll have to make do with me as a nurse.'' Anne sat on the bed and clasped his big hand in hers. ''Remember what my father said. You have to learn patience.''

Cameron had done as he'd promised. He'd convinced Governor Calvert to release Ross from the jail. Anne suspected that her father had put up his plantation as bond, and the thought that he would do so for Ross made her all warm inside.

''The governor has set a guard on the dock to

make certain Murrane obeys his instructions about not coming ashore," Cameron had said when he'd accompanied them from the jail to Brandon's manor house. "It may be months before Governor Calvert's letters reach London and he receives an answer. Meanwhile, I've asked your solicitor, Freeman, to send to Scotland for a copy of your marriage lines. The dominie who performed the ceremony may be dead, but he should have recorded and filed it with his church. I've never known a clergyman to fail to do so. When Murrane sees how long a wait he'll have before the matter comes to court, I'll wager he'll sail back to England, and you'll have heard the last of him."

Her father had returned last night, and again this morning. It was at his insistence that Dr. Johnson had come once a day to treat Ross's wound. "I've seen strong men take lockjaw and die in agony from far less than Ross's injury," Cameron had said. "Since you've had the good sense to choose a Scot, the least we can do is keep him alive to plague you."

As glad as Anne was to have Ross out of jail and with her, she was greatly troubled that he was still running a low-grade fever. And despite the fever, it was nearly impossible for her to keep him in bed.

"Ye'll make a milksop of me," Ross protested. He'd thrown Brandon's purple velvet dressing gown across the room so that he wore nothing beneath the sheets but the bandages and his own pride. She had brushed his long hair back and tied it at the nape of his neck with a red silk ribbon. Even with his unnaturally pale complexion, Anne thought he was the most virile-looking man she'd ever seen.

She smiled. "I hardly think a few days in bed

and decent medical care will turn you into a spring lamb." She raised his hard hand to her lips and ran the tip of her tongue across his knuckles. "You must be good," she teased. "I have gifts for you, and if you're bad, you'll get nothing."

"Let me guess," he quipped. "Ye have velvet slippers to match that robe." A slow smile spread over his face. "Keep doing what you're doing, hinney, and ye can join me in this bed."

She felt her cheeks grow warm. "Don't you ever think of anything else?"

"Not when I'm naked."

She laughed. "No, you must be serious, Ross. You must take the medicine the doctor left for you, and then I'll give you your presents."

"What did he prescribe—ground dog bones? Or unborn mice, seeped in wine, to be swallowed whole?"

"Ross!" she chided, only half in earnest.

"Any doctor fool enough to want to take more blood from a man who's nearly bled to death would give such nonsense to his patients."

Chuckling, Anne got up and went downstairs to the hall parlor to get the medicine. The physician had left powder to be mixed with wine for fever, as well as laudanum to help Ross sleep. She poured the correct dosages into a silver goblet, then paused, thinking how strong Ross was. If he didn't take enough laudanum, he wouldn't sleep, and if he didn't get his rest, the wound wouldn't heal. She wasn't stupid—too much could kill a man. She didn't want to put Ross in danger, but she did want him to get better as soon as possible. Pursing her lips, she added another spoonful of laudanum and the port, and stirred until the medication dissolved.

The house was unusually quiet. Sunday night

was a holiday for Brandon's servants. They attended church services in Annapolis and then stayed late in the town, visiting friends. Surprisingly, Anne didn't mind the silence. Although she'd spent her entire life surrounded by servants, she found that she enjoyed the privacy of being alone.

She glanced into the great hall and stood for a moment admiring the elegant mahogany furnishings, then went to the window and looked out. Beyond the boxwood hedge stood a man with a musket—Cameron's man. She knew a second guard was posted behind the house; both men had been sent as additional assurance that she had nothing more to fear from Murrane. Satisfied that all was well, she returned to the hall and checked the front door to make certain it was locked before she returned upstairs.

Ross grumbled bitterly as he drank the medication. "It tastes worse than horse piss," he complained.

"I wouldn't know, never having tasted the latter," she said. When he'd drained the glass, she went to a cherry highboy and returned with several objects behind her back. Her mood grew serious as she held out the first, a cream-colored envelope. "This is for you, Ross."

Anne watched with her heart in her throat as he took the letter, opened, and read it. When he raised his gaze to meet hers, his eyes were as hard as glass.

"What is this supposed to be?" he asked.

She moistened her lips nervously. "It's a deed," she murmured. "If the land is mine, as your solicitor said, then it's mine to do with as I see fit. I'm giving it to you, Ross. I . . . I thought you'd be pleased."

The deed was the reason her father had come

to King's Gift the night before. He'd had the papers prepared by Freeman, and all she'd had to do was sign. "If the wording isn't correct, we can have it done again." Her voice was so low it was barely audible. "You went to Scotland . . . you married me to try and buy the land. Now it's not necessary." The knot in her throat made it hard to talk, and her eyes stung with unshed tears. She was giving Ross everything he wanted, knowing that by doing so she was taking the chance that he wouldn't need her anymore.

"What else are ye hiding behind your back? A bag of coin?" There was no hint of tenderness in his tone—his rising fury was evident in the chill of his words.

"Why are you angry with me?" What was wrong? She'd been so certain he'd be happy if she turned the property over to him.

Ross ripped the parchment in half and threw it into the empty fireplace. "To bloody hell with the land," he said. "Do ye think that's what matters to me? Do ye still believe that I count your worth by the gold guineas in your dowry?"

"I . . . I didn't say that." Bewildered, she backed away from the bed. Pain, sharper than any grief she'd ever known, knifed through her.

"Nay, hinney." Gritting his teeth against the discomfort, he got up and came toward her. "Ye didn't say so—I can read it in your eyes."

"Don't," she whispered. "You'll hurt your wound." The ache in her heart had become a numbness that spread through her body like seeping cold.

He took another step and held out his arms to her. "I be not angry with ye, hinney. 'Tis my own harvest I'm reaping." Ross began to weave, and she ran to steady him. "I've wronged ye, Anne," he said.

"You mustn't be up."

"Hist now," he rasped. "It's warm in here—is it not? What did . . ." He blinked and rested his cheek against the crown of her hair. "Ye always had hair like a *silkie.*" He chuckled sleepily. " 'Tis a Scottish mermaid. They be so beautiful that a man canna look upon them without being enchanted." He kissed her hair. "I'm talking nonsense, am I not, sweeting?" He drew in a deep, ragged breath. "What did ye put in that goblet, hinney-lass? Be it aqua vitae, 'tis the strongest I've ever let slip down my . . ."

Anne struggled to lead him back to the bed. "Please, Ross, you'll tear open your wound."

"And what is this?" He captured her hand in his and lifted it so that he could see what she was hiding. "A child's moccasin?"

"Lie down," she insisted.

"Dinna fash me, darlin'. Ye said two gifts, did ye not?"

"You great braw of a man—back to bed, I say." Tugging at him was like trying to move an ox. "If you really love me, Ross, you'll do as I say. Please . . . get back into bed." He licked his lips and swallowed. She knew the laudanum was taking effect quickly.

He grinned. "As ye wish, m'lady. At your service, m'lady. Your wish is my . . . my . . ." He staggered and fell on his hands and knees across the bed. "I love ye, Anne. Do ye understand?" Ross sighed and raised his head. "Love . . . the . . . lady wife." He yawned and pushed himself up on one hand. "Anne! Anne!" he roared.

She started and scrambled across the bed to him. "Shhh, I'm here," she soothed, cupping his chin in her hand. "I'm here. You don't need to shout."

"Mmm." His eyes were heavy lidded. "Don't

want your money," he mumbled. "No money
. . . just my bonny Annie. Keep the land. Keep
it." His deep voice rose to a bellow. "Keep the
bloody land."

She threw her arms around his neck and pulled
him against her. Tears streamed down her cheeks,
and she rocked to and fro cradling him. "Fie on
you, Ross Campbell," she murmured, "for you're
so drunk on laudanum that you can't hear what
I'm saying to you."

"I . . . I can hear," he answered sleepily.

She recovered one baby moccasin from the cor-
ner of the bed and held it inches from his eyes.
"This is your gift," she managed between sobs.
"I'm with child, Ross . . . your child."

He chuckled. "It's . . . it's about . . . time."

She took his face between her hands and shook
him. "So it's all right about the land," she said.
"I don't care. I'm staying with you forever, Ross.
Do you hear me? Forever. I don't care if we live
in a wigwam or a hollow tree. I just want to be
with you."

"Hollow tree," he repeated. "Live with my
bonny Annie in a hollow tree." He closed his
eyes, and his breathing grew deep and regular.
Then, just as Anne started to ease his head onto
a pillow, one dark eye snapped open. "Give the
land to the baby," he whispered. "A christening
gift . . . from a beautiful . . . *silkie.*" He shut his
eye; his features relaxed, and he sank into a
drugged sleep.

For a long time, Anne held him, watching the
steady rise and fall of his bare chest. Then, when
his weight cramped her arms, she lowered his
head onto a pillow and covered him with a sheet.

"What have I let myself in for?" she asked, and
then she laughed softly. She leaned over and
kissed his lips, then wiped her tearstained cheeks.

At least life will never be boring, she thought. She looked around for the mate to the moccasin and found it on the floor beside the bed. "Will you remember in the morning?" she asked him, "Or will I have to tell you all over again that you're going to be a father?"

She felt as though a great burden had been lifted from her shoulders. Murrane's threat meant nothing if Ross really loved her. And he had refused the land that meant so much to him.

She stretched and ran her fingers through her hair. Twilight was fast fading. She sighed, feeling the weariness in her muscles despite her inner elation. It was too early to retire for the night, and she knew she needed to give him another dose of medication later, but . . . It wouldn't hurt to lie down, she thought, just for a few minutes. Removing her shoes, she climbed into bed fully dressed, molded her body to Ross's, and dropped off to sleep in minutes.

"Anne. Anne, where are you going?" Her mother's voice called to her from the shadows of the orangery. "You can't go to the party dressed like that."

Anne looked down at the doeskin dress she was wearing. The front was beaded in red and blue leaves to match her soft, high moccasins. She glanced back at Barbara and laughed. "Of course I can," she answered. "I can wear anything I want. It's my birthday party."

Barbara came closer, and Anne noticed for the first time that the paint and powder on her mother's face were smeared. Her gown was patched and torn, and the heels of her red shoes were run down. "Give me the amulet, Anne," her mother said. "Give me the amulet, and you can wear anything you like."

Anne laughed. "I don't need your permission, Mother. My father said I could go. My father gave me the amulet, and he said I could wear it to my party."

"You can't. If I say you can't . . ."

Anne walked away, out of the orangery and into the bright sunlight. As she walked, Barbara grew smaller and smaller, and her voice grew fainter. Ahead of her were dozens of laughing children running on the thick green grass. There was a Punch and Judy puppet show, and jugglers, and a dancing bear. Her sister Leah was there, and Cameron, and Ross, all laughing and calling to her. Ross was sitting on his big, black horse, waiting for her. She ran to him, and as he lifted her into the air, she looked back over her shoulder. And where the orangery had been, where the manor had jutted into the sky, there was nothing but a crystal clear lake with swans swimming on it.

Anne sat bolt upright in bed and listened. Her heart was pounding, and her mouth was dry. Something had startled her from her sleep. She held her breath and strained to hear. But there was nothing save the soft hoot of an owl and Ross's steady, deep breathing beside her.

She sighed and closed her eyes, snuggling against him. The dream came back to her in bits and pieces. She'd dreamed of Barbara . . . but this was different. She touched her amulet for luck and wiggled deeper into the feather mattress.

From the far corner of the room came the rusty squeak of a cricket. Anne's lips turned up in a smile as she remembered Ross's intoxicated rambling. They'd live in a hollow tree, would they? "If I have anything to do with it, you bonny man," she whispered to her sleeping husband, "I'll fill that house of ours with furniture as fair as any that graces the manor of an English lord."

She had almost drifted off again when the quiet autumn night was shattered by a musket shot.

Chapter 23

Heart pounding, Anne scrambled from the bed and ran to the window. In the moonlight, she could see dark figures running toward the house. One man in the lead brandished a flaming torch. There was a loud scream, and then another shot. "Ross! Ross! Wake up," she cried desperately. She returned to the bed and shook him. "Ross!"

He groaned but didn't move.

The sound of wood splintering made the hair stand up on the back of Anne's neck. There was no doubt in her mind who the attackers were—it had to be Fitzhugh Murrane and his soldiers.

"Ross, please," she pleaded urgently. "You've got to wake up!" Grabbing a pitcher of water off the table, she threw it over his face. He coughed and mumbled something in his sleep. Water soaked the sheet and pillow, but still he lay in deep sleep.

The laudanum, Anne remembered with horror. She'd given him too much, and now when they were in terrible danger, she couldn't wake him. Her fear was so real she could taste it.

She heard glass breaking in a first-floor window and the heavy thud of men's boots in the hall parlor. Frantically, she made her way to the highboy and felt for the third drawer. Ross's pistol was there. She knew it was loaded but not primed. Ross had taught her how to fire a pistol. She'd watched him prime a flintlock a hundred times, but she'd never done it in pitch darkness.

"Campbell! I've come for my wife!" It was Fitzhugh Murrane's voice.

"Bastard," Anne whispered into the darkness. "You spawn of the devil." She smelled smoke. Had they set the house on fire? The walls of the manor were eighteen-inch brick and plaster— would they burn?

Gripping the pistol and the powder horn, she ran back to Ross. His breathing was still unnaturally heavy, and he hadn't moved. "Oh, Ross," she whispered. "What shall I do?" Murrane wanted her. She'd be safe enough, but if he found Ross helpless, she knew without a doubt that he'd kill him.

Downstairs, heavy objects crashed to the floor as furniture was overturned and the house ransacked. Curses and harsh laughter filtered through the wide boards beneath Anne's feet. The thick, acrid scent of smoke was stronger.

"Upstairs! Find them!" Murrane's voice.

With trembling hands, Anne slipped her necklace off over her head and put it around Ross's neck. "Please, God, keep him safe," she whispered. Using all her strength, she wrapped him in the wet sheet and rolled him across the bed and off the far side onto the floor. Ross groaned as his head hit, but he didn't regain consciousness. I must háve given him enough laudanum to fell a horse, she thought.

She got down on her knees and pushed him under the bed, then recovered the pistol and powder horn and hurried out of the room through the side door that led to a dressing chamber.

Moonlight spilled through the single twelve-paned window, and she crouched before it and measured out a small bit of fine black powder into the frizzen pan. Anne's fingers were shaking so hard that the first dusting spilled onto the floor, and she was forced to repeat the process. Loading the gun a second time would be impossible. She knew she'd have only one shot—but one would be enough if she could put that through Murrane's black heart.

A red glow in the window drew her attention, and she stared out at flames leaping from the shake roof of one of the stables. Half-dressed men ran toward the barn with buckets of water but were driven back by the soldiers' musket fire. A woman's scream of terror pierced the hue and cry. Anne saw a slight figure fleeing across the yard with two soldiers in hot pursuit.

Sickened by the senseless violence, Anne ducked away from the window and hurried into the adjoining chamber. She could hear shouts in the upstairs hall, and she knew Murrane was closing in on her. She had to draw him away from Ross, but if she stepped into the hallway, she knew she'd be seen and captured.

Darting to the back right window, she forced it open. Below her, sloping toward the back, was the steep roof of a story-and-a-half-high wing of the main house. Holding tightly to the pistol with her left hand, Anne lowered herself through the open window and dropped onto the roof. She hit the hand-hewn cedar shakes and began to slide toward the edge. A heavy shower just that morning had made the shingles slippery and nearly impossible to hold on to.

Splinters dug into her palms, but she gritted her teeth against the pain and scrambled for a hold on the sharp pitch. She pressed her face against the rough wood, regaining her balance just as her bare toes reached the edge.

"Damn you to hell!" Murrane roared. China crashed, and Anne heard the sound of wood splitting. Torchlight gleamed from Ross's bed-chamber window above. A pistol shot rang out, and Anne stifled a scream as a man cried out in agony.

As she stared up, she lost her grip on the damp roof. She screamed as she slid off and tumbled into thin air. Branches from a cedar tree dug into her legs and arms, scratched her face, and yanked strands of her hair. She remained caught in the tree for what seemed like an eternity before she fell and landed with a thud in a shallow puddle. Miraculously, Ross's pistol was still gripped in her hand.

Sucking in deep lungfuls of air, she stumbled to her feet and took a few steps—right into the arms of a man.

A hand clamped across her mouth, muffling her outcry. The musty smell of man-sweat and fear filled her nostrils. Fury gave her strength, and she clawed at his face with one hand and lashed out with the pistol with the other.

The heavy object glanced off his head. "Uhhh!" her assailant groaned. "Shhh, Lady Anne," the man hissed in pain. "Be still. I won't hurt ye. It's Jacob—footman to Viscount Brandon. What in God's name is happening here? Who are these people? What do they want? They've killed Brian and set fire to the stables."

Anne stiffened and stopped struggling. She re-membered a big footman. "What color is your hair?" she demanded.

"Brown, m'lady," came the puzzled reply.

She breathed a sigh of relief. She couldn't remember the tall footman's name, but his hair was dark brown.

"Did you jump out the window, m'lady?"

"Something like that," she replied.

He took hold of her hand. "This way. I don't think they—"

The darkness exploded with gunshots. Jacob moaned and fell to his knees. A soldier in a leather helmet leaped forward and slashed a sword across the back of the fallen man's neck. Anne shrieked as the footman's head hit the grass with a sickening plop and rolled to her feet.

"Here! Lord Murrane!" John Brown yelled. "Campbell's dead and I've got the woman!" Brown sheathed his sword and lunged for Anne.

"You bastard," she said softly. Leveling the pistol at his midsection, she pulled the trigger. Flame and shot spat from the barrel of the gun. The recoil knocked her flat on the ground.

John Brown clutched his stomach and gave a gasp of astonishment. "Christ," he moaned. "I've been shot."

Anne scrambled to her feet and stared at him.

"I'm hit!" Murrane's lieutenant cried. "In the name of God—I'm hit bad." A dark stain widened on the front of his shirt. Blood seeped between his fingers and dripped onto his loose-fitting soldiers' breeches.

Flames from the burning stable had lit the yard so brightly that Anne could see the whites of Brown's eyes. His face contorted in pain as he staggered back away from her. "Lord Murrane . . ." Brown's voice cracked to a hoarse whisper. "She's here . . . she's . . ." Small trickles of blood ran from his nose and the corners of his mouth. "The woman . . ."

Another soldier materialized from the shadows. He seized Anne's shoulder, and she whirled and smashed him in the face with the pistol. She sprang away before he could recover and dashed across the yard toward the burning barn. A horseman galloped toward her.

"I've got you now, you bitch!" Murrane shouted.

An explosion shattered windows in the house. Anne spun on her heel and screamed Ross's name as she saw flames shooting from the second floor. Then something hard struck her head, and the world dissolved in skyrockets and black velvet.

Pain knifed through Anne's head. As she drifted in and out of consciousness, she was aware of rhythmic movement under her, and the slap of a horse's hooves hitting dirt. She opened her eyes with a start as her mind cleared, and found that she was dangling facedown across the front of a saddle.

"Be still," Murrane ordered, grinding his fist into the center of her back. "Or you'll get the same as your lover."

"Let me go!" she cried. Other horses galloped on either side of her. Two soldiers on foot ran on Murrane's left. "You can't do this," she protested.

"Hold your tongue, slut." Murrane wrenched her head back and struck her jaw so that she saw stars. Her tooth cut the inside of her mouth, and she tasted the salt of her own blood.

"Lord Murrane." A soldier reined his horse close. "Brown's dead. They want to know what to do with him."

"Leave him." Murrane's fist slammed into Anne's shoulder. "You murdering bitch, you've killed the best lieutenant I ever had." His hard fingers tangled in her hair and lifted her head.

"Don't play games with me," he growled. "I know you can hear me."

She kept her eyes shut.

"I'd meant to kill you here—did you know that?" he said. "It would have been easier for you that way, believe me." He shook her head. "Now, I'm taking you home to England, dear wife." His voice was cold. "You'll be seen there at my side, so that no one can deny our marriage. And then . . ." He laughed. "Then you'll suffer an unfortunate accident, and I'll be left a very rich widower."

She swallowed the gorge rising in her throat. Murrane thought Ross was dead. If it was true, nothing Murrane could do to her could hurt her any more than losing the man she loved. But she remembered Ross's unborn child with a rush of fierce protectiveness. Murrane would never let her carry the babe to term . . . or if he did, he would kill it at birth. Never! she decided. If the baby was all she had left of Ross, she'd guard it in this life and the next. Murrane wouldn't live to harm her child.

"We sail with the tide," Murrane continued. "And it will be a very interesting voyage . . . for me." Then he struck her again, and she lost consciousness.

Minutes later, Ross choked and gasped for air.

"Lay him down there," Cameron ordered.

Strange hands were carrying him, lowering him to the ground. Groggily, Ross opened his eyes. A fit of coughing seized him, and he sat up and leaned forward. His eyes stung from smoke, his lungs seemed full of the foul stuff. The sword cut across his ribs burned like fire. He drew a hand across his face. "Anne." His fingers closed around her amulet.

"Ross." Moonfeather's voice penetrated his fogged mind.

"Moonfeather?" His throat was dry and swollen, his speech like that of an old man. He tried to rise, and gentle hands caught him.

"Easy." Cameron's voice. "Easy, Ross. You've breathed in a lot of smoke, and that wound in your side is bleeding again."

Someone—a woman by the feel and scent of her—bathed his face with cool water. Ross blinked again, and his irritated eyes focused on Moonfeather. "What . . . what do ye do here?" he rasped. "Where's Anne?" He rubbed the ancient golden charm. Strangely, he found it comforting.

"Murrane attacked the plantation," Cameron said. "Some of my people saw the fire from the barn. We came as quickly as we could, but we got here too late to catch Murrane and stop him from carrying Anne off." The older man's face was grim. "I've sent a rider to the governor, and another to organize an armed rescue party." He put one arm around Ross and helped him to his feet.

Moonfeather handed Ross his kilt and moccasins. Clenching his teeth, he forced himself to stand alone and put them on as Cameron continued his explanation.

"When we arrived, Leah, Niipan, and another man were bringing you out of the burning house." He motioned toward the blackened walls of the building. "We were able to put out the fire, but the inside's a hell of a mess."

Ross leaned over as another choking fit seized him. His head felt as though it were full of moss, and his tongue seemed too thick for his mouth. The pain in his side was a throbbing ache, but he could bear it. Taking a deep breath, he looked questioningly at Moonfeather. "How did ye know I was still in the house?" he asked.

"I just knew." She touched the amulet around his neck. "Perhaps the Eye of Mist called to me." She grasped his arm. "You must find Anne," she said in a low, tight voice. "She carries your child. If this evil one who has taken her learns of it, he will kill her." Moonfeather's face was pale in the firelight. "If she left you her amulet, she did it out of love, so that the magic would protect you."

Niipan approached and passed a handful of dry leaves to Moonfeather. She nibbled the edge of one, then handed them to Ross. "Chew these," she ordered. "They will clear your head and give you strength." She motioned toward the house.

Ross obeyed without hesitation. The leaves were bitter on his tongue, but he chewed them all and swallowed, washing it down with water from a wooden bucket. The necklace seemed to settle around his neck as though it had always been a part of him. She loved him enough to leave him the amulet she cherished more than anything in the world. Anne, he thought. My Anne. He looked up with a start, realizing that Moonfeather was talking to him.

"We came home early to my Brandon, the children and I," Moonfeather said. "I thought my sister would be waiting here for me. I brought with me an escort of twelve Shawnee warriors to ensure our safety. Take them with you. They are fierce fighters, and they will gladly wet their knives with the blood of Murrane and his followers."

Ross turned hard eyes on Cameron. "Ye be Anne's father. If ye care for her, why are ye here and not hot on Murrane's trail?"

"We came to fight a fire, not a battle," Cameron answered sharply. "We must have weapons and enough men to go against professional soldiers. Murrane hasn't lived to be the age he is without being tough and smart. If I ran off half-cocked against him, chances are my people would be slaughtered uselessly and Anne might be killed in the process. I want my daughter back as much as you do—but I want her alive." He frowned. "Beside, when Murrane and his men rode out of here, they took the road south, away from Annapolis. I want to know why."

Moonfeather handed Ross his knife belt, a Shawnee axe, and a pistol. "I need a bow," he said, "and a good musket."

"Are you fit to ride?" Cameron asked Ross.

"Aye—fit enough for this." Moonfeather's leaves had dissipated the fog in his head, but they had done nothing to calm the raw fury rising in his chest. Murrane had dared to come and take Anne. Even now, while he stood here doing nothing, she was at that butcher's mercy.

Someone shoved a bow and quiver full of arrows into his hands, and he slung them over his back. A musket with a leather strap and a powderhorn followed. Grimly, he loaded the gun, ramming home the lead slug and priming the pan. Anne . . . his Anne. When he caught up with Murrane, the Englishman would wish he'd died on Sheriffmuir Field.

Hoofbeats heralded the coming of a rider on a fast horse. The man yanked the animal up hard, and Ross recognized the horseman as the guard from the Annapolis prison. "Lord Dunnkell," Tom Pate shouted. "M'lord. I rode to Gentleman's Folly, but they told me I could find ye here. The *Cumberland* upped anchor and sailed out of the harbor, sir. On the tide, three—four hours ago." He looked around him at the smoking remains of the barn. "Saints in heaven—what's happened here?"

"Murrane's ship sailed?" Cameron said.

"Three hours ago? That's not possible. He attacked King's Gift less than an hour ago." He ran a hand through his hair. "For the love of God! They rode south—toward the bay."

"He's moved the *Cumberland* and anchored her somewhere off the shore," Ross finished. "Murrane had to break the governor's law to come after Anne. He'd not be fool enough to return to Annapolis Harbor after raiding the plantation and kidnapping Anne."

"I've a fast sloop at my dock," Cameron replied. "The *Cumberland* wasn't built for speed. We can catch her before she gets out of the Chesapeake." He turned back to Tom Pate. "You'll be rewarded for taking the trouble to find me. I want you to ride back to the governor's house and tell him what's happened—wake him if you have to. Tell him we need ships with cannon and men to take the *Cumberland* and save Lady Anne."

Moonfeather stepped close to Ross. "Murrane took the south road. On the shore of King's Gift, in the marsh along the bay, Brandon and I keep a canoe for duck hunting and fishing. Niipan can find it in the dark."

"Bring your sloop," Ross said to Cameron, "and all the fighting men you can gather. I'll track him overland."

"Are you mad, Ross?" Cameron cried. "You can't attack a three-mated merchant vessel with a canoe full of Indians."

But Ross had already yanked Tom Pate from the saddle and swung up in his place. He pulled the horse's head around and dug his heels into the animal's sides. Niipan galloped after him on a gray horse with another Shawnee riding double behind him.

"Good hunting, *jai-nai-nah*," Moonfeather

whispered as her remaining warriors took up the trail at a hard run.

"Crazy fool," Cameron said.

"Aye," Moonfeather agreed as she clasped her amulet in her fist, "that he may be, Father. He could well be riding to his death—but since he is Ross Campbell, he has no other choice."

Murrane was sick. He leaned over the edge of the captain's bunk and threw up into a bucket. "Bring me wine," he ordered Anne as he raised his head and wiped his mouth on his sleeve.

Anne glared at him. She was sitting on the floor as far from Murrane as she could get in this small cabin. Her face was swollen, and one of her back teeth felt loose. She was covered with bruises. Her head ached, and her stomach was none too steady—but her mind was clear. "Go to hell," she answered. The way Murrane was sweating and clutching his chest, his agitation, all pointed to a weak heart. She knew that deliberately provoking him could earn her another beating or even cost her her life, but she had to chance it.

She didn't know if Ross was dead or alive. She prayed that someone had rescued him from the burning house—and that Murrane hadn't shot him upstairs. If her father came looking for her, he'd go to Annapolis. That meant any rescue party would come too late. If she was to save her life and that of Ross's unborn babe, she had to rely on her own wits.

Murrane had ordered the *Cumberland*'s captain to bring the vessel down the bay. They'd anchored as close to shore as possible, lowered the small boats, and come ashore. Anne didn't know where they'd procured the horses some of the them had ridden—she supposed they were stolen, or perhaps Murrane had arranged for part of his force to come overland from Annapolis and meet him.

According to the captain, the *Cumberland* had sailed from Annapolis harbor on the outgoing tide. The ship had ridden at anchor while Murrane and his soldiers attacked King's Gift. They'd used the small boats to return to the *Cumberland,* and then Murrane had expected to set sail before any pursuers could catch up with him.

What they hadn't counted on was a sandbar and an unusually low tide—a combination that had grounded the *Cumberland* until the next incoming tide lifted them off the bottom.

Murrane had gone berserk when he'd learned the ship was stuck. He'd ranted and raved. He'd cursed the crew and the captain—he'd even put a pistol to the master's head and threatened to blow his brains out if he didn't find a way to get the *Cumberland* off the sandbar immediately.

Anne was certain Murrane's tantrum had brought on his sudden illness. He'd dragged her below and locked her in the cabin with him. For the past half hour, she'd been watching him without the slightest trace of pity—hoping his heart would fail and he would die before they could sail for England.

Swearing foully, he staggered to his feet and stood there swaying, clutching his left arm with his right hand. "You bitch," he muttered. "You thought you'd make a fool of me with that half-breed Scot, didn't you?" His face was chalk-white, and his bulging eyes revealed his suffering. "But John Brown made a cannon ball of Campbell's head before you killed him. That was a sight for you, I'll wager."

Anne tensed her muscles and scanned the room for some weapon to use against him if he tried to harm her again. He looked like a man with one foot in the grave, but even if he was dying, he was still dangerous.

"I'm not a well man," he complained in a guttural voice. He waved toward the bottle on the table. "Fetch me wine, woman."

"You're mad," she said defiantly. "You've no right to order me about as though I were your servant. I'm not your wife, Fitzhugh—I never was. God help any woman under your roof."

"Get! Me! Wine!"

"I'd sooner bring you coals in hell." Warily, she got to her feet and took a few steps toward the table. Murrane began to choke again. His roupy cough grated on Anne's nerves and raised gooseflesh on her skin. "You're dying," she taunted him. "You'd be better to spend your last hour praying for forgiveness for your black sins than drinking and cursing."

He lowered himself onto the bunk and sat facing her, panting for breath. "You . . . you think you'll be free if I die?" he gasped. "You're wrong. I've promised . . . promised your services to my men if anything happens to me. It's . . . it's a long voyage . . . to England." He leered at her. "Soldiers need entertainment . . . to keep them from . . . getting stale." He wiped his mouth again with his damp sleeve. "A lady would be . . . a novelty. Don't you think?"

"I won't whore for you, and I won't whore for the filth you employ," she flung back. Anne reached the table and uncorked the decanter. She'd give him the wine if he wanted it—a pity she couldn't lace it with poison. "I'd sooner be dead," she added softly as she approached him with the brimming cup.

He laughed. "You may learn to like it. Soldiers are hard men." He laughed louder at his crude jest. "The softer the lady, the rougher they like their men."

"You swine." She threw the contents of the cup into his face and dodged away from his swinging fist. Murrane let out an angry roar and lunged at her. She ran around a chair and overturned it so that he stumbled over it and fell flat on the floor.

"I'll kill you!" he screamed hoarsely. The veins stood out on his forehead as he rose on one knee and pulled the sword from his sheath. Anne grabbed the wine decanter and hurled that at his head, then ran for the bolted cabin door.

Ross dipped the paddle deep into the water and drove the canoe toward the stranded *Cumberland*. His face and body were smeared with black mud to make him invisible against the dark water. His eyes were fixed on the ship; his ears strained to hear every sound. He was beyond feeling the pain of his wound—every fiber of his being was concentrated on reaching the ship before the sailors in the longboats could tow the vessel free of the sandbar.

Behind him, he heard the rhythmic swish of Niipan's paddle. The third man, Manese, crouching in the center of the canoe, made no sound. He waited, bow in hand, for Ross to give the signal.

The *Cumberland* had anchored where Ross had expected it—had prayed for it to be. His heart had skipped a beat when the clouds had parted long enough for the pale crescent moon to show the silhouette of the three-masted vessel lying only a hundred yards off shore. He knew then that if Anne lived, he would wrest her from Murrane, and if she didn't, he would take many of them with him before he died.

Ross ceased paddling and raised his hand. Deftly, Niipan steered the canoe around the stern of the ship. The *Cumberland* was listing hard to the shoreward; the top deck was barely ten feet above water. Ross laid his paddle in the bottom of the canoe and touched Anne's amulet for luck. Then he handed Manese his pistol. "Give me the time it takes to skin a deer," Ross whispered in the Shawnee tongue, "then fill the sails with fire arrows."

Manese grunted, taking care not to lower the deerskin vest he held over his lap as a shield. Beneath it, glowing coals nestled in a hearth of wet mud between the Shawnee's outspread legs. On either side of the warrior's legs, heaps of dry marsh grass lay ready to fuel the infant fire. The points of Ross's arrows were already wrapped with cedar shavings and leaves.

Ross glanced back toward the shore. It was so dark that it was impossible to tell where water left off and land began—too dark for anyone on the ship to see the ten Shawnee braves swimming toward the merchant vessel from the marsh.

"Watch your back," Niipan warned softly.

"And yours, my brother." The two Indians braced themselves as Ross lowered himself over the left side of the canoe. He let himself sink down, then kicked to propel himself underwater until his hands touched the side of the ship. He took a gulp of air and looked back—the canoe was gone.

Inching along the barnacle-encrusted wood planks, he reached out searching fingers and found a closed cannon port. Cautiously, Ross pulled his hatchet from the tie at his belt and used the blade to pry open the port. Once the cover came loose, it was a simple matter to sink the hatchet blade into the wale and heave himself up and through the open port. He was halfway through when he heard Anne scream.

The sound of her voice stripped away Ross's last vestige of civilization. With the instincts of a hunting wolf, he loped through the darkness of the gundeck. A soldier moved from the shadows to bar his way, and Ross felled him with one blow to the throat. The mercenary went down like a poled ox, his would-be cry of warning strangled as the man's lungs struggled for air. Ross took the ladder to the next deck two steps at a time.

Anne screamed again. Ross flung open the cabin door, and she burst into the dark passageway with a cursing Murrane close on her heels. She stared up at Ross's blackened face in confusion, slowly recognizing him in the dim light, then shrank back against the wall.

Like a shadow that had taken on solid form, Ross leaped through the doorway and met Murrane's sword thrust with the oak handle of his steel trade hatchet. The sword blade cut through the seasoned oak, but not before Ross's left fist arced forward to connect with Murrane's chin. The Englishman's head snapped back, and Ross brought his knee up hard into Murrane's groin. As Murrane fell, Ross twisted the sword from his limp hand.

"Ross." Anne touched him to see if he was real. "You're alive!"

"Aye, hinney," he said. "So it seems. Has the brute harmed ye? Are ye all right?"

"I am now."

His powerful mud-streaked arm clamped around her, and he pulled her against his chest. "Anne," he said. "I feared that ye . . ." He swallowed hard, unable to voice his feelings. "No time . . . We maun get ye out of here before the—"

He broke off as two armed soldiers appeared in

the passageway that led toward the gundeck ladder. Ross pushed Anne behind him and raised
Murrane's sword.

"Help!" Murrane called from the cabin. "All
hands!"

"Topside," Ross said. "Quick now."

Anne dashed for the steps leading to the top
deck. The two soldiers charged Ross. He gave the
leader four inches of steel through the chest; the
second backed away and took aim with a flintlock
pistol.

"Look out!" Anne cried. She yanked the lantern off the wall and heaved it over Ross's shoulder toward the gunman. The glass smashed
against the wall, leaving the passageway black for
an instant, then enveloping it in flames as the
whale oil spread.

The topdeck exploded in a volley of musket
shots and shouting. Bare feet and hobnail boots
pounded overhead. Men screamed, and Anne
heard the shrill whistle as a ship's officer sounded
the alarm. "Fire! We're under attack!"

"Man battle stations!"

Ross grabbed Anne's hand. Together they ran
up the steps and out onto the deck. "Keep low,"
he ordered.

An aft staysail and the mainsail were already in
flames. Anne ducked as a fiery arrow flew into
the rigging over her head. Ross knocked a sailor
out of the way and gathered a boarding net off
the deck. Before anyone could stop him, he
heaved it over the starboard side.

A soldier rushed at him with drawn sword. Another man ran toward Anne. She dodged around
the mast and collided with a ship's officer. Anne
ducked under his arm, and the soldier ran him
through with the sword.

Smoke was pouring from the hatchway leading

to the captain's cabin, and bits of flaming sails were drifting down to the deck. One sailor had climbed halfway up the mizzenmast to throw water on the burning sail.

"To me!" Murrane shouted.

Anne whirled to see the baron standing in the hatchway, a pistol in his hand. He leveled it in Ross's direction, and Anne screamed a warning. The air rang with the clash of steel against steel. Three of Murrane's soldiers backed Ross toward the railing; one blocked Murrane's line of vision. Murrane turned and fired at Anne. She threw herself facedown to the deck and rolled. Murrane came after her. She scrambled to her feet as a shout of alarm went up from the crew.

Shawnee war whoops echoed over the deck. Two of the soldiers fighting Ross backed away as painted, axe-wielding Indians swarmed over the starboard rail.

A smoldering yard fell onto the deck with a crash, trapping Anne with her back against the quarterdeck. Her breath caught in her throat as Murrane slid a wicked-looking knife from his belt and staggered toward her.

"If I'm bound for hell," he taunted her, "I'll take you with me."

"Ross," she cried. "Help!" She turned to run to the rail, but Murrane seized her arm. Slowly he brought the point of the knife down until it rested against the hollow of her throat.

"Beg," he commanded. "Beg for your life, slut."

A wall of flames framed Murrane's scarred face as he leaned close enough for Anne to smell his foul breath. I'm going to die, she thought, and suddenly the fear trickled away, leaving her breathless but defiant. Her gaze locked with his stubbornly, and for a heartbeat she read a haze of bewilderment in his eyes.

"Beg," he repeated. He pushed the knife tip into her skin, and she felt a warm drop of blood well up on her throat.

"Whoreson," she whispered boldly. "Do it if you dare."

Then Ross appeared in the flames, as beautiful as the fallen angel she'd once accused him of being. A war cry issued from his lips as he grabbed Murrane and hurled him to the deck.

"It's you," Murrane gasped, recognizing Ross for the first time. "You're supposed to be dead." Ross wrenched his wrist, and Murrane's knife went spinning over the edge and into the bay.

"Not dead enough," Ross answered between clenched teeth.

Anne covered her mouth with her hands as Ross lifted his sword over Murrane's head. The steel blade flashed down, then veered aside and cut into the deck beside Murrane's head. "I've no wish to take a coward's scalp," Ross said with contempt. "It would soil my honor." He flung down his sword. "Besides, dying would be too easy for ye—I'll leave ye to live and reap the harvest of your own black soul." Ross turned to Anne and flashed her a crooked smile. "Care to go for a swim?"

She nodded, and he caught her hand. Together they ran to the port rail. Swiftly, Ross slit the material at the back of her dress and helped her pull it down and step out of it. She removed her petticoats, leaving just her thin shift to make it easier to swim.

"Jump as far out as ye can," Ross warned. "Once we come up, ye can hang onto my back, and I'll carry ye to shore."

"Damn you," Murrane swore.

Anne glanced back over her shoulder to see him climbing to his feet. "Ross," she said. "Murrane—"

Ross jumped, pulling her with him. They hit the water and sank down, then surfaced a few yards from the ship. Anne looked back at the fiery deck. Murrane stood at the rail, sword in hand.

As she watched, he toppled forward and fell overboard. Halfway down, he struck the side of the listing ship with a sickening thud. Anne shut her eyes, and when she opened them again Murrane's body had sunk beneath the surface of the bay.

"Come, hinney, we'd best away from here."

As they swam around the stern of the ship, Anne heard the boom of a cannon across the water. In the distance, she could see the lights of another ship. "Your father," Ross said. "A little later, and he could have stayed in port."

When they waded ashore, minutes later, Cameron's sloop was already closing in to pick up survivors from the burning ship. Niipan and four of the Shawnee were waiting at the water's edge.

Ross wrapped his arms around Anne and crushed her against him. "I thought I'd lost ye, hinney," he said huskily. "Both of ye." His dark eyes shimmered like stars as he took the amulet from his neck and slipped it around Anne's. "This is yours. Don't ever take it off again—ye get in too much trouble without it, woman. Next time, it might be more trouble than I can get ye out of."

"Why you . . . you great barbarian . . ." Her words were lost as she looked up at him with love. Moonlight shone on his smoke-stained face, and his hair hung loose and wild around his shoulders. He's mine, she thought, forever and ever . . . Anne's vision blurred with tears of happiness as she tilted her chin to stare into his haunting eyes. "If anything happened to you," she murmured, "I wouldn't—"

"Hist now, hinney," he said. "I'm here and whole, and so are ye. We've another chance to put right all we've turned asunder. If ye'll still have me . . ."

"Will I have to live in a hollow tree without a stick of furniture?" she demanded.

"Nay, lady. Ye shall have a bed—a muckle bed with a feather tick as soft as swans' down."

"For your pleasure?" she teased.

"Aye, hinney, and for yours."

"And shall I come to Annapolis and visit with civilized folk whenever I wish?"

"Aye, hinney. I'll build ye a road the king would not scruple to travel on, and I'll buy ye a golden coach to ride in."

"With my money, I suppose?"

And then he silenced her teasing with a slow, tender kiss, and, laughing, they turned west and walked hand and hand over the new land toward the future.

Epilogue

Gentleman's Folly on the Chesapeake
February 1724

Anne lay in Ross's arms in the master's chamber of her father's manor house. There was no light in the room save that offered by the crackling logs on the wide brick hearth and a single flickering candle beside the bed.

Softly falling snowflakes patted against the glass windowpanes and piled in miniature drifts on the outside sills. The snow muffled the night sounds of the plantation, wrapping the house and the bedchamber in a blanket of white, until it seemed to Anne that she and Ross were the only two people in an enchanted world.

She sighed and snuggled against his bare chest, running her fingers across his skin. He chuckled deep in his throat and caught her hand in his big one.

"Hist, hinney," he teased in a deep rumble, "you've wearied me sore. Do ye keep that up, and I'll be forced to try again what we've already done twice this night."

She giggled. "Three times." She flicked his left nipple with the tip of her tongue.

"I warn ye, woman." He lowered his head and kissed her in that slow, sweet way that sent chills running up and down her spine. The quilt fell away, and he pulled it high around her neck. "Not that I don't want to look at ye," he murmured, "but I'll not have ye catching a chill."

"It's my big belly that offends you," she teased, placing a hand over her swollen middle.

"Nay." His warm hand covered hers.

"I'm fat and ugly," she insisted lightly.

"Nay, never say it," he whispered into her ear. "For it makes ye glow with such beauty that every man's head turns to look at ye." He trailed feather-light kisses down her cheek and neck. "Ah, Anne . . . sweeting . . . I do love ye." He cupped her chin and tilted her face up so that he could look into her eyes. "I love ye and the little one ye carry under your heart . . . and I will care for ye both so long as I draw breath."

A warm bubble of happiness rose in Anne's chest. She sighed and laid her cheek against his chest, listening to the strong, regular beat of Ross's heart. He makes me feel so safe, she thought, blinking back the tears that rose in her eyes. "I love you, too," she answered huskily.

He brushed aside a lock of her loose hair and lifted her amulet to kiss the spot on her throat beneath it. "If the child is a girl, will ye pass on the necklace to her?" he asked.

Anne swallowed. It was a question she had asked herself many times. If the power of the amulet were real, it had caused her great unhappiness . . . and wondrous joy. Knowing the risk, could she pass the charm to her own daughter? "If we have only boys," she hedged, "I wouldn't—"

He laughed. "Boys? This one is not yet hatched, and already ye talk of more?"

"Well, I should hope we'll have more than one child. It's lonely growing up without brothers or sisters."

"Ye have a sister."

"Now I do." Anne smiled. "The most wonderful sister anyone could hope for. I only wish she and Barbara could meet someday—I'm certain Leah would be more than a match for my dear mother." She took Ross's hand and raised it to her lips. "Once, I had another sister . . . Father told me on Christmas Day. He drank a glass of wine to her memory. He says it's a custom he never neglects . . . on her birthday and on Christmas."

"To her memory? She's dead then?"

Anne nodded, unable to resist a feeling of intense sadness for the tiny red-haired infant girl she had never known. "Her name was Fiona O'Neal," she said. "Father said she was born on my birthday, and if she'd lived, she'd be younger than Leah by seven years."

"O'Neal?"

"Irish. Father's wife owned estates near Dublin. He went there when he left America."

"Your father seems to have left a trail of daughters behind him like the beads of a broken necklace."

Anne covered Ross's lips with her fingertips. "Don't joke about it," she said, "please. Whatever Father's done wrong in the past, he's made up for it. I love him, Ross."

"Aye," he agreed, "there's right in that. Cameron Stewart is a good man—one ye can be proud of for a father." He kissed her fingertips. "I only hope our child will come to my defense as stoutly when she is grown."

"He," she corrected.

"We'll see." He cradled her against him. "Lad or lassie, my daddy will be glad to see the bairn. We'll carry our babe home to him in springtime, when the grass comes green and the woods are alive with birdsong. Ye'll like Wanishish-eyun in the spring, hinney. It's the nearest place to heaven on earth I've ever seen."

Anne snuggled tighter against him. "I'm glad we stayed here on the Chesapeake this winter," she whispered. "Until the baby comes."

"Aye, 'tis only right. Ye need to be with your family now. Besides"—he smiled down at her—"Moonfeather is the only one I'd trust to deliver ye safely of this babe." He stroked her hair. "Ye be everything to me, hinney. I'd not risk a hair on your head for hope of eternal life."

"That's nice," she murmured sleepily, "but what I'd really like—"

"Is furniture," he finished for her. "Aye, bonny Anne, and ye shall have enough for ten houses, does it please ye."

"And china," she reminded him. "My children shall not eat off leaves like squirrels. And knives and forks."

"Of purest silver." He chuckled again. "So long as your fortune suffices."

The babe in her womb kicked hard enough for Ross to feel it, and they laughed together and whispered honeyed words of love late into the cold and snowy night. And when Anne finally drifted off to sleep in Ross's strong arms, her dreams were of all the days and nights to come . . . and of the high, sweet laughter of a dark-eyed baby boy.

Avon Romances—
the best in exceptional authors and unforgettable novels!

DEVIL'S MOON   Suzannah Davis
76127-0/$3.95 US/$4.95 Can

ROUGH AND TENDER   Selina MacPherson
76322-2/$3.95 US/$4.95 Can

CAPTIVE ROSE   Miriam Minger
76311-7/$3.95 US/$4.95 Can

RUGGED SPLENDOR   Robin Leigh
76318-4/$3.95 US/$4.95 Can

CHEROKEE NIGHTS   Genell Dellin
76014-2/$4.50 US/$5.50 Can

SCANDAL'S DARLING   Anne Caldwell
76110-6/$4.50 US/$5.50 Can

LAVENDER FLAME   Karen Stratford
76267-6/$4.50 US/$5.50 Can

FOOL FOR LOVE   DeLoras Scott
76342-7/$4.50 US/$5.50 Can

OUTLAW BRIDE   Katherine Compton
76411-3/$4.50 US/$5.50 Can

DEFIANT ANGEL   Stephanie Stevens
76449-0/$4.50 US/$5.50 Can

If you enjoyed this book, take advantage of this special offer. Subscribe now and . . .

GET A *FREE* HISTORICAL ROMANCE
—— NO OBLIGATION(a $3.95 value) ——

Each month the editors of True Value will select the four best historical romance novels from America's leading publishers. Preview them in your home Free for 10 days. And we'll send you a FREE book as our introductory gift. No obligation. If for any reason you decide not to keep them, just return them and owe nothing. But if you like them you'll pay *just* $3.50 each and save at least $.45 each off the cover price. (Your savings are a minimum of $1.80 a month.) There is no shipping and handling or other hidden charges. There are no minimum number of books to buy and you may cancel at any time.

send in the coupon below